L

Born in Suffolk, Alice Marlow attended the University of Sussex and worked in Hertfordshire as a primary school teacher for many years before giving up teaching to concentrate on her writing. She includes amongst her interests reading, drawing, pottery and clay sculpture and animals, with four Burmese cats of her own and two donkeys who visit on holiday from Weston-Super-Mare. She lives in Wiltshire with her husband and their two children.

Alice Marlow is the pseudonym of an author who has, under the name Pamela Belle, written many acclaimed historical novels.

NO LOVE LOST

When Harriet Smith catches her lover, Edward, in flagrante with a tarty local girl, it's the last straw. Now, the worm has turned, and Harriet's off — with their four-year-old child, Toby, and with Edward's gleaming BMW. Edward is outraged. What is all the fuss about? He wants Harriet back, pronto, running his house and his business. Harriet is not open to persuasion. Especially after she runs into Morgan Price, who abandoned her without explanation ten years ago after a passionate affair, and who's just as charming as ever. But Harriet doesn't want another broken heart.

Books by Alice Marlow
Published by The House of Ulverscroft:

MERMAID'S GROUND

ALICE MARLOW

NO LOVE LOST

Complete and Unabridged

ULVERSCROFT
Leicester

First published in Great Britain in 1999 by
Headline Book Publishing
London

First Large Print Edition
published 2001
by arrangement with
Headline Book Publishing
a division of Hodder Headline Plc
London

British Library CIP Data

Marlow, Alice
    No love lost.—Large print ed.—
    Ulverscroft large print series: romance
    1. Love stories
    2. Large type books
    I. Title
    823.9'14 [F]

    ISBN 0–7089–4409–4

Published by
F. A. Thorpe (Publishing)
Anstey, Leicestershire

Set by Words & Graphics Ltd.
Anstey, Leicestershire
Printed and bound in Great Britain by
T. J. International Ltd., Padstow, Cornwall

This book is printed on acid-free paper

For Hugh and Patrick, for their patience
in letting me have so much time on the
computer.

Author's Note

Residents of Seend, in Wiltshire, may recognise some of the features of their village described in my fictional Sanden. I would like to assure them that none of the characters depicted in this book are intended to have any resemblance to anyone living in Seend, whether in the present or in the past.

1

'Mummy?'

Harriet Smith raised her head from exasperated contemplation of her elderly Metro's gently smoking radiator, and smiled at her small son. 'What is it, Toby?'

He came out of the front door and walked towards her over the weed-strewn gravel, his pale face frowning doubtfully. 'Mummy, why *is* Daddy bouncing around on top of that lady?'

Eleven words, spoken in four-year-old innocence. Eleven words that dropped like stones into Harriet's mind, and sank there. Eleven words that finally, after more than five years, announced the end of an affair that should have died a long time ago. And Toby, the result of it, and the reason she had ignored her misery and stayed, would now be the unwitting cause of its demise.

Harriet straightened up. Everything suddenly seemed very clear, and hard-edged, and absolute. She had persuaded herself to ignore so much, but she could not ignore this. And the Harriet Smith who had acquiesced in an essentially loveless and sterile relationship for the sake of her son stepped aside and watched, with remote and wondering interest, to see what the new Harriet, the avenger, the tigress, would do now.

'I've no idea, sweetheart,' she said calmly. 'But I'm sure he's got some excuse. Tell you what, why don't you go and sit in his car for a while, and I'll sort it out.'

'In his car?' Toby was uncertain, but obviously intrigued by the thought of such a unique treat. 'In his *new* car?'

'Of course his new car, it's the only one he's got. It's in the garage, and it isn't locked — go and get in.'

'Can I hold the steering wheel?'

'Of course you can.'

'Can I beep the horn?'

'I don't think that'd be a very good idea. Go on, Toby, I'll be along in a minute.'

With one last glance to ascertain that she really meant it, her son turned and ran off to the garage at the side of the house. Harriet stood still on the brink for a few seconds longer, while the enormity of what she was about to do seemed to suffocate her.

It was only ten o'clock, and even without this, it had already been a bad day. Edward had told her that he was going to shut himself away with the accounts, and she could go to the cash and carry. As it was Friday, there was a long list of orders from next week's hirers to fulfil, and an even longer one for cleaning materials. And when she'd asked Edward if she could borrow his BMW, he'd flatly refused. 'No, Hattie. You know I don't want anyone else driving it. And certainly not to the cash and carry. Take yours.'

There was no point in arguing. He had stopped listening to her long ago, and his insistence on calling her Hattie, which he knew she hated, was the proof. In any case Toby was there, bright-eyed, sensitive, listening. To protect her son, Harriet would have thrown herself into a lion's jaws, so swallowing her anger with her partner, for the umpteenth time, was simple by comparison. She had set off for Trowbridge with rage simmering just below her calm, organised surface. And after two miles, she'd glanced at the temperature gauge and seen it climbing inexorably towards the red. Cursing inwardly, she had turned round and nursed her ailing, panting car gently back home to the boatyard. Like it or not, Edward was bloody well going to have to lend her the BMW, or the hirers, turning up tomorrow morning expecting their boxes of groceries neatly stowed in the galleys of their boats, would be disappointed.

Much to her relief, she had made it back

before the car actually boiled over. As she opened the bonnet for an inspection, Toby had run indoors. Presumably, he had gone upstairs, and found Edward and . . . and some woman.

It wasn't as if she had honestly believed that Edward was faithful to her. On some deep, almost subconscious level, she had known that he hadn't been, for a long, long time — since shortly after Toby's birth, in fact. At first, aware of how much the knowledge would hurt her, she had refused to contemplate the possibility. Later, when all love, even affection, had withered away, when her unhappiness with her situation had grown to almost unmanageable proportions, she had managed to pretend that the truth didn't exist.

But she couldn't deny it now. And accepting that bitter, unpalatable fact was such a relief that she felt completely different, as if she'd sloughed off the old, exhausted, trapped, downtrodden Harriet and become vigorous and all-powerful, like some avenging Valkyrie. She didn't need to stay any more. She could go, with a clear conscience. And she knew that she, and Toby, both deserved more than this.

Quickly and quietly, she ran into the house, her mind churning. She paused at the foot of the stairs, to listen. From above came the unmistakable sounds of passion. Harriet crept upwards, taking care to avoid the two steps that creaked.

She was not in the least surprised to see that the object of Edward's lust was Gina, the girl who worked in the boatyard's gift shop. Gina was twenty, with firm young flesh and a down-to-earth attitude to sex that Harriet, in more innocent days, had found refreshing. She'd been giving Edward the come-on ever since she'd started working for him: the only wonder was that it had taken this long for him to respond. Granted, he usually liked them more sophisticated than Gina, but he wasn't one to spurn anything thus blatantly offered.

They were thrashing around so urgently on the bed that neither of them noticed Harriet, peering through the gap between the door and the jamb. Her heart pounding, she slunk down the landing to Toby's little room at the end. It took only a few moments to grab some essentials: clothes, favourite toys, shampoo and toothbrush. Of course, she wouldn't be able to get any of her own things, because they were in the bedroom she shared with Edward. But Harriet wasn't concerned about that. At this precise moment, all she wanted was to leave this tainted, unhappy house for ever.

The moans of ecstasy were rising to a climax as she hurried lightly down to the hall, a bag slung over one shoulder and a box of toys in her arms. She ran outside and into the garage. Toby was kneeling up on the pale-blue leather driver's seat of the BMW, wiggling the steering wheel and making muted 'brrm brrm' noises. He jumped guiltily as Harriet entered, and then smiled in relief when he saw who it was. 'What have you got there, Mummy?'

'Just some things, darling. Hop into the back seat and strap yourself in, I won't be a moment.'

'Are we going in this car, then? I thought Daddy didn't want you to drive it.'

Four-year-olds could be incredibly sharp. Harriet smiled at him, fighting her panic, the growing urge to flee. But she didn't have the keys. They should be on the hook in the kitchen, by the back door. She didn't want to think about the possibility that Edward had for some reason picked them up.

'Back in a minute, sweetheart,' she said, and ran.

The house was quiet, the air heavy, to her abnormally sensitive imagination, with the aftermath of passion. Gina smoked, and so did Edward, so they were probably enjoying a post-coital cigarette. In *my* bed, thought Harriet, with sudden fury. And he *knows* I can't stand the smell. She went into the kitchen. Thank God, the keys were where she'd hoped. She whipped them off the hook and stuffed them in the pocket of her jeans. What else? She needed something, some way of making him understand the strength and depth of her anger, and the enormous injustice of his betrayal.

Her eye fell on the bucket of dirty, scummy water which she had earlier used to wash the kitchen floor. A sudden wild, gleeful impulse took hold of Harriet. She heaved it out of the sink and carried it, with care, into the hall and up the stairs.

It was like a scene from some tacky soft-porn movie, she thought as she walked in. The handsome man, his broad chest furred with plentiful dark hair, reclining against the pillows, an expression of smugly sensual satisfaction on his face. And the beautiful, brainless bimbo beside him, her bleached-blonde locks strikingly arranged against his distinguished head, while his free hand fondled her plump, pneumatic breasts.

They saw her about half a second before she threw the filthy water over them. Gina screeched with shock and outrage, and Edward shouted something. Harriet dropped

7

the bucket over his head, and ran.

Breathless with hysterical laughter, she hurled herself down the stairs and back to the garage. With any luck, it would take Edward a few precious moments to recover, and find his trousers, and come in pursuit. And by then, she'd be gone.

Fortunately, Toby's natural habit of obedience had overcome his curiosity, and he was sitting where she had told him to, securely strapped in, although the seat belt cut across his face because he wasn't on a booster cushion. She got in, rammed the key in the ignition, and turned it. A dreadful image of a furious Edward, shouting as he dragged her out of the car, made her shake with apprehension. If it failed to start . . .

The engine roared exultantly into life. Harriet put it into gear, released the handbrake, and slipped the clutch. Like a liberated animal, the BMW leapt out of the garage, spraying gravel. Pete, one of the boat mechanics, was standing by the wharf, spanner in hand, his mouth open with astonishment. Harriet gave him a cheerful wave as she drove into the lane. Behind her, in her rear-view mirror, she saw Edward, still struggling to do up his trousers, emerge dripping from the front door and stare in horrified disbelief as his partner, his son and

8

his precious car disappeared out of the gate.

Too late: he'd never catch up with her, the Metro would boil over after a hundred yards of his driving. Something in Harriet's heart began singing an anthem of freedom. *All my trials, Lord, soon be over . . .*

She had turned right, going up the hill towards Sanden Row, straggled along the ridge above the canal. It wasn't the quickest route to her destination, but she didn't want to make it too obvious. At the top, where the houses began, she turned left, down the little back lane called The Croft, which came out just by the entrance to Forfar Towers. As she emerged without stopping, a big silver and black 4 × 4 swept past, flashing its headlights at her impertinence, and vanished down the tree-lined drive. Harriet ignored it, and floored the accelerator.

'Don't drive so fast, Mummy,' Toby pleaded from behind her. 'Please don't drive so fast.'

With a pang of remorse, Harriet eased her foot up. 'Sorry, sweetheart. I wasn't thinking. Is this better?'

'Slower,' said her son firmly. 'I want you to go *slower*.'

She took the sharp walled bend around the park at less than twenty miles an hour. In a quarter of a mile, the lane would join the main road, running between Trowbridge and Devizes, where the main part of Sanden, the posh bit, started. But at the old quarry, she turned left, down a steep and very narrow little by-way, so unfrequented by traffic that tufts of grass grew at intervals along the middle. With luck, Edward would think she'd gone to her sister in Bath, or even to her parents in Bristol. It would take a long time for him to realise that her refuge lay only half a mile up the canal from the boatyard.

Trees overhung the lane, just growing fuzzy with new April leaf. At the bottom, by the canal, lay two houses, set well back from the road, with large gardens. Both were Victorian, built in a pastiche, cottagey style with ornamental barge boards and gabled porches, and they had originally been identical.

But no longer. The nearer house, neatly hedged in trim, alien stripes of green and gold conifers, had been renovated and extended and double-glazed until the original gamekeeper and his family would no longer have recognised their humble home. In contrast, the one beyond, next to the canal, lay unseen behind the exuberant thicket of trees — holly, ash, elder, hazel — which had been allowed to grow up all around it. Harriet checked her rear-view mirror. No one was following them: the grey, unkempt little lane stretched out deserted behind her. With a sigh of unutterable relief, she turned left, into the grounds of the second cottage.

'Why are we here, Mummy?' Toby asked curiously.

Harriet, engaged in manoeuvring the car between two huge old pear trees, did not answer at first. She pulled up in the yard behind the cottage, switched the engine off and turned to face her son. His eyes, blue as harebells, stared back with interest. She said carefully, 'We're just going to see Daphne for a while. You know Daphne, I do work for her sometimes. You've played in the garden.'

Toby craned to look out through the car window. With his wide, sparkling eyes and hair the exact colour of vanilla ice cream, he was a very engaging child, and Harriet loved him with a fierce, astonished passion that ruled her life. 'I remember,' he said. 'She's got a big white dog.'

'That's right, Maggie. And here she is now.'

A very large pale-yellow Labrador came galumphing across the rough grass, barking without much conviction. Her tail, enthusiastically waving a welcome, was a much more accurate guide to her true feelings. Harriet got out of the car, hand outstretched. 'Hallo, Mags. Where's Daphne?'

'Here,' said a deep but still female voice,

11

and the owner of Holly Cottage, and Maggie, came striding out of the wilderness of garden to greet them.

Six months ago, Harriet had answered an advertisement, pinned up in Sanden Post Office, requesting secretarial assistance. She hadn't even known why she had rung the number: most of her days were spent either running the boatyard or looking after Toby. Now, she recognised that this had been the first symptom of her desperate need to escape from the trap into which Edward, and Toby's birth, and her own conscience, had sucked her. But at the time, she had told herself that she must be mad, wanting to add more work to her already busy life.

At first encounter, Daphne James, with her deep, upper-class voice, her air of command, her man's shirt and ripped, mud-stained camouflage trousers, had been an intimidating sight. Harriet had never met her before, but she knew her by reputation, as the mad old woman who lived in the ramshackle cottage at the bottom of Stony Lane. Four hundred years ago, the villagers would have thought she was a witch. Now, they just gossiped about her in the post office.

Harriet, fresh from sorting the boats because Charmian the cleaner had gone home with a migraine, had herself been in jeans and a T-shirt. With her long, curling dark hair firmly controlled by a French plait, and her round tortoiseshell glasses, she probably looked absurdly young to Miss James, who must be well into her fifties. She had held out her hand. 'Hallo. I'm Harriet Smith.'

'Hallo,' said her prospective employer, looking her up and down. 'You did say you could do word-processing?'

'I can. And database, spreadsheets, mail-shots and desk-top publishing,' Harriet told her, with pride. 'I've got the certificates with me, if you want to see them.' She was glancing covertly round the crowded living room, wondering if she had ever seen quite so many books packed into a private house before, apart from the library at Longleat. There was a radio, but no television. In a corner stood an enormous old roll-top desk, with a pale-grey PC perched incongruously on top. The fireplace was rather more recent than the house, with smooth beige tiles framing an elderly Parkray solid-fuel boiler. Above it, the chimney breast was adorned with a splendid set of Victorian engravings of British butterflies, beautifully drawn and coloured.

'Don't worry, I'll take your word for it,' said Miss James. 'That's the computer, there.

Do you think you can use it?'

'I expect I'll manage,' Harriet had said, smiling. 'What exactly is it that you want me to do?'

'I'm in the throes of writing a book. I need someone to tidy up my rough draft, sort out the grammar and the spelling, and generally give it a bit of spit and polish. Do you think you can do that? I warn you, my writing's atrocious — even worse than my typing.'

'I used to work for a bloke whose memos looked as though they were in Hebrew. Once I get used to it, there'll be no problems,' Harriet told her, with rather more confidence than she actually felt. 'What's the book about?'

'I'm creating a wildlife garden here, and making a study of the flowers and insects I find. It's reached the stage where I need an organised mind to help me pull it all together. I borrowed the computer from my nephew, who's just upgraded, but I don't like using modern technology any more than I have to. Whereas you, obviously, are quite at home with it.'

'I did several courses, a few years ago,' Harriet said. 'I've worked for an engineering company, an accountant, and a holiday firm, and now I help my partner run Wonderland Boats.'

14

'Oh, yes. Doing quite well now, so I hear.'

'Yes, since Edward took it over, it's been very successful,' Harriet had said, failing to add the undeniable fact that she had worked much harder in the business than her partner did.

'Are you sure you'll find the time to help me? I need someone who's reliable, and prepared to work at least a couple of mornings a week. And you've got a child.'

'Yes, but he's at playgroup every morning during term-time. Don't worry, Miss James. I'm sure I can fit it in. If necessary, I can take some disks home and do it on my own computer.'

'It's quite a challenge, you know.'

'I like challenges.' Harriet smiled at her. 'I'm looking forward to it — if you give me the job, that is.'

'Oh, I'm giving you the job,' Daphne James had said briskly. 'You look exactly the sort of person I need. Six pounds an hour all right? Good. You can start next week if you like.'

That had been six months ago, back in October. She hadn't told Edward that she was moonlighting, knowing that he wouldn't like it. He had always resented any time she spent away from the boatyard, and he certainly wouldn't approve of any of her precious few hours of freedom being spent working for someone else, especially the eccentric Daphne James. Once she had assumed that it was love for her which made him so possessive. Now, she knew better. Edward liked to be in control, to dominate, to have all his minions — including the mother of his child — at his beck and call. He probably counted her in with Pete and Gina and Charmian and all his other employees.

Nor would he approve of Miss James. She was far too old, plain and unfeminine to interest him, and he would probably find her blunt, forthright manner positively threatening. And as Harriet and her employer became better acquainted, all through the long, dark days of winter, she began to gain the impression that Miss James wouldn't approve of Edward either. She didn't actively dislike men, although she had never married: her academic career had always been more important to her than the desire for a husband. But although Harriet loyally tried not to discuss her partner to his detriment — and sometimes it was very difficult not to — she knew that even the fact that her work for Daphne had to be kept secret from Edward was a significant point against him.

Instinctively, she knew that Miss James was on her side. And that was why, desperate for refuge, she had come here, to Holly Cottage, rather than to her sister Georgia, or her parents. He didn't even know that she had met Daphne, let alone worked for her for six months. And while he rampaged across Wiltshire and Somerset, looking for her, she would have a few days' respite, in which to take stock and think about her future, and her son's.

'Hallo, Harriet,' Daphne said, raising her eyebrows in surprise. She was wearing a pair of very old trousers and a big dark-blue jumper that had started to unravel round the hem, and she was carrying a trowel and a large bunch of uprooted plants. 'This is unexpected.'

'I know.' Harriet glanced at Toby, who was just emerging from the car. Maggie, who knew a sucker when she saw one, immediately flopped down on to the ground and rolled over, presenting an ample and rather dirty chest for inspection. Giggling, the little boy crouched down and began stroking her. Harriet, reassured, took a couple of steps towards Daphne and said softly, 'I've come to ask a very big favour.'

'Yes?'

Fortunately, Harriet was used to Daphne's abrupt manner by now. Undaunted, she said quietly, 'Can we stay here for a couple of days?'

Her friend and employer's thick grey eyebrows climbed towards her hair. 'Have you fallen out with Edward?'

'In a manner of speaking,' Harriet told her, and explained, as concisely and calmly as she could, what had happened less than half an hour before.

There was a pause. Daphne stared at her, frowning, while behind them Toby was talking to Maggie in a soft, delighted undertone. A horrible twinge of doubt assailed Harriet suddenly. Had she presumed too much on the growing friendship between the two women? It was one thing, after all, to chat comfortably over cups of coffee about academic life, and old novels, and how to put the world to rights, and the almost human idiosyncrasies of the computer; but quite another to invite herself and Toby to stay.

It didn't *really* matter if Daphne said no; Georgia would gladly provide a haven. It was the fact that Harriet's sister had always loathed Edward, and would be incapable of resisting the temptation to say 'I told you so', that had prompted her to go to Holly Cottage first. Just at this moment, her nerves and her emotions felt raw and vulnerable, and she didn't want to face her bossy elder sister's scathing judgements for a few days yet.

'Of course you can stay, my dear,' said

Daphne, and her rather severe face broke out into a sudden smile. 'That's if you can put up with me and Maggie, of course.'

'Oh, that's wonderful — thank you so much,' said Harriet, her words stumbling over each other in her relief. 'Just until I can find somewhere else, even if it's only my sister's — we don't want to impose — '

'Nonsense. For as long as it takes, my home is yours,' said the older woman, still smiling. 'Apart from anything else, your sister lives in Bath, doesn't she? And Toby will be better off here, close to his friends and familiar things. You don't want to uproot him entirely.'

Mention of his name had made her son look up. Harriet beckoned him over. 'Listen, sweetheart, how would you like to stay here with Daphne for a while?'

The child stared up at her in bewilderment. 'Will you be staying here too, Mummy?'

'Of course I will, darling.'

'Good,' said Toby. 'But when are we going home?'

He was only four years old, and she didn't know how to explain what had happened. She said reassuringly, 'Not just yet, sweetheart. It'll be fun staying in Daphne's house, won't it?'

'Ye-es,' said Toby doubtfully. 'But what about Daddy?'

'Daddy's going to stay at our old house, because he's got to look after the boats.'

'Why can't he come here too?'

'There isn't enough room for him, sweetheart. Daphne's house is lovely, but it's only got two bedrooms.' And no television either. Toby, in common with every child of his age, was addicted to a variety of entertaining cartoons, not to mention *Teletubbies*, and the sudden withdrawal of his favourites would undoubtedly cause trouble.

'Is Gina going to stay at home with him?'

So he had seen enough of them, bonking away on the bed, to identify Edward's latest conquest. A wave of fury flooded Harriet, but she clenched her fists and forced herself to stay calm and controlled. At all costs, Toby must be protected as much as possible from the damaging, terrible consequences of what he had witnessed. And she had no intention of involving him in the deeply sordid dispute which must surely lie ahead, for he was utterly blameless.

'Of course not, sweetheart, she's got her own home to go to,' she said. 'Don't worry about Daddy, we'll see him very soon, I expect.'

'Will he take me to the toy shop?' asked

Toby, his face lightening slightly.

Harriet, her heart breaking, laughed and hugged him. Her eyes were wet, but she hoped neither he nor Daphne would notice. 'Of course he'll take you to the toy shop, sweetheart. But that's another day. Shall we get your things out of the car? I've brought some clothes for you, and some toys — '

'Have you brought Lambkin?'

'Of *course* I've got Lambkin, I wouldn't leave him behind,' said Harriet stoutly. She got to her feet, still holding his hand, and glanced at Daphne. 'Thank you — thank you so much. I can't begin to tell you how grateful I am — '

'Don't bother,' said her employer firmly. 'The very least I could do. Now, Toby, I've got some lemonade and biscuits in the kitchen — would you like some? I thought so. Come on in, both of you, and I'll put the kettle on. Everything looks better over a mug of hot tea. And then we'll sort out the spare room — I've got a little put-you-up bed that Toby can have.'

Her brusquely practical, down-to-earth manner put fresh heart into Harriet. She had made the right decision, she was certain of it. Right to leave Edward, in the face of his gross provocation; and right to put her future, at least temporarily, into Daphne's hands. At

21

this moment, she couldn't have cared less if she never saw her former partner again, although she knew that for Toby's sake, if nothing else, she would have to face him soon, and make some sense of the wreckage of their life together. But she didn't regret leaving: not one iota. And at the memory of his outraged face, disappearing behind a curtain of dirty water, Harriet could not help smiling. He deserved every drop of it, and more, and I hope he gets double pneumonia, the rat! she said to herself fiercely. I wonder what he's thinking now?

2

At that precise moment, Edward, still wet but now decently clothed, was trying to calm his indignant inamorata. 'Oh, come on, Gina, what's all the fuss about? It was only a drop of water.'

'It was filthy!' Her blonde hair in dripping rats' tails, her mascara smudged and her lipstick smeared, Gina had lost every vestige of glamour. 'I *told* you we shouldn't have used your bed!'

'Eh?' Edward stared at her, astonished. 'Where else was there?'

'But you wouldn't listen, would you?' Gina, by now in full spate, was warming to her theme. 'No, you had to have it then and there and sod the risk. Well, I've had enough. That's it, Teddy boy.'

'But Gina, darling, why are you blaming me? It wasn't me who threw the water.'

'No, it was Harriet, and if I'd been in her shoes I'd have done the same. You stupid prat, you can't see further than your own prick, can you? Well, I'm out of here for good.' Gina wriggled into her brief skirt and shoved her bare feet back into the black leather boots she always wore in temperatures less than tropical. 'And you can stuff your bloody job an' all. I don't want to be around when your lady gets back — *if* she does, wouldn't blame her if she buggered off too. See ya — *not!*'

Speechless, Edward stood and watched as she flounced out of the door. He heard her clatter down the stairs, and then the decisive, contemptuous slam of the front door.

It was only then that the enormity of what had happened smote him. He sat down on the wet bed and put his head in his hands with a groan. Oh, God — Harriet!

Once, long ago, it had all seemed so perfect. Fate had smiled kindly on him, delivering Harriet to him like some perfect, gift-wrapped present, the day after his birthday. Not only was she a brilliant organiser, adept on the computer and intelligent enough to contribute her own ideas to the business, but she was stunningly attractive. It had taken a connoisseur's eye to spot it, of course: most men wouldn't have looked beyond the glasses and the severe hairstyle. But her eyes were beautiful, very large and a lovely green-flecked brown, and her face reminded him of those Edwardian belles in old erotic photographs: serene, wistful, yet hinting at hidden fires beneath.

She was ten years younger than he was, of course, but Edward liked his women to be inexperienced and slightly naïve. The older ones had not only lost the bloom of youth, but were usually much more resistant to his charms, and harder to manipulate if they did succumb.

He had set out to woo her, gently and tenderly and romantically, and he had won her. The first few months had been idyllic. Where did it all go? he wondered now with furious despair, but he already knew the answer. It was her fault, letting herself get pregnant so quickly. A difficult birth and the demands of combining motherhood and her essential business duties had turned his gorgeous, flatteringly passionate lover into a boring, plain and unresponsive frump. She obviously didn't understand that men had important needs, which must be satisfied: and Edward liked to think that he was more virile than most. He prided himself on his abilities in bed, and resentfully took the view that it was her loss, not his, if she wasn't interested.

So, with a clear conscience, and a certain amount of discretion, he had embarked on a series of extremely pleasurable and short-lived affairs, secure in the knowledge that Harriet couldn't possibly find out, and if she did, couldn't reasonably object to them either.

But she had, and she did. And now he was sitting here, without her, or Toby, or the car in which he had taken so much pride, that he'd only had for a few weeks, with leather seats and personal numberplate. It was the symbol of his success, so sweet after all the past failures, it had cost him a fortune, and she had taken it.

Stupid girl, Edward thought furiously. Silly hysterical little fool. What's all the fuss about? It's not as if she's been any good in the sack for years — she can't blame me if I take advantage of what's on offer, can she? And if she's damaged my car . . .

It was his car, just as it was his house, and his business, and she had no right to take it. She'd have to give it back to him, or face the consequences. And he knew exactly where she would go. He threw Gina's discarded tights into the waste-paper basket, and went downstairs to the phone.

Her sister Georgia's home number was ex-directory, but Edward knew where she worked. He looked in Yellow Pages, and dialled the number belonging to one of the many firms of solicitors in Queen's Square, Bath.

The receptionist who answered had the

26

same bright manner that Harriet adopted on the phone to prospective customers. 'How may I help you, sir?'

He asked to speak to Miss Georgia Smith, on a private matter, and gave his name. After a few moments, the receptionist came back on the line. 'I'm sorry, Mr Armstrong, but she's in a meeting.'

They always were, when you most wanted them. Edward could feel his anger rising again, and squashed it. 'When will she be available?'

'I'm afraid I don't know, Mr Armstrong. She's very busy today, but I'll get her to give you a call when she's free. Has she got your number?'

Knowing Georgia, she wouldn't have it on principle. Through clenched teeth, Edward gave it, thanked the receptionist for her trouble, and banged the phone down.

As he turned to leave the office, he glanced out of the window and saw a scruffily dressed couple, with rucksacks on their backs, hovering outside the gift shop. Of course, Gina had gone, so the place was unattended. He'd assumed she had locked the door, but as he watched one of them opened it and went in. If he didn't intervene, they'd probably pinch all the stock.

With a growl of anger, Edward stamped

out of his house and across the yard. After all the other upsets of the morning, having to serve in the gift shop seemed like the final humiliation. He strode into the little room, crowded with china animals, models of canal boats, and the beautifully painted bowls and buckets that had occupied Harriet all winter, and glowered at his prospective customers. 'Can I help you?'

Fortunately, his manner failed to put them off, and they bought a water scoop, a book on the canals of southern England, and a couple of postcards. Smiling fiercely, Edward bid them goodbye, watched them walk over the road to the Wharf Inn, which was just opening up, and then had to run back inside the house to catch the phone before it stopped ringing.

Georgia's voice was neither bright nor helpful. 'Edward. You called. Make it quick, I've got a client waiting and I'm due in court this afternoon.'

'It's Harriet,' he said, thinking fast. 'I'm worried about her.'

'Really?' said his partner's sister, with cool disbelief. 'What's happened?'

'She's gone off somewhere in a huff, and she's taken Toby. I'm afraid that she might do something stupid.'

'That seems highly unlikely,' said Georgia.

'Anyway, what do you want me to do about it?'

'Tell me if she turns up at your place, of course,' said Edward angrily. 'For God's sake, she's gone missing, aren't you concerned about her?'

'Of course I am. When did she leave?'

Edward looked at his watch. 'About an hour ago. She's got Toby with her — if anything should happen — '

'Don't be ridiculous, of course it won't. Harriet isn't the suicidal type, and you know it. Don't worry about her. Anyway, why did she go?'

'I've no idea,' said Edward mendaciously. 'She just got the hump about something and took off. And she's taken my new car — '

'Oh, has she? Now I know why you're worried.' Georgia's voice had become spiky with contempt. 'You couldn't care less about Harriet, or Toby, you just want your precious car back. Sorry, Edward, but I can't help. I've no idea where she is, and if I find out, I'm not at all sure I'll tell you. I have to go now. Goodbye.'

He was left listening to the dialling tone. Sick with helpless rage and frustration, he threw the receiver down on the desk and put his head in his hands.

'I feel awful about this,' Harriet said. 'It isn't fair to dump myself and all my problems on you. I'll find somewhere to live as soon as possible.'

'Stop worrying about it.' Daphne lifted a pile of books off the spare bed, put them down on the Victorian walnut chest of drawers, and smiled at her. 'I won't hear any more on the subject. What are friends for, if they can't help in times of trouble? Anyway, if I'm honest I'll be quite glad of some congenial company. After two years away from the groves of academe, intelligent conversation is at a premium, believe me.'

'So why did you leave?'

'I'd had enough of it. I'd spent almost thirty years amongst all the bickering and the in-fighting and the petty rivalries, and I can assure you, the most mild-mannered don can be worse than any woman when it comes to malicious gossip.' Daphne shook out a sheet and handed one end of it to Harriet. 'Anyway, I had a dream. A cosy little cottage, peace and quiet, the chance to put my theories into practice. Marcus is an old friend, and he told me this place was up for sale.'

'You know Sir Marcus Grant? The owner

of Forfar Towers?'

'Indeed I do. We met at Cambridge back in the late fifties, when we were students. I had invited him over for dinner tomorrow, but if you don't feel up to it I can always ring and put him off for a bit.'

'No, honestly, that's fine, as long as I won't be in the way. And if you like, I could help with the cooking.'

'Ah. You can cook?'

'A bit. Whether I'd produce something fit for a genuine sir, of course, is another matter.'

'If you dished up baked beans on toast, he wouldn't mind. Poor Marcus, he finds that big house and all the rest of his inheritance rather embarrassing — that's why he's so generous. He'd really much rather be plain Mr Grant and live in a nice little cottage like this one. But then people always tend to want whatever they can't have, don't they?'

'They certainly do,' said Harriet, thinking of Edward, who always seemed to get what he wanted anyway, however impossible.

But he's not having me, she thought, with renewed determination. Never again. I *might* let him have the BMW, eventually, when he's learned his lesson. But I am never going back there. Never, never, never.

Toby watched from the doorway as the two women put sheets and blankets on the spare

31

bed, his bright-blue eyes very serious. 'Where am I going to sleep?'

Harriet smiled at him warmly. 'In the little bed over there, in the corner. I'm going to have this one. Is that OK?'

'Can I bounce on it?'

His mother laughed. 'No, sweetheart, or it might break.'

'Oh.' Toby digested this information, and then added wistfully, 'Kings can bounce on the bed, can't they? *I* can't, but they can do what they like. They have very posh black shiny boots, don't they, Mummy?'

'Yes, I expect they do, but anyway, sorry, bouncing's banned. This is Daphne's house, remember, and she doesn't want anything broken.'

'OK, Mummy.' Toby wandered across and sat down on the Z-bed, giving an experimental bounce with his bottom and glancing slyly at Harriet to check her reaction. She grinned at him. 'All right, like that won't do any harm. But not with your feet, OK? And *certainly* not with black boots on. Are you going to put Lambkin on your pillow?'

Toby laid his most precious toy reverently down as she suggested, and kissed the worn black nose with love. Now this was truly his own bed. It didn't make Daphne's house home, but it would help. So would the clothes neatly stowed in the chest of drawers, and the box of Duplo and his cars and favourite books. He'd need the rest of his things in a few days, but not yet. His mother, however, didn't even have a pair of knickers to her name.

Daphne had gone to fetch more blankets from the airing cupboard in her room, and Harriet went over to the window. It was at the front of the house, facing east. The overgrown trees in the hedgerow would block most of the view, once they were in full leaf, but she could still see the fields alongside the canal, and in the distance, blue and hazy in the morning sunshine, the distinctive flat top and scattered, windtorn beeches of Oliver's Castle.

'Did you do those, Mummy?'

Harriet turned, and saw him gazing at the beautiful pictures of butterflies decorating the plain white walls. 'No, sweetheart, they're not my style,' she said, laughing. 'Anyway, they're prints, not paintings.' She glanced at Daphne, who was putting the pile of blankets on the bed. 'They're lovely. Are they very old?'

'About a hundred and fifty years, I suppose. Part of my leaving present from my colleagues, along with the ones downstairs.'

'That was very generous,' said Harriet, impressed.

'Hardly. Not so much a 'We're sorry you're going' as a 'Thank God we've given the old bat the push at last'.' The older woman smiled with a warmth that entirely belied her words. 'I should warn you, I'm not an easy person to get on with, let alone live with.'

'That's all right, I'm very tolerant,' Harriet said. And I had to be, to share a house with Edward for five years, she thought wryly. 'Hopefully it won't be for long — just until I find somewhere else.'

'Don't worry. As I said, stay for as long as you have to. I honestly don't mind — in fact, I'm looking forward to it.' Daphne surveyed her. 'I didn't realise you painted. What sort of things?'

Harriet felt herself blushing. 'Oh — water-colours. Landscapes, flowers, stuff like that. But I haven't done anything for ages, apart from canal ware.' Not since I met Edward, she thought, and was pierced with a sudden, desperate longing to take up her brushes again, and produce something more creative, more individual, than the mechanical roses and castles with which she had adorned the buckets and dishes in the boatyard's gift shop.

'Hmm.' Daphne was looking at her speculatively. 'Did you go to art school?'

'Yes, but I dropped out halfway through

34

the course. It just wasn't my sort of thing.' It wasn't exactly the whole truth, but Harriet still, after ten years, shied away from telling anyone, especially this abrupt yet sympathetic woman, the real reason for her departure. She grinned, hiding her unease. 'I wasn't into cutting cows in half or videoing my most intimate moments. I liked *painting*. And my stuff's quite figurative and realistic.'

'In other words, things that people can recognise and relate to,' said Daphne. 'Don't worry — as you can probably guess, I'm not into modern art. Have you brought any of your work?'

'I haven't brought *anything* — not even a toothbrush! I'll have to think of some way of getting my things. Perhaps my sister could go over for me. I don't fancy facing Edward myself at the moment — I'd rather lie low for a few days until I simmer down.'

'It's all right, I understand,' said Daphne. 'Do you want to ring your sister now?'

'I will, yes, thanks, but not yet. This evening, perhaps. If Edward gets in touch with her to tell her that I've gone, she'll be worried.'

'Will he?'

'He'll think I've taken refuge with her. I used to share her flat, years ago, before I moved in with him.' Harriet smiled rather wistfully. 'I've never had a place that's really my own.'

She wanted it more than almost anything else, apart from the chance to start painting again. A little cottage, just for her and Toby, which would truly reflect *her* tastes, *her* personality: with a garden big enough to grow vegetables, perhaps even keep a few chickens. But no matter how she yearned for such idyllic surroundings, she knew that the best she could realistically hope for would be some damp bedsit in a seedy part of Bath.

3

Unfortunately, try as she would, Harriet couldn't see any alternative. Despite the older woman's warm words, she couldn't live indefinitely with Daphne at Holly Cottage. Harriet suspected that after a week without TV, Toby would definitely have outstayed his welcome. Georgia's immaculate flat, full of fragile, beautiful things, wasn't suitable for a small child either, and Fu-Ket, her neurotic Siamese cat, loathed Toby and his enthusiastic attempts to be friendly. Last time they'd visited, the little boy had been badly scratched.

She didn't want to call Georgia just yet. Georgia, from the best possible motives, would want to map out her sister's future in precise and excruciating detail. And now that Harriet had at last wrenched back control of her own destiny, she was certain that she didn't in the least want to hand it instantly on her bossy big sister.

Freedom was a frightening thing, she thought that evening, as she bathed Toby. If she had still been single, there would be no problem. But she was responsible for her son's happiness, and she couldn't afford to make any mistakes. Whatever happened, she would never return to Edward. With an intensity that astonished her, she wanted to make him understand how despicable his behaviour had been. She wanted some financial recompense for all the effort she had put into running his business. And she wanted, if she was honest with herself, to make the bastard really suffer.

'Bang bang BANG!' Toby cried, breaking into her thoughts with alarming aptness. 'The goody's shot the baddy and he's dead. Can I get out now, Mummy?'

She dried his small slippery body, all clean and warm and rosy from the bath, and reminded herself that it wasn't fair on her beloved son to embark on a bitter battle with his father. She couldn't do it, for Toby's sake. He was the innocent party. He loved Edward, despite the fact that his father had had precious little to do with him in his brief life. And she would have died rather than expose him to any more hurt than was absolutely necessary to separate herself from her expartner.

As she helped him into his pyjamas, the phone began to ring downstairs. She heard Daphne's voice, answering it, and, then her call. 'Harriet? It's your sister!'

Well, at least it wasn't Edward. She grinned at Toby. 'Auntie Georgia's tracked us down. Do you want to say hallo?'

Toby was a little in awe of his mother's elder sister. 'No thanks, Mum,' he said, his beautiful harebell eyes wide and serious. 'When's Daddy coming?'

'I don't know,' said Harriet, with a sigh. Before long, she would have to give her son a simple version of the truth, but she wasn't ready for it yet. 'You'll see him soon, I promise.'

'Toby, would you like some warm chocolate to drink?' Daphne stood at the foot of the stairs. 'And if you want, I'll read you a story while your mummy's on the phone.'

'*The Enormous Crocodile!*' Toby cried at once, and ran to fetch it from his room. With a grateful smile for Daphne, Harriet went down to speak to her sister.

'How did you find me?' she asked at once.

'Easy, really. Not me, not Mum and Dad — don't worry, I didn't spill the beans, I know how Mum's fussing gets on your nerves. So there was only one other option. I looked her up in the phone book. Harriet, are you all right?'

'I'm perfectly OK, honestly. Couldn't be better.'

There was a doubtful pause. '*Really?*' said

Georgia, disbelievingly. 'And you've really left him? For good?'

'Definitely. Absolutely. Completely.'

'Wonderful,' said Georgia. 'You should have done it years ago. He's a total loser. So, come on, tell big sis. What happened?'

Harriet glanced round, but the hall was empty, and Daphne's voice, bravely embarking on *The Enormous Crocodile*, came from the sitting room. Keeping her voice muted, she gave Georgia a pithy account of the morning's events.

'Jesus Christ,' her sister said, when she'd finished. 'The complete and utter bastard. He just told me you'd gone off in a huff. No wonder. I think a bucket of water was very restrained, in the circumstances — I'd have cut the bugger's goolies off with a *very* blunt knife. So who was the totty?'

'Gina, the gift shop assistant. Young and tarty, not really Edward's type at all. He likes a bit of class.'

There was a pause. 'Are you telling me,' Georgia demanded, 'that he's done it before?'

'Yes. Lots of times, probably.'

'Then for God's sake, girl, why did you *stay*? Because of Toby?'

Because of Toby. Everything she'd done, for nearly five years, had been because of Toby. And he lit up her life: she would never,

40

ever regret having him.

'Of course,' she said, knowing that it would have been easier, and better, to have left ages ago, before her son was old enough to miss Edward. But then, she had thought that she could still make it work, still recapture some of the original magic. She had been deluding herself, but it had been worth trying. And if she hadn't, she would have regretted it later: just as she still regretted the end of that other, long-ago affair, so abruptly and brutally terminated at its passionate height, rather than being allowed to fade away with time.

'I see,' said Georgia, though as a fully paid-up member of the Herod Appreciation Society, she was hardly likely to understand the power of maternal feeling. 'So, what are you going to do now?'

'Find somewhere to live. And sort things out with Edward.' Harriet took a deep breath. This was probably on the tip of Georgia's tongue, but she was going to suggest it first, and thereby preserve the illusion, at least, that she had resumed control of her life. 'The success of the boatyard is almost entirely down to me, and he knows it. So I want some financial acknowledgement of that, as well as maintenance for Toby.'

'And quickly, before he lets the business slide back into the red again,' said Georgia, who had an even lower opinion of Edward the entrepreneur than of Edward the partner. 'You'll need a good lawyer. I can't really act for you, unfortunately, unless he's done something criminal — you want someone specialising in marital and property. Don Potter's our man — he's excellent.'

'That would be great, but I certainly couldn't afford it.'

'We might be able to wangle you some legal aid. Anyway, what are you going to do for money?'

Most of the wages Daphne had paid Harriet over the past six months had been spent on Toby: shoes, clothes, playgroup fees. She had a little over two hundred pounds saved, in a building society account that Edward didn't know about, but that wouldn't even pay the deposit on the meanest bedsit. 'I'll have to get a proper job,' she said, determined to sound cheerful and optimistic. 'Though I haven't finished Daphne's work yet. Toby starts school in September, so that should help. Anyway, compared to the wonder of being free at last, my financial problems are positively minute.'

'Well, remember that I'm always here if you need me,' Georgia informed her. 'After all, what are sisters for?'

'Thanks, George,' Harriet said, with

genuine gratitude. 'And you haven't even said 'I told you so' yet.'

'I assumed you'd take it as read. Anyway, consign the dirty low-down, two-timing, double-crossing, adulterous rat to the sewer where he belongs, and think about yourself for a change. That's the trouble with you, Harry, you never *have* thought about yourself, not for years and years. Edward, Toby, the boatyard, you've put them all first. Well, now's your chance to be selfish again, and I should bloody well take it.'

'I intend to.' Harriet, grinning to herself, was thinking that of all people Georgia, with her luxurious single life and her almost total lack of real responsibility, was in a supreme position to know about selfishness. But that was being unfair: George simply didn't know what it was like to have someone utterly dependent on her. She just had her cat to care for. And although she was only thirty-three, and very attractive, she had made it quite clear, years ago, that she wasn't interested in marriage, or children, or even in long-term relationships. 'Look, George, can you do me a big favour?'

'Gladly.'

'Can you go over to the boatyard and get some things for me? I don't fancy meeting Edward just yet, and anyway, if I turn up in the BMW he'll grab it back, and I want to hang on to it for a bit.'

'Bargaining counter?'

'Exactly.'

'It'll give me the greatest pleasure,' said Georgia, with lip-smacking satisfaction. 'When's the best time?'

'Depends whether you want to come face to face with him or not. Tomorrow's Saturday, changeover day, so he's got to be there, to sort out the boats.' Harriet realised, with a splendidly liberating sense of wonder, that for the first time in more than five years, she wouldn't have to do it. She wouldn't have to say goodbye to the old customers, check the boats, make sure the inventories were complete, see that Pete had serviced the engines thoroughly, oversee the cleaning, sort out the grocery orders for the new hirers, greet them, show them round the boats, and even, when Pete was too busy, give them basic instructions in canal etiquette and how to work a lock. Edward would have to do it. It would be absolute chaos, she was certain of it. And she didn't give a toss: they could leave all the paddles up and empty the canal from Sanden to Caen Hill, and she wouldn't care.

'He'll probably be too busy to notice you,' she added. 'And I could really do with some clothes and my toothbrush and things like that.'

'Sure thing, kid. Just tell me where to find them, and what you'd most like, and I'll write it down.'

Harriet listed the basic essentials of her life: jeans, trousers, blouses, jumpers, underwear, T-shirts, toiletries. Deliberately, she omitted the expensive, formal clothes that Edward had liked her to wear to impress his posh friends, and which she had secretly hated. Never again would she have to wear the mustard-coloured suit that made her look a frumpy forty-five, or the tight black dress which, he had claimed, was so sexy, and which Harriet knew revealed all her most unlovely bulges.

'Is that all?' demanded Georgia, who was a snappy dresser, always smart and elegant. 'Haven't you even got a skirt? If you go for interviews, you'll need something a bit better than jeans.'

'I'll buy anything else I want. Then it'll be my choice.'

'Aha,' said Georgia, light dawning. 'I can take you shopping — that'll be fun.'

'It's a deal,' Harriet said. 'But remember — *my* choice. No pressure, no vetoes.'

'OK, OK, I promise not to be bossy,' said Georgia cheerfully. Evidently, she was so delighted that Harriet had finally taken the plunge and dumped Edward that she was prepared to forgo her usual big-sister role.

'World first if you can keep it,' Harriet told her. They had always had this bantering, knowing, argumentative relationship. As children, the fights had been serious, but now they were adults, and each recognised the other as sister, confidante, comrade and best friend. She added, 'There's one other thing. My watercolours and sketch blocks. They're in a box in the office, up on the highest shelf above the fax machine. Could you get those as well? And all my old paintings too, they're in some folders on the top.'

'He put your watercolours away in a *box*?' Georgia sounded horrified. 'Dear God, kid, is that how bad it was?'

For the first time, the true realisation of how her life and her talents had been wasted under Edward's thumb smote Harriet. She felt hot tears of self-pity spill on to her cheeks, and wiped them fiercely away. 'Not any more,' she said stoutly. 'I'm not looking back, I'm looking forward. I'm going to paint again, properly. You never know, I might even sell some stuff. The whole world's waiting for me out there, George, and I'm not going to waste any more time — I'm going out and grabbing whatever I can, and sod anyone who tries to stop me now.'

But she knew, as she put the phone down, that despite her brave words, leaving Edward had been the easiest part. From now on, her life would certainly become very difficult. The world wasn't kind to unemployed unmarried mothers, especially those who had left an ostensibly stable relationship for what seemed like selfish reasons. She didn't know if she would be able to cope with all the troubles that undoubtedly lay ahead. But for Toby's sake, she must do her best. And no matter what happened, she would never go back.

4

At half past ten on Saturday morning, Georgia Smith drove her Vauxhall Tigra into the yard of Wonderland Boats, and parked with a flourish next to the dejected, rusty little Metro that belonged to her sister. She got out, ready to do battle on Harriet's behalf, and looked around for the enemy.

There was no sign of Edward, but there was a knot of people standing by one of the bigger boats tied up at the wharf, and there appeared to be an argument going on. Georgia had no intention of getting involved. She marched up to the front door of the house that Harriet had called home until yesterday, and leant heavily on the bell.

Rather to her surprise, it was answered almost immediately. Edward peered cautiously round the door, and his expression, when he saw who it was, came down across his face like a steel shutter. 'Oh. It's you. Where is she?'

'Enjoying a well-deserved rest, and some peace and quiet,' said Georgia pointedly. 'And she said most particularly not to tell you where. I've come for her things, and some more of Toby's. Are you going to let me in?'

A shout came from behind her. She turned, and saw a young man in mechanic's overalls hurrying across the yard to the house. 'Mr Armstrong — there you are! We need your help!'

'Oh, buggery,' Edward muttered. 'I was hoping to avoid this.' He glared at Georgia, and she smiled blandly back.

'I think you're wanted. Shall I go in and get Harriet's clothes?'

'If you must,' said Edward ungraciously. He edged past her and faced the mechanic. 'Now what is it, Pete?'

'Mr and Mrs Thompson don't like the state *Queen of Hearts* is in. They reckon it isn't clean enough. Could you come and sort it?'

'I blame *you* for all this,' said Edward, rounding on Georgia with a savagery that startled her. 'If you'd been a bit more supportive with Harriet, none of this mess would have happened.'

'*My* fault?' Georgia stared at him, her jaw dropping. 'What the hell has it got to do with me? *You're* the one she caught shagging someone else, Edward, not me. You've no one to blame but yourself, and you know it.'

But Edward, unwilling or unable to argue the point, had already turned away, and was striding over to the wharf. Pete gave her an

49

eloquent glance and scurried in pursuit.

'God, what a bastard,' said Georgia. She removed a couple of pristine cases from the boot of the car, and walked briskly into the house.

It had been built for a canal official, nearly two hundred years previously, and age had not treated it kindly. Georgia knew that the determinedly cheerful yellow paintwork, the brightly striped throws and rugs, the block-printed curtains and the charming collection of lace-edged plates were all the marks of Harriet's gift for colour and design. Without them, the house would be a drab and comfortless place.

She stuck her head round the sitting room door. The table next to the sofa bore mute witness, in the form of an unpleasantly overflowing ashtray, an empty bottle that had once held vintage claret, an unwashed glass and a bag full of the sourly aromatic debris from an Indian takeaway, to how Edward had spent the previous evening.

Criminal waste of good wine, Georgia thought. She withdrew, wrinkling her nose at the stale stench, and carried the cases briskly upstairs.

It did not take long to find and pack Harriet's clothes. As instructed, she left the racks of frumpy, 'classic' garments untouched, and took the trousers, jumpers and shirts. Folded away inside the first case, it didn't seem very much. A couple of boxes of jewellery, mainly cheap necklaces and earrings, sat forlornly on top. There was a copy of the latest Joanna Trollope paperback on the bedside table: it didn't look as if her sister had read more than a couple of pages, and it had dust on it. Georgia put it in as well, and zipped up the case. She glanced around, remembering how Harriet, with much laughter, had described the lurid pink and purple colour scheme she had found in here, and her efforts to conceal it with a liberal application of blue paint and a new carpet, despite Edward's protests at the disruption and expense. And even then, when her sister had been in the first passionate stages of the relationship, Georgia had wondered how long a union between Harriet, who loved beautiful things, and Edward, who was entirely indifferent to them, could possibly last.

Well, she'd finally seen the light and got out, thank God. Georgia picked up the cases and went out on to the landing. There were towels hanging over the banisters, and an extremely large and hairy spider glaring balefully down at her from a place which would require a very long brush to reach. She put the full case down at the top of the stairs and went into Toby's room.

Here, Harriet's eye for colour and her gift for drawing had been enchantingly united. The pale-blue walls were scattered with fat white clouds, and a profusion of hot-air balloons, brilliant and beautiful, floated amongst them like vivid teardrops. The theme was echoed in the curtains, which looked as if they had been hand-stencilled, and in the intricate mobile drifting thoughtfully in the air above Toby's bed. Georgia stood staring round, filled with admiration for her sister's talent, and also with fury at how it had been wasted. Then she dropped the case down on the bed and began to fill it with what had been left behind.

Five minutes later, she was loading everything into the car. She couldn't see Edward by the wharf, so he was presumably inside the boat, placating the customers. I hope they fry him, Georgia thought vengefully. And that'd be no more than the bastard deserves.

There was still one more thing to find, and then she could get the hell out of here. Not that she was frightened of a further confrontation with Edward: far from it, she'd relish the chance to tell him exactly what she thought of him. But Harriet had asked for her watercolours, and they were in the office.

Georgia slammed the car door and went back into the house.

The door on the right was firmly closed, but she opened it anyway and went in. This was Harriet's domain, so there was a place for everything, and everything apparently in its place. Trays marked *Urgent* and *Later*; box files ranged neatly on the shelves, containing bookings dating back several years, wages and personnel information, boat records; a small photocopier and a fax machine; and the top-of-the-range PC, its screen blank and slumbering, which held all the current details of Wonderland Boats within its smooth grey case. Georgia would have liked to have wiped it clean, but her knowledge of computers went no further than Word for Windows, and in any case Harriet, acutely aware of how easily her chief work-tool might crash, would undoubtedly have kept back-up disks of everything important.

Georgia looked round for the box of watercolours, and found it exactly where her sister had said, on the highest of the shelves above the fax machine. She had to stand on a chair to reach it, and a choking cloud of dust, and a lot of dead flies and cobwebs, came down with it.

Harriet, once asked what she would take to a desert island, had unhesitatingly named her

53

painting kit. All too obviously, this hadn't been touched for years. Georgia, whose fierce desire for independence would allow no interference with the pleasures of her life, could not comprehend the level of devotion, or unselfishness, or submissiveness symbolised by the abandonment of something which had once been the guiding star of Harriet's life. She brushed the rest of the dust off the folders and the old envelope, presumably full of paintings, which lay on top, and carried them and the box of watercolours out to the car.

She was just getting in when she saw Edward actually running across the yard towards her. She slid behind the wheel, put on her seat belt and coolly watched him approach. Granted, he had a nice voice and abundant charm. When it suited him to use it, and the confident, man-of-the-world air that went with money. To the younger Harriet, his obvious interest must have seemed flattering and exciting.

Well, she knows better now, Georgia thought. But too late — she's lumbered with a child, and no job, and nowhere to live. And she was aware of an unworthy feeling of smugness, that she herself had always been careful to avoid such a trap.

'You've got to tell me where she is!'

Edward cried through the open car window. 'She's got my *car*, for Christ's sake! And my son,' he added, clearly as an afterthought.

'You're only worried about your precious BMW,' Georgia said coldly. 'You couldn't care less about Toby.'

'That's not true!' Edward was plainly hurt. 'He's my son, and I love him.'

'Not enough to make sure he didn't find you bonking some tart in his mother's bed,' Georgia said, callously plunging in the knife.

To her extreme gratification, Edward went grey with shock. '*What?*'

'*He* found you yesterday. Not Harriet. Toby went upstairs and saw you. God, Edward. I knew you were a rat but I'd no idea how deep your particular sewer was.'

'He can't have done! She's lying! I didn't see him!'

'I gather you had other things on your mind at the time. Anyway, you know as well as I do that Harriet isn't a liar. Naïve, trusting, loyal to a fault, certainly, but she's truthful and always has been. She wouldn't make a story like that up for effect — and definitely not if Toby was involved. She'd lay down her life for him, which is a damn sight more than you'd ever do, you selfish pig. Oh, look, I think those people want to talk to you.'

Edward glanced round, his expression

hunted and haggard. The couple who had hired *Queen of Hearts* were advancing purposefully across the yard, and the husband, a big man with tattoos along each forearm, looked alarmingly fierce.

'Oh God,' said Harriet's former lover in panic.

'Well, I must be going,' Georgia told him, with cheerful unconcern. 'Looks as if you're going to need all your slippery charm to get out of this one, Edward. Have fun!'

She drove away with a contemptuous roar of the engine. As the Tigra paused at the gate into the lane, she couldn't resist a glance in her rear-view mirror. The tattooed man was looming over Edward, and gesturing vehemently. With a grin, Georgia turned right, over the canal bridge and past the Wharf Inn, as if she was heading for Melksham and Bath. At the sharp left-hand bend just before New Farm, however, she turned right up Stony Lane, towards Harriet's refuge.

Straight after the canal bridge, her sister had said, but at first sight there was nothing except a lot of very overgrown trees, hanging over the road and obstructing the view. Beyond, however, there was a neat hedge and a strip of closely mown grass, with four staddle stones placed along it to prevent anyone driving or parking on the verge. A slab of rustic sandstone, propped against a large classical urn full of military tulips, was carved with the name *Cypress Lodge*, and a middle-aged woman was standing beside it, cutting the hedge. She looked round as Georgia halted the Tigra and leaned out of the window. 'Excuse me?'

The woman switched off the hedge-trimmer and approached. Her flowery blouse and pleated skirt looked more appropriate for a tea party or a shopping trip than for gardening. She said, in very wellbred tones, 'Can I help you?'

'I'm looking for a place called Holly Cottage,' said Georgia. 'I was told it was along here. A Ms James lives there?'

The woman's face, heavily powdered, changed instantly from polite helpfulness to excitement. 'Are you from the council?'

'No, I'm not,' said Georgia, raising her eyebrows. 'I'm just a visitor. Is this the right road?'

The eagerness faded rapidly, to be replaced by disapproving hostility. 'It's there,' she said, gesturing back down the lane. 'Next door.'

'Good grief.' Georgia turned and peered behind her. 'Is there a house behind all that lot?'

'Yes. My point *exactly*,' the woman snapped. 'Five complaints I've made to the council now, and they won't do anything about it. They said they'd send someone round, but that was days ago and I haven't heard a thing. Well, *something* ought to be done about it. I ask you, would *you* like to live next door to that mess?'

Her well-bred voice had become much more ordinary under the pressure of her indignation. Georgia said mildly, 'I don't think it would bother me much, personally. Live and let live, that's my motto. Anyway, thanks for your help. Can I turn round in your driveway?'

'I'd very much rather you didn't,' said the woman, who had obviously now ranked her with the enemy. 'You'll find a gate just up the road. Good day.'

Eyebrows raised at her rudeness, Georgia carried on up the lane. The gateway proved to be at the narrowest stretch, hemmed in with high banks on either side, and it took a lot of manoeuvring back and forth before she was able to turn the Tigra in the right direction. The woman was still clipping her already manicured hedge, and gave Georgia a hard, hostile stare as she drove past.

There was a gap in the trees, just before the lane rose up over the canal, and she slowed right down. Yes, sure enough, some were holly trees, and there did seem to be a house in

58

there. Good grief, it's like Sleeping Beauty's castle, she thought, turning cautiously in under the sagging branches. Well, she couldn't have chosen a better hideaway — I doubt Edward even knows this place exists.

The dirt track led round the side of the house to a rough, bare area at the back. A sleek silver-blue BMW, its gleaming paint-work blotted with bird droppings, was parked under a gnarled pear tree next to an old red Golf. Georgia slid the Tigra into the remaining space and got out, looking round with considerable curiosity. Despite the jungle of trees at the front of the house, this side showed definite signs of love and care, although no one could have called it tidy. The house itself was almost completely covered with climbing plants, amongst which Georgia, no gardener, could recognise wisteria, just coming into gloriously fragrant bloom, honeysuckle and summer jasmine. Outside the back door, there was a paved area, bounded by a low dry-stone wall, and enlivened by a profusion of crimson, bronze and golden wallflowers, growing in a very assorted collection of pots, mostly old-fashioned terracotta, interestingly lichened. A wooden table and four matching chairs indicated that the unknown Ms James sometimes ate outside. Beyond the cars, a rough area of grass, bordered by overgrown shrubs and strewn with late daffodils and other less showy flowers, stretched for fifty yards or so along the side of the canal. On this bank, free of the towpath, the ground straggled untidily into the water, the boundary irregularly marked by tall reeds and other wet loving plants. Beyond the hen-run and the hawthorn hedge at the bottom of the garden, the park belonging to Forfar Towers sloped up towards the distant, hidden houses of Sanden Row.

Georgia was a city-dweller, by upbringing and inclination, but even she could understand the peace and beauty of this place. And Harriet, painter of flowers and landscapes, would surely feel utterly at home here. Smiling, she turned back towards the house, and saw her sister approaching.

5

All morning, Harriet had been both dreading and looking forward to this moment. Despite the quiet, and the deep darkness, she had slept very little the previous night: she had been too busy thinking about what had happened, and what would happen, and what she would now do with her life. Then, too, she had felt this strange, exhilarating mixture of excitement and fear. In the coming days and weeks, her decisions would have momentous consequences both for her and for Toby. For someone who had been a slave to routine and duty for so long, it was at once a glorious and a terrifying prospect.

'Hallo,' she said, almost shyly. In these very rural surroundings, Georgia's smart tailored trouser suit and crisp white blouse looked so incongruous that she was tempted to smile; and also so dear and familiar and welcome that she felt like crying. 'It's great to see you.'

'Likewise.' They had not come from a particularly demonstrative family, but this seemed the right moment for a brief embrace. Harriet smelt her sister's expensive perfume, felt her slender bones and the warmth of her hug, and heard her voice, unusually soft and affectionate. 'Has it been really bad?'

Her obvious sympathy almost undid Harriet's avowed intention to look forward rather than back. Her eyes prickled, but she said firmly, 'I don't want to think about it. It's gone now, forever.'

Georgia privately thought that the furious, bitter Edward she had left at the boatyard would not disappear so easily from his former lover's life, and certainly not while she was still hanging on to his car. She said, 'I've got all your things. Shall we take them inside?'

'I'll give you a hand.' Harriet was glad of something to do, and to think about. She carried the precious box of paints and sketches into the house, while Georgia followed with the cases. It didn't seem much baggage for thirty years, and once more she was conscious of her deep desire to make a real, permanent home for herself and her son.

Toby was sitting at the kitchen table with a half-empty glass of milk and a nibbled biscuit in front of him, looking expectantly at the door. When his aunt came in, his face visibly fell. 'Where's Daddy?'

For once at a loss, Georgia glanced at Harriet. She said gently, 'I told you, sweetheart. You'll see him soon.'

'Soon's a long time,' Toby said wistfully.

But he was soon diverted by the sight of the rest of his car collection, and was sorting eagerly through the contents of the case when Daphne James entered the kitchen. 'Hallo,' she said to Georgia, with a smile. 'You must be Harriet's sister. I'm Daphne.'

They shook hands, while Harriet watched them rather warily. Despite the vast difference in age and appearance, both were women who spoke their minds and refused to suffer fools gladly. But at least they shared a common cause, although Harriet hoped, without much confidence, that they wouldn't take it upon themselves to interfere too much. Granted, she had asked for their help, and she was very grateful for what they had done, and would do, but she intended to assert her own independence as soon as she could. Which, of course, was very much easier said than done.

Toby went out to the patio with his box of cars, and Daphne made coffee and produced biscuits in a rather battered old tin with a bold yellow sunflower design on the lid. Harriet, cradling her mug, smiled at her sister. 'So you found the place all right, then. My directions couldn't have been too bad.'

'Even so, I nearly missed it. The woman next door put me right, but when she found out I wasn't from the council, just an ordinary visitor, she wasn't exactly friendly.' Georgia paused, and glanced at Daphne. 'Have you been having trouble?'

The older woman cast her eyes up in exasperation. 'To put it mildly, yes. Heather has a thing about tidiness. And, as you have no doubt ascertained, I haven't. I bought this house precisely because the garden was overgrown and neglected. The holly trees at the front are wonderful — a perfect ecosystem in miniature. So is the hedgerow between us. Elm, oak, silver birch, hawthorn, ash — a linear wood. But she wants me to uproot them all, and cut the birch down because, if you please, its seeds are littering her patio.' She gave the sisters a rueful smile. 'Still, I've got much better things to do with my life than worry about what she thinks of me. More coffee, anyone?'

As she poured out the rest of the cafetière's contents, Harriet took the opportunity to thank her sister for fetching her things. 'Did you see Edward?'

'Unfortunately, yes.'

'How was he? Did he seem . . . upset at all?'

'Absolutely furious is a better way of describing it. He wants his car back, of course. And he accused me of interfering. A lot of it was bluster, I think; he knew he was in the wrong.'

'Edward's very good at taking up attitudes,' Harriet said quietly. 'He gets on his high horse about something and then thinks it'd damage his manhood to back down. I know I shall have to talk to him eventually, but not until I've sorted out what I want to do. Otherwise he'll try and persuade me to go back to him, and then get even more angry when I refuse.'

'And you're not even the teeniest bit tempted?' Georgia enquired, with raised eyebrows indicating that it'd be more than her sister's life was worth to give in to her ex-partner's bullying.

'No,' said Harriet firmly. 'No, no and definitely no. Even if he lays on the guilt with a trowel, I've had enough. Gina was the last straw. I may be homeless and broke, but at least I'm free. And quite honestly, I think Toby's better off without him, too.'

'Are you sure about that?' Daphne asked. 'He's been talking a lot about wanting to see Daddy. You can't just cut Edward out of your life completely, however much you might want to.'

'I do know that.' Harriet took a deep breath. 'I don't mind if Edward sees him. After all, it's only fair and right. But on *my* terms. And he'll have to pay me maintenance as well — that's fair too. But he never took much interest in Toby before we left, so he can't complain I've deprived him of his son's company. I suspect he thinks of him as a nuisance.'

'Wouldn't surprise me, the rat,' Georgia said. 'Well, now we're all here, we'd better decide what to do next.'

'You've got it slightly wrong.' Harriet was sitting very upright in the old Windsor chair, her pale hands clasped round her mug of coffee and her hazel eyes clear and determined behind the round glasses. As her sister looked at her enquiringly, she added, 'Change the pronoun, please. *I'd* better decide what to do next. My life, remember? So my choices.'

'OK, point taken,' said Georgia, rather irritably.

'Sorry, George.' Harriet gave her an apologetic smile. 'It's not that I'm not grateful for all you've done, and Daphne's been brilliant. But I'm sick of having other people run my life for me. I don't want to have to impose on your kindness.'

'I've told you — you're not imposing,' Daphne put in.

'At five foot two, I'm certainly not,' Harriet said, with a sudden flashing grin. 'And, like I

66

said, I really really do appreciate what you've done. But we can't stay here forever. We need our own space. I know you'd have us, George, and so would Mum and Dad, gladly, but that isn't the point. I'm thirty, and I've never had a home that was truly *mine*. I want to be in charge, not a guest. The house at the boatyard wasn't *ours*, it was Edward's. I wanted to do much more than slap some paint on the walls, but he barely noticed when I did, and he said new windows and refurbishing the kitchen would be a waste of money.'

'And buying a forty-grand car wasn't, I suppose,' Georgia muttered.

'Even renting somewhere will be expensive,' Daphne said practically. 'Edward will have to pay you maintenance eventually, but what do you do in the short term?'

'I've thought about it. I'll have to do all the boring things like signing on and claiming benefit. I'm going to register with all the employment agencies, though I know I don't stand much chance of getting anything worthwhile because of Toby. He's at Sanden playgroup every morning, and I want that to continue, to give him *some* stability. So if that's OK with you, Daphne, I would like to stay here for a while, but it won't be for long, I promise. Ideally, I'd like to find somewhere to rent in the village, but I know even the cheapest place will be far more than I can possibly afford. I've got hardly any savings, and no job. But I've got the time now to enjoy Toby's company, and time to paint.'

'Did Georgia bring any of your paintings back?' Daphne asked her. 'I'd love to see them.'

'Oh, yes. Pretty well everything I've ever done that was any good came with that box.' Harriet smiled. 'That's one advantage of working in watercolours — the results don't take up much space.'

It didn't seem a lot for a lifetime's work, she thought, laying the three fat folders on the table, which Daphne had just cleared of everything remotely spillable. She put aside the old envelope which lay on top, and was nothing to do with her, and opened the first folder. 'This is what I was doing when I was at art school. I couldn't find anyone prepared to teach me the techniques, and I couldn't afford to go to evening classes on my grant, so I got a book out of the library and taught myself. Now, of course, you can get videos and it's much easier to learn. And I made all sorts of stupid mistakes — a purist would be horrified. You're meant to work from light to dark, you see, and I started out doing it the wrong way round.'

'That's the view from your bedroom window at home,' Georgia said. 'I can remember you doing that.'

'It took ages. I hated it by the time I'd finished, but I was determined to get it done. These are of the pub we all used to go to in Clifton, remember? I did a whole series of them, inside and out. I used to love the look of it on a Sunday lunchtime, with the sun shining through all the cigarette smoke.'

'Now that is good,' said Daphne, with genuine admiration. 'I love that couple with their heads together, completely absorbed in each other.'

Harriet had forgotten the picture, but never the subject. Suddenly it was all coming back to her, with bitter, desperate clarity. His voice, soft and dark and passionate, with the Welsh lilt that he had never managed to lose, although he'd left Cardiff at the age of fifteen.

'That's us, isn't it?' he had said. 'In the beer garden at the Goat. I recognise your hair.'

Well, no one would recognise it now. Ten years ago it had been cut very short and dyed brilliant red, in a conscious attempt to electrify her image. Only Georgia remembered her in her rebellious phase, before she bowed to the pressures of conformity. And even the dye had been nothing unusual amongst the other students. Sian, her flatmate in the second year, had had hair bleached white and a complexion to match. Harriet could recall nothing else about her appearance now except her nose-stud, which had looked like a drop of bright blood. She herself had drawn the line at piercing anything more than her ears.

Strange, and terrible, how nostalgia had the power to grab you by the throat and urge you to go back. But no matter how hard she might wish for the power to shed ten years and choose differently, she could never return to that earlier, more innocent Harriet, still supremely confident in the prospect of happiness.

Quickly, she riffled through the pictures until she found some that were less painful. Jug after bowl after vase of flowers, pansies and irises and daffodils, beautiful and unthreatening, carrying no burden of memory or betrayal; the back yard at her sister's flat, full of geraniums and tomatoes and terracotta pots; studies of Fu-Ket, with his slitted, sinister blue eyes and attenuated body; and then, as she grew more confident and competent, street scenes in Bath, Abbey Green and the Pump Room and odd, overlooked corners revealing a hidden charm that the famous tourist attractions no longer possessed; vistas from the hills around the city; a dead tree in a hedgerow, its naked branches like arms crying for mercy; the steep lane down to the Pack Horse in South Stoke; autumn trees in the valley at Claverton, their gold and amber leaves reflected in the canal below.

'But these are absolutely stunning,' said Daphne. 'When I asked if you painted, I had no idea — '

'You thought she was just a weekend amateur,' Georgia told her, grinning.

'But I am,' Harriet pointed out. 'I've never sold a picture in my life.'

That wasn't quite true. She had given one away, long ago, along with her soul. It had been a bad bargain.

'Only because you couldn't bear to part with them,' Georgia said. 'Come on, Harry, these are wonderful. When I think of the badly drawn, amateurish junk I've seen at craft fairs and exhibitions selling for three or four hundred a throw, I could weep. Honestly, you'd have no problem getting just as much for these, if not more.'

'I don't know.' Harriet looked doubtfully at the final folder. A painting of the Wharf Inn, opposite the boatyard, lay on top. It had been the last thing she'd ever done, five years ago, before the demands of work and motherhood had hijacked her art and left her barren. 'I want to start again. But I'm not sure if I can.'

'Nonsense!' said Georgia robustly. 'A gift like that can't just abandon you. You don't need a job at all — you just need to paint. Get this stuff properly framed and in a gallery, and you'd be made. People come to Bath from all over the world, and they want to take something of it home with them. All you'd ever need to do would be the Abbey and the Pump Room.'

'For the rest of my life? Get real, George. Perhaps I could make my living as an artist, but even if I manage it eventually, how do we exist in the mean time? Galleries, paper, framing, it all costs far more than I can afford. At the best, it'd be precarious. And I can't take risks, I really can't. I could if it was just me, but I've got Toby to think about.'

'And he was the biggest mistake of all, if you ask me.'

The sisters glared at each other. Georgia, as ever, was cool, stern, in control. Harriet's hair was coming out of its plait, and two bright spots of colour blazed in her cheeks. 'How *dare* you say that! He's the best thing that ever happened to me. I can't ever regret having him, not *ever*, and if you want any part in my life you'd better get that perfectly clear.'

'OK,' said her sister, after a brief, eloquent pause. 'I'm sorry, I shouldn't have said that. Harry, I don't want to quarrel, but you do need to sort yourself out. You've got a wonderful gift, you're brilliant, you really are, and it'd be criminal to waste it. All it takes is a bit of push.'

'Which you're ready and willing to provide, of course.' Harriet caught Georgia's eye and grinned suddenly. 'I'm sorry too. I just need a bit of space, OK? Time to think it all over. Can you just step back a bit and give me the chance?'

'Of course I can,' said her sister, with sincerity. 'Let's just hope that we can persuade Edward to be understanding and reasonable too.'

But there was, thought Georgia, as she helped Harriet to pack away her paintings, precious little chance of that ever happening.

6

'Look, Mummy!'

Harriet had been sorting out the clothes that Georgia had brought into neat piles on the bed. She turned, startled, and beheld her son striking a dramatic pose. He was wearing a blue sweatshirt and trousers, with a pair of red shorts over the top, and a red patterned tea-towel tucked into his collar. 'Guess what I am, Mum!'

Laughing, Harriet pretended ignorance. 'Goodness, I can't think. Batman? Robin Hood?'

'No, Mum,' said Toby in exasperation. 'I'm *Superman*!' He twirled round the bed and flopped down on it. 'Are these your clothes, Mummy?'

'Yes, they're what Auntie Georgia brought from home.' There was a small silence. Toby sat up and looked at her very seriously. 'Mummy, when are we going to go home?'

Now. Now was the time to tell him. Harriet took a deep breath and said gently, 'I don't think we are, sweetheart.'

'Oh.' His blue eyes stared at her intently.

'But I want to go home.'

'We're going to make ourselves a new home, just for us.'

'Here?'

'No, not here — Daphne's house is lovely, but it's much too small to fit us in for very long. And it's hers.'

'And Maggie's.' Toby paused, frowning, and then added, 'If we have a home of our own, where will Daddy live?'

'At our old home.'

'Won't he be with us, then?'

'I'm afraid not, sweetheart.'

'Why not? Will the new home be too small for him?'

'It probably will, so Daddy is going to be staying with the boatyard so he can carry on working there.' And that'll bring him down to earth with a crash, Harriet thought, not without some vengeful satisfaction. Actually having to *work* for a change.

'But why can't he be with us?'

'I know it's difficult for you to understand, but Daddy and I have decided that we don't want to live in the same house any more. Don't worry, you'll still be able to see him, of course you will. We just won't be living together, that's all.'

'Oh.' Toby digested this momentous information very seriously, and then added,

'Lots of people living together — that's family, isn't it?'

'Yes, it is. And you and I will still be a family, even though there are just the two of us.'

'I want to live with *you*, Mummy.'

Harriet laughed, her eyes prickling, and hugged him close. 'And so you shall. We'll find a little house somewhere, with a garden — '

'Can we have a kitten? *Please* can we have a kitten?'

'I don't see why not. But it'll have to wait until we've got our own home. Daphne doesn't like cats — they kill birds, you see.'

'And mice,' Toby said. 'But our kitten won't catch birds if we tell it not to, will it?'

'It's a nice idea,' Harriet told him. 'But I shouldn't rely on it. Cats do their own thing, they don't take much notice of what people tell them to do.' She smiled at him. 'Look, the sun's out, why don't you go and play with Maggie in the garden?'

'I want *you* to come too, Mum,' Toby said, his voice teetering on the edge of a whine.

Harriet sighed. She loved him dearly, and she knew that he needed her very much at this difficult time, but at moments like this she could not help looking forward to September, when he would be starting

76

school, and growing more independent.

Still, she thought as she followed him downstairs, he seemed to have taken the news that his parents had split up with remarkable sang-froid. But she knew that most of her carefully positive explanation had gone well above his head. At the moment, he was too excited by the novelty of living in Daphne's house, full of unexpected wonders: the chickens at the bottom of the garden, the big box full of antique metal soldiers and farm animals, the amiable presence of Maggie the Labrador. But soon he would begin to question the reasons for their departure from the only home he had ever known. He would want to see Edward on a regular basis. And she wondered if Edward, who had greeted the news of the forthcoming baby with dismay, who had blamed her pregnancy for Harriet's 'letting herself go', and who had never taken much notice of Toby once born, would welcome the opportunity of frequent contact with him.

Well, that was his problem, not hers. At this moment, still full of anger, she wouldn't care if she never clapped eyes on Edward again. But Toby was his son, whether he liked it or not, and all the surveys showed that children who remained in contact with a departed parent were happier and better adjusted than those who didn't. She wanted what was best for *Toby*, even more than for herself, and if that meant she had to negotiate things like access and maintenance with her expartner, then she would try to conquer her bitterness and rage, and be reasonable.

Outside, Toby found an old tennis ball buried in the grass, and threw it for Maggie to fetch. He couldn't propel it very far, but the dog charged off in pursuit with the unstoppable momentum of a tank, rolling over and over in her eagerness to stop and snatch it. With her prize clenched in her jaws, she panted up to him and dropped the ball at his feet, then sat back, her ears cocked and her tail wagging, poised for the next throw. With joyful excitement, Toby picked it up and hurled it wildly into the air.

Unfortunately he had aimed in completely the wrong direction. Harriet gave a cry of dismay as it plummeted beyond the hedge on their left, just inside next door's garden.

'Oh,' Toby said, crestfallen. 'Sorry, Mum.'

'It's all right,' Harriet reassured him, with more confidence than she actually felt. 'I'm sure they won't mind. Poor Maggie, though — look, she doesn't know where it's gone.'

The dog was bounding about, searching fruitlessly for the ball amongst the bushes along the boundary between Daphne's garden and her over-tidy neighbour's. 'Try throwing a stick or something for her,' Harriet said. 'I'll go and ask if I can get the ball back.'

A few days ago, this suggestion would not have perturbed Toby in the least. Now, with his world turned upside down, he was evidently feeling considerable insecurity. 'No!' he wailed, running after her. 'Wait, Mum, wait, I want to come with you!'

Harriet looked quickly round for Daphne, but she was nowhere in sight. Firmly, but without much hope of success, she told the dog to stay, and then, hand in hand with her son, went out of the garden to beard the ferocious Heather in her den.

On foot, she had time to take note of the extreme contrast between the two cottages. As if the borderline had been drawn with a ruler, the overhanging branches and tangled growth of Daphne's domain gave way to a severely clipped hedge of alternate green- and gold-leafed conifers. A new wooden five-barred gate was shut across the immaculately gravelled drive. Toby, a neat and observant child, glanced round approvingly. 'It's very tidy,' he said as Harriet lifted the catch.

'The people who live here must work very hard to make it look so nice.' She could see no sign of life, so perhaps Heather and her family were out. In that case, it surely wouldn't do any harm just to have a quick look for the ball.

She rang the front doorbell and waited. No response. 'Isn't anyone at home?' Toby asked, a wobble in his voice. 'But I want to get the ball back.'

To make sure, Harriet rang again, with the same lack of result. 'Come on, sweetheart,' she said. 'Let's go round to the back.'

A new wing had been built on to the rear of the cottage, in yellow, reconstituted stone that almost, but not quite, matched the mellow blocks of the original. Beside it, a pristine Victorian-style conservatory, in anachronistic white plastic, filled in the gap between new and old. Harriet caught a glimpse of abundant foliage, and the bright plump cushions of expensive cane furniture. Resisting the temptation to have a quick peek, she walked firmly across the patio and over the expanse of emerald turf to the boundary hedge.

After some searching, they eventually located the ball under a roundly clipped bush of flowering currant, some distance from where Harriet had thought it would be. With glee, Toby picked it up and clutched it to his chest. 'Come on, Mum, let's go back!'

'May I ask what you're doing?'

The voice was loud, and sharp with animosity. Startled, Harriet whipped round, and saw three people marching across the lawn towards them. Her heart sank. This must be Heather and her family. And to judge from the expressions on their faces, her unauthorised presence in their garden was not exactly welcome.

Oh, Christ, Harriet thought. This'll mean more trouble for Daphne. But she had learned, at the boatyard, that a pleasant manner could smooth over all sorts of difficulties, so she smiled and went to meet them. 'Hallo, I'm Harriet Smith. Sorry, we rang the doorbell and there was no reply, so we — '

'So you just thought you'd have a snoop round,' said the woman. 'Shall I call the police, Keith?' she added to her companion, presumably her husband. He was a short, spare man in his early fifties, with square, dark-rimmed glasses, greying hair swept back, and a distinctly harassed expression. 'She was probably trying to steal something.'

The woman's sweeping assumption that she was up to no good annoyed Harriet intensely. She clamped down on her anger and tried to remain calm for the sake of Toby, who was clinging tightly to her hand. 'I'm sorry,' she said again. 'I know we shouldn't be here, but we were only trying to find our ball — my son accidentally threw it over the hedge.'

Three hostile pairs of eyes bored into her. Toby's voice, small with fright, wobbled into the silence. 'Mum, I'm scared. Can we go?'

'Are you staying with Miss James?' the man demanded suspiciously.

'*Please*, Mum, can we go?' Toby was pulling frantically at her hand. Harriet gave Daphne's neighbours a placatory smile and said brightly, 'Just for a few days. I'm sorry I upset you — I'm sure it won't happen again. Goodbye.'

As she walked briskly out of the garden, she could feel their animosity focused like a laser on the vulnerable spot between her shoulder blades. Her hands were shaking as she shut the gate behind her. Toby glanced back, and said, fortunately not very loudly, 'I don't like those people, Mummy. They weren't very nice.'

'Well, we were trespassing, even if it was just to get the ball back.' Harriet sucked in a deep, shaky breath. 'Look, there's Maggie, waiting for us by the hedge. Do you want to throw some more balls for her?'

'Not really,' said Toby sadly. 'Mum, can I watch a video?'

'Sorry, sweetheart — you know Daphne

hasn't even got a TV, let alone a video.'

'Oh.' His voice was woebegone. 'Why hasn't she?'

'She likes to read and do things, she says she doesn't need one.'

'But *I* need one.' He was dangerously on the verge of tears, and her heart contracted with love and grief and pity. His world had been shattered, and although the absence of TV and video was hardly significant, it must seem like the final straw to him.

'No you don't,' Harriet said, determined to be cheerful even if she felt like weeping herself. 'Listen, I've got a much better idea. Why don't we finish unpacking all our things, and then we can get Daphne's game box out and play snakes and ladders?'

To her intense relief, Toby brightened at once. 'Oh, yes *please*, Mum!'

If only, she thought as he towed her eagerly indoors, all their problems could be so easily solved.

They went back upstairs to their bedroom, and Harriet resumed the task of sorting out her clothes, while Toby, in earnest imitation, did the same with his. A pile of jumpers over one arm, she opened the door of the old walnut wardrobe. As she had hoped, it had shelves running up one side of it, and a rail on to the other. A few garments that must be

Daphne's drooped sadly from their hangers, all in dismal shades of black, or grey, or an unfortunate olive green.

All, save one. Her attention grabbed by the sight of brilliant colour, she pushed the jumpers on to the nearest shelf and gently parted the clothes so that she could see. Then, with reverent care, she lifted it off the rail and brought it out into the room.

It was a dress, made of some slippery, sheeny stuff that might be silk. Harriet possessed only a vague knowledge of changing fashions, but the fitted, sleeveless bodice and the extravagantly long, full skirt surely belonged to the forties. A little short-sleeved jacket sat jauntily on top. And the material . . .

'Oh God, how beautiful,' she breathed, in wonder. The background was white, thickly strewn with bright flowers in vivid primary hues. It was not a dress to hide in; it was a dress designed to be noticed, made for dancing and delight. And by the longest and wildest stretch of her leaping imagination, she could not envisage Daphne ever wearing it.

'That's pretty, Mum. Is it yours?'

'Oh, no, of course not, sweetheart. It's much too old.' Harriet did a quick calculation. 'And it's probably much too old to be Daphne's. She must have been about your age when it was made.'

'It was my mother's.' Her friend came into the room, smiling. 'I'd forgotten all about that. Beautiful, isn't it?'

'Utterly gorgeous,' Harriet said, stroking the skirt gently. The material rustled faintly under her fingers, as if it was alive. 'Have you ever worn it?'

'Oh, no. Much too showy for my taste, I'm afraid, but then I'm not at all like my mother. She was a very lively woman, always the centre of attention. She was wearing it when she met my stepfather — my real father was killed in the war, before I was born. She always called it her garden dress, and she kept it because she said it reminded her of happiness. I found it amongst her things after she died, and I couldn't bear to get rid of it.'

'I don't blame you.' Harriet laid the dress reverently on the bed. 'No, Toby, don't touch it unless your fingers are *absolutely* clean.'

Without waiting to be asked, he ran off to the bathroom to wash his hands. Daphne said, 'I should think it would fit you.'

'*This?*' Startled, Harriet glanced up at her. 'Oh, no, I'm sure it wouldn't. I'm at least a fourteen.'

'My mother was taller than you, and carried herself well, but she must have been about your size. Try it on, see how it looks.

Marcus always hosts a charity ball at Forfar Towers, at midsummer. You could wear it then.'

'Thank you,' said Harriet, with genuine gratitude. She knew that her chances of being able to attend such an event were slender, to say the least, but it did not harm to indulge her fantasies, once in a while. '*If* it fits. Are you *sure* you wouldn't mind? What if I spilt something on it?'

'Then it won't be the end of the world. That dress is meant to be worn, not to hang in the dark for years and years. Go on.'

Feeling suddenly shy, Harriet gestured to the door. 'Thank you. Give me a few minutes?'

'Of course,' said Daphne, and withdrew. As she pulled off her jeans and sweatshirt, Harriet could hear her telling Toby to wait, and Mummy would have a surprise for him.

It had an underarm zip, which she undid. Then she slipped her head into the rich, cool folds of the skirt, and up towards the neckline.

There was no sound of ripped seams, although it seemed very snug around the waist. With care, and a powerful intake of breath, she pulled up the zip. Tight, but not impossibly so. She wriggled into the little bolero jacket, and then, on a sudden impulse, undid her thick plait of dark hair and shook it loose. Only then did she look in the mirror.

It was wonderful. It was glamorous, entrancing. She felt different: she wanted to waltz, in diamonds and sapphires, long white gloves and satin slippers, with a man who would lover her. This was not a dress for Harriet Smith, unemployed, impoverished and scruffy single mother; this was a film-star frock.

There was a fusillade of knocks on the door, and Toby, demanded excitedly, 'Mum, Mum, can we come in?'

'Yes, I'm ready now!' Belatedly, she remembered that she still had her socks on, and was bending, trying to remove them without falling over, when her son burst in, Daphne behind him. She straightened, and spread the skirt, like two great multicoloured wings, out on either side of her. 'What do you think?'

'Oh, Mum!' Toby, touchingly, was lost in admiration. 'You look like a *princess*!'

'It suits you,' Daphne commented approvingly.

'It doesn't, you know,' said Harriet. 'I'm simply not the sort of person who would ever wear this.'

'You know that, and so do I, but that's not the point. You *look* as though you are. It might be better without the socks, though.'

'I'll try and remember to take them off next time.' Harriet said, laughing.

She let Toby touch the material, and then pirouetted in front of him, the full skirt flowing out around her legs. It was definitely too long, and she'd need quite high heels if she ever wore it in public, but with every moment that passed she felt more and more comfortable inside the dress, as if it welcomed the warm, living presence of her body within the silk.

She took it off with surprising reluctance, and hung it back in the wardrobe, hoping that she would indeed be wearing it at Sir Marcus's summer ball. Daphne's mention of his name had reminded her that he was coming to dinner that evening, so she found some clothes that would look suitably smart with the right accessories, and placed them on one side for ironing later. Then, with a pleasant feeling of anticipation, she finished putting the rest away, and went downstairs to introduce Toby to the delights of snakes and ladders.

7

Sir Marcus Grant was not in the least as Harriet had imagined him. He was a small, lean man about the same age as Daphne, with white hair only just thinning back from his forehead, a neat beard, and goldrimmed glasses. His skin had the russet, shiny look bestowed by years under a tropical sun, and he was wearing a brown tweed suit with a bright-yellow waistcoat. Harriet, looking at him, thought it should have been plus-fours: she was sure she had seen someone very similar in *Tin-Tin*. He greeted Daphne with a kiss on the cheek, and shook hands with Harriet. His grip was firm and warm, a good sign, and he looked her up and down with a smile. 'Daphne speaks very highly of you.'

Harriet felt herself blushing. 'I'm just a minion,' she said. 'I obey orders.' And knew, as she spoke the words, how well they described her life, up until now.

'Well, as any old soldier will tell you, that is a considerable talent,' said Sir Marcus.

'And she's much too modest,' said Daphne briskly. 'Right, Marcus, what will you have?

Sherry? Or I've still got some of that malt . . . '

'In that case, you shouldn't need to ask. Mmm, something smells good. Better than Mrs Young's steak and kidney pie, anyway.'

'Cassoulet,' said Daphne, leading the way into her sitting room. She was wearing the least flattering of the dresses that Harriet had seen upstairs, a shapeless knee-length shift in a raw, drab green silk that would have looked unbecoming on a supermodel, and did her tall, sturdy frame no favours at all. But for Daphne, clothes served only one purpose, to protect her from the weather, and she made no concessions to fashion, or to beauty. Harriet thought of the garden dress, hanging like a garland in the wardrobe upstairs, and wondered how the woman who had loved it could ever have given birth to someone so resolutely uninterested in personal adornment.

Apart from her brief time at art school, Harriet herself had never been a fashion victim, but beside Daphne she knew that even her plain white cotton blouse and black trousers must seem chic. She wore the gold and jet necklace that Georgia had given her for her twenty-first birthday, and her favourite earrings, in the shape of Egyptian cats. She had twisted her long dark hair into its accustomed plait, and finished it off with a velvet bow. Toby, inspecting her judiciously, had given her his verdict. 'You look very smart, Mum.'

'I wish.' Harriet had bent to kiss him good night. He smelled of soap, and the appley shampoo with which she had washed his hair, and his slender arms wound round her neck with love, unstinted and unconditional. 'Still, it's not the clothes that matter, it's the person inside them.'

'Do I *have* to go to sleep, Mum?' her son asked wistfully, but with a yawn. 'It's not dark yet.'

'It soon will be.'

'The weather's light blue,' said Toby, who sometimes employed a delightfully poetic turn of phrase. 'When it's dark blue and silver — I mean gold — then it's night-time, isn't it?'

'That's a nice way of putting it,' Harriet said with a smile. 'Good night, sweetheart, sleep tight.'

'And don't let the bugs bite,' Toby said, giggling sleepily. 'You're not going *out*, are you, Mummy?'

'No, of course not. I'm going to be downstairs with Daphne and her friend. If you want me, just call.'

'OK, Mum,' said her son, and curled up with another wide yawn, cuddling Lambkin.

She wondered now, sipping a tiny crystal glass of excellent sherry, how much Daphne had told Sir Marcus about her situation, and found that she really wasn't bothered. He obviously knew something, for he had greeted her without surprise, and his hostess had offered no explanation. But she did hope that he had been asked not to mention her presence here to anyone else, at any rate for the moment. Edward had dropped his name several times, and she knew that both men were part of that vast masculine web of connection and networking, on the golf course or in the squash court or the Rotary Club, which occupied so much of her former partner's life.

'Daphne tells me you paint,' said Sir Marcus, interrupting her thoughts.

'I try to,' Harriet told him, thinking of her art report, long ago at primary school. *Makes fairly good attempts.*

'In what field?'

'Watercolours.' The sherry was beginning to glow nicely below Harriet's throat, and she felt more relaxed. 'Mostly landscapes.'

'You're young for that,' he said, with a shrewd glance. 'I thought figurative art was the exclusive preserve of old codgers like me and Daphne. So — where have you exhibited?'

Harriet gave him an apologetic smile. 'Nowhere, I'm afraid. I'm just a hobby painter.'

'You're selling yourself short,' said Daphne. 'This young woman has real talent, Marcus. Her sister and I have been trying to persuade her that she won't be wasting her time if she starts again.'

'You don't need to persuade me,' Harriet said. 'But I'm just trying to feel my way gradually back into it, that's all.'

'Why did you give up?' Sir Marcus was smiling at her, his face full of friendly interest, and she gave him an expurgated version of her reasons. 'I had a baby, and a lot to do. I don't know who commented on the pram in the hall being the enemy of female creativity, but it's true. Everything's different now, though, and Toby's older, and my fingers are itching to hold a brush again.'

'Well, if you like doing views, you can come and paint in the park,' said Sir Marcus. 'Up by the old quarry, looking north, there's all the land between Sanden and Bowden Hill laid out before you. And you can see over to Oliver's Castle, as well.'

'The old quarry? Isn't that where you're putting the underground house?' Daphne enquired, returning from the kitchen, where she had been checking on the cassoulet.

'Underground house?' Harriet echoed. 'That sounds intriguing.'

'I'm surprised you haven't heard about it,' said Sir Marcus, drily. 'Half the village was up in arms — surely you remember?'

'I think I do,' Harriet said, though in truth she could recall only the vaguest details. She didn't read the local papers, and had never had time to stand gossiping with the other mothers at playgroup or in the post office. 'Did you get planning permission eventually, then?'

'A couple of weeks ago, after a lot of wrangling. God knows what they were imagining — something like a nuclear bunker, I suspect. It's long been an interest of mine, energy efficiency, and the most energy-efficient houses are underground, insulated by the earth. I had a good site in the park, and a chap my stepdaughter knows — her boyfriend, in fact — to design it for me. Interesting chap. He's Welsh, did architecture at Bristol, and then spent ten years in the States. That's where Selina met him, in fact, out in California.'

Harriet was overwhelmed by a most peculiar feeling. She knew the name he was about to say, and the words chimed together, inside her head and in the air. 'Morgan Price, he's called, couldn't get much more Welsh than that, could you? But he's gained quite a reputation over there — built a dozen or more underground houses, in places like Montana and Wyoming. When Selina ran across him, though, he was in Los Angeles. She took up with him, brought him back here, introduced him to me at Christmas.'

'What — what's he like?' Harriet asked. Her voice sounded very remote, and she felt as if she might faint, but neither Sir Marcus nor Daphne seemed to have noticed anything amiss.

'Morgan? Tall, early thirties, dark hair — sounds American rather than Welsh, of course, after all that time over there. Temperamental, according to Selina, but then she's not exactly placid herself. I've seen the sparks fly between them, several times.'

'Think she'll settle down with him?' Daphne enquired.

Sir Marcus laughed ruefully. 'Selina? She wouldn't settle down with anything less than twenty bedrooms and a thousand acres. I love her dearly, don't mistake me, but Morgan isn't the man for her. Anyway, he's the rootless type, moves from job to job. He'll probably go back to the States when the house is completed.'

'So are you going to live in it when it's finished?' Harriet said. She wasn't interested in the underground house, she only wanted to know more about the man who had designed it, the man who had haunted her memories for ten years. But she couldn't explain, to these kind, middle-aged people, the agonies she had endured because of Morgan Price, still less the fact that after all this time, after so much else had befallen her, the mere mention of him still had such power over her emotions.

I was only twenty, she thought. Calf love, infatuation, that's all it was. Come on, Hal, get a grip on yourself, and pretend he doesn't matter.

'I don't know,' Marcus was saying reflectively. 'I intended it as an experiment, really. I've got the Towers, of course, but it's so huge that Selina and Mrs Young and I rattle round it like dry beans in a pod. The place Morgan's building is much more compact — the quarry isn't very big, and anyway I didn't want to go too much over the top. I might rent it out, or keep it as a sort of guest house, perhaps, if Selina ever does settle down.'

'When does the building start?' Daphne enquired.

'It's started. We've got a couple of JCBs up there, levelling off the site. Morgan reckons it'll be finished before winter, but I'll believe it when I see it, quite frankly. If you do want to paint,' he added, turning to Harriet, 'don't worry, you won't be in the way — unless you sit on one of the diggers, of course!'

'If,' she said. 'I've got to find the time first.'

'I thought playgroup started again on Monday?' said Daphne. 'If it's a nice day, I should take the opportunity.'

'I should be signing on,' Harriet pointed out. She didn't care about that, of course: it would be perfectly possible to take Toby with her to the job centre. But she didn't want to disclose the real reason for her sudden reluctance to go anywhere near the place where she might risk an encounter with Morgan Price.

To her relief, Daphne decided that it was time to eat, and they went into the dining room. As her contribution to the meal, Harriet had laid the table and prepared the starters, a simple array of sliced vegetables and dips. A bowl of brilliantly striped and fringed parrot tulips graced the centre, and she had shown Toby how to fold Daphne's damask napkins and arrange the cutlery and glasses.

For a while, there was a pleasant silence as they ate, broken only by appreciative comments on the food. Although she was desperate not to think about him, Harriet found her mind ruthlessly invaded by the image of Morgan Price. She could remember, as clearly as if it had happened only a few hours ago, her first encounter with him.

He had been serving behind the bar of a cider pub in Clifton. Harriet had come in with her friends, a large and boisterous group of secondyear art students like herself. It was her turn to be in charge of the communal kitty, so she collected the money, took the orders, and made her way to the counter.

The place had been crowded, and Harriet was only five foot two, and slightly built. Her cropped vermilion hair should have made her conspicuous, but the staff seemed unable to notice her. She couldn't even wave a valuable note under their noses, because the kitty was all in pound coins. Thirsty and seething, she stood on tiptoe and hailed the barman coolly pulling a pint for someone who'd come in only seconds ago. 'Hey, am I invisible, or what?'

'Something spoke to me,' said the young man, putting the pint of sweet cider — another black mark against the queue-jumper, in Harriet's opinion — on the bar in front of her. 'But I can't see anyone.'

'Then get your eyes tested,' Harriet had

said forcefully. 'Five pints of dry and two of mix, *please*.'

'Oh, it's a leprechaun,' the young man said, with a grin. 'Sorry, *cariad*, didn't notice you down there.'

From that, and the slight lilt in his voice, she deduced that he was Welsh — there were a lot of them around, taking refuge from Cardiff, although Harriet had never been able to understand why they thought life in Bristol was so much more attractive. And despite his infuriating manner, she had to admit that she liked the look of him. He was taller than Welshmen were popularly supposed to be, with longish, curling dark hair and brilliant blue eyes that possessed an unholy glint of mischief. His T-shirt bore the legend *For Fox Sake Ban Hunting*, which was, as far as she was concerned, another definite point in his favour.

'Then I must have had my cloak of invisibility on by mistake,' she said tartly, unwilling to reveal that she fancied him. 'Or a big sign above my head saying, 'Please serve the person standing behind me'.'

'Yes, sir, what'll you have?' said the Welshman, his eyes fixed on someone else. Furiously, Harriet turned round, saw there was nobody there, and burst out laughing.

'A gullible leprechaun as well,' he said,

already pulling the first pint of her order. 'But one who can take a joke.'

'A rare creature.' Harriet was beginning to enjoy herself. 'A non-Irish leprechaun. Only one in the world, in fact.'

'And does this one-off have a name?'

'Harriet Smith.'

'And is it at the art school?'

She laughed. 'How did you guess, Sherlock?'

'Scarlet hair, lots of earrings, lots of make-up, lots of black. You don't need a sign above your head. And my name's not Sherlock, it's Morgan.'

'Lucky your Mum didn't like Porsches. Or Ford Prefects.'

'It was a toss-up between Morgan and Lotus, actually. So, are you really a pretentious art student, or just pretending to be one?'

Harriet grinned at him. 'What do you think?'

'Well, if you wanted to see a film, which would it be? The Chinese one with subtitles at the University Cinema Club tomorrow night, or *Robocop*?'

'Neither. The new Woody Allen is on at the Odeon.'

'Are you asking me out, Harriet Smith?'

'I thought you were asking *me* out.'

'It's a deal, *cariad*.' And he had leaned over the counter and kissed her with lingering, exploratory passion, earning himself a derisive whistle from the other barman, and a smudge of her black-grape lipstick all round his mouth.

Slightly dazed, she had returned to her friends thinking that she must be quite mad. She didn't know anything about him. He could be a rapist or a drug addict or just a boring, self-obsessed creep. He could have a hairy back, or cut his toenails in bed, or like heavy metal. He could live in a squat, or have a string of simultaneous girlfriends, or an intense personal relationship with his computer.

But in the space of a few words and a kiss, her whole world had tilted, and begun to dance to a different tune. And he had fulfilled all of her hopes, and none of her fears, except one.

Helping Daphne to clear away the plates, she wondered what he was like now, ten years later. Would he still be the careless, thoughtless, entrancing boy she had loved so much? Would he still be long and lean, with hair down to his shoulders and that wild, exuberant way of talking?

No, she thought, with sad realism. He'll be fat, and balding, and full of his own importance. Or even worse, he'll have a ponytail and leather trousers and a mobile phone. Or be seriously, instead of slightly, weird. And from what Sir Marcus said, he's lost his Welsh accent. What else has he lost, in ten years?

She should be able to contemplate the inevitable changes with equanimity. He was nothing to do with her any more. He had ceased to be anything to do with her when he had disappeared from her life, without word or farewell or explanation, and left her devastated. And in the process of picking up the pieces and dusting herself off, she had abandoned art school, abandoned Bristol, and reinvented herself. Hal, the deliberately unconventional and rebellious student, had been transformed into Harriet, conscientious and efficient computer expert. It had not been easy, but she had achieved it with single-minded determination.

So successfully, in fact, that she wondered suddenly if he would even recognise her, if they ever met again. And following hard on that thought came the desire to see what he had become. Curiosity, nothing else, she told herself, carrying in a basket of hot fragrant bread. Pure nosiness. He's probably forgotten I ever existed. We were only together six months, that's all.

Only six months. But that brief span had had such an effect on her life, then and after, that it seemed like much longer.

The cassoulet was delicious: despite her disclaimers, Daphne was not at all a bad cook. The conversation drifted cheerfully over subjects that were interesting but, to Harriet, seemed curiously unimportant compared with the news that had shattered her earlier. She concentrated on the food, and uttered a few polite comments here and there, but it was obvious that her hostess and Sir Marcus were extremely comfortable in their own ecological world, which wrapped them up like Daphne's battered old waxed coat.

I won't think about him, she told herself fiercely, spreading butter on her hot bread. I won't, I won't, I *won't*!

But of course she did. It was typical of Morgan: even in his absence, he had the power to dominate any situation, from sheer strength of personality. Her friends had either loved him or loathed him: there were no half-measures with Morgan, nothing wishy-washy, no compromise. Her flatmate, Sian, had moved out in a huff after objecting to his drawing equipment, which had gradually infiltrated the living space until there was scarcely room to move. Morgan had promptly left the seedy squat in St Paul's where he had been living since before they'd met, and moved in, complete with a small holdall full of tatty clothes, several boxes of surprisingly intellectual books, a record collection notable for its eclectic components, a very varied assortment of posters advertising art exhibitions, anarchist demonstrations and rock gigs, six flourishing cannabis plants and a portable flashing blue light he'd once nicked off a plainclothes policeman's car.

The memory brought an involuntary smile. His misdemeanours had been increasingly outrageous, but he'd never been caught, although he fully deserved a criminal record several sheets long. Just as well for him, she thought wryly. They'd never have let him into the States if he had.

Living with Morgan had been wonderful: exhilarating, nerve-racking, and above all *fun*. It was easy to look back on it with the golden glow of ten years' nostalgia, and sigh with regret. But Harriet knew, realistically, that it could never have lasted. He would have discovered her secret, sooner or later. He would have realised that the scarlet hair and the gothic clothes were only a pose: that locked away inside the trendy art-school rebel was a dull, boring, conventional little product of bourgeois society, determined to get out.

Well, she had got out. But reverting to her

roots hadn't made her any happier. She had made one mistake after another. And the irony was that her biggest mistake of all, Toby, had also brought her the truest joy of her life. But now, at the advanced age of thirty, she didn't know any longer which was the real Harriet.

Or perhaps the real Harriet had not yet emerged.

Whatever she made of her life to come, she was absolutely certain that never again would she let it be influenced by anyone else. Certainly not by Edward. And double, treble certainly not by Morgan Llewellyn Price.

8

'I'm sure that was Sir Marcus Grant's car I saw turning in next door last night.' Heather Clark set the bowl of high-fibre cereal in front of her husband, and observed his instinctive recoil. 'Don't pull that face, Keith, it's good for you. We don't want you getting bowel cancer, now do we?'

Their son, Adam, muttered something obnoxious, but as he was bent over the breadboard, vigorously sawing away at a crusty wholemeal loaf, his parents fortunately did not hear him.

'I can't say I noticed any car.' Keith sighed, picked up the jug of milk — skimmed, of course — and poured it over the heap of pellets that looked exactly like rabbit droppings. For himself, he would much rather have died young and happy, his arteries clogged with cholesterol and his innards riddled with the consequences of a high-fat, high-sugar diet, than linger long into a miserable old age with nothing better to look forward to at mealtimes than food even a goat would have scorned, but after twenty-two years of marriage, he knew better than to resist his wife when she had a bee in her bonnet. Or a whole hive, for she was perfectly capable of fostering several obsessions at once. At present, the household was comparatively peaceful, because she had only two: the healthy eating fad, which had been in force now for six long, tedious months; and the feud with their only neighbour, Miss James, which had begun when they had moved into this house.

Left to himself, Keith Clark was a relaxed, tolerant, easy-going man who didn't ask much from life. He had married Heather because he found her very attractive and she had made it perfectly clear that it was the only way of getting her into bed; and also because, as he admitted to himself in his more reflective moments, he sensed that her drive and energy and ambition amply compensated for his own deep lack of these things. Without her pushing furiously from behind, he would never have risen to the dizzy heights of a senior partnership, never have been able to afford this house, and above all, would never have been able to call himself successful.

He should have been happy, but he wasn't. He thought of his adored, pretty, clever daughter Jessica, who had escaped to university at the earliest opportunity and who only came home now, very grudgingly, at Christmas; of Adam, aged fifteen, desultorily studying for his GCSEs, whose idea of a good time seemed to be hanging around with his mates in the bus shelter outside the King's Arms on the Devizes Road; and of the beautiful, lavishly decorated home where he hardly dared sit down for fear of disarranging the cushions.

'I can't imagine why a man like that should want to visit *her.*' Heather sat down in front of her own breakfast, a slim slice of toast, topped with such a liberal thickness of low-fat spread that a generous portion of butter would probably have been less calorific. 'Whatever can they have in common?'

'I've no idea, and I've no interest in finding out,' said Keith, doggedly chewing the rabbit droppings.

'Well, he wanted to build that underground house, didn't he?' Adam volunteered, in his usual thick mutter. 'And that's sort of alternative, innit?'

'Do talk properly, Adam,' said Heather, her lips compressed. 'You sound like some dreadful oaf. And that was a fix. It's the same old story — it's not what you are, it's who you know that counts. I expect he'd been to school with the chairman of the planning committee.'

'I doubt it,' said Keith drily. 'Sir Marcus is an old Harrovian, and the chairperson of the planning committee is called Helen Kingston.'

'The district council hasn't been the same since this lot got in,' Heather went on, regardless. 'You don't know where you are with them. Wasting money on women's refuges and making such a fuss about equal opportunities. If a woman wants to get on, she will. Look at Mrs Thatcher.'

'I'd rather not, thanks,' muttered Adam, who had finished spreading his doorstep slice of bread with lavishly unhealthy amounts of peanut butter, and was about to cram most of it into his mouth at once.

'Anyway, I'm sure I don't know why Sir Marcus would even give the time of day to a woman like that. She looks like a gypsy, her fingernails are always filthy, and her garden's no better than a rubbish tip.'

'Perhaps he came round to ask her to clear it up,' suggested Adam, who had a subversive sense of mischief. He finished eating the bread, and sat down beside his father with a bowl of officially approved cereal. 'Anyway, short of asking her, you'll never know, will you?'

'And who *was* that girl?'

'The one in the garden yesterday? Haven't a clue,' said Keith, hoping, probably in vain, that he would soon be left in peace with the *Sunday Telegraph*.

'She could be *her* niece, I suppose. Or a friend. Not that I suppose she can have many, living like that.'

'Honestly, Mum, anyone would think we were next door to a travellers' camp!'

Heather glared at him. 'At least they were *born* dirty. *She*'s chosen it.'

Jessica had kept her opinions to herself, before her escape. Adam had done so too, until recently: he didn't know whether it was because he had grown less tolerant, or because his mother had got worse. He said, with deceptive meekness, 'It isn't anything to do with us, anyway.'

'Of course it is! We have to live next door, don't we? And you're at school for most of the time, you don't have to look at all those trees, and clear up the mess they make with all their leaves and seeds and twigs, or try and see past the undergrowth when you're coming out of the drive, or wonder why you should bother to keep everything nice and tidy when it changes into wilderness five yards down the road.'

'I bet the real reason you'd like her to cut

110

all the trees down,' said Adam gleefully, 'is because you want a better view of what she's doing.'

'Adam!' Heather drew herself up to her full height, her prominent bosom jutting out indignantly. 'That was very rude, and hurtful, and untrue.'

'No it isn't. You could be nosy for England. You were *born* nosy, and you'll die nosy. We'll have to remember to put a peep-hole in your coffin so's you can see what the worms are getting up to.'

'That's quite enough, Adam. Go to your room.'

Keith rarely spoke out, but his son knew that this time he had overstepped the mark. He didn't regret one word of it, though, he decided, as he climbed the stairs, thinking with anticipation of a whole morning working on his cartoons, which amongst other things featured a cruelly dysfunctional family with certain marked similarities to his own. It was true. His mother was a nosy, interfering, bossy old bag, and he couldn't wait to escape, as Jess had done, to university, or college, or even the streets of London or Bristol: anywhere, so long as he didn't have to listen to her rantings.

Downstairs, Keith shook out the paper, but to no avail. Heather was appalled and outraged by her son's comments, and demanded his support. 'Where did we go wrong? We've done *everything* for them, and they've thrown it back in our faces!'

Keith forbore to point out that his wife's oscillations between stricture, indifference and indulgence, throughout the children's lives, might have something to do with their present attitude. Adam, in particular, seemed to be honing a nice collection of one-liners, largely at Heather's expense. He said mildly, 'You know what teenage boys are like. He didn't really mean it.'

'Just as he didn't really mean it when he asked if I'd got my new hat from Oxfam? Sixty pounds it cost me! Or when he told that story about how his bike had been stolen, and he'd actually swapped it with a friend for CDs? I could have *died* with embarrassment when the policeman got the truth out of him. You should be more strict with him, Keith, you really should.'

'I do my best,' said her husband, with patent untruth. 'Goodness, is that the time? I'm due to tee off in half an hour. Sorry, dear, must dash. And don't forget, I'm having lunch at the club, should be back about three. See you later!'

Fuming with angry frustration, Heather watched his new Mercedes rolling out of the gate. Keith was spending altogether too much time on the golf course these days. He claimed that it was healthy exercise, and helped his business contacts into the bargain, but surely he didn't need to play three or four times a week? What with that and the Rotary Club and the Freemasons, he was hardly ever home. No wonder Adam seemed to be running wild. He needed a father's firm hand, and Keith was not providing it.

Grimly, she cleared breakfast away and put the plates into the dishwasher, wiped the table and swept the floor. Her cleaner, Maxine, came three times a week, and was extremely thorough — Heather would not have employed anyone who was not — so very little needed doing, but she still spent a brisk half-hour with duster and vacuum cleaner. Then she poured herself another cup of tea, and took it and the *Mail on Sunday* out on to the patio to enjoy some April sun.

Unfortunately, peace and quiet was not an option. Just as she had taken the cover off the floral hammock and arranged the cushions comfortably, the sound of childish laughter shattered the silence. 'Mu-um! Come and get me!'

Fuming, Heather sat down and tried to concentrate on the paper. There was a very illuminating article about single mothers, and how most of them were teenage girls who had only had babies in order to qualify for housing benefit. Heather had long ago formed the opinion that children needed two parents, and that any other situation should be severely discouraged. That girl staying next door, with her noisy brat and her habit of trespassing on other people's gardens, was almost certainly a single mother. *She* would probably be inviting homosexuals and Asians next. Really, it was like living in the inner city. The effect on the value of their house must be disastrous. Keith had recently begun to contemplate his future retirement, and a move, once both the children had left home, to a smaller but no less luxurious house. The money gained by such a step would supplement his pension, and he had painted a wonderful picture of idyllic holidays, luxury cruises, a trip on the Orient Express . . .

But if they couldn't sell Cypress Lodge because of their neighbour, all that glorious vision would remain just a pipe dream. Heather's fertile imagination supplied them with a poky little semi in Trowbridge, hardly the smartest Wiltshire town, rather than the bijou Georgian house, in Marlborough or Bradford-on-Avon, that she had set her heart on. And instead of the Mediterranean, in the company of like-minded souls of taste and refinement, a coach tour of the Lake District with fifty other pensioners, all complaining about their bunions and hernias, and discussing the latest episodes of *Coronation Street*.

She had tried everything to persuade Miss James to change her ways, and Miss James, at first politely, later more forcefully, had utterly refused to budge. Letters to the planning department, the highways department, and the parish council had had no result. Heather had even consulted her solicitor, who had advised her, regretfully — for disputes between neighbours were famously lucrative — that she didn't have a legal leg to stand on. Miss James owned her house outright. As long as her garden wasn't a health hazard, and as long as her trees weren't taking Heather's light or their roots causing damage to her house, there wasn't anything the law could do. She would just have to put up with it, and live and let live.

The phrase, recalled now, reminded Heather of the young woman who had visited Miss James yesterday morning. Something was going on next door, she was sure of it: something suspicious. Perhaps *she* was thinking of starting up a commune. The thought of drug-taking undesirables, perfectly placed to corrupt her teenage son, was so awful that Heather, for a brief instant of pure, blinding rage, was tempted to do something quite drastic.

But of course she was a moral, upright pillar of local society: she was president of the WI, ex-chairwoman of Sanden St Lawrence PTA, and secretary of the village hall committee. She was not a common criminal, and she would not stoop to such methods, however provoked. She would *shame* her neighbour into conformity. She would get the whole village behind her. And she knew exactly how she would do it.

★ ★ ★

Monday dawned a perfect April day: birds sang joyously, the trees had been freshly air-brushed in a hazy, delicate green, and the sun shone warmly from a mother-of-pearl sky. After consultation with Daphne, Harriet had decided not to use the BMW to take Toby to playgroup. She didn't think Edward would have realised that term started today, and she hoped that he still assumed her to be in Bath with her sister. But she didn't want to risk the possibility that he would be waiting for them when she and her son turned up at the village hall at half past nine as usual.

So she had borrowed Daphne's car, which

was a VW Golf, middle-aged, dull red and very anonymous. It's silly, really, all this cloak-and-dagger stuff, she thought, driving up Stony Lane. And rather childish. But I want to keep the upper hand, and while he doesn't know where I'm staying, while I've got the BMW, I've got him on the run.

But there was no sign of her former lover in the little car park outside the hall, only the usual gaggle of familiar faces. She exchanged brief greetings and pleasantries with the other mothers, few of whose names she even knew. It would have been nice, she thought wistfully, as she watched Toby settle down with a jigsaw, to have made friends with some of them. But she had never had the time: she had always had to rush back to the boatyard, and after a while the offers of cosy chats over cups of coffee had dried up. They probably thought she was standoffish or snooty. And yet nothing, thought Harriet sadly, could be further from the truth.

But one of the other mothers did stop her, as she walked out of the door. 'Harriet? Would Toby like to come back for lunch after playgroup?'

It was Juliet Moss, the chairperson of the playgroup committee. She was a tall, willowy woman with short blonde hair, who had an older boy at the village school, and a younger one roughly the same age as Toby. Harriet had always warmed to her: she combined energy and organisational ability with a sunny, down-to-earth personality that it was impossible not to like.

'I'm sure he'd love to,' said Harriet. 'Thank you very much.'

'A pleasure. Nicholas gets really bored when his brother's at school all day, he's desperate for someone to play with. Do you know where we live? In Manor Close, number forty-seven, it's right at the end opposite the little green. You go and do some shopping or whatever, and pick him up any time between two and three. If you come early, we can have a cup of tea and a chat. See you later!'

She went off to her car, and Harriet nipped back into the hall to tell Toby about the revised plan for his day. To her relief, he sounded enthusiastic at the prospect of playing with his friend, and she left him with a clear conscience, her heart lifting already at the thought of four and a half hours stretching gloriously in front of her, with only herself to please.

There were things to do, of course. She would have to sign on, and start looking for a job. She needed to try and find somewhere else to live. All of the problems she had created for herself, in the act of leaving Edward, seemed to crowd in menacingly around her like a thicket of thorns.

'No,' Harriet said fiercely, aloud — fortunately there was no one within earshot. 'No, no, no. First I please *myself*.'

She drove back to the cottage. Daphne had spread a pile of rough notes all over the kitchen table, and was swearing quietly over them as Harriet came in. 'I can't find Chapter Three anywhere, bugger it.'

'It's the last one I transcribed — I think it's by the computer.' Harriet went to check, and came back waving a thin sheaf of paper. 'Here you are. Do you want any help?'

Daphne glanced up over her small, rectangular glasses, that gave her a definite look of Hinge, or was it Bracket? 'I thought you were going to do some painting this morning,' she said severely. 'And you really couldn't have better weather for it. Go on, scarper. I need to do this on my own, or I won't be able to think straight.'

So Harriet packed up her equipment. Yesterday, she had taken the precaution of soaking and stretching a rectangle of thick, creamy paper on her drawing board, and it was now dry and ready to be used. She wrapped it in a protective plastic, bag, and placed it in a rucksack. Her box of watercolours followed, an old cracked white saucer for mixing paints, a couple of soft pencils and a rubber, a small sponge and some pieces of clean rag, a notebook, an old mustard pot and a plastic squash bottle full of water. She never used an easel, even when working out of doors, preferring to find a position where she could rest the board on her knees. The ground was sure to be wet, but she had her waterproof jacket to sit on.

'Any idea where you're going to go?' Daphne asked, as she came back into the kitchen, with Maggie jumping around in joyful expectation of a walk.

'Not a clue. I'll find somewhere good, I'm sure of it.' Harriet grinned at her, feeling suddenly more light-hearted and optimistic than she had done for a very long time. 'Serendipity, that's the key. Seeing the possibilities of a place or a view, and seizing the right moment. And I've got all morning, Toby's going to a friend for lunch.'

'Well, good luck, and good hunting,' said Daphne, and returned, frowning, to her book.

The air outside smelt damp and earthy, and a cuckoo called jauntily in the distance. Harriet walked up the lane with the dog, humming to herself. She couldn't resist a quick glance into the garden of Cypress Lodge as she passed, but there was no sign of the redoubtable Heather.

Fifty yards further up the lane, a footpath sign pointed across the park belonging to Forfar Towers. Harriet climbed the stile and glanced around. A wide swath of rough grass, studded with venerable oaks and jewelled with pale-purple flowers, stretched in front of her. Further up the hill, sheltered by a belt of graceful young beech trees, she could see an area of rough ground and, just, the angular yellow shape of a JCB digger. That must mark the site of the underground house, where Morgan Price, who had once been the love of her life, would probably be working.

For a moment, Harriet hesitated. The pull of his presence was so strong that she actually took a step in the direction of the old quarry. Then her hard-won common sense reasserted itself. She was here to *paint*, not to spy on her former lover. He didn't matter any more, he was past history, out of her life by his own choice. If they met, it must be as strangers. And even if curiosity didn't kill the cat, it would certainly be the downfall of Harriet Smith, should she give way to it.

Resolutely, she turned away from the quarry, and began to walk up the hill, seeking a vantage point which would afford a good view of the fields and hills beyond the canal, and give her the opportunity to paint the picture which would prove, to herself and to the world, that her gift still lay in her possession.

9

The bright-yellow digger tore up great heaps of the reddish Sanden soil, burying the grass and desecrating the peace and beauty of the park. But Morgan Price knew, from what Sir Marcus had told him of Sanden's history, that this image of untouched nature was deceptive. A hundred years previously, a huge ironworks had stood on these verdant slopes, belching smoke and polluting the canal. A tramway had run down to the wharf where the boatyard now lay, taking ore to be loaded on to the boats which would carry it to Bristol or Reading or London. The line of it could still be seen, a green ramp running up the side of the hill above the canal, but unless you knew what had made the irregular humps and bumps that lay all around, you would never guess that this part of Sanden had once been an industrial complex, and Forfar Towers built by a Scottish entrepreneur — Sir Marcus's great-great-grandfather — who had seen the potential of the iron-rich soil, and decided to exploit it.

It had always been a marginal enterprise, and by the end of the nineteenth century cheap imports had made the ironworks redundant. The quarries remained, scattered round the village, and the houses where the workers had lived, stoutly built in local stone. But the remains of the foundries had been carted off for scrap, and nature, with some help from the original iron-master's son, who didn't want the ugly evidence of his father's trade disfiguring the view from his house, had obliterated all remaining traces of the works with remarkable thoroughness.

This quarry had been the first to be dug, and quickly abandoned when better ore had been discovered half a mile away, near the main road. It was small, perhaps thirty yards by twenty-five, and hardly more than ten feet deep. Morgan would have preferred it to face south, but, as his patron had drily pointed out, he didn't own any land that faced south. Everything on the other side of the hill on which Sanden lay, looking over to Westbury and the first bleak ridges of Salisbury Plain, belonged to Sanden Manor, and Geoff Bentley, who owned it, was a deeply conventional millionaire property developer whose wife had been one of the most vociferous opponents of Sir Marcus's plans.

Morgan sat down on an outcrop of rock at the edge of the quarry, and studied the plans. A breeze was blowing from the west, soft and warm, speaking of rain later, although the sky was still almost clear of cloud. The paper flapped, and he put it down on the grass beside him and anchored it with a couple of pieces of iron slag. It was a good design, even if the site did face north-west, and he was pleased with it. The quarry floor was almost level, and allowed space for two large bedrooms, arranged on either side of a generously proportioned living room, and all with superb views across the valley beyond. Sir Marcus had insisted that the house should blend in with the hillside as much as possible. He had even asked, hopefully, if trees could be planted on top of it.

'Not a problem,' Morgan had told him, smiling at the older man's surprise. 'Especially if I use the arched construction for the roof — much stronger than straight beams. And less like a concrete bunker, as well.' He had sketched out the shape of it, swift, sure lines gently mocking the lumps and bumps around it on the hillside. 'There you are. Hobbit Hall. Bag End.'

Sir Marcus, who had not read Tolkien, gave him a slightly quizzical glance. 'There's an underground house up near Tetbury called Mole Manor. A trifle twee for my taste.'

'And mine. You could be really unoriginal and call it Hill View.'

'I think that between us, we should be capable of coming up with something a bit less banal than that. Perhaps inspiration will strike. What do they tend to call these places in America?'

'The Robinson House. The Jones Cave. The Cliff House.'

'That nation,' said Sir Marcus resignedly, 'has no sense of poetry. Well, I shall keep thinking, and you can too. It'll probably come to me in a dream.'

'I get most of my best ideas in the bath,' Morgan told him, adding a whimsical chimney to the nearest lump. 'There. All ready for Bilbo Baggins to move in. And if we can't think of anything else, why not call it The Pits?'

Fortunately, Sir Marcus was becoming accustomed to his architect's quirky sense of humour, and laughed. 'Don't tell anyone in the village, or it'll be christened that for ever more. My house is already known as Fawlty Towers by almost every inhabitant of Wiltshire.' He glanced down at the sketch. 'But it's a good design. I like it. In a couple of years, you'll hardly know it's there, and that's what I want. And almost entirely energy-efficient into the bargain.'

'It's what you pay me for,' Morgan had said, with a lift of the brows that could almost be called arrogant. 'And rest assured, I shall deliver.'

And so he had. Three months later, with planning permission at last granted, the concrete and steel ordered, the heating pipes, solar panels, glass and window frames commissioned, and the JCBs hard at work on the site, the underground house still known, privately, as The Pits was poised to leave the realms of fantasy and assume reality at last. Morgan should have felt entirely satisfied. Sir Marcus was a generous and imaginative patron, and he was earning more money from this commission than he had ever achieved in the States, and with less hassle. He was back in England, where he had always felt, Welsh ancestry and upbringing notwithstanding, more truly at home than in the brown, open landscape and lunatic lifestyle of California. He had a considerable and growing reputation amongst the more unconventional members of his profession, and a brilliant future seemed assured.

Then why this nervy, almost anxious sense of impending change? Why did he feel as if he was balanced on the edge of something so desperately important to his life that any choice he made might have catastrophic effects? Why did he always wake at dawn, and prowl the empty corridors and echoing halls of Forfar Towers, as restless as an unquiet ghost?

He had been so self-assured for so long that he could still keep up the pretence of it, like wearing another skin. But inside, all the past certainties had dissolved into a quivering morass of unease and doubt. He hadn't felt like this for ten years or more, and he didn't like it in the least. What was happening to him?

He looked up, and saw at least part of the answer riding down the hill towards him.

Selina Grant was beautiful, and it had been lust at first sight: she had been at a party thrown by the minor Hollywood celebrity for whom he had designed a beach house, hidden in the dunes of the Pacific coast. She was tall, slender, a classic English blonde, her sleek pale hair knotted in a sophisticated chignon and her supple, athletic figure clothed in understated black silk that made her stand out against all the overdressed, overtanned women trying too hard to be noticed. She had seen him looking at her, and had smiled, so subtly that he almost missed the significance of it. Then she had turned away to talk to the star of the year's hottest TV comedy show. If it had not been for the glance she threw over her shoulder, he would have assumed that she was not interested.

Later, bored with insincere and pretentious chatter, he had been standing alone on the terrace, listening to the distant hum of traffic on the freeway competing with the incessant and infuriating chirping of the crickets, when he felt her presence at his shoulder. 'Nice view,' she said softly, and he realised only then that she was English, and thought wryly that he should have guessed.

'Only after sunset.' He turned, smiling, and held out his hand. 'Morgan Price.'

'The architect. I've heard all about you from our host. I'm Selina Grant. You're from my part of the world, aren't you? The West Country?'

'You could say that. You could say it's a small world, but you look like a woman who avoids clichés. And I could ask what brings you here, but clichés have never been my strong point either. Do you dance?'

'Only with people I like,' said Selina, and as the band inside began to play something soft and romantic, she swept him into her embrace.

That had been six months and six thousand miles ago. In the crazy, exotic warmth of California, it had all been so easy, so wonderful. Back in England, he had quickly realised that they didn't have enough in common to sustain the relationship. Sex

129

was as good as it should be between two widely experienced adults, but not the best, and no substitute for true compatibility. He no longer felt that unbearable frisson of desire when he looked at her. And besides, he knew now what had attracted her to him, and he had far too much self-esteem to put up with being her bit of rough any longer.

She looked superb in her cream jodhpurs and tight-waisted hacking jacket, and sat Hadrian, her sixteen-hand bay hunter, with magnificent assurance, as much in control of half a ton of horse as she was of her life. 'Hallo. Hard at work?'

'Of course,' said Morgan, rolling up the plans and inserting them back into the cardboard carrying tube. 'And you?'

Selina worked, if it could be called that, in a gallery in Bath, allegedly selling antique paintings and sculpture at inflated prices to wealthy overseas visitors who wanted an expensive souvenir of their trip. She didn't need the money: her indulgent mother, who had died some years ago, had left her millions, salted away in an offshore trust fund. The interest alone more than paid for her expensive habits: the couture clothes, the parties, the extensive foreign holidays, the top-class horses, and other, less permissible, interests. Morgan had often wondered whether Sir Marcus was fully aware of what his stepdaughter got up to in her ample spare time. His patron had surprisingly unconventional views, but despite his globe-trotting past, he retained an air of genuine innocence.

'I've told Sebastian I'm not going in today,' said Selina, waving an airy hand. 'It's far too nice to be cooped up indoors.' She paused, frowning slightly, and then added, 'I've been meaning to tell you. I'm going to look at a flat in Bath this afternoon. A friend of mine works for Cluttons, I rang her yesterday to see if she had anything suitable.'

Suddenly, the air between them seemed charged and tense. As if sensing it, the great horse shuffled and side-stepped, chewing his bit. So this is it, Morgan thought, and instead of sadness or despair, a vast feeling of relief swept over him. He said calmly, 'A flat for one, is it?'

Selina's face cleared, and he realised that she had thought he would take it badly. 'Yes. I think we've come to the end of the road, don't you? It was fun while it lasted. But that's all, really. Sorry, Morgan.'

'I'm sorry too. But not devastated.' He gave her his sudden, brilliantly mischievous smile, and for a moment, obviously, she felt a pang of regret. But the cool, sophisticated façade resumed almost immediately: she gathered up the reins and smiled back. 'Good. I'm glad you can be mature about it.'

'You thought I wouldn't be,' he said. 'That says it all, really. Goodbye, Selina.'

'Goodbye,' she said, and suddenly, unexpectedly, blew him a kiss. 'And thanks. Marcus will understand, he always does.'

Morgan watched her canter away up the hillside, and found that it was possible to admire the perfect union of woman and horse without involving any deeper, more complicated feelings. She was beautiful, desirable, gorgeous, but ultimately she wasn't what he wanted. Nor were any of the other women — Kim, Jonie, Robyn, Marta, Hazel — whose vague, smiling faces crowded his memory. He knew, with sudden and surprising bitterness, that he had spent the last ten years looking for something that didn't exist. He knew it didn't, because he had held it in his hand once, and then wilfully destroyed it.

A hundred yards away, the bay horse swerved suddenly, and came to a rearing halt. Selina, who hunted side-saddle, was far too expert a rider to fall off, but she had evidently been alarmed, for Morgan could hear her shouting. For a moment he thought she was berating the horse, and then a dog began barking. A figure rose up from the bushes beside Hadrian, and began shouting back.

Morgan watched with interest. Behind him, one of the JCBs started up again, drowning the sounds of argument. He saw Selina gesticulating with her whip, while a large cream-coloured dog frisked at a safe distance.

In his present mood, anyone who made Selina cross must have something in their favour. Grinning, Morgan made his way across the rough grass towards his girlfriend — his *former* girlfriend, he reminded himself — to investigate.

At closer quarters, Selina's adversary proved to be a young woman in jeans and a madras check shirt in faded pinks and blues. Morgan didn't recognise her, and he wondered, with considerable interest, who she was. Not only was she very pretty, despite the glasses and the shabby clothes, but clearly she was quite capable of giving the aristocratic Selina a really hard time.

'I could have been *killed*,' she was saying, as Morgan approached. 'And your clumsy great animal has ruined my work!'

'I told you, you shouldn't be here. This is private property. And that wretched dog should be on a lead.' The incident had obviously shaken even Selina's self-control: she was pale with repressed fury, and a bright spot of red stood out on each flawless cheek. 'So it's hardly my fault if I nearly ride you down, is it?'

'I've a perfect right to be here. There's a public footpath across the park.' The young woman grabbed the dog's collar, and stared belligerently up at her opponent. She was not very tall, which should have put her at a disadvantage, but she did not seem in the least disconcerted by Selina's haughty manner. 'Anyway, Sir Marcus said I could paint anywhere I liked.'

'Sir *Marcus? He* gave you permission to be here?' Selina broke into disbelieving laughter. 'Now I *know* you're lying. I'm his stepdaughter, and he hasn't said anything to me.'

'Well, he did. I'm staying with a friend of his, Miss James. He came round for dinner on Saturday, and he told me then. Ask him, he'll remember. And I'm sorry I startled your horse, but perhaps you should look more carefully where you're going.'

'I shall check with him now,' Selina said. 'And if you're lying, I shall call the police.' With an ostentatious flourish, she pulled a mobile phone out of the inside pocket of her hacking jacket, and punched in a series of numbers. There was a long wait, and then she spoke. 'Marcus? Selina. There's a woman here claiming to be a friend of Miss James — says you gave her permission to paint in the park.'

In the brief pause, Morgan, now only a few yards away, had leisure to study the other woman, who was belatedly securing the bumptious Labrador on a stout lead. She was generously and pleasingly proportioned, and he liked the long, curling brown hair, inadequately confined in a thick French plait. The face behind the round, owlish glasses was beautiful, in a rather old-fashioned way, with thick straight brows and large dark eyes. Like Lillie Langtry, he thought, and realised that, whoever she was, he was interested in her.

Didn't take you long to get over Selina, did it? he reflected ruefully. Three minutes after she's dumped you, you're fancying someone else.

'Really? I see. Thank you. No, I won't be in for lunch. 'Bye.' Selina shut the phone with a snap and replaced it. 'Well, apparently you do have permission. I should be more careful where you sit, in future. And kindly keep that dog under proper control — there are usually cattle in the park.' She gathered up the reins and smacked the horse smartly on the rump. With a snort, he sprang off across the grass, his huge hooves scattering a liberal helping of earthen clods over the young woman as she stood beside the bushes.

With an exclamation of annoyance, she

brushed herself down, and then gave a cry of anguish. 'Oh, God, my *painting*!'

She didn't seem to have noticed Morgan, so he walked forward. Strewn on the ground beside her was the familiar paraphernalia of an artist, but the sketchpad was disfigured by a large hoof-print, and the water pot had overturned, spilling a great splash of liquid across the half-finished picture, along with copious dollops of mud. The girl knelt down and picked it up. 'That's an hour's work down the pan. God, I could *kill* her! And she didn't even say sorry!'

'Being Selina means you never have to,' said Morgan drily.

The girl's head jerked up: she obviously hadn't realised he was there. He had time to notice that her wide, startled eyes were not brown but in fact a warm greenish hazel, fringed by very long lashes, and to feel a strange shock as she stared at him. Then she said fiercely, 'God, don't *do* that!'

'Do what?' said Morgan, raising his eyebrows quizzically.

For some reason, this seemed to infuriate the young woman still further. 'You know perfectly well what I mean. *Smirking* at me like that. Why don't you go away and leave me in peace?'

Surprised by this unprovoked onslaught,

Morgan said mildly, 'Don't you want any help?'

'I can manage perfectly well, thank you very much. Oh for God's sake, Maggie, calm down and just *sit*, will you?'

'I'll take her,' Morgan offered.

'It's all right, I can manage.' Furiously, she was stuffing her paraphernalia into a rucksack obviously too small to hold all of it comfortably. Morgan caught sight of the ruined painting as it was ruthlessly jammed in with the rest. One corner was untouched, and the tawny, unmistakable shape of Oliver's Castle lay in perfect miniature on the paper, given substance by the dark woods behind it and the ethereal sky above. He said, 'It's a real shame. It looked good.'

'And what would you know about it?' For some inexplicable reason, the girl seemed determined to be as rude as possible. Morgan rose with delight to the challenge. 'Quite a lot, as a matter of fact.'

'Oh, really? Well, tough. Maggie, leave him alone.'

'It's OK, I like dogs,' Morgan said, bending to pat the Labrador, who was eagerly sniffing him. 'So, you're staying with Miss James? Is Maggie yours, or hers?'

'Hers.' The girl finished, and slung the rucksack over one shoulder. Her eyes, lustrous with anger, met his unflinchingly. 'Not that it's any of your business, of course.'

'Of course not,' said Morgan, smiling. 'I just can't help being nosy, that's all.'

'What a sad life you must lead. And do thank your girlfriend for ruining my morning, won't you? She looked as if she really enjoyed it. Goodbye. Come *on*, Mags.'

Slightly bemused, Morgan watched her stride away across the rough grass towards Stony Lane, her head high and the rucksack banging vehemently on her back. He liked her. He liked her fierce spirit, and her unmistakable talent, and her complete disregard for the looks which she undoubtedly possessed. He wanted, very much, to know her better, and yet he felt as if he knew her already. And despite her anger, he had enough confidence in his own powers of attraction to be sure that, sooner or later, he would win her round.

10

Harriet didn't dare look back until she had reached the comparative shelter of the trees growing along the edge of the park by the lane. Then she took the risk of stopping, and turning. He was still just in view, walking back to the quarry, but as she watched, a clump of bushes hid him from sight.

Only then did she realise that her knees were shaking and her palms slick with cold sweat. Oh my God, Harriet thought, with something close to panic. Whatever possessed me to pick a fight with him?

She knew, though. All the anger, pent up and penned in for ten long years, could no longer be contained at the sight of him. He hadn't changed for the worse. His hair was short now, and his clothes were smarter, but he wasn't bald, or fat, or greying, or *safe*. He was still devastatingly attractive, but with one crucial difference. The boy she remembered, wild and eager and graceless, had become a man. A physically impressive, formidable, arrogant, self-assured man, who had left behind his old student identity, just as she had shed hers, but for different reasons. Her growing-up had been done privately and painfully, and at the bitter cost of all her illusions. Whereas Morgan looked as if he'd never known a moment of doubt in his life.

She wanted to shout and scream her rage at him, she wanted him to understand exactly what he had done to her, ten years ago, when he had abandoned her without a word and gone off to America to further his career. She wanted to take him by the scruff of his neck and shake that insufferable arrogance out of him until he had the grace to apologise. And then . . .

And then, she realised with shame, she wanted to take him to bed.

But it was too late for that now, ten years too late. They were different people, with ties and responsibilities and the emotional baggage of all their mistakes and memories weighing them down. And when he discovered her identity, as he inevitably would, he wouldn't want to know. She would be past history, consigned to the dustbin of previous affairs. If the superb, elegant Selina was the sort of woman he could attract now, then he wouldn't look twice at an impoverished single mother with cheap, unflattering clothes, no makeup, and an inconvenient longing for revenge.

It hadn't been like that then. For six

months, they hadn't been able to take their hands off each other. She was caught by a sudden, unbearably vivid memory of a Christmas party at someone's house. She was standing in the kitchen, talking to one of her friends, with Morgan beside her, his arm around her, and his fingers gently stroking her shoulder, over and over. Then the music in the front room had changed from thumping bass to something softer and more romantic, and they had danced together, melded close, breast, hip, thigh, their lips touching, and she had seen passion and love and desire in his eyes, reflected in the mellow golden glow of the candles along the mantelpiece. Words were unnecessary, a look enough. Unable to wait any longer, they had slipped out into the garden, and made love on the dark grass, just out of reach of the light from the coloured lanterns strung across the windows. It was a clear, frosty night, and the sky had been swarming with stars, strewn thickly over their heads, and reflected, with wonderful brilliance, around and within her heart and soul. She had had dead, cold leaves in her hair and mud on her dress, but she hadn't cared. He had made her warm: he had made her whole body, her whole self, right down to the soul, melt with rapture and longing and desire, with the glory of being loved. She could still recall, with desperate clarity, what it felt like to lie in his arms, to feel him around and inside her, his voice whispering Welsh endearments to her mouth, his fingers weaving passionate enchantments on her bare skin. He had said, '*Rydw i'n dy garu di*,' which meant 'I love you' in the language of his childhood. And the tears, unnoticed, slid down her face as she remembered.

She had been as certain of his feelings as she was of her own. But she had been wrong, and her mistake had skewed and distorted her whole life afterwards, however much she had refused to admit it at the time.

And Morgan? All too obviously she had made so little impact on his own life that he hadn't even recognised her. Admittedly, she looked very different now, but her stubborn heart refused to acknowledge that someone who had once professed to love her so much would feel not the slightest frisson of remembrance.

'Oh, sod him!' she said aloud, to Maggie's evident bewilderment. 'So what if he didn't know me? I don't care!'

But she realised, as she climbed the stile into Stony Lane, that she still cared, very much, about what he thought of her, and was furious with herself for being so affected.

By the time Harriet reached Holly Cottage, the tears had dried, and the face she presented to Daphne was back to normal. 'I knocked over my water pot,' she said, in explanation of her early return, and was relieved when the older woman accepted it without question. She didn't want, just yet, to bring all the tangle of emotion and anger and betrayal with which she had surrounded her memory of Morgan Price into the open.

In any case, he was not the only complication in her life, and the phone call, which came just as she was occupied in stretching another piece of paper in readiness for any further attempt to resume her painting, was an unwelcome reminder of it. 'Harry? George here. Look, I've just had your ex on the line with all sorts of threats.'

'My ex? You mean Edward?'

'Of course I mean Edward, you haven't got any more tucked away, have you?'

Little do you know, thought Harriet ruefully. She dragged her mind away from Morgan and back to the other man who had occupied her life, also to its detriment. 'What sort of threats?'

'Don't sound so worried, it was all bluster, you know Edward. But he's obviously getting desperate for that bloody car. Take some advice from big sis?'

'That's what I spend my life doing,' said Harriet. She had no intention of mentioning Morgan: Georgia had never approved of him anyway, he was far too alternative and unconventional for her tastes.

'Well, give him a ring and tell him he can have it back. You don't want to antagonise him too much, do you? Or he'll probably refuse to pay any maintenance for Toby. I know he wouldn't have a leg to stand on, but that won't stop him trying to wriggle out of his obligations if he gets really stroppy. You know how pig-headed he can be.'

Harriet knew, only too well. She said reluctantly, 'OK. Though I really don't want to see him at the moment. It's wonderful here, pretending he doesn't exist.'

'If only!' Georgia gave an unkind cackle. 'Look, why don't you come into Bath now and we'll work out a strategy over lunch? I've got a free hour or two, a client cancelled. There's a new place just round the corner, does great pizza, I'll treat you.'

'I've got to get back to pick up Toby before three,' Harriet said. 'But yes, that'd be brilliant. Thanks, George.'

'The least I could do,' said her sister. 'And maybe we could fit in a little shopping, if your bank balance is up to it.'

'It isn't up to much more than a jumble

sale,' Harriet reminded her.

'All the more reason to sort something out with Edward ASAP, then. I'll lend you some dosh. See you shortly!'

She rang off before her sister could inform her, briefly and forcefully, that she had no intention of surviving on anyone's charity. But I'll have to, Harriet thought, as she went in search of Daphne, who was in the garden. Little as I like it, I've got to accept her help. As soon as I'm settled, though, I shall pay her back — and everyone else, too, according to their just desserts!

⋆   ⋆   ⋆

Edward Armstrong had spent a miserable, anxious and frustrating weekend. Saturday had been a complete nightmare, full of argumentative, fussy clients whose every wish, however unreasonable, he had been forced to satisfy for the sake of his business. Sunday had seemed to promise a brief respite, but at nine in the morning the people who had hired *White Rabbit* had rung in, complaining that they couldn't get their boat started. He had tried in vain to contact Pete the mechanic, but he, so his wife informed Edward with some satisfaction, had taken advantage of one of his few Sundays off to go sea-fishing from Weymouth, and wouldn't be back until the evening. Cursing Pete, his wife, Harriet, all pernickety customers and anyone else who might conceivably be responsible for his plight, Edward had crawled out of bed, trying to ignore the headache which drinking a bottle of wine and several whiskies the previous evening had bestowed on him, located Pete's well-thumbed and extremely oily engine manual from his insalubrious workshop, and driven off in the Metro to find *White Rabbit*, apparently moored at the top of the Caen Hill flight in Devizes.

By the time he managed to locate it, the little car's bonnet was belching steam, and the needle had climbed well into the red. Once more cursing Harriet, he had done his best to get the boat started, and after a messy and painful hour — he had taken all the skin off his knuckles on a sharp edge, and covered his Calvin Klein jeans in oil — he had succeeded, much to his own and his customers' surprise. With a relieved and cheerful wave, he watched them chug away towards Pewsey. At last something had gone right.

That turned out to be the only success of the day. The Metro gave up its labouring ghost halfway home, and he was forced to summon assistance. The mechanic took three hours to turn up, only to pronounce the car well and truly deceased. 'We might as well tow it to the scrapyard now, mate, it'd save us both a lot of time and trouble.'

My BMW! Edward thought, with anguish and longing. No matter what it takes, I'll get it back off Harriet if it's the last thing I do!

By the time he had arranged for the disposal of the Metro, and the hire of a substitute vehicle at outrageously exorbitant rates, it was late afternoon. Tired and hungry, he drove back to the boatyard. There were seven messages on the answerphone, three making bookings, the rest asking for information. It was the sort of thing that Harriet would have dealt with in a few minutes, but Edward, hunting through the computer for the standard letters, trying to find where she'd put the new brochures, and entering customers' names on the log, took nearly two hours to sort it all out. Too weary and dispirited to do anything except flop in front of the television with a lasagne from the freezer and another bottle of wine, he had gone to bed early, vowing vengeance against the woman whose departure had had such a catastrophic effect on his lazy, pleasant life. And on Monday morning, breathing fire and brimstone, he had rung Georgia at her office, demanding to know the whereabouts of

Harriet, Toby and the BMW, though not necessarily in that order.

Georgia's manner had been so frostily unhelpful that he knew at once that she must be sheltering the miscreant. Edward did not have her home number, but he knew where she lived. Within half an hour, he was hammering on the door of her pleasant little flat, not far from the Royal Crescent. When his efforts brought no response, he peered through the windows. The place was unquestionably deserted, and there was no sign, in either of the unnaturally tidy rooms which he could see, that anyone except Georgia was living there. He walked up and down the street, and found only one BMW, older than his, and a different colour. And the nosy neighbour who came out to investigate at his second attempt on the door told him that Georgia had had no visitors in the last few days.

So where in God's name had Harriet gone? To her parents in Bristol? By now desperate to locate her, he went there as well. Again, no answer, no BMW, no trace. Sick, disbelieving, furious, he drove home along the M4, much too fast, and was stopped by the police. By the time he reached Sanden again, it was late afternoon, and the answerphone was winking at him busily, telling him, if he could be bothered to count the flashes, that he had eleven messages.

Five provisional bookings, three information requests, two cancellations, and suddenly his vanished partner's voice, clear and accusing, at the end of the line. 'Edward? Harriet here. As you're not around, I'll ring back later. We have a lot of things to discuss, and I hope you'll be reasonable and civilised about it. I'll certainly try to be. *If* I can, in view of your behaviour. Goodbye.'

Incandescent with rage, he glared at the machine. It blinked imperturbably back at him. Then, so unexpectedly that he jumped, the phone rang. He picked it up and spoke automatically. 'Wonderland Boats.'

'Oh, hallo, Edward. Have a nice day?'

'*No*, as a matter of fact,' he said, through clenched teeth. 'Dear God, Harriet, what the hell d'you think you're playing at? Where's my bloody *car*? I've had to use your old wreck and it finally conked out yesterday, and the hired one's costing me a fortune — '

'Calm down,' she said mildly. 'No need to make such a fuss.'

Edward had heard her use a similarly soothing tone to Toby, and it was the final straw. Suddenly, he exploded with the hoarded rage of three nightmarish days. '*Fuss?* You think I'm just making a *fuss*, you

149

deceitful, stupid little cow? You're bloody lucky I haven't reported you for stealing my car. I want it back, and I want it back *now*, or I'll contact the police.'

'It's all right, don't lose your rag. You can have it back tomorrow. I'll bring it round.'

'Thank God. About bloody time too. I knew you'd see sense in the end. Have you any *idea* what a nightmare I've been through here? There's bookings piling up, all sorts of trouble with the boats, I don't know where anything is and the computer might just as well be in Greek for all I can understand of it — '

'Well, you're going to have to learn,' Harriet said.

It took a while for the import of her words to sink in. Then Edward said grimly, '*What* did you say?'

'I said, you're going to have to learn. About the business and everything. I'm not coming back, Edward. I've had enough of being your skivvy. You're a big boy now and you're perfectly capable of managing on your own. You've leant on me for far too long, and I was a complete mug to put up with it. I'm sorry, but that's it. Finish. End of story.'

'But . . . but . . . ' At last, a small thread of concern for someone other than himself had entered Edward's mind. 'But what about Toby?'

'He's fine. He's been asking for you, and I'll bring him over to see you as often as you want. I'm not going to cut you out of his life, no way — you're his father, and he loves you, and you've got rights as well as responsibilities.'

'Responsibilities?'

'Well, he's your son, so of course you'll have to pay maintenance for him.'

'*What?*'

Harriet took a deep breath. 'I can't exist on nothing, Edward, and nor can he. And it's not as though you can't afford it, after all. The boatyard must have been coining money, the past three or four years.'

'And if I refuse? *You* left *me*, remember.'

'Only because of your intolerable behaviour. Anyway, refusing to pay isn't an option. If you do, you'll have the Child Support Agency breathing down your neck. You really can't get out of it, Edward, I do have the law on my side. I haven't got any income, I shall have to find a job, and childcare for Toby, and somewhere to live — '

'Well, you bloody well should have thought of all that before you buggered off and left me in the lurch!' Edward shouted furiously.

I will *not* get upset or angry, Harriet told

herself desperately at the other end of the line. Aloud, she said, keeping her voice level, 'You're talking as if I'm one of your employees, and that just about sums it up. We had a relationship once, remember? And a son. But you've been unfaithful to me for years, haven't you, and Toby finding you screwing Gina was just the last straw. So what the hell was the point in me staying? I'd rather be penniless and homeless. At least I'm free.'

'It was your own stupid fault,' Edward said viciously. 'If you hadn't been so bloody frigid — I mean, what do you expect when you fall asleep every night before I get to bed? Eh? You wouldn't let me near you — '

He found himself talking to the dialling tone. Harriet, goaded beyond endurance, had put the phone down.

She sat for a while, persuading herself that throwing things round Daphne's hall would not make her feel better, or help her win the argument with Edward, or find her a new life. But it was hard, hard indeed to deal with the rage which had flooded her when he had offered his excuses. How *dare* he call me frigid? she thought, incensed with the injustice of the accusation. I was too bloody knackered looking after his house, his business and his son. Too bad he wanted a mistress as well as a wife and a secretary and a mother and a doormat.

And then, unwelcome, sad and yet exultant: Morgan could say a lot of things about me, but he'd never have called me frigid.

Though what he would say when, as would inevitably happen, Sir Marcus told him her name, she could not imagine.

11

It was a beautiful room, looking out over the gently sloping expanse of the park. The canal gleamed fitfully beyond the distant trees, and then the fields merged into the misty blue of Sandridge Hill, on the northern horizon. But Morgan did not notice the view, nor had he paid any attention to Selina's clothes, laid out neatly on the bed they had shared for more than three months, ready to go to her new flat in Bath. His mind was entirely, catastrophically occupied with the information which Sir Marcus had divulged in answer to his curious question.

'Oh, you mean Harriet, I expect. Harriet Smith. She's staying with Daphne, wanted to do some painting in the park. Apparently she's very talented. Nice girl, quiet, a bit shy I think.'

The name sunk like a stone into his heart. Harriet. It couldn't be. It could *not* be. His Harriet had been vivid, lively, never shy. He remembered the bright hair, the huge earrings, the weird clothes. No way, *no way*, could she have mutated into the angry, ordinary, yet beautiful young woman he had met in the park today.

And yet . . . and yet, he had felt he had known her already. So had his senses remembered what his conscious mind had forgotten? Had that instant attraction, so strong and mysterious, been a sign of the truth?

Unwillingly, he faced the possibility, and all its consequent ramifications. He hadn't recognised her, but had she known who he was? Quite likely, if Sir Marcus had mentioned his name at Daphne's dinner table. And that explained her baffling and disproportionate anger with him.

An anger which was, he knew, absolutely justified, even after ten years. He had treated her like shit. He had swept her into a passionate and all-enveloping relationship, and then dumped her without a word as soon as the chance to further his career came along. Selina had her faults, but at least she had had the courage, and the honesty, to give him notice that their affair was over. He had claimed to love Harriet, but he hadn't even had the guts to say goodbye.

Well, he could apologise. If he were Harriet, he'd take great pleasure in throwing it back in his face, but it was the very least he could do. And besides, he wanted to make sure that still, somewhere beneath that apparently conventional exterior, lurked the sensual, wonderful, vibrant girl he remembered.

The door opened: he hadn't heard a knock, so he was not surprised to hear Selina's cool, well-bred voice. 'I didn't know you were in here. Indulging in nostalgia?'

He turned, his face serious. 'Hardly. How did the flat-hunting go?'

For answer, she held up a keyring. 'I can move in any time. I thought I'd make a start now. What are you going to do?'

Over lunch, he had explained the situation to his employer. As he had expected, Sir Marcus had been his usual tolerant and understanding self. 'Well, I can't say I'm exactly astonished. I trust this won't make any difference to your work for me?'

'Of course not,' Morgan had said, and had managed to convey, with a lifted eyebrow, his surprise that the older man could ever have imagined that he would be so unprofessional as to let his personal feelings get in the way of his contract. 'But if you would rather I found somewhere else to live — '

'Only if you want it. If Selina's going off to Bath, I shall be rattling round this place on my own. Seems ridiculous to kick you out — you're welcome to stay here until The Pits is finished.'

'I'm moving my things over to the stable flat,' Morgan said now to his former lover. 'I thought that would be best.'

'Fine by me.' Selina opened one door of the wardrobe that ran the length of the wall between door and window, and removed a nest of Louis Vuitton luggage. 'If you don't mind, I'd rather pack in private.'

He should have been angered by her politely indifferent tone, as if they were strangers: but he was not. And that, he knew, was a symptom of how their relationship had degenerated over the past few weeks. Now, he didn't care what she said or did. But, he realised, he still cared very much about Harriet.

He said a brief, unemotional goodbye to Selina, aware that she would probably have gone to Bath by the time he returned, and went out. It was still a pleasant afternoon, although the wind had risen in the last couple of hours, and the clouds rushing across the sky were thicker now, and burdened with grey. He walked down to the quarry and spent some time going over the plans with Mick, the building foreman. But all the while, the same restlessness was simmering in his mind, making him fidgety and ill at ease. He wanted to see her. He wanted to make sure that the Harriet Smith staying with Daphne was the same girl with whom he had fallen so deeply in love, long ago. His brain told him that it was a common name, there must be hundreds of them about, that it was a coincidence too great to be possible. But his heart, yearning and desperate and guilty, told him otherwise.

It was nearly five o'clock before his self-control at last capitulated. He exchanged a final word with Mick, and then set off across the park, towards the distant hedge that bounded Stony Lane.

He had never met Daphne James, although Sir Marcus had told him something about her. He knew that she had been a high-powered academic, and that she had retired to write a book. Not by any stretch of his vivid imagination could he imagine his Harriet even knowing such a person, let alone being on sufficiently friendly terms to be staying with her. It was another reason to doubt that the woman he had met this morning was his long-lost lover.

And yet, and yet . . . his Harriet had worn contact lenses. He remembered her familiar shout, in pub or dance hall or common room: 'Stop, everyone! Stand still, one of my lenses has come out!' And she had painted, quick, beautiful watercolour sketches of the life they led, which at this distance seemed to have been a never-ceasing round of bars and parties and clubs.

The girl this morning had worn glasses. And she painted in watercolours. There surely couldn't be *two* short, short-sighted artists called Harriet Smith.

Well, there was only one way to find out. He vaulted over the gate into the lane, and walked briskly down it.

There was a little huddle of teenage boys and bikes in the gateway of the first house he came to. They looked so guilty and furtive as he approached that he knew they must be up to no good, and felt a pang of nostalgia for his own nefarious youth. Sure enough, his nose caught the unmistakable aroma of cannabis, and the tallest boy whisked what must be a spliff out of sight behind his back.

'Hi,' said Morgan, unable to resist teasing them. 'Is this where Daphne James lives?'

For some reason, the simple question seemed to cause the lads considerable amusement. The tall boy, still sniggering, said, 'You mean the mad woman?'

'I mean Miss James,' Morgan said patiently. 'She lives round here somewhere.'

'Adam! Adam, what are you doing?'

'God, that's your mum,' said the tall one. 'Better go, Ad. See ya.' They leapt on to their bikes and pedalled urgently off up the lane, leaving the one who must be Adam standing rather forlornly in the gateway.

'So where does Miss James live?' asked Morgan hastily: he had no wish to encounter the large and intimidating lady just emerging from her porch.

'Down there,' Adam said, pointing towards the canal bridge. He turned and wandered sulkily back into his mother's domain. Morgan, with memories of his own tyrannical father unpleasantly vivid in his mind, gave him a sympathetic glance and went on to find Daphne James's house.

Within Holly Cottage, Harriet was cooking Toby's tea. The mundane task, carried out with unusual vigour and much energetic stirring of scrambling eggs, had done a little to exhaust her anger with Edward. It didn't matter, after all, what he called her, what he thought of her. She knew, with towering certainty, that she was right: that he had treated her badly and that he must do something to support his son. She was still smarting with the injustice of his accusations, though, and also with the information that Georgia had given her over lunch that day. 'Sorry, Harry, but I've been taking advice, and you haven't got a claim on the business. If you were married to him, that'd be different, but of course the cunning sod never popped the question, did he?'

'I brought it up when Toby was born,' Harriet had told her, blushing to remember how she had been deluded and strung along. 'And he said that what we had was so beautiful, it was a shame to spoil it.'

Her sister's raucous, unkind laughter had echoed all round the restaurant. 'And you fell for it! Oh, Harry, how could you? But then you never did have much luck with men, did you?'

There were times when Harriet felt an active pang of dislike for her forthright sister, and this was one of them. She said defensively, 'No more than you.'

'I take damn good care never to get involved,' said Georgia. 'And at least I haven't got a kid holding me back.'

'If I didn't have Toby, I think I'd give up,' Harriet told her forcefully. 'Will you please stop treating me like a stupid child and tell me exactly what I am and am not entitled to?'

'OK, OK.' Georgia had thrown up her hands in mock surrender. 'Sorry. You're entitled to maintenance for Toby, of course, and you can sue the pants off him if he tries to wriggle out of it. But as you're not his wife, and not his business partner, you've no stake in the boatyard. I know it's unfair, given all the hard work you've put into it, but you just count as an employee, and an unpaid one at that. Your only consolation will be watching it all go down the pan without you.'

Which, thought Harriet now, putting a slice of bread to toast under Daphne's ancient grill, was poor payment for her years of labour. But at least she knew where she stood.

There was a knock on the front door. Daphne, who was very nobly helping Toby with a jigsaw at the dining-room table, went to answer it. Harriet heard a masculine voice, and suddenly the timbre of it struck at her heart. Oh God, she thought, her knees trembling. He's here. He knows. What shall I say to him?

'Someone to see you, Harriet,' said Daphne at the kitchen door, her face expressing what in anyone else would be described as intense curiosity. 'It's that architect, I think. Are you all right?'

'Fine. Show him in. Can you keep Toby occupied?'

'Of course. I'll finish his tea, if you like.'

'No. It's all right. I can manage. He won't be staying long, anyway.' Harriet grasped her wayward emotions and shook them vigorously into something resembling normality. 'Hallo, Morgan.'

In Daphne's small kitchen, he seemed

much bigger than she remembered: taller, broader, more intimidating. Behind him, she caught sight of Toby's anxious face, and her heart sank with the prospect of all the explaining she must do. She said calmly, 'Can you shut the door, please? Thanks. What are you doing here?'

'I've come to see you.' His eyes were still that alarming, electrifying blue. 'I'm sorry I didn't recognise you this morning. What have you done to your hair?'

'This is what it's supposed to be like. It isn't really scarlet, you know.' She knew she must seem rude and hostile, but she couldn't help it: the wounds that she had once thought healed were now newly and agonisingly raw, as if he had abandoned her only last week. And suddenly, with frightening perspicacity, she realised that Edward, too, might be feeling like this.

'You look completely different.' Morgan was staring at her as if he still couldn't believe that this Harriet and the one in his memory were one and the same.

'I grew up,' Harriet said shortly. 'Have you?'

He frowned. 'I don't understand.'

'Then you haven't.'

'Look, *cariad* — '

'*Don't* call me that!'

'I'm sorry I hurt you.'

'Sometimes,' said Harriet, with cold dignity, 'the word 'sorry' is totally and ludicrously inadequate. I haven't ever forgiven you for what you did to me, and I don't honestly think I ever will. Now please can you go away and leave us alone?'

'The toast is burning.'

'Oh, *shit!*' Harriet leapt to the grill and pulled the smoking slice out. 'We're getting low on bread, too.'

'And the eggs look as if they could do with a stir.'

'Oh, for God's sake, bugger off.' She whipped the pan off the ring, banged it down on the table and glared at him. '*Please,* Morgan, just *go.*'

'Is that kid yours?'

Furiously, she met his eyes. 'Yes. Look, you can't *begin* to understand how much I've changed in the last ten years, and if you think I'm going to let you back into my life then you've got another think coming, you arrogant, lying toad.'

'So how about coming out for a drink tonight?'

For a moment, Harriet stared at him, and then began to laugh in astonished disbelief. 'God, you're *impossible!* I wouldn't have thought that even you would have the effrontery. Can't you take no for an answer, or do I have to ask Daphne to help me throw you out?'

'No.' For an instant, she saw something more serious in his face. 'It's all right, I'll go. But I *am* sorry, for what I did. Will you let me explain some time?'

'There's nothing to explain.' Harriet walked over to the back door and held it open. 'And I don't want to hear your pathetic excuses. Goodbye, Morgan. And don't get the idea into your head that you'll be welcome here — you're not.'

'I got the message,' he said drily. 'Goodbye, *cariad*.'

And before she could protest again, he had gone.

Her hands shaking and sweaty, she put another piece of bread under the grill, stirred the eggs and found a plate and a knife and fork. Her limbs obeyed her automatically, while her mind seethed. How *dare* he? How *dare* he come here and try to justify himself?

The door from the dining room opened cautiously, and Toby put his head round it. 'Mum, where's my tea?'

'Here — it's almost ready.' Furiously, Harriet buttered the toast and dumped a dry mountain of overcooked scrambled egg on top. 'Ketchup?'

'Yes, *please*.'

She settled her son with his supper, glad of the chance to be busy. As he began eating, she found Daphne at her elbow, with a steaming mug of tea. 'You look as though you need it,' the older woman said sympathetically.

'I do.' Knowing that she would have to explain, Harriet moved into the kitchen. She added, 'Sorry about that. He won't be coming here again.'

'I didn't realise you knew him,' said Daphne, who had obviously arrived at some understanding of the situation.

'Yes, but a long time ago. We lived together for a while when we were students.' Harriet directed a wry glance at her through the steam from the tea. 'A bit of unfinished business, I suppose you could call him. An old flame, now well and truly extinguished.'

But, remembering Morgan's legendary stubbornness, she knew that he wouldn't see it like that. He'd always wanted to have the last word, and this time he hadn't. And if he was going to be here in Sanden all summer, they were bound to encounter each other again.

And a part of her, small, obstinate and unrepentant, welcomed the prospect.

12

Harriet had wanted to return the BMW to Edward by herself, but Georgia, over their Monday lunch, had pointed out the flaws in this plan. 'For a start, you need some moral support, not to mention a witness. And then how are you going to get home, if he's managed to wreck your poor old Metro? Walk back to Daphne's? That'd be a dead give away if you don't want him to know where you're living.'

'There isn't much point in *not* telling him — he's bound to find out sooner or later. Anyway, I can't break off all contact with him, because of Toby.'

'You can communicate through your respective solicitors — that's what most people do.'

'Yes, but at what cost? You've said yourself I'm not entitled to any share in the business, and he's legally bound to pay me maintenance, so I don't actually *need* a solicitor, do I? They just end up making more work and hassle, and anyway I can't afford one.'

Georgia, eyebrows raised at her sister's unworldly and trusting naïvety, had spent the next five minutes explaining exactly why she did need professional legal help. 'If you don't have a solicitor, he'll feel he can walk all over you,' she had finished. 'He'll think he can get away with all sorts of outrageous things. There's nothing like an official letter to keep an errant ex-partner's mind on his responsibilities. And as you've got no savings and no income, you'll qualify for legal aid, no problem.'

In the end, reluctantly, Harriet had agreed. She knew that Georgia spoke sense, but still a part of her, perversely childish even as she claimed to be grown-up, wanted to escape the role of little sister, in which Georgia had persistently cast her.

At half past ten, early enough to have plenty of time to pick up Toby from playgroup at twelve, late enough to, as Georgia had put it, 'make the bugger sweat', Edward's cherished BMW rolled elegantly into the yard at Wonderland Boats, and ground to a halt with a crunch of gravel in front of the garage. Her heart pounding, Harriet switched off the engine and got out. Strangely, although she had only been away for a few days, the place where she had spent five increasingly unhappy and frustrating years seemed already to have become part of her past, and she no longer felt any sense of belonging there. She glanced round, wondering where Edward was, as Georgia's Tigra and Don Potter's Rover pulled up alongside.

In spite of her protests, her sister had brought along the practice specialist in what were still, apparently, called rather coyly 'matrimonial affairs'. He was a large, middle-aged and patronisingly avuncular man, and Harriet had taken an instant dislike to his smile, his glasses and his damp, rather too lingering handshake, but she was getting quite good at hiding her feelings. Certainly Georgia was, for she behaved as if she actually liked the man: which Harriet, suppressing a shudder, could not possibly believe. But there was no doubt that he was good at his job: in the space of five exhausting minutes, he had given Harriet all the information she required, and a great deal she didn't, about her rights and Edward's, and her confidence had consequently received a much-needed boost.

Edward opened the door as they advanced on it. He had obviously expected to see Harriet alone, for his face registered surprised and disapproving suspicion at the sight of the two solicitors. 'Is this necessary?' he demanded of his former lover, with heavy sarcasm. 'I'm not under arrest, am I?'

'I thought it would be best to bring my

representatives along,' Harriet said. She indicated the BMW. 'Here you are. As agreed.'

'If you've put just *one scratch* on it . . . ' Edward pushed past her and examined his treasure with hungry eyes. Harriet and Toby, with much laughter and the expenditure of many buckets of soapy water, had given it a good clean the previous evening, so it was almost devoid of bird droppings and pear blossom. At last, reluctantly satisfied, he turned back to her. 'Thank God. Well, are you going to see sense and come back?'

'No,' Harriet said firmly. 'I've already told you I'm not, and the reasons why.'

'God, Hattie, you've *got* to come back, I need you!' Edward cried, with a pathetic look of appeal on his face. Obviously, he had decided that since indignation wasn't working, he would try a different tack.

'Perhaps this discussion would better be conducted indoors,' said Don Potter, with calm authority. 'We have quite a lot on our agenda, Mr Armstrong, so if you would be so good?'

Harriet was almost tempted to feel sorry for Edward. Outgunned and outnumbered, he was plainly unprepared for this assault. However, she suspected that it would not be long before he reverted to the defensive

170

bluster with which he met unwelcome facts.

In the office, perched nervously beside the computer, Edward listened as Potter outlined the settlement which he, Georgia and Harriet had concocted that morning, and pointed out the advantages of acceptance. 'My client is asking for no more than your discharge of your legal responsibilities towards your son, Mr Armstrong. In the circumstances, you will save a great deal of time, money and inconvenience to yourself if you acknowledge this undeniable fact and agree to what she is asking.'

'I'm not going to be bounced into agreeing to anything until I've seen my own solicitor,' said Edward, his back metaphorically to the wall. 'But I think Harriet is being very unreasonable. She upped and left without any explanation or warning, she took my car, *and* Toby — '

'You can have him this afternoon if you like,' Harriet said. 'He'd love to see you, he's been asking for you.'

'This afternoon?' The wind taken thoroughly out of his sails, Edward stared at her in dismay. 'But I'm not sure . . . I'd thought . . . I mean, where would I take him?'

'Oh, just use your imagination,' said Harriet, with a ruthlessness Georgia might envy. 'Victoria Park in Bath is nice, or you could take him swimming, or fly a kite up by the White Horse, or just go for a walk along the canal and feed the ducks. It's up to you. Give him tea and drop him back at five.'

'Wait. Stop. You can't spring it on me at a moment's notice. I'm up to my eyeballs here without you.' He cast a look of anxious appeal at Harriet, but she remained resolutely impervious.

'You claimed my client was keeping your son away from you,' said Potter heavily. 'But although she has very generously offered you free access, you don't sound very keen to take advantage of it. Hardly the best note on which to start, in my opinion.'

'Of course I'll have him!' Edward cried. 'But not today.'

'Tomorrow?'

'Sunday,' said Edward desperately. 'I'll have him on Sunday afternoon.' He gave his former lover a look of boyish helplessness, designed to soften the stoniest heart. 'Please, Hattie, won't you think again about all this? After all I've done for you . . . Please, come back, and I'll try to be better, I promise. I can't do without you — '

'Of course you can,' Harriet said briskly, ignoring the melting appeal in his eyes. 'Come on, Edward, act your age. What are you, forty-two? Of course you can manage without me. Please understand, I am not coming back. This is for ever. And a few apologies and promises aren't going to win me over. They might have done once, but I know better now — if I was mug enough to believe you, you'd be up to your old tricks by the end of the week. This isn't something I've done out of spite, or even a capricious whim — you've *driven* me to this, Edward, you made my life so unbearable that I *had* to leave, or I think I'd have gone mad. If it wasn't for Toby, I'd be quite happy never to clap eyes on you again. But as you're his father, and he wants to see you, I'm prepared to keep in contact and be civilised, for his sake. And if you love him as you say you do, then you're going to have to do the same, OK? Because I don't want him hurt or upset by all this. And if you try practising your little power games on him, then I'll make sure you don't get the opportunity again. Understand?'

Edward stared at her, his mouth open in astonishment. With an effort, he said at last, 'Go. Go on, all of you. Get out and stop harassing me, do you hear? Out!'

'Goodbye, Mr Armstrong,' said Potter, with extreme politeness.

Edward ignored his outstretched hand.

'You'll be hearing from my solicitor tomorrow. In future, Harriet, all legal arguments will be conducted through him.'

'Fine by me,' she said cheerfully. 'So unless I hear otherwise, I'll bring Toby over on Sunday?'

'I repeat — I'm only communicating through my solicitor, from now on,' Edward said, as if this statement was sufficient to protect him from further hassle. 'Now will you all *kindly* leave, before I have to throw you out?'

It was curious, Harriet thought, as she climbed into the Tigra beside her sister. This encounter with Edward at his worst should have left her shaking and weepy. But instead she felt invigorated and optimistic. She'd been right, absolutely and incontrovertibly right, to leave him. Whatever the material costs, and the catastrophic effect on her standard of living, poverty and the long, hard struggle of single parenthood would be an absolute doddle compared to the grim realities of life with a man who, she now saw, had always tried to manipulate or bully her.

'OK?' Georgia asked, as they drove out of the gate. 'I must say, I thought you did very well back there. I'd have hit the bastard.'

'I know what Edward's like. He puts on

174

that little-boy lost act, and promises every-thing under the sun, but it's just to get what he wants, and it doesn't wash with me any more. Then, when he sees it doesn't work, he takes refuge in angry bluster, and it's all a front. Just as long as he realises that he can't escape his responsibilities towards Toby, that's all I'm after.'

'So you're not even bothered about the business?'

Harriet shook her head. 'Not now. If I'm honest, I'm glad to see the back of it. And if having to run it all by his poor little self makes Edward grow up a bit and realise that the world isn't put there for his convenience, then it'll be a good thing.'

* * *

To Harriet's considerable surprise, it was a different, more pleasant Edward, though, who greeted her and Toby, as arranged, on the following Sunday afternoon. By that time, the legal brains had managed to sort out a settlement that was, more or less, acceptable to both sides. Toby would see his father every weekend, at a time convenient to both parents: and Edward had, with great reluctance, agreed to pay Harriet regular maintenance. It was a sum much larger than

175

he would have liked, and rather smaller than Harriet needed, but at least she was no longer penniless. She would not have to sign on, or submit herself and her circumstances to the humiliating scrutiny of the benefit office.

So she was feeling happily optimistic as she knocked on Edward's door, and greeted him with a smile. 'Hallo, here's Toby.'

Their son, who had been in a state of high excitement all morning, and who had skipped along the canal towpath in Maggie's large white wake, now seemed to be overwhelmed by this longed-for meeting. He clung tightly to Harriet's hand and stared resolutely at the ground.

'Hallo, Toby,' said Edward. He was obviously making a supreme effort to be natural, and in consequence the artificiality of the occasion seemed to prickle in the air around them. 'I thought we'd go swimming at Chippenham, you know, with the flumes, and then feed the squirrels in the park. And perhaps we can go to McDonald's afterwards for a burger, how about that?'

'Don't like burgers,' said Toby, to his shoes.

Edward stared at Harriet, his eyes desperately signalling for help. Since he really did seem to be trying, she took pity on him. 'No, but you like chicken nuggets, don't you? And you *love* swimming, and you haven't been for ages.' A thought struck her suddenly. 'Edward, have you got his trunks and armbands?'

'All packed and ready to go,' said her ex-partner, with disproportionate pride in his achievement. 'Come on, Toby, or we'll run out of time.'

The little boy ignored his outstretched hand and turned to Harriet. 'But I want you to come too, Mum.'

'I've got things I have to do,' Harriet told him firmly. 'Go on, sweetheart, it'll be fun. And I'll pick you up at six.' She gently disengaged her hand, and stepped back.

For a tense moment, Toby hesitated, his wide blue eyes urgently seeking reassurance. Harriet smiled at him. 'Go on. You've been looking forward to seeing Daddy for days. Have a good time, and I'll see you later.'

'I want *you*!' Toby cried. '*Why* can't you come too, Mum?'

The situation was suddenly threatening to become difficult, and Edward, evidently completely at a loss, wasn't doing anything to help. Harriet said gently, 'I explained. I've got lots to do. I thought you'd enjoy seeing Daddy, and he wants to see you. And you never know,' she added, not without a certain touch of mischief, 'he might even let you ride in his front seat if you're *very* good.' And she glanced significantly at Edward.

With, obviously, considerable reluctance, he took the hint. 'Come on, Toby, I'll put your booster seat in the front for you.'

'And he might,' Harriet said, with a wink at her unfortunate ex-partner, 'even let you beep the horn.'

'*Can* I, Dad? *Please* can I?' cried Toby eagerly. Without a backward glance, he grabbed Edward's hand and towed him over to the BMW, crouched sleek and ready by the garage door. As the loud blast of the horn shattered the rural peace, Edward sent Harriet an indignant and reproachful glare.

'Did you *have* to?'

'Well, it worked, didn't it?' said Harriet cheerfully. 'You should know by now, distraction is ninety-nine per cent of successful child care. Have fun, and see you later!'

She glanced back at the gate, and saw that Toby, engrossed in working the windscreen washer to fountainous effect, hadn't even noticed her departure. With a light heart, she crossed the road and walked past the Wharf Inn, Maggie ambling lethargically at her heels.

She heard her name called and stopped, before she realised who had done the calling. Then, her cheerful mood in tatters, she averted her head and walked firmly on.

'Harriet! Hal, *wait!*'

Once, she had done everything at his behest: her whole world had been encompassed in his. Now, she could not even bear to look at him. She heard his running steps coming up the road behind her as she crossed the canal bridge, and steeled herself to be ruthless. 'Go away, Morgan.'

'No, I won't.' He came past her and stopped right in front, blocking her way. 'Not until you've given me the chance to explain — '

'For God's sake, you don't need to explain anything! It's all over, done, finished, and wrapped up ten years ago. And if you haven't moved on by now,' Harriet said, warming to her theme, 'then you must be a sad and pathetic person indeed.'

'You haven't moved on either, have you?' Morgan's blue eyes were brilliant and challenging. 'You can't have — you're still too angry.'

'I'm just trying to get it into your thick head that you're a complete bastard,' Harriet said, between her teeth. 'Once I've done that, you'll be finished business. Now go away and leave me alone.' She stepped out into the road to get past him, and a familiar horn blasted at her. Morgan grabbed her and pulled her painfully against the parapet of the bridge, as Edward's BMW, with Toby waving gleefully at her through the window, shot past and off towards the main road.

'That hurt,' said Harriet, rubbing her bruised elbow, while Maggie, who had come within a whisker of being knocked flying, grinned at her cheerfully, quite oblivious to the danger she'd been in.

'Less than being run over would have done,' said Morgan. 'Was that your kid in that car?'

'Yes,' said Harriet, deliberately uninformative.

'So who was the maniac? His father?'

'None of your business. Now piss off.'

'No. Not until you've agreed to be civilised.'

She could be reasonable and pleasant to Edward, if she tried hard enough: and the wounds he had dealt her were still raw and agonising. So why couldn't she be nice to Morgan?

And she was so sick of dispute and confrontation: she seemed to have done more quarrelling, these past ten days, than she had ever done in her whole life before. It was all very well to be assertive and defend her rights, but it didn't come naturally to her, as it did to Georgia: she liked to get on with people, and to face life with a smile, not a belligerent frown.

A frown, in fact, not unlike the scowl which Morgan was at present bestowing on her.

But she couldn't forgive him, not yet. After what he'd done, he didn't deserve such a swift capitulation. She said coldly, 'I don't think you've any right to expect that I'll welcome you back with open arms, as if you'd just gone out for a quick pint.'

'I'm not expecting that. I know I did you wrong, and I'm sorry. Sorrier than you can ever guess, believe me.'

'I doubt it.'

'So will you come and have a drink and let me explain?'

'How many times do I have to tell you? No, no and *no*!' Harriet glared at him. 'You may be on a full-blown nostalgia trip, but I'm not. Now if I were you I'd go back to your posh girlfriend and just leave me to get on with my life in peace.'

Amazingly, he stood back and let her pass. Aware, as she was aware of the sun's rays coming from the same direction, of his eyes boring holes into the back of her head, she ran down the steps leading from the road to the towpath, and walked briskly away towards Daphne's cottage. She stopped, twenty yards along, to let Maggie off the lead, and risked a glance behind her. He was still standing there, on the crown of the old brick bridge, watching her. When he saw her looking, he raised a hand in farewell, or acknowledgement, and turned away.

It should have been enough. But, knowing Morgan, it wouldn't be. And she didn't know whether she found the prospect exciting, or alarming.

13

Sanden parish magazine was not usually noted for its humorous content, but something in it was certainly amusing Daphne. Harriet, coming into the kitchen to find out what was happening, discovered her sitting at the table, cackling with merriment.

'What's up?' she asked, bewildered: the older woman had a dry, robust sense of humour, but she had never heard her actually laughing before.

'I can't believe that woman's effrontery,' Daphne said, shaking her head. 'Read that!'

Still puzzled, Harriet took the magazine from her. It was generally filled with times of church services, forthcoming events, applications for planning permission, and advertisements for local businesses. It was apparently one of these, occupying a whole page, that Daphne had found so funny.

But it didn't advertise the services of the village hairdresser, or the man who made bird tables and garden furniture. It was a notice announcing the formation — with superb disregard for the unfortunate acronym — of the Sanden Neatness Action Group. The immediate aim of this organisation was to ensure that Sanden would win the Best Kept Village award this year, and members of the group had already compiled a list of sites which needed immediate attention. Parishioners were asked to keep their gardens neat and their verges mown, and to take to task anyone they saw dropping litter. Starting the following weekend, a working party, to tidy various village eyesores, was to meet at the war memorial outside the church every Sunday afternoon, armed with gloves, shears, and rubbish bags, under the direction of the chairperson of SNAG, Mrs Heather Clark.

'You know what this means,' said Daphne, as Harriet reached the foot of the page.

'War?'

'In a manner of speaking, yes. She's using this as a lever to make me cut my hedge back, and if I won't, she can point the finger at me as the wicked person who lost Sanden its chance of winning the Best Kept Village competition.'

Harriet looked at Daphne narrowly. 'And do you care?'

'Of course not! I've no patience with these people who think that rural areas ought to be as neat and tidy as a town park. If only she would *think* before climbing on to her white charger and waving her sword about.'

Harriet giggled at the idea. 'A sort of Joan of Arc, waging war on mess.'

'Well, she won't make any impression on me. There are eight species of birds nesting in that hedge between us, and even more in the holly at the front — not to mention the butterflies and insects. I saw a weasel slinking through the back garden the other day, and there was a fox trying to make off with one of Maggie's bones last night.'

'Could it lift it?' asked Harriet, thinking of the huge shins and knuckles which the Labrador spent days gnawing under the shade of the apple trees.

'They're stronger than you think. It *dragged* it off into the shrubbery at the bottom, and I found it there this morning — the bone, I mean, not the fox — with not a scrap of meat left on it.' She chuckled suddenly. 'That would be one way of annoying Heather. If I made sure there was food out in the garden every night — '

'You'd have every fox in Sanden queuing up at the door.'

'Precisely. And Heather can't stand foxes. Vermin, she calls them. And she thinks that because I keep a few hens, I ought to feel the same.'

'But you don't?'

'Of course not. Foxes aren't evil, whatever

the hunting lobby may say — they're opportunists. If one of them pinches a couple of chickens, it's because I've forgotten to shut them up, and so of course the fox has taken advantage. No, I like foxes. Born survivors. *And* they've got a sense of humour, too. Which is more than you can say for Heather.' She glanced at Harriet. 'It's five to two, by the way.'

'Oh, God, so it is! I'd better go and find Toby.' Harriet had forgotten that she was supposed to be delivering him to Edward in a few minutes' time. 'Daphne, can I take your car?'

'Of course, my dear. Will you be long?'

'Only a few minutes,' said Harriet apologetically. 'I wish I didn't have to keep doing this — I must use it more often than you do.' She was trying to save up for her own car, but Edward's maintenance money, although it was arriving regularly so far, left little spare cash once essential bills, and Daphne's rent, had been paid.

'I'm not bothered about the car,' Daphne said, glancing at Harriet speculatively. 'But there's something I'd like to discuss with you, and I thought a child-free environment would be more appropriate. I'll put the kettle on.'

She got up and went into the kitchen, leaving Harriet rather disconcerted. What did

Daphne want to talk about? Wildly, she wondered if her friend was going to ask her to find somewhere else to live. A moment's reflection convinced her that this was hardly likely, but she couldn't think what else it might be.

Whatever it was, it could wait, unlike Edward. She grabbed the keys and called Toby, who was upstairs.

It was his third Sunday visit to his father, and he had been looking forward to it all morning. He scrambled eagerly into Daphne's car, and when they drew to a halt at the boatyard, a few minutes later, he leapt out and hurled himself at Edward with cries of delight.

Endearingly, Edward also seemed genuinely pleased to see his son. He swung him round, lifted him up, and kissed him. 'Hello, rascal, how are you today?'

'I'm fine,' said Toby. 'You've got a sandpapery chin, Dad.'

Harriet watched the scene with slightly bemused interest. It was evident that absence had definitely made her former lover's heart much fonder of his son. Once, he had had to be reminded to read Toby a story, or to answer his questions with rather more than a grunt. Now, he was chatting cheerfully to the little boy, as if he had been doing it all his life.

Gratefully, Harriet knew that Edward could have made things very difficult for her, the past few weeks. She had feared that he would vent his anger at her departure on Toby. But instead, the relationship between father and son had blossomed, and Harriet wryly found herself wishing that this could have happened years ago, before it became too late.

'Hallo, Hattie,' he said, with the smile that had once delighted her. 'You're looking very well. Have you lost weight?'

From someone who wouldn't previously have noticed if she had grown three heads, Harriet thought ruefully, this was quite a compliment. 'I've no idea,' she said, trying not to sound pleased. 'Where are you taking him this afternoon?'

'I thought we'd go ten-pin bowling,' said Edward. 'You've never tried that before, have you, Toby? It's a lot of fun.'

Harriet privately thought that his small son would have a job just to lift a bowling ball, never mind propel it in the right direction, but Edward was trying so hard to entertain Toby that she hadn't the heart to point it out. 'Enjoy yourselves,' she said, smiling at them both. 'I'll pick him up about six.'

'Don't worry, I'll bring him back and save you the journey,' said Edward, beaming. 'Come on, rascal, race you to the car!'

'He's a different man these days,' she said to Daphne on her return. 'Kind to Toby, considerate — he really does seem to have turned over a new leaf.'

'Don't question it, enjoy it,' said her friend. 'Are you having second thoughts, then?'

'Good grief, no! The trouble is, I'm sure that if I went back to him, he'd soon return to his bad old ways. I don't *think* he's being nice to me because he hopes I'll change my mind, but on past form I can't help being suspicious. Anyway, it's a treat to see him and Toby together, they're getting on far better than they ever did when we lived at the boatyard. Whatever else happens, at least that seems to have come right, and I'm actually very grateful to Edward. But it's not enough of a base on which to reconstruct our relationship, not by a long chalk.' She paused, and then added, rather apprehensively, 'What was it you wanted to talk to me about?'

'Don't look so worried!' Daphne exclaimed. 'I'm not going to give you your marching orders — far from it. I've got a proposal to put to you, that's all. Sit down and have some tea.'

'God, is it that bad?' Harriet said, determined to be light-hearted. She took the steaming mug and gazed at Daphne over the top of it. 'Fire away, then.'

'This isn't charity, so don't throw it back in my face,' Daphne said, sitting back in the other armchair. 'I've been thinking about this for a while now, ever since you started painting again, and I think it kills a whole flock of birds with one stone. The book will need illustrations, of course, and I'd like you to do them.'

Harriet stared at her in astonishment. 'You're joking!'

'I can assure you I'm not. I've already had a word with my editor, and she's keen to see your stuff.'

'But I thought you were going to get a photographer — '

'This is better. I've seen what you can do. Your work is exactly right — really detailed, yet so vivid and lively. I thought a variety of views of the garden at various seasons, and close-ups of the plants and animals. And I wouldn't be asking you if I didn't think you were the best person for the job. You're a very talented artist, my dear, and it's about time you faced up to that, or you'll regret it for the rest of your life.'

For some reason, Harriet felt dangerously close to tears. She said, 'Are you *sure*?'

'Of course I am. And if it all goes well, as I'm sure it will, you'll get other work on the strength of it. But it's up to you.'

Harriet took a deep breath. This was the challenge for which she had longed — and yet it all seemed too easy. She didn't like the way it had dropped into her lap: she had thought that her chances would only come if she went out and hunted them down. But she knew Daphne well enough by now to know that she meant what she said. And that she would be a complete and utter fool if she turned down the opportunity of a lifetime.

'I'll do my best,' she said. 'I just hope I'll be good enough. You've been so kind, and I really don't want to let you down.'

'You won't,' said Daphne, with absolute certainty. 'I've been keeping an eye on what you've been doing, and it's perfect. In fact, that painting of the garden you did from upstairs would make a wonderful cover for the finished book. And if you want to get going now, the sun is shining and the king-cups are looking their best.'

Still unable to believe her good fortune, Harriet settled down by the canal, on an old stool which buried its feet into the soft, marshy ground, and painted the king-cups in pure and utter yellow, and the soft pastel lavender of the cuckoo-flowers against the young spring green of Daphne's flower meadow, and out of pure joy in her skill, put in a pair of sulphurous brimstone butterflies dancing in the warm air above. Where her art was concerned, Harriet was a ruthless perfectionist, but even she had to admit, as she studied the finished picture, that she was pleased with the result.

Daphne was delighted. 'My dear, that is absolutely wonderful — you've captured the atmosphere of the place to a T. I can't believe it's only taken you a couple of hours.'

'I work fast when I'm keen,' Harriet said. 'And I've been thinking — shall I do some holly? After all, we ought to have an illustration of it somewhere, as it's Holly Cottage, and the flowers are out now. Perhaps I could put one of those little blue butterflies in it as well, if I can persuade it to stay still for long enough for me to draw it.'

'Holly blue, you mean? I've got a photograph if you want.'

'Great, that'll do to capture the detail, but I'd like to observe it in flight as well. There's bound to be a couple about.'

'You don't need to start another one now,' said Daphne. 'Take a break, have some more tea.'

'It's OK,' Harriet assured her. 'I've got all enthusiastic now, and Toby won't be back for ages, so I'm going to pack as much into my free time as I can.'

Sketchpad and pencil in hand, she went

round to the front of the house. The holly grew so thick here that very little light could reach the windows. There was no denying, if this was her cottage she would be sorely tempted to have some of the trees cut down, or at least ferociously pruned. And she could, if she were honest with herself, see why Heather Clark, obsessively tidy in her own life, got so upset over the overgrown, shaggy boundary between the two cottages.

But it isn't my house, it's Daphne's, Harriet reminded herself as she walked out into the road. Stony Lane was lovely in early May, the hawthorn drenched white with blossom like snow, the cow parsley frothing creamily along the verge, and the morning sun shining down on the holly's gleaming dark-green leaves. She stepped back and squinted upwards. Yes, there were a pair of holly blues, right up at the very top. Typical, she thought ruefully. They must have known I was coming.

She waited to see if they would fly lower, or if any more would appear. It was wonderfully pleasant here in the sun, listening to the country sounds. A tractor several fields away; two robins arguing over territory inside the trees; a cuckoo hiccuping in the park; the swallows swooping high in the air; and, rather less rural, the intrusive thump of Heather Clark's son's hi-fi, blasting out the latest Oasis album. Harriet was tempted to go and ask him to turn it down, or at least shut the window, but it wasn't up to her to make the point. And in any case, she heard Heather's unmistakable voice, quite close, telling Adam in no uncertain terms to do just that. Briefly, the music soared in a crescendo before sinking into oblivion, and Harriet grinned to herself. In his place, she'd have done just the same, before she obeyed.

Another sound shattered the peace: a car's horn, approaching the bridge on her right. Just in time, Harriet jumped back on to the verge as a big silver and black 4 × 4, of the type more usually seen on fashionable city streets, bounced over the hump and slammed to a halt beside her. As she stared at it in bewilderment, the window glided down and the driver leaned out.

It was Morgan, looking aggravatingly cheerful. 'Just the person I wanted to see. How are you?'

'Fine,' said Harriet shortly. 'What are you doing here?'

'Coming to see you, of course.'

Harriet, unwilling to meet his eyes, allowed her gaze to wander over the 4 × 4. Its underside was caked in mud, and there was something very long and slender strapped to the roof-rack. She said curtly, 'Why?'

'To see if you wanted to come out for the afternoon.'

'Haven't you got work to do?'

'It's Sunday,' said Morgan, with untypical patience. 'Builders tend to put their feet up on a Sunday.'

'Sarcasm doesn't suit you. Anyway, you may not be busy, but I am.'

'Too busy for a picnic up on the hill?'

'Which hill?' An unwelcome yearning was beginning to wake within Harriet, a longing for the days, long gone, when only love had lain between them.

'That one.' Morgan waved a hand in the general direction of Oliver's Castle, four miles away. 'You must have noticed it. Big, bare, perfect for hang-gliding.'

'*Hang-gliding?*'

'Yes. It's what the phallic symbol on the roof-rack's for. You had noticed that, hadn't you? You've got your glasses on.'

'I didn't know you did hang-gliding,' said Harriet, diverted in spite of herself.

'Oh, there's a lot you don't know about me, *cariad*.'

'Tell me about it,' said Harriet, with repressive significance. 'Anyway, it's not on. I've got a lot to do.'

'Then why are you mooching about out here, Minnie?'

'I'm looking for holly blues. Like that one, in fact.' One of the butterflies, with infuriatingly good timing, danced past between them. 'I'm painting it, for Daphne.'

'Looks a perfectly good colour already to me.'

'Oh, will you just sod off and leave me in peace!' Harriet cried in exasperation. 'You can't take *anything* seriously, can you? I wish you'd just get it into your thick skull that you broke my heart ten years ago, you almost *destroyed* me, and nothing, absolutely *nothing* you can say or do will mend it, do you understand?'

The maddening gleam of mischief had faded abruptly out of his eyes. 'I understand,' said Morgan, in quite a different tone of voice. 'And I am sorry for it. I *am, cariad,* believe it or not.'

Harriet made an incredulous noise in her throat.

'So you won't come and watch me hang-gliding? It's a dangerous sport, you know — you might even have the pleasure of seeing me crash to my death.'

'Oh, I don't want that,' Harriet said. 'Much too quick and easy. Seriously hurt will do nicely, thank you. Preferably something extremely painful, very slow to mend, and permanently crippling.'

Morgan laughed suddenly. 'You're brilliant, you are! I haven't been so insulted since the last time we met. Well, if I can't persuade you to come out today, perhaps this will do instead.' He reached back into the car and proffered two large white envelopes. 'And before you throw them back in my face, they're not from me, they're from Sir Marcus. Another time, perhaps, *cariad*. Goodbye!'

The 4 × 4 roared off over the bridge. Harriet, watching it as it disappeared, found herself laughing in rueful exasperation. He was absolutely impossible: he always had been, but now that self-assurance, so compelling ten years ago, had changed into outright arrogance.

She looked down at the two envelopes he had given her, and slid her thumb under the flap of the one marked, in a rather old-fashioned black script, *Miss Harriet Smith*. There was a card inside, and she pulled it out.

It was an invitation to the Third Midsummer Charity Ball, to be held at Forfar Towers on Saturday 20 June, in aid of the Air Ambulance and other worthy local causes. At the top, Sir Marcus had written, 'I do hope you can come.'

Well, Harriet decided at once, she certainly would, come hell or high water, whether she wore Daphne's garden dress or someone else's cast-off, whether she could afford the price of the ticket or not. She would undoubtedly meet the haughty Selina Grant again, and Morgan as well, but she didn't intend to let that, or anything else, stop her having a very good time. And in the intervening six weeks, a great deal might have changed.

'Thank you, Marcus,' she said aloud, in the general direction of Forfar Towers. Then she stuffed the envelopes in the back pocket of her jeans, and set about finding the elusive and restless holly blues.

14

Heather Clark thanked the last member of her work-party and watched in considerable satisfaction as he trudged wearily away towards his Range Rover. It had been a good day — no, an *excellent* day. At two o'clock that afternoon, she had arrived at St Lawrence's church to find a gratifyingly large number of people waiting for her. True, it was more than their lives were worth for any of the half-dozen committee members of SNAG to be absent, but in addition she had counted another fourteen eager participants, plus several children, all from the handsome and extremely expensive houses along the village's main street. And, a considerable feather in Heather's cap, even Helen Bentley, who lived in Sanden Manor, was there, in headscarf and corduroy slacks and green wellies.

With absolute aplomb, Heather had directed her minions. First, the rough area opposite the school, which belonged to no one in particular, would be cleared of rubbish, nettles and brambles. There was supposed to be an old pond in the middle of it somewhere, so they could tidy that up as well. The bus stop on the main road was in a disgusting state, foul with graffiti and horrible smells, and she dispatched a small group with a large can of whitewash and three huge brushes to paint everything over. She herself, armed with a clipboard and accompanied by her friend Christine Howell, who lived in Sanden Row, set out in the car to tour the village, making a note of all the eyesores which needed attention.

By five, they had been down every lane, road and cul-de-sac in the village, and Christine had covered three pages of lined A4 paper with her round, neat handwriting. The bus stop looked splendidly fresh and clean in its new coat of dazzling white paint, and when they arrived at the area opposite the school, a huge bonfire was smoking sullenly, while a pile of hideous rubbish — plastic bags, old buckets, half a bicycle, pieces of scrap metal and other assorted junk — had been heaped in the corner of the plot, waiting for the skip that Heather had ordered for tomorrow.

'*That* looks better,' Christine said in admiration. 'It's been an absolute disgrace for years.'

'Well, all it needed was someone to *do* something,' Heather said. She stopped the car and got out, beaming, to congratulate her workers on a good job well done.

There was one dissenting voice: the small boy who stood disconsolately by, complaining that the pond was *his* secret, *his* den, and what had happened to the tadpoles? Apparently, Helen Bentley told Heather, he had made some camp in the thick of the undergrowth, and all his treasures had been put on the bonfire before he could stop them.

'Treasures?' Heather had said in disbelief. 'What sort of treasures?'

But the boy, sullenly, had refused to elaborate, and Heather had declined to offer any apology or sympathy. The child was much too young to be going around unsupervised, and anyway, all unsupervised boys were potential vandals and hooligans.

'So,' she said to Christine, on their way back to Cypress Lodge for a well-earned sherry, 'a very good start, don't you think? And if only we can persuade That Woman to cut those wretched trees back and mow her verge, we'll stand a much better chance of winning.'

Christine, who was normally a rather shy and retiring person, ventured the opinion that the judges would probably keep to the main part of the village, and would hardly bother to come all the way down Stony Lane just to look at a couple of cottages.

'They should investigate *every corner* of the village,' said Heather robustly. 'Otherwise, all sorts of horrors could be going on that they wouldn't have noticed, couldn't they? Which reminds me, did you *see* the mess Row Farm was in? Mud everywhere. That man ought to do something about it.'

'Well, it *is* a farm,' said Christine, rather hesitantly. 'I thought farms were meant to be muddy.'

'Not to that extent, certainly not. *And* he persists in driving his cattle all along the Row, leaving it absolutely filthy. I'm sure it's quite unnecessary, and I told him so a few months ago.'

'What did he say?'

'He was *disgracefully* rude to me. Asked me whether I wanted him to beam them into their field like Captain Kirk, whoever he is. Still, he can't fob me off with excuses. I shall have another word with him next week. Make a note of it, will you, Christine?'

Dutifully, her friend wrote it down. 'But I should be careful,' she warned, as the Peugeot swung into the driveway of Cypress Lodge. 'Mr Sanderson does have a very quick temper.'

'Well, he doesn't frighten me. All bluster and no gumption. Really, Christine,' said Heather, pursing her lips disapprovingly,

202

'anyone would think that you weren't *wholeheartedly* committed to the cause when you say things like that.'

Her friend flushed. 'Oh, I am, Heather, you know I am! But sometimes . . . ' She paused, searching for the right words, that would convey what she wanted without offending the other woman. 'Sometimes people do need handling with kid gloves. I can always get my girls to do things for me if I set about it the right way. Tact and diplomacy can work wonders.'

Heather made a disbelieving noise. 'Sanderson wouldn't know the meaning of tact. Plain speaking, that's what I've always believed in. No point in beating about the bush. Let people know where you stand.'

Christine thought of the collective backs which Heather had put up over the years, the toes she had trodden on, the egos she had bruised, in the WI, the PTA, the village hall committee, the Guides and the junior football club. But her approach did seem to get things done. And certainly they had made a splendid difference today to one of Sanden's biggest eyesores.

'Hi, Ma,' Adam greeted them as they entered the hall, having carefully removed their shoes in the porch. 'What's for tea?'

'There's a hotpot in the oven, I left the

timer on. It'll be ready in ... ' Heather glanced at her gold watch, a fiftieth birthday present from Keith, 'an hour and twelve minutes.'

'But Mum, I'm *starving!*'

'Then have a nice piece of fruit. If you start on the biscuit tin now, you'll ruin your teeth and your appetite. Sherry, Christine?' Heather led the way into the large, pleasant room she liked to call the drawing room. Although part of the new wing which they had added to the cottage, it was traditionally decorated, with chintz swagged curtains, matching settees, and a picture rail from which hung several large prints of well-known Impressionist works of art. The immaculate cream carpet, the gleaming brass around the fireplace — fuelled by gas: Heather disliked the mess associated with real flames — and the carefully arranged vases of dust-free silk flowers were ample evidence of her desire for a clean, neat and ordered life.

Adam, always ill at ease in this formal and unnaturally tidy environment, left them to it and sneaked off to the kitchen. The smell of the hotpot, which had been cooking by itself for three-quarters of an hour, pervaded the air. He spread a thick layer of butter and strawberry conserve over a hunk of bread, crammed it all into his mouth, and selected a banana. Then, bored, he ambled out into the garden, barefoot. But there was no respite here either in the straight edges, the manicured green velvet lawn, the chemically protected roses and the clipped hedge. Still chewing, he wandered aimlessly down the gravel path to the end of the herbaceous border.

'Excuse me?'

It was a female voice, young, well-spoken, polite. Although it was coming from next door, it certainly wasn't the fearsome Miss James, so it must be the woman who was staying with her. Adam had heard vaguely that she was connected with the boatyard down at the wharf, and that she'd left her partner or husband or whoever he was, and now she and her small son were living at Holly Cottage. From the little he'd seen of her, she looked OK, and certainly easier on the eye than Miss James. Adam ran a hasty hand through his hair, hoped the new zit on his chin wasn't too prominent, and said loudly, 'Yeah?'

'Hallo.' The tangled hedge parted and Harriet's face peered through. 'You couldn't throw Toby's ball back, could you? I kicked it over by mistake.'

'What? Oh, yeah, sure thing.' Adam looked round and spotted it, lying innocently in the rose bed. He picked it up and passed it over the fence that his father had erected to keep the undisciplined shrubbery on the other side from encroaching on their garden.

'Thanks. Did you have a good day?'

'Eh?' Adam stared at her in bewilderment.

'Your mother's clear-up party. Was it successful?'

'I dunno,' Adam said. 'I s'pose so. She looks pretty pleased with herself, anyway.'

Since that was Heather's usual demeanour, Harriet didn't invest this fact with too much significance. 'You mean you didn't go along?'

The surprise in her voice made Adam blush. He mumbled defensively, 'It's not my sort of thing, is it?'

'Sounds like it could be fun,' said Harriet cheerfully. 'Getting muddy, making bonfires, and all in a good cause.'

'You what?' Adam stared at her in astonishment. 'I thought you'd be against all that.'

'Oh, no,' Harriet told him. 'And neither is Daphne. Heaps of rubbish and litter are disgusting, and dangerous to children and animals. Your mum's doing a grand job, and you can tell her I said so.'

'But . . . ' Adam was still staring at her, unable to get his head round the fact that

206

Miss James didn't like untidiness either. 'But why is her garden like that, then? Ma says it's because she's too lazy to clear it up.'

'Miss James is an expert in British ecology,' Harriet said patiently. 'In her field, she's quite famous — she was a professor at Cambridge. Now she's writing a book about creating a wildlife garden.'

'Famous!' Adam's jaw plummeted in disbelief. 'Is she really?'

'Oh, yes,' said Harriet, omitting to mention that outside the rarefied groves of academe, Daphne was hardly a household name. 'So you see, her garden looks untidy because it has to be, to encourage the birds and flowers and insects.'

'Bugs and that wouldn't *dare* go in my mum's garden,' said Adam. 'She'd zap 'em dead, she's got more chemicals than in the lab at school.'

'Well, Miss James doesn't use any chemicals at all, even in her vegetable plot. And it works. I've never seen so many wild flowers as she's got in her garden, and birds and butterflies too. It's going to be a wonderful book.'

'A famous author,' Adam said again. 'Right next door to us. Real cool. You'd never think it, the way she dresses and all.'

'She just has a different idea to the rest of

us of what's important,' Harriet said. 'It'd be a dull world if we all looked the same, anyway.'

'Ma wouldn't reckon so,' said Adam gloomily. 'Though come to think of it, she wouldn't have anything to complain about if everyone was like her, would she?'

'I wouldn't know,' Harriet said cautiously, remembering how Edward didn't let anyone criticise his parents except himself.

'Well, take it from me, she wouldn't,' said Adam. 'Gawd, famous! Just wait till I tell Ma, that'll be one in the eye for her! She'll be well pleased.'

'Why?' Harriet demanded, bewildered.

''Cos she's a raving snob, that's why,' Adam told her dismissively. 'She's always cuddling up to the Bentleys and people like that. Now she'll have something to show off.'

'But she doesn't like Miss James very much, does she?'

'That won't make any difference,' said Adam cheerfully. 'You don't know my mum. Thanks for telling me. Cheers!'

With considerable foreboding, Harriet watched him shamble back to the house. She couldn't imagine what Daphne's reaction would be if Heather Clark appeared at the door, all smiles and apologies. And she knew that she should warn her friend of the fate in store for her, if Adam was right about his mother.

* * *

If Daphne had not already been primed by Harriet when she opened the door the following morning, she would have been stunned by the warm smile on Heather Clark's immaculately made-up face. Unfortunately, it failed to ignite a similar expression on her own, rather forbidding features. 'Yes?' she said.

'Good *morning*, Miss James,' Heather said graciously, ignoring this unpromising start. 'I have come to ask you if you would like to attend a small dinner party I shall be giving this Saturday. Just a few close friends, but we shall all be *delighted* to meet you.' Her smile was becoming somewhat fixed, but she added brightly, 'Seven thirty for eight?'

'Let me get this straight,' said Daphne, in glacial tones. 'After two years of internecine strife, during which you have several times threatened to sue me for entirely trivial reasons, incited the council to harass me without cause, hacked back my trees and trespassed on my property when you mowed my verges, without so much as a by-your-leave, you now turn round and invite me to *dinner?*' Her glare, over the top of her spectacles, would have withered the soul of anyone less armoured in righteous self-esteem.

'Of course,' said Heather. 'After all, we *are* neighbours.'

'Only in the physical sense,' Daphne informed her. 'Let me assure you, Mrs Clark, I do not feel in the least neighbourly towards you. And I can only presume that this astonishing volte-face has something to do with your discovery that I am not, after all, some batty old hippy woman with anti-social ideas, but an internationally renowned expert on British ecology. Yes?'

Heather, aghast at being rumbled, could only utter a strangled sound.

'Well, I had better disabuse you of your peculiar notions. I have no intention of accepting your invitation. I have not the slightest desire to become a prize exhibit at your dinner party. If you really want to make amends for all that you have put me through over the past two years, then you can start by apologising for your intransigent attitude and your high-handed actions. And while I am still talking to you, I would like to inform you that the pond you and your band of interfering, ignorant obsessives so cavalierly devastated yesterday was in fact one of the few remaining homes of a colony of great crested newts. They are a protected species, Mrs Clark, and I would be entirely within my rights to inform the Wildlife Trust, if not the police. Is that clear? Now good day.'

She slammed the door in Heather's face, leaving her neighbour quivering with outrage in the porch.

There was no call for her to be so rude, no call at all, Heather thought furiously, marching back to her own house. Never, never, in all my born days, have I been so insulted.

She was wrong. In fact, over the years, people had quite often spoken to Heather Clark using words just as direct, though employing a rather less impressive vocabulary. But she had forgotten the PTA treasurer whose integrity she had doubted, and the traffic warden who had taken exception to her parking for five minutes on a double yellow line, and the man in the park whom she had suspected of being a paedophile, and many, many others. She needed someone to loathe, and The Woman Next Door had filled that unenviable position for two years. This conversation, if it could be dignified with such an appellation, only confirmed Heather's worst opinion. Snooty old bag, she thought as she opened her own front door, made of rich Brazilian mahogany, and so very different from the peeling faded blue gloss of Holly Cottage. Whatever did she mean about those newts? Of course there couldn't have been any in that revolting puddle of stagnant water. How dare she threaten me with the police?

She stalked into the kitchen and put the kettle on, then, as an afterthought, switched it off again and went into the drawing room to pour herself a stiff sherry. It was only ten o'clock, but she felt she needed it, and Maxine, the cleaner, was busy vacuuming upstairs and wouldn't notice.

After a few sips, she began to feel better, but the hatred was still there, seething furiously inside. I'll get even with her, Heather vowed, trembling with indignation. I don't care how long it takes or what I have to do, I'll get even. And she'll regret the day she ever crossed me, or my name isn't Heather Anne Clark.

15

Although she had lived in Sanden for nearly five years now, Harriet had never even visited the gardens of Forfar Towers before, let alone been inside the house. It was strange, she reflected, as she and Daphne climbed the wide sweep of steps to the front door, to be so close to a place and yet know nothing whatsoever about it. And though she had now met Sir Marcus Grant several times, always at Daphne's, she felt like a complete stranger, totally out of place amongst all these beautifully dressed people, air-kissing as they greeted each other in high-pitched, elegantly insincere voices. 'Darling! How *lovely* to see you!'

Glancing at Daphne, she saw a look of slight distaste cross her friend's severe features. In deference to the occasion, the older woman was wearing an evening dress which could only be described as sensible. It was long, straight and black, with a high round neck and three-quarter sleeves, and enlivened only by a plain gold brooch. Daphne hadn't even put any make-up on, and Harriet strongly suspected that there were traces of Wiltshire earth still stuck beneath her fingernails: she had been working in the garden until half an hour before they were due to leave for the ball, weeding the lettuces.

She herself, however, had spent over an hour getting ready. Georgia, when asked to baby-sit, had accepted with alacrity. 'Thank God you're starting to get on with your life again! Who knows, you might even meet the man of your dreams!'

Harriet, on the other end of the phone, had flushed betrayingly, glad that her prying, bossy sister couldn't see her. She had indeed had a very vivid dream the previous night. Unfortunately, the man in her arms had not been some anonymous white knight, but had possessed the face, the voice, and above all the touch of Morgan Price. She had felt it so strongly, the pull of his personality, the power of his glance, swinging her round like a compass needle from the direction of sense, and calm, and stability, into wild and uncharted seas. And she had woken wishing that it could all have been different.

'I doubt it,' she had said, keeping her voice dry. 'For a start, I expect Edward will be there. It's just his sort of thing, and he knows Sir Marcus.'

'Well, you never know your luck till you've

tried it,' Georgia said briskly. 'Now, what are you going to wear? I've got a few things you could borrow — '

'It's all right,' Harriet interrupted, knowing that although she had once been as slender and bird-like as her sister, motherhood had made a permanent difference to her shape. 'I'd never fit into any of your stuff, anyway. Daphne's lending me something.'

There was a brief pause, and then the sound of Georgia's most scathing laughter came down the line. 'What is it, a sack?'

'It's OK, don't worry, I've got it all sorted.'

'I don't believe you. I like her, but she's got the dress sense of a blind sheep. Look, Harry.' Her sister's voice became suddenly and urgently serious. 'Don't spoil it for yourself. I'll lend you some dosh if that's what you're worried about.'

'I told you, no problem. I've got everything perfectly under control,' Harriet had said, with a smile that Georgia, perhaps fortunately, couldn't see. 'Just you wait.'

Whatever happened, it had been worth it to see her sister's face as she came down the stairs at Holly Cottage. She had had a bath, and washed and dried her hair, and left it flowing, thick and dark and gleaming, around her shoulders. She had spent some time applying make-up, not the dramatic black and white of her student days, but something much more subtle, her large hazel eyes shadowed with green and gold and bronze and her lips enhanced with a deep red that she had bought on her last visit to Bath. She wore no jewellery, apart from a small pair of lapis earrings: she had nothing to match the wonderful colours of the garden dress, and anyway, necklaces and bracelets would seem superfluous beside its splendour.

Assuming, of course, that she could still get into it. She didn't want to spoil the surprise by having to call Georgia to do up the zip, but fortunately she seemed to have lost a little weight, rather than gained any, over the past two months, because the buttons no longer strained across her bust. She had splashed out on a pair of high-heeled forties-style shoes to go with it, and as she twirled in front of the mirror, feeling the brilliant skirt skim her ankles, she knew that this was truly a dress to match the occasion.

As she made her way carefully and elegantly down the stairs — she wasn't used to high heels, and it would really spoil the evening if she fell and twisted her ankle — she had the supreme satisfaction of watching her sister's jaw drop. 'Good grief, Harry, what a stunning dress!'

'You look beautiful, Mum,' said Toby, who

had shared her bath, and was now pink and warm and glowing in his pyjamas.

'I feel beautiful, too.' Harriet reached the bottom of the stairs safely, and smiled. 'There you are, doubting Georgia. I told you I'd got everything under control, and you didn't believe me.'

'I'm sorry,' said her sister, with as much contrition as she ever displayed, which wasn't great deal. 'I just didn't think — '

'That I'd have a dress like that?' Daphne enquired acerbically from the dining room. 'Don't even try to apologise, I'm not bothered. It was my mother's. And you suit it splendidly, Harriet.'

'You've got taller,' her son said, as she bent down to kiss him good night. 'And the flowers on the dress smell nice.'

'Be good,' she had said, smiling to hide her nerves, or her excitement. 'Or Auntie George will eat you all up.'

'Nonsense, he'd give me terrible indigestion,' said her sister, who despite all her avowals was very fond of Toby. 'I'll read you a story before you go to bed. Goodbye, you two, and be sure and have a wonderful time!'

Admittedly, the prospect of encountering both her previous partners, with or without gorgeous women on their arms, should have been intimidating, but Harriet was determined not to let it spoil her enjoyment of the occasion. As she and Daphne walked through the front door of Forfar Towers, she looked round curiously. She had imagined that it would be decked out in Scottish baronial style, full of tartan and antlers, and was rather disconcerted by the plain dark-blue walls, the ornate plaster coving picked out in cream, and the lights strategically placed to illuminate the large, flamboyantly abstract oil paintings in tropical colours, all by the same hand. In the arched alcoves, on either side of the huge fireplace — evidently designed to hold a very large baronial log — stood various pieces of ethnic sculpture in painted wood, with crossed assegais behind them, a reminder that their host had spent many years in Africa.

He came to greet them, smiling, and Harriet was relieved to see that he wasn't wearing a kilt. 'Hallo, Daphne, I'm so pleased you could come. My word, Harriet, you're looking quite dazzling! You'll have them flocking round you tonight.'

'I hope not,' she said, with a smile, and he laughed.

'Nonsense, they won't be able to resist you. There's a buffet and a bar in the dining room, and a band in the drawing room. Make yourselves at home, and I'll come and find you later.'

'Have you never been here before?' Daphne enquired, as they made their way towards the music. 'No, I suppose you haven't.'

'It's not in the least how I expected,' said Harriet, pausing to look at one of the paintings. 'That's gorgeous, I wonder who did it?'

'He has a cousin who's quite a well-known artist — Laurence Grant.'

'I've heard of him,' Harriet said, admiring the painting. 'He had a major retrospective in London when I was a student, but I never got to see it.' She smiled. 'I wish I could paint like that — big and bold and technicolour.'

'Your work, my dear, may be very different, but it's just as accomplished, and just as full of life, if not more so. You sell yourself too short, you know.'

'I don't,' Harriet said, smiling. 'I just know my limitations, that's all. And oils were never my medium.'

A loud and familiar voice cut through the background chatter, and Daphne glanced round. 'I thought so, the Clarks are here. This could be interesting.'

'We'll just have to steer clear of them,' Harriet said. She had no desire to let unpleasantness spoil the evening, although given the probable composition of the guest list, this was perhaps unlikely. But at least Heather, clad in a long dress so luridly coloured in pink and green that it seemed to be wearing her, rather than the other way around, was not very well camouflaged, and therefore easy to avoid. 'Let's go and check out the band.'

It proved to be a competent and popular local group who specialised in re-creating long-gone hits of the fifties and sixties. 'Goodness me,' Daphne said, 'that takes me back to my youth. I suppose all this sort of thing is way before your time?'

'I'm afraid so.' Harriet thought that the tall figure in the middle of a group in the far corner might be Morgan, but when he turned, it was someone quite different, and she didn't know whether to be relieved or sorry. She mentally consigned both of her troublesome ex-lovers to the nethermost regions, and smiled at Daphne. 'I'd love a drink. Where did Sir Marcus say the bar was?'

The dining room, like the hall and the drawing room, was decorated in dark, powerful colours, in this case a deep-green silk wallpaper and huge swagged curtains in heavy brocade. The effect should have been oppressive, but the high white ceiling and numerous lights gave it a surprisingly spacious feel. A long table lay against the wall opposite the windows, supporting the lavish and luxurious buffet laid out on top. Another, shorter table, covered with a white cloth, had been pushed across a corner to serve as a bar. While Daphne sat down on a free chair, Harriet went over to join the crowd waiting to be served.

There were only two barmen, both sweating in their white shirts and bow ties, striving to keep up with the orders. Harriet's treacherous memory dredged up the inconveniently vivid picture of the cider pub where she had first met Morgan. I wish he'd appear, she thought, her whole body fizzing with a kind of angry, urgent apprehension. Then at least I wouldn't be in a state of nerves waiting for him.

Someone pushed past her, and she gave an exclamation of annoyance as her toe was heavily trodden on. The man paused, and said courteously, his voice deep and charming and cultured, 'I'm so sorry.'

It was Edward. For a second or so longer, he did not recognise her: then she nodded coolly, and he said in disbelief, '*Harriet?* What are you doing here?'

'The same as you, I expect,' she said, resisting the temptation to utter a smart remark at his expense.

'But . . . ' Edward gazed at her in what he obviously thought was flattering wonderment. 'You look stunning.'

'Don't sound so astonished.' To her surprise, there was a glint in his eyes that she had not seen turned on her since Toby's conception. Sorry, buster, she thought contemptuously. You're too late, by several years.

'But I am. You haven't looked like that for far too long.'

'Flattery will get you nowhere,' Harriet said, as crushingly as she could. She had reached the front of the queue, and quickly requested a bottle of white wine before the barman could move on to someone else.

'Are you with anyone?'

'You never stop trying your luck, do you?' said Harriet. She slipped her change back into her beaded evening bag, and took charge of the wine. 'I've come with Daphne. You know, my landlady. Who did you come with?'

'Edward, darling, who's this?'

The voice was low, seductive, drawling and somehow familiar. Harriet turned and to her astonishment saw Selina Grant, Sir Marcus's stepdaughter, taking Edward's arm in proprietorial fashion. Obviously, they were an item.

'Have you met Harriet, darling?' Edward was saying, with a lingering glance into his companion's wide blue eyes. Harriet realised, with an alarming and treacherous leap of her heart, that this very public display of affection meant that Selina could not possibly be Morgan's girlfriend any more. He was now free and unattached.

Don't be so stupid, she told herself sternly. If that's the sort of woman he attracts, why should he ever give me another glance? Even if I wanted him to — which of course I don't.

'Ah, yes, your ex.' Selina's disdainful blue stare swept Harriet from head to toe, examining, judging, assessing possible competition and, all too obviously, deciding there was no danger. Everything about her dripped class, wealth, taste. She wore a slinky dark-green satin gown that perfectly fitted her superb figure, her golden hair was arranged in an elegant chignon, and the diamonds around her long, slender neck were huge, flashy, and undoubtedly real. Beside her, Harriet felt like a small girl pretending to be a grown-up, and not doing it very well. With that trophy on his arm, she thought, I'm surprised he even noticed me.

But of course Edward had never been able to resist flirting with any woman of beddable age. Despite his pretensions, though, he was definitely playing above his game with Selina. She could eat his sort for breakfast, and probably will, Harriet decided, with a wicked smile. And good luck to them, they deserve each other.

'We have met,' she said to Selina, in a spirit of mischief. 'Don't you remember? On the hillside in the park. You nearly rode me down.'

Selina's perfectly arched eyebrows rose. 'Really? I didn't recognise you.'

You weren't the only one, Harriet thought. 'That's all right,' she said kindly. 'I often go about incognito. So nice to have met you. Goodbye, Edward. Give my regards to Gina. I *do* hope she didn't catch pneumonia.'

She returned to Daphne, childishly gleeful. 'I think I've just put the cat amongst the pigeons with a vengeance.'

'A risky business,' said Daphne, who was an excellent practitioner of the art herself. 'Did you know about Edward and Selina?'

Harriet, pouring the wine with an unwarranted sense of elation, shook her head. 'No, but don't worry, I don't mind in the least. He's obviously very pleased to have hooked her, but with any luck she'll get tired of him in a couple of months, if not weeks, and dump him.' She grinned suddenly. 'Why are the most beautiful women always the worst bitches?'

'Because they don't have to make themselves agreeable,' Daphne pointed out. 'If you

224

can get what you want — and in particular the man you want — just by looking superb and sexy, why bother to be nice? Although in Selina's defence, I must say that I have met many worse. After all, it wasn't her fault that her mother always gave her everything on a plate.'

'Well, if she does to Edward what he did to me, I shall hang the flags out,' Harriet said. She raised her glass. 'To Edward and Selina — may they make each other thoroughly miserable!'

'Is this purely a man-haters' table, or can anyone join in?'

It was Morgan. Despite all her good intentions, Harriet gasped, and choked on her wine. Coughing and spluttering, she was furiously aware that he was slapping her solicitously on her back. 'Stop that, will you?' she said, when she could speak again. 'And go away.'

'You keep saying that to me,' Morgan remarked, with some indignation.

'I wonder why.' Harriet took a long, reviving gulp of wine and glared up at him. Like all the other men present, he was wearing a black dinner jacket: unlike most, he looked superb. She couldn't get used to the fact that his hair was short, but it still had a curl in it, and the cut set off the beautiful bones of his face, the wide, mobile mouth, and the brilliant blue eyes.

The trouble is, he's drop-dead gorgeous, she thought despairingly. And doesn't he just know it!

'You must be deaf,' she added repressively. 'Or, alternatively, just plain stupid. Will you please go away and leave us in peace?'

'No.' Morgan pulled up a spare chair and sat down. He had a full glass of red wine in his hand, and to judge by the slight flush across his cheekbones, it wasn't his first. 'Not until you've promised me at least one dance.'

'Is he always like this?' Daphne enquired, her eyebrows raised. 'If so, I wonder how he's managed to live so long.'

'He has a lot in common with a rat,' Harriet told her, deliberately turning away from Morgan, on her left. 'Both unpleasant, unreliable and unprincipled beasts, but unfortunately born survivors.'

'I wish you'd agree to be civilised,' he said plaintively.

'Oh, compared to how I'd *like* to be,' Harriet said, 'this is certainly civilised. But I haven't got a dagger conveniently to hand at this precise moment.'

'She's got a lovely line in invective, hasn't she?' Morgan said to Daphne. 'I could listen to her all day.'

'I had a good teacher,' Harriet said. Reluctantly, she was beginning to realise that she was enjoying herself. Love him or loathe him — and she certainly loathed him — at least life was never dull when Morgan was around. 'I've never forgotten what you said to that bloke who crashed into the back of your old van on the ring road.'

'It's not fit for delicate ears,' Morgan said, finishing his wine. He looked hopefully at Harriet's bottle, but she ignored him, and poured a second glass each for herself and Daphne. 'You take my breath away, *cariad*, you're so beautiful, you are. Come on, Hal, please. Just one dance.'

'If you agree, he'll go away,' Daphne pointed out.

'No, he won't,' Harriet said. 'It's like Ethelred the Unready and the Danes — the more you give in to him, the more he wants to take. I mean it, Morgan. If you don't go away now and leave us alone, I'll never speak to you again — nicely *or* nastily.'

For a brief, exhausting moment their eyes met. She had a sense of something that was deeply disturbing in his gaze, but before she could analyse it, he had risen to his feet. 'Goodbye,' he said to Daphne, and was gone.

It was only afterwards that she realised that

she was trembling. But whether with rage, or regret, or relief, she had no idea. And although she kept looking for him in the crowds, she told herself it was only so that she could avoid him if she saw him again.

16

Despite the presence of Morgan, Edward and Selina, not to mention the Clarks, Harriet enjoyed herself thoroughly as the evening wore on. She danced with Daphne, a decorous jig to something she vaguely recognised from the dim and distant past, and with Sir Marcus, who waltzed her round the floor during a slow ballad, sung by the group's lead singer with rather more soul than was good for him. She had some more wine, and an excellent meal from the buffet, which she ate standing up, trying to balance plate and glass and fork, because by this time all the tables had been taken. If Morgan was still at the ball, she did not see him, although Edward and his new love were much in evidence on the dance floor, closely entwined, and eliciting several comments about their good looks and obvious interest in each other. Briefly, Harriet had wondered if Morgan's absence was due to the fact that he couldn't bear to watch his former lover so obviously wrapped up in his replacement, and had instantly rejected the idea. He was surely incapable of such vulnerability, and in any case she felt that being dumped by Selina was no more than he deserved.

After supper, she danced again with a pleasant young man who had struck up a conversation with her as they waited at the buffet table, and then with Adam Clark, who had approached her with an engaging mixture of cocky teenage bravado and considerable terror. Acutely aware of his mother glaring at them from the doorway, she obliged, and they had a brief and frenetic fling to a lamentably precise rendition of something originally sung by Gary Glitter. She grinned at him as the music finally ended. 'Thanks, I enjoyed that. Does this mean hostilities are over?'

'Eh?' Adam was scarlet and sweating, his borrowed DJ was far too big for him, and he had a large and pulsating spot right on the end of his nose. But despite his unprepossessing appearance, he had the makings of a nice lad, and she felt rather sorry for him: it couldn't be easy for a normal teenage boy, having Heather for a parent.

'Are we friends?' Harriet repeated.

Adam glanced at his mother, still glowering at the edge of the room. 'Yeah, why not?' he said, and grinned. 'Better go. 'Nother time, eh?'

She watched him return to the ample

bosom of his family, and then looked round for Daphne. She was deep in conversation with Sir Marcus, so Harriet, feeling rather hot and sweaty herself after the unaccustomed and intensive exercise, went off to the bar for something to cool her down.

She had expected it to be even more stifling in the dining room than on the dance floor, but the tall French windows were wide open, and the fresh air breathed softly against her skin. With her glass of iced orange juice in her hand, Harriet slipped outside, into the welcome dark.

Her high heels lurched on gravel as she walked along the terrace, illuminated by intermittent slabs of brilliant light from the windows. There were steps at the end, flanked by patriotically Scottish statues, one a lion and the other a unicorn. With a little sigh of relief, Harriet sat down on the cool stone, and took her shoes off.

The gravel crunched again behind her. She looked round, curious, and saw a tall figure in a white shirt and dark trousers pause at the top of the steps. And a voice, uncharacteristically hesitant, said, 'Harriet?'

Within the house, the band was playing 'Return to Sender'. She turned back to face the shadowy garden, sloping away from them down towards the park, and said firmly, 'It's no use asking me to dance. I'm exhausted.'

'I wasn't going to.' Morgan sat down beside her. 'I just want to talk to you, *cariad*. Please?'

She had never heard that desperate note of pleading in his voice before. Almost, she relented, and then hardened her heart. 'There's nothing you can say that can possibly make any difference to what I think, or to the fact that you're a complete and utter bastard. I don't know why you keep wasting your time.'

'Don't you?' He was unsettlingly close to her: her skin, abnormally responsive, could sense his warmth. 'Hal, *cariad*, just listen. Please. One minute, that's all. And then I'll never bother you again, if you don't want me to.'

'Really? Promise?'

'I promise.' He added something in Welsh. 'And that means, 'I swear by the English blood spilled by my forefathers'.'

Despite herself, Harriet laughed. 'Don't be so melodramatic.'

'I'm not, I was being serious,' He actually sounded genuinely indignant. Belatedly she realised that he must have had quite a lot to drink: and Morgan, drunk, was a reckless, unpredictable and dangerous creature.

'OK,' Harriet said guardedly, hoping he

wouldn't notice that she had unobtrusively moved a few inches away from him. 'Your minute starts now. And don't waste it — it's all you're going to get.'

'Right. OK.' He paused, as if her consent had taken him by surprise, and she pressed her lips firmly together on a rude remark and waited expectantly. 'What happened ten years ago — I'm sorry for that, more sorry than you'll ever know.'

'So am I,' said Harriet caustically.

'No, wait, listen. I never told you I was going to the States because I was too much of a coward. I couldn't face it.'

'Oh, come on!'

'It's true,' Morgan said, and she heard the desperation, hoarse in his voice. 'I knew I had to go. I'd got this job, the chance of a lifetime, to work with Rick Steinberg.'

'Who's he?'

'Just about the most famous alternative architect in the USA, if not the world. I'd sent him a sheaf of drawings and ideas, and we met in London. He offered me the job of assistant on his new project, a whole underground village in Wyoming. I couldn't pass it up.'

No, he couldn't. She could see that, from where she sat now, with her own chance of a lifetime only just accepted. And yet it still hurt, and hurt sharply, that he had not had the courage to tell her.

'You never said *anything* about this,' she said accusingly. 'Not one word. You just upped and left. Not even a note on the kitchen table.' Her voice wobbled suddenly, treacherously. 'For a couple of days I really thought something awful might have happened to you, and then I met your friend Dave Freeman and he told me where you'd gone. I couldn't believe it.' The memory was overwhelming her again, with the pain, the disbelief, the terrible, agonising knowledge that he had lied, that she hadn't mattered enough, hadn't meant anything to him. She cried angrily, 'Why didn't you *tell* me? At least you could have *told* me!'

And he said, 'Because I loved you too much, I couldn't bear it. If I'd told you, I wouldn't have gone.'

Inside, with terrible timeliness, the band had begun to play 'Don't be Cruel'. Harriet was glad of the concealing dark: she didn't know whether to laugh in scorn, or burst into tears, or hit him. And because anger was less humiliating than weeping, she said furiously, 'How *dare* you say that now! You don't know what love means, or you couldn't have gone off like that.'

'I do know.' He sounded suddenly weary. 'I

knew then, and I know now, when I've had ten years to think about what I threw away. I wanted to ask you to come with me, but you were in the middle of your course — '

'As it happens, that didn't matter,' Harriet said. 'Because when you buggered off, I was so upset I chucked it all in and went home. Do you *realise* what you did to me? You messed up my *whole life*: because of you I jacked in my course and changed my career and made myself different; because of what you did I stayed with Edward long after I should have left him because I didn't want to do to him what you did to me; and now I've finally got my act together and everything's looking great, you come swanning back telling me you *loved* me, as if that makes it all OK . . . Oh, do me a favour,' Harriet said, through gritted teeth. 'And get out of my life before you mess it up again.'

'Then I still mean something to you.'

'I won't let you,' Harriet said vehemently. 'It's too late, Morgan, too late for apologies and definitely too late to carry on where we left off. We can't go back to what we were then, it just isn't possible, there's too much water under the bridge.'

'So how about starting from scratch? Pretend we've never met before tonight. You said yourself it's all different now, so it should be easy.' His hand came out to caress her hair. 'Oh, *cariad*, how beautiful you are . . . '

'How did we get on to relationships when I thought I'd told you many, *many* times in plain English that you haven't a snowball's chance in hell of even dancing with me?' Harriet demanded. She had moved along the step until she was touching the far end, but he still seemed no further away.

'Because I never take no for an answer,' Morgan said softly. 'Particularly not where you're concerned.'

'Look, do I have to spell it out again, or do you want me to kick you where it hurts before you get the message?' Harriet was aware that her voice lacked conviction, but the memory of what they had done together, long ago, was beginning to erode her anger and her resolution. In a minute, she thought, with a mixture of panic and anticipation, he's going to try and kiss me, and then I'll be lost . . .

'Come on, Hal,' he said, in the voice she had loved so much, rough with passion. 'Just one kiss won't hurt.'

'Yes it will.'

'Only because you're frightened of what might happen to you.'

'I'm not frightened,' Harriet said. 'Just being sensible.'

'You never were before.'

'That was ten years ago, and under your influence. You've never been sensible in your life.'

'You don't know me very well, do you?'

'Oh yes I do. I know what you're like in bed and out of it, I know you can't settle to anything, you've no moss to gather, you have a cavalier attitude to the laws of the land and more than a passing fondness for alcohol and assorted illegal substances. And I've grown past that sort of thing.'

'I'm not into drugs any more,' Morgan said. 'Come on, *cariad*, admit it — you want to kiss me, but you're afraid that once you do, you'll be hooked again, just like you were before.'

'Yes,' Harriet cried. 'Yes, yes and yes! I was addicted to you, just as if you were coke or smack. I couldn't get enough, and when you left I did cold turkey big-time, for six months I hardly ate or slept, and I can't put myself through that again. I've got a new life, a different life, and it may seem boring and limited and conventional to you but that's how best to bring up children. You can't traipse them all over the world with a succession of so-called 'uncles' in tow and expect them to be happy or secure or well adjusted.'

'You've changed — well, so have I, *cariad*.'

He put his hand over hers, and she snatched it away as if it had burnt her.

'Oh no you haven't — you're just the same, only even more arrogant, if that's possible. You've all the sensitivity and understanding of a bulldozer, you're selfish and demanding, and bringing up one kid on my own is quite enough, thank you very much. I can't cope with another grown-up one. Now *will* you go away and leave me alone, before I do something I regret? And don't get any ideas: it wouldn't involve anything pleasurable to you, just something extremely painful and undignified.'

There was a taut silence, the band finished playing 'Heartbreak Hotel', and began, with telepathic aptness, on 'Lonesome Tonight'. My love life as defined by Elvis Presley, Harriet thought, with a crow of inward and somewhat despairing laughter. Talk about bathos.

'OK.' Morgan stood up suddenly, and she noticed that he was swaying slightly. 'OK, you win — for the moment. I promise not to proposition you or ask you for things you don't want to do. And if I do that, will you let us be friends?'

'You won't be able to settle for that,' Harriet said. 'You'll just want more and more and more, and I'll spend my whole life fending you off. No thank you, Morgan. Now go away and leave me alone.'

And he went, leaving a void behind him as tangible as if a hole had appeared in the air.

It was only then that she could put her head in her hands and weep, for what might have been, and missed chances, and the anguish of resisting temptation.

'Harriet, are you all right?'

It was Daphne's voice. Flushing with shame, she smeared a hand across her eyes and looked up. 'Yes, it's OK, I'm fine.'

'You don't look very fine to me,' said her friend. 'Is it something to do with that Morgan? I saw him come in, he looked positively thunderous.'

'And so he should,' Harriet said, sniffing. 'I really told him where to get off, and part of me desperately wishes I hadn't.'

'Oh dear.' Daphne sat down beside her and put a comforting arm around her shoulders. 'Mind you, I think he could do with some healthy punctures in his ego. I've met a few men with more arrogance and self-esteem, but I'm not at all sure where.'

Harriet laughed. 'I don't think I ever have. Morgan is Morgan, a law unto himself. I just wish he hadn't said . . . certain things. I think the most terrible feeling in the world is regret, wondering what might have been.

Does that sound stupid?'

'No. We've all done, or not done, life-changing things and regretted them later. The trick, I suppose, is to accept that you can't change what's happened, and build on that, instead of bewailing your fate.'

'I thought I could, but I was wrong. And Morgan definitely can't. He wants to pick up where we left off, and I told him until I was blue in the face that that wasn't possible, but would he listen?'

'No.'

'You're absolutely right.' Harriet took several long, calming breaths, and smiled at Daphne. 'Thanks. It's funny, but I'm beginning to feel a lot better. It could be something to do with the fact that I got everything off my chest, I threw at him all the pain and hurt that's been festering for ten years, and if he doesn't understand what he did to me, then he must be deaf.' She laughed again. 'But I wish the band would stop playing songs that fit. I want 'I Will Survive', something like that.' She stood up, dusting down the wide, soft folds of her skirt. 'Thanks, for being a friendly shoulder. It's nice to have someone to listen, once in a while.'

'Any time,' Daphne said, getting up rather more stiffly. 'Goodness me, that stone is hard.

I must be getting too old for this. Take my arm for a minute, will you? Thanks. I can see I shall have to start saving up for a hip replacement.'

Within the house, Heather Clark was waiting for Keith to reach the end of the queue for the bar. Bored, she gazed blankly out of the nearest window at the dark garden beyond. A sudden movement outside caught her eye, and she focused sharply on two figures at the end of the terrace. One, she was sure, was Harriet, or Hattie, or whatever she was called, the unmarried mother next door — Heather had just had a strong word with Adam about daring to dance with her, and he had been very surly in return, which showed all too clearly what a bad influence anyone from Holly Cottage had on her son. The other, an anonymous shape in black, definitely had an arm round her. Heather peered curiously round the curtain, but at this distance could not make out who it might be. She glanced at Keith, but fortunately he was still a long way from the head of the queue. With any luck, the figures would finish their embrace and return to the dining room before she had to move away from the window.

In a fever of impatience, clutching her bag until her knuckles whitened, Heather waited.

241

And just as her husband was being served with a second bottle of low-alcohol white wine, Harriet and her companion got up and began to walk, arm in arm, slowly back along the terrace.

Heather spent her life being shocked, or disapproving, or critical, but the identity of the other person stunned her. She gasped, and stared, refusing to believe the evidence of her own eyes. It was a *woman* who had been embracing Harriet — *a woman*! And, much, much worse even than that, it was *Daphne*!

Suddenly, everything fell into place. Why else would an attractive young woman leave a pleasant, charming man like Edward Armstrong, who seemed to have everything going for him, to live in the untidiness and poverty of Holly Cottage? And it explained Daphne's looks, too, her complete lack of make-up or adornment, her mannish dress. They're *lesbians*, Heather thought, with horrified fascination. Just wait till I tell Keith about this!

'Here you are, dear. What's up?'

Heather started as Keith arrived at her elbow. 'I didn't notice you there. Oh — something I've just seen,' she added, trying not to sound too excited. 'I'll tell you about it later.'

'OK, dear,' said Keith, without much

interest, and handed her a glass of wine. 'Is that all right? You're always saying we should cut back.'

'Fine,' Heather said. The wine was revolting, but she hardly noticed the taste: she was too busy going over in her mind the details of what she had just witnessed, and the implications.

She had wanted some way of getting her own back on That Woman. And chance, it seemed, had put the weapon right into her waiting hand.

17

'Well, *I* think it's wicked. I always *thought* there was something wrong about that woman.'

'There's no harm in it, surely? These days it's all over the place.'

'You always were too tolerant, Christine. It shouldn't be allowed. And as for that poor little boy — fancy being brought up by people like that.'

'She's still his mother, whatever else she is.'

The door to Sanden's only shop was open, because of the warm weather, so the little huddle of middle-aged women clustered round the fridge cabinet hadn't heard Edward come in to get the *Sunday Telegraph*. He made his way with some difficulty past the boxes of crisp packets and racks of magazines to the counter at the other end, wondering without much interest who they were gossiping about now. Mark Fennell, who ran the shop, seemed to be gesturing at his other customers, and Edward saw, to his surprise, that there was a look of acute embarrassment on his pale, rather doughy face.

'Poor man,' said Heather Clark's artificially well-bred, carrying voice. 'He must feel so *dreadful*, his girlfriend leaving him for another woman. And taking the little boy, too, *and* leaving his business in the lurch.'

A ghastly suspicion began to dawn upon Edward, a suspicion compounded of horror and humiliation, and confirmed by the sudden flurry of shushes and whispers by the fridge. His errand forgotten, he turned abruptly and saw three of the four women scurrying hastily out of the shop. Only Heather, whose hide would have seemed thick to a rhinoceros, stood her ground. 'Good afternoon, Mr Armstrong,' she said sombrely, as if they were meeting at a graveside. 'How *are* you?'

'Can I have a quiet word with you?' Edward demanded, in tones so vehement that even Heather drew back a little.

'Of course,' she said, and dropped her voice. 'I was *so* sorry to hear what had happened,' she added confidingly. 'Of course, I always had my doubts about That Woman, you know, but no one likes to have their worst fears confirmed. You must be missing your little boy dreadfully.'

Belatedly, Edward realised that to preserve some semblance of masculine pride, he must put on a brave face, and pretend that it was not the first he had heard of this unthinkable news. It was incredibly hard to appear calm and composed, but he made a valiant attempt at dissimulation. 'Naturally I am,' he said, while his mind seethed with questions that he could not ask. Did she really mean that Harriet and Daphne were having a lesbian affair? How long had it been going on, for God's sake? And how the hell did Heather and, obviously, half the village know about it when he, Harriet's ex-partner, had had no inkling of the real reason for her abrupt departure?

'I can tell you, I was devastated when I found out,' Heather said, her voice oozing sympathy. 'I could hardly believe the evidence of my own eyes, but there they were, actually embracing in public. Dreadfully embarrassing. I mean, you expect that sort of thing in London and places like that, but we don't want those goings-on in *Sanden*, do we? What an example to set our young people. I feel quite peculiar, knowing such dreadful things are going on next door, right under my nose. My poor sweet, innocent Jessica could have seen . . . ' She shuddered with exaggerated sensitivity.

From the stories Edward had heard from Keith, during their golf games, about his wayward daughter, she was hardly noted for either her sweetness or her innocence, but he let that pass. 'Mrs Clark, are you *sure* that Harriet and Miss James — '

Heather drew herself up with righteous indignation. 'I know what I saw, Mr Armstrong, and it was quite disgusting. I will not go into the unsavoury details, but believe me, I have no doubts.'

Edward did, but he shrank from expressing them in the face of her emphatic conviction. 'Please, Mrs Clark, can you do me a favour?'

'Of *course*, Mr Armstrong, I shall be only too pleased to help.'

'Can you try to restrain your friends from discussing this in public? I'm sure you understand . . . My son is very young, but even so, he might hear things at play-group . . . '

'Oh, yes, I do understand,' said Heather, secure in the knowledge that the genie had already escaped from the bottle, and was even now spreading the forbidden tidings all over Sanden, and beyond. 'I shall do my very best, Mr Armstrong, you can count on me.'

'Thank you, Mrs Clark.'

'*Heather*, please.'

'Thank you, Heather. I'm very grateful to you,' said Edward, and made his escape, his paper quite forgotten in the tumult of confusion, anger and disbelief that threatened to destroy his calm façade completely. He got into the BMW, which was parked outside, and drove off at considerable speed.

It was only when he nearly ran down a motorcyclist as he shot out on to the main road without looking that he realised that he needed to stop and regain his composure. Hastily, he pulled in at the next gateway, turned off the engine and put his head in his hands.

Harriet and Miss James. Miss James and Harriet. He couldn't believe it — not of Harriet. He had never dreamed, never suspected that she was a lesbian. He remembered her early passion, and shook his head. No, surely not. Mrs Clark must have made a mistake. Although he hardly knew her, she had the reputation of a gossip and a troublemaker. And her well-publicised feud with Daphne James was ample motive for spreading such rumours.

Telling himself it was all nonsense, he drove back to the boatyard, and tried to immerse himself in the cricket on BBC2. But all through the long, hot afternoon, certain puzzling details kept nagging at him. Why had Harriet's flattering ardour, early in their relationship, turned so cool so quickly? If she was more interested in women, he thought, pouring himself another stiff gin and tonic, but just fancied a quick fling with me, then got pregnant . . . His mind returned, again and again, to the episode Heather had described. She seemed so absolutely certain, and her revulsion had genuine conviction. *Could* she be right?

After a couple more gins, he was beginning to think that she was. Daphne James, with her cropped hair, her mannish clothes, her uncomfortably direct and masculine manner, and above all her total disregard for her appearance, exactly fitted his stereotypical idea of the predatory older lesbian. He thought of the two of them in bed together, and shuddered. In happier, more innocent days, he had actually found the idea of two gorgeous young ladies canoodling extremely exciting, and so did most men, to judge from the frequency with which such scenarios appeared in soft-porn magazines. But this was different. This was much too close to home. This was disgusting, and, worse, had dealt an almost mortal blow to his pride and his vanity. To be abandoned for another man would have been bad enough, but to be rejected in favour of a *woman*, and an ugly old bag at that . . . it was unendurable.

And Toby was in that house too, caught up in the middle of it. If he stayed there, he'd grow up warped, probably gay. Edward, whose knowledge of sexual psychology was sketchy to say the least, contemplated the prospect with absolute horror. He couldn't let it happen. He *had* to do something, and right away.

It was Sunday, but his solicitor was a personal friend — they played golf together, and both belonged to the Rotary Club, so he knew Gerald's number. With fumbling hands, he reached for the phone and began punching the buttons.

★   ★   ★

Rather earlier that same afternoon, Harriet had been happily planning a picnic tea. It was a glorious June day, the air was fresh and warm, and the sky was innocent of clouds. She hummed under her breath as she made some ham sandwiches, and packed a couple of packets of crisps, some hard-boiled eggs, a bag of chocolate chip muffins, some fruit, biscuits, a bottle of diluted orange squash and a flask of tea into her elderly rucksack. She was sorely tempted to take her painting kit, but knew it would be a waste of time. From past experience, she would hardly have got it out of the bag before Toby would be wanting her attention, to play some game, or look at a fascinating insect. She would take Daphne's camera, an elderly but still excellent Canon manual SLR, with a long telephoto lens, in case she saw anything that might make a good picture. Usually she didn't like working from photographs: so many people did, and she could always tell, because the results seemed flatter, less lively and spontaneous, than they did in life. But a photo took seconds to frame and shoot, whereas she was physically incapable of producing a watercolour in less than an hour.

It took some time to pack everything in her new car, bought last week with the money from Daphne's publisher, who had, to her wondering delight, paid her a small but very useful advance on the strength of five sample paintings and Daphne's heartfelt recommendation. 'New', of course, was a relative term: the little Polo was nearly ten years old, but it was cheap and what the advert had termed 'a good runner'. It would transport her, and Toby, and their picnic, with Maggie in the back, to their chosen place, and it would bring them all safely home again. And that, thought Harriet, is more than you could say for my awful old Metro.

Still, if the Metro hadn't overheated, that momentous day more than two months previously, she wouldn't be here now — she would still be trapped at Wonderland Boats.

No, surely I wouldn't, she decided, calling Toby in from the garden. Gina was just the excuse, I'd have got out by now anyway. Wouldn't I?

She honestly didn't know. She did know that it was quite true when she had told Morgan that it was his fault she had stayed too long with Edward. She had grieved so much for what might have been in one relationship that she had been determined not to make the same mistake again. And, she knew now, it had been the wrong decision.

But she no longer felt bitter about it. Strangely, that furious conversation, if that was the right word, which she had had last night with Morgan had purged all the resentment. Somehow, the very act of telling him how much he had hurt her had washed all the pain away, to leave a bleak but curiously comforting acceptance. It was a long time to keep such bitterness in her heart, and she was glad that it seemed to have left her at last. She had finally drawn a line, in triplicate with a very thick pen, to finish the story of their relationship. And now, for the first time in ten years, she felt she could let her past lie in peace, and look forward with a whole heart and a sense of real optimism. It was all beginning to go right.

'Where are we going, Mummy?' Toby

demanded, fetching his wellies from the porch. 'Where are we having our picnic?'

'Oliver's Castle,' Harriet told him. 'It won't be too hot up there, there's bound to be a breeze, and we can take your kite and see if we can fly it.'

'Yippee!' Her son did one of his jubilant war-dances round the kitchen table, and finished with a hug. 'Come on, Mum, let's go.'

With an almost equally excited Maggie panting in the back, they set off towards Devizes. Daphne was trying to compose her final chapter, the most important one, which would summarise all her findings and present her conclusions, and taking Toby off for a picnic would leave her with peace and quiet to get the job done. The deadline was not until the end of August, but there was still a lot of work to do, and Harriet had a long list of subjects to paint. It was looking good, though, and her mind lingered happily on visions of the finished book, replete with her illustrations, handsome and glossy on the shelves of Waterstone's.

'Look, Mum, the kite-men are up there!' Toby's high voice broke into her thoughts. They were driving up the narrow lane which led to the hill, and she could see, with a quick glance, the brightly coloured sails of several hang-gliders, turquoise and yellow and a peculiarly virulent shade of cerise, soaring in the warm thermals rising from the steep slopes of Oliver's Castle.

Damn, Harriet thought, with annoyance. She had forgotten all about Morgan's hobby. And if he was up there now, and saw her, he would think she had come up to the hill on purpose to find him. Which she most certainly had not — unless Freud was right, and her subconscious had been working in overdrive.

It hadn't, of course, because she was wearing shorts, hardly the most seductive of garments unless you were a sleek size ten with endless tanned legs. Anyway, hadn't she just been telling herself that he didn't matter any more? True, she still fancied him: and just the thought of meeting him again was enough to bring her out in a flush of anticipation. But she was grown up, she could handle it. She would show him, *if* he was there, that she could control her unsuitable urges, even if he couldn't.

He was there. As she pulled up on the verge at the end of the track, she recognised his silver and black 4 × 4 amongst the other vehicles. This was as far as you could go: the downland stretched away all around her, much of it alas cultivated, on pitifully thin chalky soil, and the rest devoted to grass, and flowers, and butterflies, and the sweet, unending song of the larks, pouring down from above them in the warm summer air.

'Come on, Mum!' Toby was at the stile before she had even got the rucksack out of the car, while Maggie, in a frenzy of excitement at the prospect of a long walk, leapt up and down in her confined space in the back.

'Wait, sweetheart!' Harriet called. She slung the bag on her back and locked up before letting the dog out. At once Maggie shot off to greet a couple of golden retrievers, returning panting from their exercise, and she wasted some time attaching her lead to the grovelling dog before turning back to the stile.

Toby had gone. Hastily, Harriet ran over to the fence, the picnic bouncing heavily and painfully on her back. As she had hoped, he was far ahead along the path towards the edge of the hill, running purely for the joy of it, his fair hair flying and his heels flashing. She let Maggie off the lead, climbed over the stile, and set off more sedately in pursuit.

By the time she caught up with him, her son was leaping wildly about on the ramparts of the hill-fort, waving his arms. 'Careful!' Harriet called, afraid that their expedition would end in grazed knees and tears before it had properly begun.

'It's all right, Mum!' he yelled back, brandishing what was apparently an imaginary sword. 'I'm only trying to kill the wind!'

'I should pick on someone your own size.' Harriet scrambled up the ramparts to stand beside him. 'Look at the hang-gliders, aren't they beautiful?'

Most of them were swooping gracefully above this part of the hill, but the cerise one was further over, above the wooded slopes of Roundway Covert, and had attracted the attentions of a buzzard.

'Look,' Toby said, pointing. 'That bird thinks the glider's another bird. It's copying it, see?'

'I can't imagine why, giant pink buzzards aren't exactly common round here.' Harriet shaded her eyes against the brilliance of the sun, and gazed at the distant sail. She would be willing to bet a considerable sum of money that it belonged to Morgan. It was entirely like him to choose the dangerous part of the hill — landing in those trees would not be comfortable — and also typical that he had hooked an admirer, albeit one with feathers, beak and talons.

'Race you to the end, Mum!' Toby cried, and set off again along the rampart, with

Maggie in eager pursuit. Harriet grinned to herself, and began to jog after them. Even up here, with the breeze cooling against her bare legs and arms, she felt too hot to be energetic.

The hang-gliders had left their paraphernalia all over the flat space within the fort. Where once Celtic warriors had gathered their flocks and families in time of danger, now spar covers, bags and rucksacks littered the long grass. As she came to the edge of the hill, one of the gliders sailed past twenty yards away, at eye-level, and landed with nonchalant grace on the path beyond.

'I wish I could do that,' Toby said. He flopped down on the ancient burial mound that crowned the escarpment, and stared enviously up at the vivid triangles of colour soaring high above them. 'Just like flying.'

'I'd love to as well, but I don't think I'd have the bottle.' Harriet slung her rucksack on the grass and sat down beside him, while Maggie exchanged greetings with a friendly spaniel further along the hillside.

'What's bottle, Mum?'

'Courage. Gumption. Being brave. I'm not that keen on heights. This is all right, though. Even though we're up here, we're still firmly on the ground. Look at that view!'

Toby was more interested in the ingredients of their picnic than in the broad prospect of Wiltshire, laid out so gloriously before them. 'I'm hungry, Mum. Can we have tea?'

It wasn't three o'clock yet, but there didn't seem any point in delaying it. Harriet glanced surreptitiously to her left. The pink hang-glider was very much closer now, and looked as if it might be going to land soon. Determined to ignore it, she unpacked the food, and at once Maggie left her new friend and came trotting back, tail wagging hopefully. At Harriet's sharp command, she retreated a few yards and sat down, her tongue hanging out and her brown eyes liquidly beseeching.

'You're trying to make out you're starving to death, aren't you?' Harriet said, putting some crisps and a sandwich on a plastic plate for Toby. 'Sorry, old girl. You might get a few leftovers, but that's all.'

'She can have some of my crisps,' said the boy. 'Here you are, Maggie.' Before Harriet could stop him, several had landed around the dog's feet, and were devoured in a single gulp.

'Like Little Red Riding Hood's grand-mother,' Harriet said. She poured out squash for Toby, tea for herself, and a small bowl of water for the dog. 'Don't give her any more, sweetheart, or she'll get fat. Fatter. And there won't be enough for us.'

'There's *loads*,' Toby protested, peering into the rucksack. 'Ooh, yummy, chocolate muffins!'

For a while, silence reigned as they worked their way through the contents of the rucksack. Even though there must have been, to judge by the cars, at least a dozen groups of people on the hill, their presence did not intrude on her sense of peace, and the only sounds, apart from contented munching, were of birdsong and the soft, high noise of the wind in the sails of the hang-gliders.

Harriet gazed at the view, entranced as she always was by the sheer splendour of so much to see. It was hazy, so the Mendips weren't visible today, but the colours of the tessellated fields — rough green pasture, emerald unripe wheat, the soft azure of flax — filled her gaze, and she knew that she could never tire of this place. Just being here, looking at that infinitely changeable yet unchanging land-scape, was enough to put all her problems, such as they were, into perspective. On a glorious day like this, she couldn't wish anyone ill.

'Look, Mum, here comes the pink one.'

It swooshed cheekily in to land, only a few feet above their heads. The pilot, if that was the right word, was wearing flamboyantly purple overalls, and even though his face was invisible behind the pink and purple helmet, she knew who it was, as if her mind possessed a sixth sense that was as susceptible to him as she was to colour, or scent, or touch.

Conflicting emotions jostled briefly within Harriet's head. Be friendly — show you don't care any more. No — give him an inch and he'll take a mile, you know what he's like. And, finally, life's too short for all this, and it's a lovely day, why not?

There was still lots of food left, enough even for a hungry hang-glider, so she packed it quickly back into the rucksack, and stood up, smiling, and holding out her hand to her son. 'Come on, Toby, let's go and say hello to an old friend.'

18

The pink glider lay tilted on the grass in the centre of the fort, and its owner was standing beside it, beginning to dismantle the harness. He still had his helmet on, and Harriet, walking towards him, wondered suddenly if her senses had deceived her, so that a complete stranger would be revealed when he took it off.

'Do you know that man, Mum?' Toby asked.

'I used to, a long time ago. Oh, Maggie, do shut up!'

The dog, who would bark at plastic bags and rubbish bins but not at anyone who came to the door, was glaring suspiciously at the pilot, all her hackles raised. 'It's his helmet,' said Harriet, as the Labrador leapt forward. 'She probably thinks he's an alien or something.'

The man turned, removing his headgear. Her intuition had not deceived her. As he saw her approaching, he grinned suddenly, and with such unfeigned and joyful delight that her heart's rhythm began misbehaving.

'Hallo,' Harriet said, hoping that her

response to him did not show in her face or in her eyes. 'I guessed it was you. Did you see the buzzard buzzing you?'

Morgan was still looking at her as if she was a winning lottery ticket. 'What are you doing here?'

'I've brought Toby for a picnic. Say hello, sweetheart — this is Morgan.'

'Hello,' said her son, gazing up in respectful awe at the man who could fly like a bird. 'I've got my Action Man socks on, *and* Action Man pants.'

Despite all the usual warnings he had received about not talking to strangers, Toby still possessed the risky but endearing habit of engaging them in animated conversation about the things that concerned him most at the time. He had once informed an old lady waiting at the chemist's that he had a sore bottom and the doctor had given him some cream for it, and did she have a sore bottom too? Before he could offer to show Morgan his underwear, Harriet said hastily, 'We've got quite a lot of picnic left. Would you like some?'

'Wow,' said Morgan. 'This *is* civilised. Or is it laced with strychnine?'

'Of course not,' Harriet said, contriving to sound hurt. 'I thought it was time to call a truce. Have a ham sandwich. Or a hard-boiled egg, they're Daphne's.'

'Laid them herself, did she?' Morgan grinned at her. He seemed very happy and light-hearted, and she put it down to the adrenalin rush of hang-gliding.

'Don't be cheeky.' Harriet sat down on the grass beside the pink bird, and unpacked the food again. She glanced at Toby, who was examining the glider with interest, and added, 'Be careful, sweetheart, and don't touch anything.'

'It's all right, there's not a lot he could do to it.' Morgan unzipped his overalls and shrugged himself out of them. Underneath, he was wearing a T-shirt that bore the logo of the Chicago Bears, and a pair of blue shorts. She couldn't help noticing that his legs were much more muscular than she remembered, though still gently furred with dark hairs. Come on, she told herself severely. You thought you could handle this, remember?

'Can I have a go? Please, Mum?' Toby stared at her, his blue eyes as imploring as Maggie's.

'Sorry, sweetheart. It's only for grown-ups.'

'But you can sit in the harness, if you like,' said Morgan unexpectedly. 'And pretend you're flying. Are you good at pretending?'

'It's my favourite thing,' said Toby, his face

glowing. 'Can I? Oh, thank you! Can we do it now?'

'Of course,' said Morgan. He shoved most of a ham sandwich into his mouth and winked at Harriet. 'I won't let go of him — promise.'

Astonished and rather bemused by this glimpse of a facet of Morgan she had never suspected, Harriet looked on as he showed her son the basic elements of the hang-glider: struts, sail, instruments, harness, and the curious bag into which he would zip himself once airborne. Toby wriggled inside this with enthusiasm, gripped the bar and made loud whooshing noises. Although he usually posed self-consciously for photographs, he was so absorbed that he didn't even notice when she surreptitiously slipped the lens cap off the camera and took several shots. And if they were carefully framed so as to include Morgan, well, he would never know.

Watching the two very different heads, one blond and silky, one dark, curly and briefly cropped, bent together over the compass, Harriet was visited by a novel and rather disturbing thought. The Morgan she had known ten years ago, impatient and irresponsible, wouldn't have known how to deal with a small child's absolute ignorance and endless questions: any more, in fact, than she herself had, before Toby's arrival. She had changed, and it appeared now that he had, too. So perhaps there might be hope for a relationship after all.

And no matter how much she tried to tell herself that Morgan meant nothing to her any more, she knew that she was deluding herself. He still mattered, very much indeed.

'Any more food left? I'm starving.' Morgan flopped down beside her and delved into the rucksack. 'And don't look like that, *cariad*, you offered it to me.'

'It's OK, go ahead, feed your face. We've finished.'

'These eggs are good. Free range?'

'Not really, they're penned in at the bottom of the garden. Daphne won't let them loose, they do too much damage, though she does turn them out in the winter. They're great at controlling slugs and snails.'

'I didn't know they ate snails.'

'They eat practically anything. You don't want to know — if you did, you'd never touch another egg.'

Morgan made a face as he swallowed a mouthful. 'I *thought* you were trying to poison me.'

'Not at all. I'm going to be civilised, remember?'

'And glad I am of it.' Noticeably, his accent

was losing its mid-Atlantic twang and reverting to his native Welsh. 'Is that flask empty?'

'There's a dreg or two left in it.' Harriet poured out the last of the tea and handed it to him. 'Or do you still prefer coffee?'

'I do, but this is fine, thanks. You have a long memory, *cariad*.'

'Yes.' She smiled at him. 'But somehow it doesn't seem to matter so much now.'

'I'm glad, I never wanted there to be any bitterness between us. And if I had my time over again, I'd do it all very differently, believe me.'

'Would you still have gone to the States?'

Morgan sipped the tea, thinking. She saw the way his hair curled against the nape of his neck, and the dark growth of beard just under his skin, and the lines of laughter, white against the tan, around his long-lashed blue eyes, and her body ached with longing. Mistake, mistake, mistake — keep it slow, keep it friendly, don't let him know how you feel.

'I'd have gone,' he said at last. 'But I'd have asked you to come with me. Would you?'

'Yes,' she said, unhesitatingly. 'I'd have followed you into an erupting volcano if you'd asked me, you know I would.' And that was another reason why you left, she thought, with a sudden flash of insight. You were afraid of the intensity between us — you didn't want to commit yourself.

But that was ten years ago. Perhaps he had changed. And it was becoming increasingly difficult for Harriet to ignore the effect his proximity was having on her senses. Sex of any kind, let alone the wonderful, explosive sex she had once had with Morgan, hadn't figured in her life for so long that she had almost forgotten what it could be like to fancy someone, until now.

'No you wouldn't,' said Morgan cheerfully. 'You'd have hovered on the edge telling me to be careful, and worrying about whether the soles of my shoes were thick enough.' He rummaged around in the rucksack, and drew out Toby's kite, neatly folded, although the string, as kite strings always do, had somehow got tangled up all by itself. 'This isn't edible.'

'By the look of it, it's not going to be flyable either.'

'You're speaking to the world-famous kite expert. Do you want to fly this, Toby?'

The little boy looked round from his fascinated investigation of the hang-glider. 'Yes *please*!'

'Then we'll fly it,' said Morgan. He licked his forefinger and held it up. 'Wind from the west. A bit on the gusty side, but we can try.

Have you ever flown it before, kid?'

'Yes, with Daddy, and my name's not kid, it's Toby.'

'Sorry. Toby. Well, I'll hold it up in the air, as high as I can reach, and you run with the string, letting it out as you go, and when I release it, it should fly.'

'Straight into the nearest kite-eating tree, I expect,' said Harriet, grinning.

'You dare to doubt my competence, *cariad*? I see you do. Well, we'd better prove you wrong. Come on, Toby, let's go to the end of the fort and have a go. And if you could hang on to that lunatic dog, I'd be grateful.'

Afterwards, the memory of that afternoon lingered in a hazy golden glow of delight in Harriet's mind, so different from what came after. Helpless with laughter, she watched as Morgan, completely on purpose, tangled himself in the string, fell over several times, and generally revealed himself to be utterly hopeless at kite-flying. Finally, Toby himself launched it successfully into the air, without realising that in fact Morgan had done all the work to make it easy for him. Harriet used the telephoto lens to take several close-ups of his rapt, wondering face as he gazed at the blue and green kite soaring as effortlessly as the hang-gliders, a hundred feet above. Then Morgan showed him how to make things travel up the string — a ring-pull from a discarded can of beer, a watch-strap, and, most alarmingly, Harriet's bunch of keys.

'If the kite takes off and drops them somewhere over the Marlborough Downs, you can go and find them,' Harriet said. 'Or lend me your four-by-four.'

'No way. That's my precious baby, bought with my ill-gotten gains.'

'Ill-gotten?'

'Oh, the proceeds of organised crime. You don't imagine I spent *all* my time in the States just designing underground houses, do you? There was the drug-running, the arms business, the Mafia connections . . . '

'You're joking, of course.'

'Only about the Mafia. The Japanese equivalent pay better.' Morgan gave her a sly sideways glance, and burst out laughing. 'You always were gullible, *cariad*! Though I don't think they'd let me back in, even if I wanted to go. A former girlfriend got busted on a drugs rap, and they put me through some fairly heavy questioning, I thought it was time to come home, before they pinned something serious on me.'

'And you were completely innocent, of course,' said Harriet, thinking exultantly, Sir Marcus was wrong — he isn't going back to America after all.

Morgan gave her another look, under raised brows. 'As it happens, yes. I've grown out of dope, and anyway cocaine's never been my scene. Another reason why I'm not shedding any tears over Selina.'

'She does coke? Does Sir Marcus know?'

'I doubt it. He's not very streetwise, and she's a good girl when she's around him. That's why she moved out, I suspect — she wanted a bit more freedom to party. And no one can party like Selina.' He glanced at her. 'Was it your ex she was with, last night?'

Harriet nodded. 'It's all right, I'm not bothered. The two of them probably deserve each other.' It was what she had thought about Selina and Morgan, she remembered wryly. 'I suspect he's bitten off rather more than he can chew.'

'And he's Toby's father?'

The little boy was some yards away, hanging on to the kite string with fervent concentration, but even so, Harriet dropped her voice. 'Yes. He still sees him, on a regular basis. Usually on Sunday afternoons, in fact, but he cancelled this week, that's why we're here. Toby loves seeing his father, and however much bad feeling there is between me and Edward, I'm determined to make sure that it affects Toby as little as possible.'

'Not everyone would be so altruistic.'

'Believe me, it isn't easy. Every time I see him I want to be rude to him.'

'Like you were to me?'

'Being nasty to you was just practice. With Edward, it's the real thing. Whatever your faults, at least you didn't let your four-year-old son catch you screwing some totty in his mother's bed.'

'Jesus,' Morgan stared at her in horrified concern. 'What a bastard. Hanging's too good for him. Drawn and quartered, minimum.'

'But at least it made me realise there was nothing left but to walk out. And now I'm quite grateful to him, in a way, for making it easy for me.'

'*Easy?*' Morgan demanded. '*Grateful?*'

Under the azure intensity of his gaze, her own eyes slid away, to where Toby was still holding the kite. The afternoon wind tugged at her hair, brushing annoying stray locks of it across her face. 'Yes,' she said. 'I can be quite philosophical about it all, really, when I try. But then, I haven't had a lot of luck with men.'

Morgan put out a hand and turned her back to face him. 'Oh, *cariad*,' he whispered, and brushed the hair away from her lips. 'Let me change that.'

For an instant, a single brief, mad moment,

she almost let him kiss her. Then her common sense reasserted itself, whispering, *No, wait, too soon.* Reluctantly, she moved out of his reach. 'Oh, Morgan, please don't. *Friends*, you said, and that's what I settled for. Stop thinking you've only got to look at me with those melting eyes to have me swoon into your arms.'

There was a brief, tense silence as they stared at each other. It was broken by Toby's heartfelt wail. 'The kite! The kite's caught in the tree!'

Once, Oliver's Castle had been ringed by beech trees, planted probably in the Victorian age by an improving owner. The ravages of time and weather, in particular the almost unceasing wind, had taken their toll, and now there were only about a dozen left, all rather the worse for wear. In one of these, over twenty feet from the ground, Toby's kite had become entangled.

'Oh, sweetheart.' Harriet knew better than to blame him: rather, she blamed herself, for being distracted by Morgan. 'Don't cry, Toby, it wasn't your fault. We'll get another one.'

'But I want *that* one! It's my *favourite*!' Toby cried. Tears spurted out from his blue eyes and ran down his face in torrents. 'I want you to get it down, Mum!'

'I can't fly,' said Harriet reasonably. She

wanted desperately to make it better for him, but that was impossible, and as always, her inability to help tore at her heart. 'We'll get another one tomorrow, from the same shop, just exactly the same.'

'No need, I'll get it,' said Morgan. He ran forward to pick up the trailing handle, lying where it had been dragged out of Toby's hands. He glanced back to where Harriet knelt beside her distraught son, and sent them a flying, reckless grin that reminded her, suddenly and poignantly, of the wild boy she had loved so much. 'Trust me!'

'Will he fly up to get it, Mum?' Toby asked, so astonished and delighted that he had forgotten his tears.

'With Morgan, almost anything's possible,' Harriet said drily. 'Or at least *he* thinks it is.'

But in the end, flight was not required. With a little judicious jiggling of the string, and a lot of coaxing, or swearing, in Welsh, Morgan was gradually persuading the kite that it would really much rather come down and be safely packed away for another day than spend the foreseeable future twenty feet up a beech tree, at the mercy of every passing gale. When it finally slid free, and fluttered meekly to the ground like an ailing bird, there was a cheer from the other hang-gliders, who had assembled to watch, and Toby ran forward to retrieve it, his eyes shining with admiration. 'Oh, thank you, *thank you*, Mr Morgan!'

'Just plain Morgan will do,' he said, handing it over, the string wound neatly back on the handle. 'There, see, not a tear in it now. You were lucky, kid. Hang on to it in future.'

'He will, don't worry,' said Harriet. 'Thanks, Morgan. You've saved us a lot of trouble and grief.'

'It was nothing, *cariad*,' Morgan said, with heavily ironic modesty. 'Anyone would have done the same, despite the mortal danger I was in.'

'It wasn't dangerous at all, you pig!'

'Oh yes it was — what would you two have done to me if I'd failed?' His hair tousled over his head, grinning in triumph, he was entirely desirable, and also, unfortunately, entirely conscious of it.

Harriet laughed in affectionate exasperation. 'Pushed you over the edge of the hill, probably. Or held your glider to ransom.' A thought struck her suddenly, and she gasped in dismay. 'Oh God — what about my keys? Weren't they still on the line?'

'Never fear — Morgan Llewellyn Price thinks of everything, does he not? Here you are.' He fished them out of his shorts pocket and handed them over. 'I found them in the grass by the handle. Lucky for you, or you'd have had to beg a lift home off me.'

'I'm surprised you didn't hang on to them, then,' said Harriet drily. She grinned at him suddenly. 'I said thank you, and I meant it. And not just for rescuing the kite, either — it's been a really nice afternoon. Toby's thoroughly enjoyed himself.'

'I'm glad,' said Morgan, smiling back. 'Because I've enjoyed myself too, and I wouldn't want to be the only one having fun around here.'

'You weren't.' She went back to pick up the rucksack, and Toby, carrying the kite as reverently as if it were truly alive, placed it carefully inside. 'It was great. We must do it again some time.'

'Really?' He looked endearingly surprised, and delighted. 'I'd like that. And I won't try anything on again, I promise.'

'Good. I'm glad to hear it.' She looked round for the dog, who was lying a short distance away, panting. 'We ought to go now, it's nearly Toby's bathtime, and he's getting tired.'

'Would you have dinner with me soon?' Morgan said quickly. 'Just a meal in a pub somewhere — I know a couple of nice places.

Good food, and good talk, and no strings attached.'

'I'd love to,' said Harriet. She scrabbled in her bag, found an old receipt and a Biro, and wrote down Daphne's phone number. 'Give me a ring and we can arrange something. Goodbye, and thanks!'

She looked back, briefly, as they were about to descend the ramparts to the path. He had begun to dismantle the hang-glider, but he straightened up and waved in farewell. Toby waved enthusiastically back, and skipped down the steep slope in Maggie's wake. Harriet's own salute was briefer, but no less joyful. It had indeed been a good afternoon. If nothing else, she had found a friend. And she realised that, for the first time in many years, she was looking forward to the future with eagerness. Against all hope, against all expectation, her luck had finally changed. It was going to come right in the end, after all.

19

It was a lesson she should have learned long ago, Harriet thought bitterly, as she put the phone down in furious and horrified disbelief. Just when she had thought she had it sussed, fate — or someone more human and more malign — had thrown everything contemptuously back in her face.

'Harriet? My dear, what is it?' Daphne paused in the doorway, staring at her in considerable concern. 'Is it bad news?'

'You could say that.' Trembling with rage, Harriet sat down by the telephone. 'I've just had a call from my solicitor. Edward's decided to apply for custody of Toby — on *moral* grounds!'

'No!' Daphne stared at her, a serious frown between her thick grey brows. 'My God. Whatever can he mean?'

'I don't know. He must have gone mad or something.' Harriet heard the fury in her voice and tried to control it. 'What a complete and utter hypocrite! He shags anything that isn't nailed to the floor, and then has the cheek to accuse *me* of being unfit to bring up Toby! Why? *Why?* What's happened, for God's sake? What's changed? He was almost *too* friendly, at the ball — in fact, I thought he was trying to make a pass at me. What have I done to make him do this?'

'Has your solicitor any idea?'

'None. He's just had a very bald letter, and when he rang Edward's solicitor he was being very cagey.' Harriet shook her head in disbelief. 'I can't understand why on earth he suddenly wants to do this. OK, he's great at sunny afternoons out, all the fun things, but surely he won't want to read stories to him or wipe his bottom or take him to playgroup, he thinks that sort of thing is demeaning to his manhood. He's always been a part-time father. *Why* does he suddenly want custody?'

'Ask him direct.'

'I don't know if I can do that. My solicitor told me to be very careful. He thinks if I lose my rag with Edward, I might say something that would prejudice my case.' She laughed incredulously. 'My *case*! I'm his *mother*, that should be enough.'

'For some children, it isn't,' Daphne pointed out gently. 'But anyone with eyes to see would know that you are the best, indeed the only person to care for Toby.'

'He must want revenge,' said Harriet. She scrabbled in her jeans pocket for a handkerchief and blew her nose violently. 'Hell hath no fury like a man scorned. This is his way of getting back at me for leaving him.'

'That doesn't seem very likely now,' Daphne said. 'If he'd wanted revenge, surely he would have applied for custody straight away, not waited nearly two months. You're right, something else must have happened.' She touched Harriet lightly on the arm. 'I've put the kettle on. Come into the kitchen and have a cup of tea and we'll have a think.'

It was at times like these that Harriet was overwhelmingly grateful for Daphne's presence. She was so direct and sensible, so matter-of-fact, and with the benefit of her superior years and accumulated knowledge, it was like having a mother to turn to. Except I'd never dream of discussing something like this with my mother, Harriet thought wryly, as she followed Daphne into the kitchen. She'd throw her hands up in horror and witter on and urge me to go round to Edward's house and confront him. She'd only make matters worse. Not for the first time, she wondered if Georgia was so adamantly in control of her life and her emotions largely in reaction to their mother, who always made such a fuss.

'Moral grounds,' said Daphne, when they were both sitting at the kitchen table, mugs of tea in front of them. It was Wednesday morning, and Toby, fortunately, was at playgroup: Harriet had two hours left before picking him up. 'Can you think of anything that's happened that will cast some light on that?'

Ever since she had heard the phrase, Harriet's mind had been revolving round and round its pivot in a frantic search for a cause. 'Not really,' she said at last. 'I haven't got anyone else — I'm not conducting orgies every night — and I'm not into drugs.'

But Morgan was, once. The unwelcome thought flashed into her mind. She added slowly, 'But he might have heard something about Morgan.'

'Ah.' Daphne looked at her, raising her eyebrows. 'Has he been a bad boy? He rather looks the type.'

For some reason, this annoyed Harriet. 'He's not up to his eyes in smack, or anything like that. He used to smoke cannabis, that's all. And he said something the other day about an ex-girlfriend of his in the States having been busted. It's one of the reasons he left, to avoid getting tarred with the same brush. But he was adamant he doesn't do anything now.'

'Edward might have been talking to Selina. They certainly seemed very close, at the ball. And she might have made it sound a lot worse than it actually was.'

'Then she'd be the world's second biggest hypocrite,' said Harriet, too angry to be discreet. 'Morgan told me she does coke.'

'Ah,' said Daphne again, with infuriating calm. 'I rather thought she might. Don't say any of this to Marcus, will you? He's very fond of Selina, and quite blind to her more unattractive aspects. And although he's seen a great deal of the world, he's surprisingly unworldly. Whereas I may be a reclusive old fogey, but after thirty years at Cambridge, not a lot escapes me. Believe me, what your Morgan gets up to is probably minuscule compared to some of the wild and well-heeled undergraduates I came across.'

'He's not *my* Morgan.'

'He thinks he is,' said Daphne drily.

'That's his problem.' Harriet took a sip of her tea, and felt a little better. 'But if we're right, if it *is* Morgan who's the problem, then that's easily sorted. Toby's only met him once, on the hill last Sunday. You can be my witness that he's come to the house a couple of times, very briefly. We're not having any kind of relationship, however much Edward might be deluding himself that we are, and I should think it would be fairly easy to prove that we're not.'

'In any case, moral grounds would have to

be pretty strong to justify taking Toby away from you, I would have thought,' said Daphne calmly. 'So, what happens now?'

'It's all rather complicated — I was so shocked by the very idea, I couldn't really take it all in.' Harriet considered for a moment, fighting her anger and her urgent desire to go and vent it on Edward. 'Edward is going to apply to the county court for something called an s.8 order.'

'And what does that mean?'

'It basically means, I think, that he's asking for custody, but that's not what it's called now, it's called a residence order. Apparently, because we were never married, I automatically have parental responsibility, but if he gets the residence order then he gets parental responsibility as well.' She shook her head, still unable to understand why Edward had done this. 'I just don't believe he could be so — so vindictive. If he'd ever shown much interest in Toby, or spent a lot of time looking after him, and been very close to him, I might just begin to see why, but most of the time he's acted as though his son's a millstone round his neck. I had to pretty well force him to keep in touch with him. And then he rang me at the last minute on Sunday morning to say he couldn't see Toby because he wanted to watch cricket, for God's sake! What kind of a father disappoints his son because of a cricket match? And then he has the nerve to accuse *me* of not being a fit parent.'

'I should try to talk to him,' said Daphne. 'In my experience, if you conduct your business exclusively through solicitors, things can quickly get out of hand. If you can just find out why he's done this, then you can prepare your defence.'

Harriet grimaced. 'You make it sound as though I'm on trial. But it does feel like that, it really does. And the worst thing is, I don't know what I'm being accused of.'

'Then find out. Pick up the phone and ring him. And try not to lose your cool.'

'Easier said than done. What I'd really like to do is throttle him, and then kick him into the canal and drive a boat over him.'

'I wouldn't,' Daphne advised her drily. 'That would certainly wreck your chances of keeping Toby.'

'I know, I know.' Harriet ran a hand through her hair, pulling much of it out of its plait. 'I'll try to control myself. After all, I've had a lot of practice, over the years.'

But when she dialled the familiar number, the only sound at the other end of the line belonged to the answerphone. She hated talking to the things at the best of times, and the cold tone of Edward's recorded voice threw her completely. She put the receiver down and found herself fighting tears. The injustice and unfairness was bad enough, but the fear that she might lose her beloved son was beginning to overwhelm her. He would be distraught, bewildered, she could imagine him torn sobbing from her arms and led away to begin a new and unhappy life with Edward, who wouldn't have time for him, who would hand him over to a succession of nannies and then probably pack him off to boarding school when he was seven . . .

It didn't bear thinking about. And she would fight with the last breath in her body to prevent it happening.

The phone rang, making her jump. She picked it up with some trepidation, wondering who it was, and heard Georgia's brisk voice. 'Harry! Don Potter's just told me. God, what a complete and utter *bastard*! Still, he won't have a snowball's chance in hell of getting the residence order. It might be different if Toby was older, but as he's only four the judge is bound to rule in your favour.'

'I'm glad you're so positive,' said Harriet, hoping that her voice wouldn't wobble.

'Oh, come on, Harry, you *know* he hasn't got a hope! You're not all upset over this, are you?'

'It was just a bit of a shock, out of the blue like that. He's seemed quite friendly recently.'

'And you've no idea what he's on about, 'moral grounds'?' Georgia gave a cynical laugh. 'I must say, that's rich, coming from him. All you'll have to do is tell the court how Toby found him bonking Gina, and they'll give his bloody s.8 application the contempt it deserves.'

'There's only one thing I can think of,' said Harriet, considerably heartened by her sister's robust attitude. 'And that's Morgan.'

There was a brief silence. Then Georgia's voice came back, loud with astonishment. '*Morgan?* But that was years and years ago. Another complete bastard, you do know how to pick 'em, don't you?'

'He's back,' said Harriet. And gave her a brief account of what he had been up to in the intervening years.

The silence this time was longer. At last Georgia said, 'If that's the only thing you can come up with, then, yes, I suppose someone vindictive and nasty enough could use that against you. But I can't say it sounds very likely. And if it *is* Morgan he's concerned about, then he *certainly* hasn't a snowball's chance in hell of getting the residence order. Just as long as you're not seen smoking wacky baccy with Morgan in public, of course.'

'God forbid! I probably won't be seeing him again anyway,' said Harriet, guiltily conscious of the lie. 'Listen, George, is it OK if I ring Edward and ask him what the hell this is all about?'

'Unwise,' said her sister unhesitatingly. 'Best to do it all via Don. You might shoot your mouth off and make things worse. That's why solicitors were invented, you know, to stop people taking matters into their own hands and murdering each other.'

'I thought they were invented to make themselves lots and lots of money.'

'You've got very cynical in your old age! But seriously, Harry, leave it to the experts, OK? You've got legal aid, so you don't have to think about what it's costing. Don's the best family lawyer in Bath, he'll sort everything out. So don't *worry*, it'll all be fine, you'll see. Just don't give him any ammunition — keep away from Morgan, and don't start yelling abuse at him.'

'At Morgan, or Edward?' Harriet enquired, thinking that she had already done it to both men, and how much they both deserved it.

'Edward, of course.'

'But I've got to see him on Sunday afternoon,' Harriet said, suddenly remembering. 'He has Toby every week, that is, if he doesn't cancel at the last minute.'

'Has he done that? The swine!'

'Last weekend. Toby was really disappointed.'

'So he's unreliable, too. Another point in your favour. You'll sail through this, Harry, you're bound to. Don't lose any sleep over it. We'll make the bastard wish he'd never been born.'

'It sounds too good to be true.'

'Trust me,' said Georgia. 'Look, I've got to go, I'm due down at the nick in ten minutes. Just don't worry, OK? It'll all come out in the wash.'

Harriet put the phone down, feeling much better. Almost, her sister's supreme confidence had made her believe that Edward would fail. Almost, but not quite. Still, a little voice in her head whispered of disaster, and tragedy.

But she couldn't believe it. Couldn't believe that Edward could be so spiteful, couldn't believe that he really wanted Toby, couldn't believe that he would succeed.

Once more, the phone rang. She wondered if it was Edward, who could have dialled 1471 to find out who wasn't leaving messages on his answerphone. But instead, her other ex-lover's voice came cheerfully down the line. 'Hi, *cariad*, guess who?'

'The Prime Minister,' said Harriet crushingly.

'Sorry, haven't got the teeth for it. Look, how about meeting for a drink at the Wharf this lunchtime? It's a nice day, bring Toby and we can sit outside and feed the ducks. Meet me at half twelve at The Pits?'

'The what?'

'The Pits. The underground house. I'm there now.' And indeed, there was a sudden roar of machinery in the background.

'I'm sorry, I can't,' Harriet said. She wanted to, she wanted to desperately, but for Toby's sake she couldn't risk it.

'How about tomorrow, then? Or if you don't fancy the Wharf, we can always go somewhere else.'

'I'm sorry,' Harriet said again. 'It's just . . . ' She swallowed, acutely aware of how dangerously close she was to tears, and went on bravely, 'Something's happened, and I don't think I can see you for a while.'

'Hal?' Even on the mobile's dodgy line, she could hear the acute concern in his voice. 'Hal, what's wrong?'

She couldn't, in all fairness, keep him in ignorance. 'Edward's applied for custody of Toby.'

'*What?* Jesus, the bastard!'

Harriet thought that people tended to use a

very restricted vocabulary when referring to Edward: but, on the whole, he entirely deserved it. 'That's not the worst of it. He's applied on 'moral grounds'.'

'Why, for God's sake?'

'I don't know. The only reason I could think of was you.'

The silence at the other end was so long and so profound that she could hear some building worker shouting instructions. At last, Morgan said, 'God, you really know how to hit below the belt, don't you, Hal? Are you making this up?'

'I only wish I was. Look, Morgan, as far as I'm concerned I've no worries about you — I *know* you're not a pervert, or a druggie, I trust you. But Edward doesn't. And perhaps Selina's been telling him tall tales. Is that likely?'

'Could be, but I wouldn't have thought there was enough bad feeling between us. The affair was cancelled due to lack of interest.'

'But it was the only thing I could come up with. And whatever he thinks I've done, or am doing, it must be pretty serious.'

'Surely he doesn't have a hope, does he?'

'My sister says not, but I can't take the risk. You do see that, don't you? Until I find out for sure why he's done this, I've got to be really, really careful. I *can't* let him have Toby, I can't.'

He must have heard the desperation in her voice, because his own was suddenly full of a gentleness that made her eyes water. 'It's OK, *cariad*, I understand. I know how much he means to you, and I can wait. We've got all summer to make friends again, haven't we? And that bastard will get his comeuppance in the end.'

'This is real life, Morgan, not a film.'

'Yes, but real life sometimes needs a helping hand.'

'Don't.' Harriet shuddered at the implications. 'For God's sake, keep away from him. The last thing I need is anyone else interfering, however well-meaning.'

'It's all right, I didn't mean it. My joke lights were on.'

'Maybe they were,' Harriet pointed out with some asperity. 'But they're not visible down the phone.'

'Damn! I *knew* this model didn't have all the features I needed. It's OK, *cariad*, I understand, I really do. Don't worry. It'll all be fine in the end, you'll see.'

But she wished, as she put the receiver down, that she shared his optimism.

20

Despite Georgia's advice, Harriet was determined to talk to Edward. She tried to contact him four times during the rest of that day, in between attending to more mundane matters, such as picking Toby up from playgroup and doing some essential shopping. Her first call was answered again by the machine, and she spoke, as calmly as she could, the message which she had written down on a piece of paper. 'Hallo, Edward, it's me, Harriet. I would very much like to know why you have suddenly decided to ask for custody of Toby. Please can you ring me as soon as possible, so that we can have a talk. Thank you.'

But the day wore on and there was no response. She tried again at three o'clock, half past four, and at six. Where in God's name is the man, she wondered, as she put the phone down for the fourth time, without bothering to leave any further message. Is he trying to hide from me or something?

She slept very little during the night, and should have felt exhausted, but the following morning was so gloriously sunny that she could not help feeling a fresh surge of hope.

As she fed Toby his usual Weetabix and banana, the desperate fears that had kept her awake seemed no more substantial than the half-remembered monsters of a bad dream.

At ten past nine, the phone rang, and Daphne answered it. She came back into the kitchen, where Harriet was washing up and Toby, fierce with concentration, was sitting at the table, crayoning a picture. 'For you. It's your solicitor.'

Her heart banging against her ribs, Harriet wiped her wet hands on her jeans and went to answer it. 'Hallo?'

'Miss Smith? Good morning, Don Potter here. Look, I've just had a call from Mr Armstrong's solicitor. He claims you've been harassing his client.'

'*Harassing?*' Harriet said incredulously. 'Of course I haven't. I just tried to ring him and find out what was going on, that's all.'

'Apparently you left a message on his answerphone.'

'Yes, I did, but I wasn't *harassing* him,' Harriet said. 'In fact, I've got the message I left written down right here.' She picked it up and read it down the line. 'Surely he couldn't describe that as harassment.'

'Well, that's just what he is doing, I'm afraid.'

'I was only trying to get him to *talk* to me!'

Harriet cried in despair. 'How are we ever going to get all this sorted out if he won't tell me what's wrong?'

'I would strongly suggest,' said Don Potter, 'that it would be wiser, in future, to address all contact with your ex-partner through myself. That way, no one can be accused of harassment.'

'Well, please could you find out what's upset him?'

'I have already asked. He apparently takes the view that you would know very well what it's all about.'

'But I *don't*! I've racked my brains and I can't come up with anything more than an old friend of mine who's got a bit of a past.'

'May I enquire what sort of past?'

Harriet gave him the bare facts about Morgan. 'But that was ten years ago, and he seems to be a reformed character now. Anyway, quite honestly, when you look at what Edward's done, Morgan's transgressions pale into insignificance.' She couldn't help a wry smile at the thought. Insignificant was not a word usually associated with her flamboyant, turbulent and outspoken former lover.

'I agree with you entirely there, Miss Smith,' said Don Potter. 'But let's not rock the boat too much, eh? Keep your distance 'and let the professionals sort all this out.'

'There's a big problem, though,' Harriet said. 'What about next Sunday? Edward's supposed to be looking after our son that afternoon. It's a regular arrangement, and he cancelled last time, so I really want Toby to go. He was so disappointed.'

Potter asked for the details, obviously noting them down. 'If Mr Armstrong starts to make a habit of this, obviously his unreliability will count against him. Anyway, I would suggest that on Sunday you get a third party to take and collect your son. Perhaps your sister, or someone similar?'

'Are you sure that's a good idea?' Harriet said doubtfully, thinking of Georgia's fervent dislike of Edward. 'She's even more likely to say something unfortunate than I am.'

'Now, now, Miss Smith. Your sister is a very professional woman. She won't let her personal feelings interfere with her duty.'

'All the same, I'd like my landlady, Miss James, to do it. She's very mature and sensible, and she's got no axe to grind. Can you pass on the message that she'll take him over at two o'clock, and pick him up again at six, as usual?'

'Of course,' said Potter. 'Now don't worry, Miss Smith. Personally, I think Mr Armstrong is being very unreasonable about this, and I'm sure you'll find that there's been some ridiculous misunderstanding. Given your son's tender years, and Mr Armstrong's own past behaviour, I really don't think you run any risk of losing him. Now don't forget, will you? No phone calls, for whatever reason. Stay aloof. And I'll keep you posted about the date of the hearing. It probably won't be for a couple of months, there's always a backlog of these cases, so hopefully we can sort it all out before it ever comes to court. OK? Fine. Goodbye, Miss Smith, and please don't worry.'

Patronising man, Harriet thought, putting the phone down. Perhaps his age and class influenced his avuncular attitude towards her. But, she reminded herself, Sir Marcus was older than Don Potter, and he treated her as an equal, with her own thoughts, rights and opinions.

The call had taken the joy right out of the day. There was a rush to get up to playgroup in time, exacerbated by the temporary loss of one of Toby's shoes. Then, as they were going into the village hall, they met Cindy Bates, one of the other mothers, coming out. Harriet remembered that she'd arranged to have the other woman's son to play the next day: she smiled at her, and said, 'Still OK for tomorrow?'

Mrs Bates was a large and loud young woman whose mother was a pillar of the church, and also one of Heather Clark's cronies. To Harriet's surprise, she shook her head. 'Sorry, I'm afraid he can't.'

'How about some time next week, then?'

'Sorry,' said the other woman again, and pushed hastily past. 'It's not on, I'm afraid.'

Bewildered and dismayed, Harriet stared at her retreating back. But Toby, who hadn't paid any attention to this encounter, was pulling her on into the hall.

She settled him down at the play-dough table, with cutters and a big lump of bright-red squidgy stuff to roll and mould, and kissed him goodbye. Then, as she turned to go, she became aware of a little knot of mothers clustered by the book corner, and whispering to each other, with curious glances in her direction. As soon as they saw her looking, they broke up so abruptly that it was obvious that Harriet had been the subject of their conversation. Resolutely ignoring them, she waved goodbye to Toby, and went thoughtfully back to the car, wondering why she had suddenly become interesting to people who hadn't really taken much notice of her before. Did it have something to do with the mysterious reason for Edward's application for custody?

Whatever it was, it must be bad: when she returned, two and a half hours later, to pick Toby up, all the other mothers seemed to be avoiding her. Even Juliet, whose son Nicholas was Toby's best friend, rushed past her without pausing to say hallo, muttering something about a dentist's appointment.

Harriet walked home across the fields, thinking hard, and paying very little attention to the chattering child beside her, or to her surroundings. It *could* be Morgan. People might have heard something dubious about him, and made a very large mountain out of a very small pimple. But somehow she doubted it. Someone, somewhere had got hold of the wrong end of the stick about her, and that was why Edward had suddenly asked for custody. But although she had racked her brains for some clue, some hint, as to what was wrong, she was still no nearer the answer.

She climbed the gate into Stony Lane, and spent some time persuading a panting, weary Maggie that it was possible to squeeze her bulk through the small gap under the fence. At length, after enthusiastic persuasion from Toby, the dog managed to crawl underneath, and they walked down towards Holly Cottage.

Heather Clark was outside her gates, vigorously pushing an electric mower, on a dangerously long cable, up and down the already immaculate verge. Live and let live, Harriet thought, and gave her a wave and a cheery smile. She expected to be ignored, but she was not prepared, even after recent events, for the look of complete disgust that came over her neighbour's heavy, powdered face.

'I don't know what I've done,' she said despairingly to Daphne after lunch, at the end of a brief report of her various encounters that morning. 'But it seems to be something really awful. I just wish I could find out what it is, and put people right.'

'Well, there's been no further word from your solicitor,' said Daphne. 'And I haven't heard anything untoward — not that I've been out and about at all this week, of course. And I don't exactly make a habit of gossiping in the village shop anyway.' She smiled. 'It makes a change. I'm sure *I* used to be the subject of most of it, but I really couldn't care less what people think of me.'

'I couldn't either,' Harriet said. 'But when Toby's affected by it, then I've got to get to the bottom of it all.'

'Well, hopefully your solicitor will be able

to shed some light on the matter,' Daphne said. 'And in the mean time, don't worry. I'm sure everything will come right in the end.'

'You sound exactly like Mr Potter,' said Harriet, only half joking.

'Don't be insulting,' Daphne said briskly. 'But, like it or not, despite what I said to you yesterday, I've come to the conclusion he's right. I know you want to go round to Edward and have it out with him, but if he's intent on being absolutely unreasonable, it will probably do more harm than good. When so much depends on his attitude towards you, you can't afford to risk it. I'll take Toby on Sunday — at least he doesn't have any quarrel with me.'

'You make it sound as if I'd be threatening him with a carving knife or something.' Harriet got up and went to make the coffee. 'I feel so frustrated, I just want to clear it all up and get *on* with my life, and I can't.'

'By this time next week,' Daphne said, as the coffee machine began to cough and gurgle through its cycle, 'you'll be wondering what all the fuss was about, and why you were ever so worried.'

'I'm sure you're right,' Harriet said, with much more optimism than she actually felt. 'But I've gone to a lot of trouble constructing a nice new secure world for Toby. I really don't want it shattered again, and if it happens because Edward just feels like being belatedly spiteful, then I shall find it very hard to forgive him.'

21

'You've got a nerve, coming here.'

For once in her life utterly taken aback, Daphne stared at Edward, standing belligerently in the doorway of his house. She said, in her most majestic Lady Bracknell voice, 'I *beg* your pardon?'

'You know what I mean,' Edward growled. 'And if you think I'm going to stand here making polite conversation, you've got another think coming. Come on in, Toby.'

The little boy stood uncertainly between the two adults, his face a picture of bewildered distress. 'I don't want to,' he said, although he had been looking forward to this visit for days.

'I've got a new video for you,' said Edward, who had learnt a little cunning over the past few weeks, if nothing else. 'It's all cued up and ready to play.'

Toby still paused, turning back to Daphne to seek her reassurance. Concealing her considerable misgivings, she smiled at him. 'Go on, Toby, go with your daddy.'

'That's right, come on,' said Edward, giving the child what he obviously believed to be an encouraging grin, rather too full of teeth. 'It's a new Tom and Jerry.'

To Daphne's relief, this proved a successful lure. 'Yippee!' Toby cried, and hurried indoors before she could say goodbye.

'And don't bother coming back,' Edward snarled. 'I'll drop him off when it's time.' And he shut the door in Daphne's face.

Angered and astonished by his rudeness, she considered ringing the bell and telling him what she thought of him, but that would do Harriet's cause no good at all, so she walked thoughtfully back to the car. Obviously, he considered Daphne to be Harriet's partner in whatever crime she was supposed to have committed. But he had given her no chance to ask why he was so upset.

Although she did her best to make light of the episode to Harriet, it worried both women. It was a dull afternoon, lightly overcast, and Daphne spent it in the garden, surveying and recording. Her book was planned to cover the span of a year, to run from January to December, but she had actually begun the notes and research last June, so it was all but finished. Still, she could not resist investigating the progress of her favourite corners: the bog area by the canal, the rabbit colony in the ditch beyond the hedge which separated her garden from the park, and the meadow flowers in her unmown lawn, now at their summit of glory.

Harriet, meanwhile, was sitting at the patio table, trying to concentrate on a painting of ox-eye daisies. Normally, she would not be anxious while Toby was visiting his father, but Daphne's account of Edward's manner was so alarming, despite her attempts to play the incident down, that she could not help fearing that he would refuse to return the child to her. And still she could not think of any reason that could rationally justify the sudden alteration in his behaviour towards her, and Daphne.

She was inexpressibly relieved when, at five minutes past six, she heard a horn out at the front of the house. She ran round to the gate and was just in time to see the BMW accelerate away, over the canal bridge. And Toby, beaming, rushed to hug her. 'Look, Mum, Dad took me to McDonald's and I got this cool toy!'

All seemed well, and her worst, wild imaginings appeared ridiculous now. Smiling, Harriet took him up for his bath. Highly excited, he took a long time to calm down for bed, but at last she had tucked him up with Lambkin, warm and clean and drowsy after several stories, and bent to kiss him good night.

'Mum?' Toby enquired sleepily, as she turned to go. 'Mum, *you* like Daphne, don't you?'

Harriet's heart clenched with apprehension. 'Of course I do, darling. You do too, don't you?'

'Yes, but Daddy doesn't.'

'I'm sure he likes her really.'

'No, he doesn't, he was horrible to her today.'

'I expect he was in a bad mood about something,' Harriet said reassuringly. 'Nothing to do with Daphne at all. He hardly knows her, how could he dislike her? Now don't worry about it. Good night, sleep tight — '

'And don't let the bugs bite,' said Toby, completing the ritual phrase. ''Night, Mum.'

He sounded more cheerful, but she went downstairs only partly comforted. More than ever, she longed to storm round to the boatyard and find out what on earth Edward was playing at. How dare he upset Toby, when she had gone to such great lengths to ensure that the split between his parents affected him as little as possible?

But she couldn't do anything. She was forced to be passive, to remain silent, to keep her rage in check at the injustice, because to express her opinions would not only endanger her chances of keeping Toby, but would also distress him considerably. Once, perhaps, she had found it too easy to swallow her feelings for the sake of the status quo. Now, after two months in which she had taken her life by the scruff of its neck and shaken it into a new pattern, she seemed to be suddenly locked back into the old one. And she didn't like this terrible feeling of helplessness one bit. There was no one who could give her an answer, it seemed, no one to whom she could turn.

She was wrong, though. And the solution came from a source which she had never suspected.

On the following Tuesday, it had started to rain heavily in the middle of the morning, so she drove up to the village hall to collect Toby from playgroup. To her surprise, as she left the hall with her son and a large sticky collection of boxes glued together to make what was apparently a space ship, Juliet came up to her. 'I should have rung and saved you the journey up here, but I've mislaid your number. Would Toby like to come and play with Nicholas?'

'Now? Do you want to, sweetheart?'

'Yes *please*, Mum!' her son cried jubilantly.

'Thank you very much, Juliet,' said Harriet, with real gratitude. 'That's wonderful.'

'Not at all,' said the other woman, with a smile. 'The least I could do.'

Well, that was one in the eye for the gossips, Harriet decided, as she watched Toby climbing into the back of Juliet's car. She had noticed several mothers looking askance at her as she talked to Juliet, and hoped that now they would follow her lead. Juliet was an energetic, popular young woman, and her continued friendliness towards Harriet was deeply heartening.

As she turned into the village street, she noticed Adam Clark walking along the narrow pavement opposite, looking distinctly miserable, his thin shoulders hunched and a morose expression on his face. Harriet had long since decided that having Heather Clark for a mother would make the most determinedly cheerful person contemplate suicide, and felt a pang of pity. On impulse, she stopped the car and wound down the window. 'Do you want a lift home, Adam?'

He came over to the passenger door, looking marginally less depressed. 'Don't mind if I do.'

'No school today?' Harriet enquired brightly as he fastened his seat belt.

'Got sent home, didn't I,' said Adam glumly. 'Got flu.'

He did look rather flushed, and to confirm

it, he blew his nose with a blast that could have felled the walls of Jericho.

'You should take a hot lemon and go to bed,' Harriet advised him, waiting until a stream of traffic went by before pulling away. 'Or do I sound too much like your mother?'

Adam gave her a rather shame-faced grin. 'A bit, yeah.'

'Well, that's what mothers are for, I'm afraid. Anyway, everyone needs pampering when they're feeling down.'

'Yeah, right,' said her passenger, staring dejectedly through the windscreen at the wet road ahead. To the unenlightened, his manner verged on the half-witted, but Harriet, with acutely embarrassing memories of her own and her friends' adolescent years, knew that this was normal teenage boy behaviour.

Well, she thought, its not his fault. Determined to draw him out of his shell a little, she added, 'You must be taking your GCSEs this year.'

'No, not till next summer.'

Good grief, thought Harriet, almost a proper sentence — *and* a word of more than one syllable! Encouraged, she went on. 'I bet you get sick of people asking, but what's your best subject?'

The answer was quite unexpected. 'Art,' said Adam, with slightly more animation. 'I really like that. Painting and drawing and stuff.'

'Do you want to go to art college when you leave school?'

'Might, yeah — *if* Mum'll let me.'

There was real resentment in his voice. Sympathetically, Harriet said, 'My parents weren't too keen on me going to art school either, but I managed to talk them round in the end.'

'You went to art school? Which one? What did you do?' Suddenly, the flood-gates were open, the questions came tumbling out. Amazed, and rather pleased, Harriet said, 'I went to Bristol, to do fine art. But I gave it up halfway through — it wasn't really my sort of thing.'

'Do you paint stuff, then?'

'Yes — I do watercolours, flowers, land-scapes. Much too old-fashioned for most of my teachers. What do you want to do?'

'Cartoons, illustrations, 'n' things. I'd like to draw comic books, Tank Girl, stuff like that. Mrs Field, she's my teacher, she says I'm really good, but Mum thinks I ought to get a proper job like Dad's. And he's an *accountant*,' said Adam, with as much disgust as if Keith Clark had been an axe-murderer or a child molester.

'If it's what you really want to do, then try

to persuade her. I know she's quite a determined sort of person — '

'Too right!' Adam muttered.

' — but once she sees you're serious, then perhaps she'll change her mind.'

'Mum's never changed her mind in her life.'

'Well, there's always a first time. But anyway, if you want to be a graphic artist, then go all out for it. Or you'll wake up in twenty years' time and really regret you never did. That's what almost happened to me, but I was lucky — I landed the job with Daphne.'

'Job? What sort of job?'

'Well, you know she's writing a book about her garden? I'm helping her — I'm doing the typing and the illustrations.'

'You're living there because you're *working* for her?'

'Well, not quite — I needed somewhere to live after I split up with Edward, and Daphne came to my rescue, but, yes, it is quite handy being able to work at home.'

'Then it's not true, what Mum's been saying about you and Miss James?'

They had reached the top of Stony Lane. There was a gateway on the left, and Harriet swerved into it, stopped the car and turned to face him, suddenly afraid of what she was about to learn.

To her surprise, he had gone bright red, and he seemed considerably embarrassed. 'I don't know what your mother's been saying about me and Daphne,' she said quietly. 'So I don't know whether it's true or not.'

'She saw . . . she says . . . she's been telling everyone . . . ' Adam gulped and blurted out at last, 'That you're lezzies.'

Utterly dumbfounded, Harriet gaped at him. 'That we're *what*?'

'You know. Lezzies. Dykes. Gay.'

And suddenly everything became appallingly clear. Harriet said angrily, 'Why, for God's sake?'

'She said she saw you. At the ball. Cuddling and that.'

Harriet remembered, suddenly, her distress on the terrace at Forfar Towers, after she had told Morgan to go, and Daphne's warm, affectionate arm comforting her. She said slowly, 'I was a bit upset that evening, and Miss James just gave me a hug, that's all. Your mother must have misunderstood what she saw. I'm not gay, Adam. I can't vouch for Daphne, but I've never fancied a woman in my life, let alone slept with one. Anyway, whether I'm gay or straight, what business is it of your mother's?'

'She thinks it's disgusting.'

'That's her opinion, and I suppose she's

entitled to it, but that doesn't give her the right to tell the whole village. Especially when it isn't true, and when it might do a lot of harm.'

'What sort of harm?' Adam still, obviously, couldn't look her in the eye.

'Well, for a start I'm pretty sure it's the reason my ex-partner has just decided he wants to take Toby away from me. *And* the reason why one or two of the other mothers are giving me the cold shoulder at playgroup. *I* don't particularly mind if people think I'm gay, but the trouble is that some of them are a bit bigoted about it. And Toby's the one who'll suffer, and whatever I'm supposed to have done, *he* surely doesn't deserve it.'

'Mum wants everyone to be just like her, and if they're not she hates them,' said Adam. 'Look at Miss James.' He glanced sidelong at Harriet. 'Is *she* gay?'

'I haven't a clue,' Harriet said, with perfect truth. 'And if she is, what business is it of mine? She's a friend. And believe me, Adam, right now I need all the friends I can get.'

'I'm your friend,' said the boy, blushing, if possible, an even deeper red. 'I mean, I like you. As a friend, I mean. Could — could you give me lessons, do you think?'

'Lessons?' said Harriet. 'You mean drawing

lessons? But you already have them at school, don't you?'

'Yeah, well, Mrs Field's ancient, she's retiring next year, she don't know nothing about comic books and all that.'

'I may be thirty years younger than she is, but I don't know all that much either,' Harriet said, grinning. 'Look, Adam, normally I'd love to, but at the moment I don't think it's a very good idea. Your mother would never allow it — '

'Don't have to tell her, do I?'

'Well, what would she do if she found out I'd been teaching you behind her back? I can't do that, Adam, I'm afraid. I like to be straight with people.'

'You can't be straight with Mum, or you'd never do anything 'cept what *she* wants.'

Harriet could see he had a point, but although she sympathised with his plight, she couldn't do anything about it.

She could try and do something about the rumour-mongering, though. She paused, thinking hard. It might completely backfire on her, but at least it meant that she didn't have to be a passive victim of gossip and circumstance.

'Is she likely to be in?'

'What, you mean now?' said Adam. He evidently wasn't as half-witted as he appeared, for a look of acute alarm came over his face. 'Look, Miss Smith — Harriet — please, don't say nothing about any drawing lessons to her, not now. She'd go ballistic, and she'd want to stop me doing it at school an' all.'

'Don't worry, I'm not. I just want to tell her the truth about me. It's OK, I won't be rude or anything.'

'I wish you would,' Adam said. 'Someone ought to stand up to her.'

'Perhaps, but that someone isn't me. I just want to put my side of the story, OK? And if I can persuade her that I'm not a lesbian, then perhaps she'll try and undo some of the harm she's done.'

But even if I do get through to Heather, I'll still have to convince Edward, Harriet thought. He must have heard the gossip, too, and that's why he applied for custody of Toby. And the thought that he had been rejected in favour of another woman had evidently dealt a terrible blow to his masculine pride. Harriet hoped that she would be able to persuade him otherwise, but she knew that once he had struck his attitude, that same pride made it very difficult for him to back down and admit that he had been wrong.

'Come on,' she said, starting the engine. 'I'll drop you home, and have a word with your mother. And don't look so worried, Adam. I'm really glad you told me, because now I can do something about it, even if I have to take out a full-page ad in the local paper to deny all the allegations. So thanks, OK? And if you do need any help with your drawing, I'm always here to ask. I just want everything open and above board, that's all.'

'Wish my mum thought like that,' said Adam, with such a look of despair that despite all her bold resolution, her heart faltered a little at the thought of what lay immediately ahead.

Get it over with, Harriet told herself sternly, as the car drew up outside Heather's house. And for God's sake be as tactful as you possibly can. No throttling the bloody woman, however much you're tempted.

But she noticed, as she stood on Heather's doorstep, that the hand she reached out for the doorbell was shaking with nerves.

22

Heather had had a bad morning. Her cleaner had rung to say that she was giving in her notice, with immediate effect, because she'd got a 'proper job'. This had meant, of course, that Heather had had to go round the house herself this morning, tidying and cleaning. At least she had been able to have a good poke-about in Adam's room, but if he had any drugs or condoms hidden, she couldn't find them, only a sheaf of those revolting cartoons stuffed under the bed. With a feeling of self-righteous disgust, she had consigned them to the dustbin. It was about time he got his ridiculous ideas about going to art school out of his head. It was Ben Jarvis's bad influence, she was certain. Adam was easily led, and he had somehow got in with a very dubious crowd. She still believed him to be a good, obedient lad at heart, but you could never tell these days — look at Jessica.

And that was another source of discontent. Jessica had rung the previous evening, to say that she'd got herself a job over the summer holidays — at a *holiday camp*, for goodness' sake — and wouldn't be coming home at all.

For Heather, who had been looking forward to showing off her clever daughter to all her cronies, this was a blow only partially mitigated by the thought that if Jessica still dressed like a bag-lady and smoked and drank and swore like the proverbial trooper, then a potentially major cause of conflict would be averted. Though what kind of holiday camp would ever employ such a scarecrow was impossible to imagine. Heather was unaware that Jessica had long ago divided her life into watertight compartments, and the dreadful clothes and obnoxious behaviour were exclusively reserved for the one marked 'home'.

When the doorbell rang, she was giving the downstairs toilet a good seeing-to: Maxine, her newly ex-cleaner, was thorough and conscientious, but even she could not match Heather's exacting standards. Puffing with annoyance, she put down the brush, took off her rubber gloves, laid them precisely in the basin, untied her apron, glanced in the mirror to check that her hair was still perfect, and went to answer it.

The young woman from next door stood on the step, wearing loose navy-blue trousers, a pretty floral top, and a confident smile. Beside her, looking distinctly nervous, was Heather's son.

A riot of conflicting reasons for this unlikely association ran wildly through Heather's mind. 'Adam?' she said sharply. 'Why aren't you in school?'

'Got sent home, didn't I,' said her son sullenly. 'Flu. Harriet gave me a lift from the high street. Thanks,' he added, rather belatedly, to his benefactress.

'Well, come in,' said Heather. She reached out and grabbed her son's arm, to pull him across the threshold. With a grunt, he twisted out of her grasp, and said irritably, 'Get *off*, Mum.'

'And what are you doing here?' Heather demanded, turning to Harriet. 'I'd have thought you'd have known you wouldn't be welcome.'

'I'd like to have a word, if I may, Mrs Clark.' Harriet's voice was calm and sensible, belying the seething bubble of anger and apprehension within. 'It won't take long.'

Something in her manner made Heather, all set to slam the door in her face, pause. Adam said suddenly, 'You ought to hear it, Mum.'

'*I'll* be the judge of that, young man. Now get inside out of the rain, or you'll catch your death.'

'She didn't have to give me a lift,' Adam said doggedly. In his mother's presence, it was noticeable that his diction had improved somewhat. 'If she hadn't, I'd have got pneumonia or something, walking home.'

'Don't be so silly. Come on in, Adam.'

'Not till you've heard her,' said the boy, sticking out his lower lip. ''S only fair — you've had your say all over Sanden, now let her have hers.'

'I understand you're under the impression that Daphne and I are lesbians,' Harriet said quickly, before Heather could speak. 'And I'd like to tell you that we're not.'

'Don't be ridiculous! Of course you are, I saw you with my own eyes. It was quite disgusting, a public exhibition.'

'Where? At the ball? If it's the incident I think it is, then I was upset about something — a man, as it happens — and Daphne was offering me a friendly shoulder to cry on. And on that flimsy evidence, you've been spreading gossip about me.' She knew that she should choose her words more carefully, but she had Heather's attention now, and she couldn't waste time pausing to think. 'Normally it wouldn't bother me, but I think you should know that because of the rumours, my ex-partner is now trying to obtain custody of my son.'

'And a good thing too, in my opinion,' said Heather righteously. 'People like you

318

shouldn't have children.'

'I have just told you, Mrs Clark. I am not a lesbian. I have never been to bed with a woman. I am exclusively heterosexual. You have got hold of the wrong end of the stick, because of some silly misunderstanding, and on that basis my ex-partner is trying to take my son away from me. I'd managed to come to an amicable arrangement with Edward for Toby's sake, and now your gossip has ruined all that.'

'You can't pull the wool over my eyes,' Heather said. 'I *saw* the two of you, carrying on, plain as the nose on my face! And then you have the cheek to come here and deny it! I've never heard such rubbish!'

'Listen,' said Harriet, with such desperate vehemence that it gave even Heather pause. 'It shouldn't matter whether I'm a lesbian or not — what really counts is whether Toby's better off with me, his mother, than with a father who's too busy shagging everything in a skirt to care about looking after him properly. Do you know why I finally left Edward, Mrs Clark? I left him because *Toby* — not me, *Toby* — found him in bed making love to another woman. And she wasn't the first, not by a long chalk. Do you *really* think he's the best person to look after a small boy? I certainly don't.'

'What malicious lies! Mr Armstrong would never do such a thing!'

'Oh, wouldn't he? And you know all about malicious lies, Mrs Clark — you've been spreading them with a vengeance, all round the village. That's called slander, and it's not a very nice thing to do. I really do think you ought to apologise, and start trying to undo some of the harm you've done to me and Daphne.'

'I'll do no such thing,' Heather said fervently. 'Now let me tell *you*, Miss High-and-Mighty Smith, you've both got no more than you deserve, and if your poor little boy is taken away, then as far as I'm concerned that's the best thing for him.' Her cheeks burned brightly under the powder, her blue eyes were distended with rage, and small flecks of spittle had gathered at the corners of her lipsticked mouth. 'It's a disgrace.'

Harriet saw her expression and knew that she was making very little impression on Heather's armour of bigotry. Suddenly, she wanted no more of the ugly confrontation. 'Please have a good think about it,' she said urgently. 'I'm sure when you've calmed down a bit, you'll realise I'm telling the truth. And if you do, it'd be nice to have an apology, at the very least.' She glanced sympathetically at Adam, who was scarlet with embarrassment

— or perhaps, she realised as she saw the look in his eyes, with anger. 'Goodbye, Mrs Clark. And thank you for your time.'

She glanced back as she walked away down the drive. Heather was still standing in the doorway, staring at her. Then Adam left his mother's side and came sprinting across the gravel towards her. 'You were great, really great! You really laid it on her!'

'She won't listen,' said Harriet. She was shaking, and close to tears, and desperate to get away before the reaction caught up with her. 'She's still convinced she's right. I'm sorry, Adam, I've probably completely scuppered your chances of drawing lessons.'

'Don't worry, it'll be OK,' said Adam, with an encouraging grin. 'Fast as she's telling lies, I'll be telling the truth.'

'I don't want to be the cause of any bad feeling between you and your mother,' said Harriet firmly, although the look on Heather's face, even from this distance, indicated all too clearly that there was going to be plenty of animosity between her and Adam, very shortly. 'Look, I'd better go before there's any more trouble. Thank you, Adam. And I'm really sorry about all this.'

'Adam! Come here *at once*!'

'Better do as I'm told,' said the boy, and, with a final grin and a wave, went back across the gravel. He pushed rudely past his mother and vanished into the house.

As the door slammed behind them, Harriet ran through the rain to the car and scrambled inside. She was frightened by the intensity of the rage that filled her. It had taken a supreme effort of self-control to restrain herself from punching the fanatical glare from Heather's face. She leaned her forehead on the steering wheel, and took several deep, calming breaths. And then, with the smell of burnt boats wafting acridly round her mind, she drove the few yards back to Holly Cottage.

Inside her own immaculate abode, Heather poured a very generous sherry, still trying to calm herself. What a dreadful episode! What a very rude, unpleasant young woman! How *dare* she speak like that! And her accusations had been deeply upsetting. *Malicious lies,* indeed — when she, Heather, had only been telling the truth.

But as she sank into her soft, enveloping armchair, and tried not to listen to the shattering thud of Adam's stereo, turned up aggressively loud in his room above, unaccustomed doubts began to crowd in on her feelings of self-righteous rage. Miss Smith had been so heartfelt in her denials that she had almost seemed convincing. And what about Mr Armstrong? He was a very charming man, of course, but she had heard a lot of gossip about him over the years, and he had a considerable reputation as a ladies' man. If the little boy *had* found him in bed with some woman, then Miss Smith's anger would be entirely justified.

Appalled, Heather considered, very briefly, the possibility that she might have been mistaken, and then flung the idea away in revulsion. I will *not* apologise to her, she thought vehemently. Not after the way she spoke to me.

But the very fact that she could even contemplate the humiliating idea of being in the wrong was an indication of the effect Harriet's impassioned argument had had on her.

*   *   *

Daphne was in the kitchen, slicing bread: she looked up as her lodger burst in. 'You're in a rush! What, no Toby?'

'At his friend Nicholas's for lunch.' Harriet shut the door behind her and took a deep breath. 'I've found out what all this trouble's about. And I think you ought to sit down.'

Daphne stared at her in concern. 'What on earth is it? Are you all right?'

'I'm fine. Just very, very angry. And you will be too, in a minute, so I should put the bread knife away and sit down.'

Obviously bewildered, Daphne did as she proposed. 'Come on,' she said, as the younger woman still hesitated. 'It can't surely be as bad as all that.'

'Oh yes it is,' said Harriet. And as calmly and dispassionately as she could, told Daphne what Adam had said.

As she spoke, disconcertingly, Daphne began to laugh. 'She thinks we're *lesbians*! Oh dear, the stupid, silly, pathetic woman. So that's what this is all about!' She glanced at Harriet's face and added, 'What's the matter?'

'I'm sorry — I can't laugh about it. All the trouble she's caused between me and Edward, I could throttle her.'

'Oh, come on, anyone with half an eye will realise it's all nonsense! And anyway, why should being a lesbian mean you're a bad mother?'

'It's what Heather thinks. It's what Edward thinks. And it could be what the judge will think, too. If he's some crusty old bigot with a moral viewpoint straight out of the ark — '

'No reason why he should be. They're trying to get that sort off the bench and into retirement. Anyway, it isn't true, is it? Not about you, anyway.'

Harriet had taken off her glasses to wipe her eyes with a rather damp tissue. She stared at Daphne in surprise. 'What do you mean? Are you . . .'

'A lesbian? No, as it happens — but not entirely straight either. Don't look so shocked, it's not unusual. I'm not some crusty old spinster straight out of an ivory tower, you know. I packed a fair bit of living into my years at Cambridge — mostly men, I grant you, but one or two women as well.'

Harriet continued to stare at her in astonishment. She had always thought of her friend as essentially sexless, a creature of the intellect, not of the senses. And now she was sitting there, calmly admitting to a string of affairs that would have done credit to a woman half her age. At last she said, 'I didn't know.'

'Young people can never imagine the older generation having any kind of sex life,' said Daphne, with some asperity. 'Let alone a full and varied one. Anyway, that doesn't matter. What matters is that you've found out why Edward wants custody of Toby, and now you know the reason, you can fight him. I should ring your solicitor at once.'

Harriet glanced at her watch. It was only half past twelve. Less than half an hour ago, she had been waiting at playgroup. And in that brief time, her world and her perceptions had been turned upside down and thoroughly shaken.

She dialled the number without much hope of getting straight through to Potter, but to her surprise he was available. Briefly, she explained the situation, and found him surprisingly helpful. 'And these allegations are completely untrue?'

'Of course they are,' Harriet said vehemently. 'Anyway, it shouldn't make any difference to my case, even if I was a lesbian. What should matter is whether I'm the best person to bring Toby up.'

'Unfortunately, in the past that was not always the most important factor,' said Potter. 'For instance, some judges have thought that the child in question may suffer long-term psychiatric harm from living in such circumstances. Even now, many people feel that a child brought up by a lesbian mother may suffer problems in acquiring a sexual identity, or be teased or bullied at school. However, in these more enlightened times, I am bound to say that recent decisions have gone in the mother's favour, although sometimes not without a considerable battle.

In a case a few years ago, for instance, a consultant psychiatrist spoke in support of the mother's application and stated that fears of stigma or sexual identity problems were unfounded, and the mother and her girlfriend were granted custody. If the mother can be shown to be the best and most fit person to have care of her child, then her sexual orientation should not of itself be a bar to granting her custody.'

'Anyway, that's all quite irrelevant,' said Harriet, wondering if he was quoting at length from a textbook: it certainly sounded like it. 'I'm not a lesbian, and I'd be happy to swear to that on oath, if necessary.'

'I'm sure it won't be, Miss Smith. It seems to be purely a case of a simple misunderstanding, unfortunately compounded by malicious gossip. I shall ring Mr Armstrong's solicitor immediately, and acquaint him with the facts. Don't worry, my dear, I'm sure it will all be sorted out without ever having to go to court. Mr Armstrong is a reasonable man — '

'Not about this, he isn't.'

'Well, he of all people must be well aware that you are not a lesbian.'

'You don't know him,' said Harriet. 'Once he's got an idea fixed in his head, it can take an earthquake to shift it. But at least I know

now what the problem is, I can do something about it.'

'I should acquire a passionate boyfriend as soon as possible,' said Potter, laughing with a cheerful insensitivity that set her teeth on edge. 'And make sure you're seen with him in public.'

Georgia, a few minutes later, was thinking along the same lines, although rather more specifically. 'I should give that Morgan bloke a ring, if he's still sniffing about. He must be good for something, after all.'

'No,' said Harriet, with a firmness that surprised both her and her sister. 'I wouldn't dream of using him for anything like that. It'd leave a nasty taste in my mouth.'

'Good grief, you've become very scrupulous all of a sudden! I thought there was nothing you wouldn't do to keep Toby.'

'There isn't, but I don't like the thought of using Morgan for my own ends.'

'Why not? *He* used *you*, didn't he? Ate you up and spat you out. Give him a taste of his own medicine.'

'I already have,' said Harriet, thinking of that intense conversation on the steps at Forfar Towers. 'Anyway, do as you would be done by, and I don't like being used myself. I got enough of it from Edward to last a lifetime.'

'Listen, take it from big sis, the world is divided into two — the users and the used. Join the sharks, for a change.'

'No,' said Harriet again. 'Sorry, but I'm going to do this my own way. And I'll only drag Morgan in as a very last resort.'

'Well, don't come crying to me if it all goes pear-shaped,' said Georgia, her scorn rather obvious. 'Anyway, from what I remember of him, he's not the type to fade away into the background, is he? So take my advice and take advantage.'

But Harriet thought, as she put the phone down, that Morgan deserved more, much more than that. She remembered how gentle and understanding he had been, when she had explained about her fear of losing Toby. She was acutely aware of the irony, that somehow, against all her inclinations, against all that had happened in the past, she had come to like and respect him again. And he was not in fact the cause of her present predicament. Indeed, if she listened to Potter and Georgia, he could be her salvation.

But I don't want it to be like that, she thought. If there's ever anything between us again, I want it to be open and honest and straight, right from the start, or it won't be worth it.

And the very fact that she could contemplate the renewal of their long-ago
relationship was an indication of how very
much her feelings had changed, over the past
few days.

23

After lunch, which was a rather quiet, thoughtful affair, Harriet told Daphne that she was going to take Maggie for a walk. 'I suppose I ought to be sitting by the phone, waiting for some response from Edward's solicitors, but they probably won't be in touch before tomorrow, and I feel I have to get out, or there's a risk of me going bananas.' She grinned at Daphne. 'I hate sitting around waiting for things to happen.'

'I agree entirely. Has it stopped raining?'

'Yes, but it wouldn't make any difference if there was a monsoon out there,' Harriet told her. 'Come on, Mags, let's go!'

The dog, of course, was keen to go out whatever the weather, and as she hadn't had a walk yet that day, her frisking was more than usually exuberant. Harriet clipped the extending lead on to her collar, and glanced at her watch. Half past one. She had well over an hour before Juliet was due to drop Toby back. She could go along the towpath, east towards Devizes so as to run no risk of encountering Edward. She could walk along the footpath that ran below Sanden on its ridge, across the fields towards the village hall and the playing fields.

Or she could take Maggie across the park towards Forfar Towers, and see if she could find Morgan.

I should tell him Edward's custody application is nothing to do with him, Harriet justified the idea to herself as she climbed over the gate into the park. It's only fair. More than that, she would refuse to ask, although already her heart was beating faster at the prospect of seeing him.

There were cattle grazing in the park, so she kept Maggie on the lead, much to the dog's disgust. It was just as well, because the beasts were young, and extremely curious. Feeling rather like a bovine Pied Piper, Harriet walked briskly along the path, stalked, rather more closely than she would have liked, by a dozen heifers, breathing heavily and following Maggie's every move with their soft, long-lashed brown eyes. Far from being frightened, the dog was just as fascinated as the cows, and kept trying to turn back to investigate. If I'd come with the band of the Royal Marines, fifty majorettes and a banner over my head, I couldn't have announced my arrival more clearly, Harriet thought wryly as she cut across the side of the hill to the site of the underground house that was apparently called The Pits.

In the four or five weeks since she had last seen it at close quarters, the site had changed out of all recognition. The mounds of earth were still there, grouped around the edge of the quarry, but the scraped-out hole in the ground had been filled with what looked at first like three huge grey bubbles, blown in cement. To Harriet's relief, the area was now surrounded by a single-strand electric fence. She ducked underneath and walked with Maggie towards the underground house, leaving the cows staring disconsolately after them.

The three bubbles had been sliced down their outer edges, leaving three wide, arched openings, looking down the hillside, over the canal and across the valley to Sandridge and Bowden beyond. Harriet paused, letting her eyes travel across the green Wiltshire countryside. She could imagine the house finished, grassed over so that from a distance no one would know it was there, and put herself sitting on the terrace — that further corner would be a morning sun-trap — eating her breakfast, drinking coffee, and gazing at that glorious view. The picture was so vivid and powerful that for a moment she blinked, surprised that it was not real.

Someone emerged from within the house,

wearing jeans and an open-necked shirt, and carrying a yellow hard hat. She recognised Morgan in the same instant that Maggie, with her usual overwhelming friendliness, rushed to greet him, tail wagging, and nearly pulling her over in the process.

'Hallo, dog, you're pleased to see me!' Morgan bent to fondle her ears and pat her. Maggie, in an ecstasy of obeisance, promptly flopped down on to the wet ground and rolled over, displaying a rather large and grubby white stomach for his delectation. The lead by now was hopelessly tangled round her legs, and Harriet knelt to unwind it. 'Stupid dog!' she said. 'Sorry — she can be such a nuisance.'

'I don't mind.' As she got up, reeling in the surplus yards of lead, she met his eyes, and felt herself blushing. He added, the Welsh lilt much more pronounced than usual, 'I thought you didn't want us to meet for a while, *cariad.*'

'That's all changed,' Harriet said. 'I came up here to tell you — I thought you ought to know. I've found out what the problem was, and it's nothing whatsoever to do with you.' She smiled at him, rather shyly. 'I'm really sorry, Morgan, I was almost certain it wasn't, but I couldn't be a hundred per cent sure.'

'And you couldn't afford to take the risk. I

know, *cariad*, I do understand.'

'Thank you,' Harriet said. 'I mean, even if it *was*, *I* know you're OK, you were so good with Toby that day on the hill, I could tell . . . ' Her voice trailed away in confusion. 'Sorry,' she added again. 'I hope you don't mind too much. I'd better go now.'

'No you don't,' said Morgan. 'Not now you're here. So what was the problem really, or don't you want to tell me?'

Harriet's blush became, if anything, even deeper. She realised, with horror, that there was a real danger that she would cry, and that would be the crowning humiliation. Her whole strategy with Morgan depended on her being confident, bright, in control. Once give him a hint that she was vulnerable, and he'd leap in, never taking no for an answer, someone else who wanted to run her life for her. She said, 'It doesn't matter. Come on, Maggie, we ought to get back.'

'It very obviously does matter,' said Morgan. 'Aren't we friends again? Can't you tell me?'

With a desperate effort, Harriet banished the tears and kept her voice firm. 'OK,' she said, as casually as she could. 'It's all a stupid misunderstanding. Somehow Edward has got it into his head that Daphne and I are having a lesbian affair.'

For an instant there was complete silence. She could hear the traffic on the main road, far away, the cawing of some rooks, someone hammering something inside one of the bubbles. Then Morgan shook his head in disbelief. 'Jesus, where did he get that idea from? *Nothing* could be further from the truth.' He grinned at her suddenly. 'I can vouch for how extremely heterosexual you are, *cariad*.'

'That won't be necessary,' said Harriet drily, her composure restored. 'I'm sure I can convince the judge by myself.'

'But it's serious, though, isn't it?' Morgan's eyes were resting on her thoughtfully. 'What a criminal waste. I mean, there you were, shacked up for years with a man so stupid and imperceptive that he honestly thinks it's your fault rather than his.'

And there he had cut to the heart of it. Harriet thought of those brief, impersonal and pleasureless couplings that Edward had inflicted on her in the dying stages of their relationship. And rather than believe that his own deficiencies were to blame for her abrupt departure, he had assumed that her alleged lesbianism was the reason.

'And the real irony is that he's applied for custody on 'moral grounds', while leading a less than moral life himself,' she said, trying not to sound too bitter. But why shouldn't I? she thought. I have every right to feel like that.

'You deserve a lot better,' Morgan said softly. 'And I shall give serious consideration to punching his teeth down his throat, the next time I meet him.'

Despite herself, Harriet laughed. 'And when's that likely to be? You don't exactly move in the same circles.'

'On the contrary — Marcus had him and Selina over for dinner the other night.'

'Could have been awkward. So what did you do?'

'Well, since Selina and I split up, I've been living in the stable flat, so I tactfully made myself scarce. I am not without resources, you know.'

'I do know. But listen, Morgan, seriously — *please* don't get in any kind of fight, or even an argument, with Edward. I've had enough of trouble in that department, I'm up to here with it, and I just couldn't take any more, OK?'

'Anyway, he's hardly likely to win, is he?' said Morgan. 'Sooner or later, he's got to realise he's made a major error of judgement — and preferably before it ever comes to court.'

'That's what my solicitor thinks, but I can't

help feeling frightened — the thought of what would happen if Edward took Toby away from me — '

'He won't,' Morgan assured her, with his usual arrogant confidence. 'Because I'm going to make damn sure he doesn't. Starting now. Have you got time for a drink at the Wharf?'

Startled, Harriet looked at her watch. 'Yes, if it's a quick one, but I don't think that's a very good idea — '

'Tough, you're coming with me. I'll run you back in the Shogun.' He took hold of her hand, and his expression became suddenly wild and joyful. 'Come on, *cariad*, let's give the gossips something to think about!'

Which was how, a few minutes later, Harriet found herself steered into the Wharf Inn, Morgan's long arm curved protectively round her shoulder. The dark, smoky, low-ceilinged bar was still crowded with lunch-time drinkers who had nipped out from Melksham or Devizes for a quick pint and one of the excellent meals for which the pub was justly famous. Harriet glanced round quickly, but could see no one she knew, which rather removed the point of the exercise.

But it was quite like old times, to stand here at the bar, feeling his vivid warmth so close to her, their bodies almost touching. She glanced surreptitiously sideways at him as he leaned across the counter to attract the landlord's attention. At this proximity, she could see the subtle lines of laughter around his eyes, and the tucked corners of his mouth that made him look as if he was about to smile, even at his most serious moments, and a renewed wave of longing engulfed her. I have never stopped loving him, she thought. After everything he's done, all that has happened, despite the gulf lying between us, I still feel the same about him as I did ten years ago.

'Half of cider,' said Morgan, passing the tankard to her. 'Anything to eat? I'm going to have a ploughman's.'

She shook her head. 'No thanks — I've had lunch already.'

'Then you'll have to share my pickled onions,' said Morgan, grinning. 'Because you won't want me kissing you unless you've had one too.'

'And who said I'm going to let you kiss me?' Harriet demanded indignantly, while within, her heart leapt at the prospect.

'I did. We're going to go outside, and sit in full public view of anyone passing by, and I'm going to kiss you again and again until they all get the message.'

'No, you can't!'

'Why not? I can't think of a better way to spread the word that you're no more a lesbian than I am. Unless, of course ... ' The mischievous look that she loved so much infused his face. 'How about the war memorial by the church, twelve o'clock Sunday, clothes optional? I've always fancied doing it in front of the vicar.'

'Morgan!'

'Well, perhaps not, as there's probably a law against it.'

'Since when has that ever stopped you?'

'More times than you'd think, *cariad*. Come on, let's get started, and perhaps the odious Edward will look out of his window and see us.'

Still protesting, Harriet was towed outside, attracting not a few curious glances, and installed at one of the tables grouped on the terrace between the pub and the road. As Morgan sat down beside her, she said vehemently, 'No, I can't let you do this!'

'Why not, *cariad*? It'd solve everything.' He grinned at her again. 'Proves you're not gay, and gives me the chance to succumb to temptation.'

'No, you mustn't,' Harriet said. 'Listen, I don't *want* to make a great show of it like this.'

'Why not?'

'You always say that.' Harriet took a deep breath. 'Because it isn't fair on you. I'd just be using you.'

'And if I want to be used, isn't that my business?'

His eyes were bright, and hungry, and compelling. She could smell the tang of some very expensive aftershave, mixed lightly with sweat and the scent of the flowers profuse in their tubs all around them. She said stubbornly, 'No. I want it to happen because it's spontaneous and inevitable and *right* — not like this.'

The admission had been a major mistake, she saw it at once in his face. 'Oh, *cariad*,' he said, so softly that she could hardly hear him, and suddenly his arms were around her and his lips were seeking hers. 'It has always been right.'

She had no idea how long the embrace lasted: only that the feelings which flooded her were almost more than she could contain. Then something banged down on the table, someone coughed pointedly, and she drew back in time to see one of the pub's kitchen staff, a middle-aged woman who had once worked as a cleaner at the boatyard, staring at them with raised eyebrows.

'Thanks,' said Morgan casually, with the

smile that had charmed many far more hostile than this. Harriet, feeling she ought to acknowledge the woman's presence, added shyly, 'Hello, Yvonne. This is Morgan, he's an old friend.'

'And a very good one, by the look of it,' said the woman caustically. 'Still, better than some, eh? Enjoy your meal, sir.' And she turned and went back inside the pub.

'What did I tell you?' said Morgan, gleefully triumphant. 'Worked a treat. It'll be all over the village by tea-time.'

'They'll probably just think I'm AC/DC.'

'Isn't that a bit sophisticated for Sanden?'

'Undoubtedly.' To her relief, Harriet had managed to recover some of her composure, though part of her, a very substantial part, wanted to invite him to rip her clothes off and make love to her, there and then on the splintery old table, in full and glorious view of everyone in the pub, not to mention passing traffic.

'You know what I'd like to do now?' Morgan murmured, ignoring his plough-man's, rapidly warming up in the sun. 'I'd like to take all your clothes off and make mad, passionate love to you, right here.'

'What a very strange man you are.'

'And what a strange woman you are, not to want it.'

342

'Who said I didn't want it?'

'*Do* you?' His hands slid seductively around her, and one inveigled its way between the buttons of her shirt. 'Darling Hal, there's more of you than there used to be.' He was doing things to her breast that made her gasp. 'And don't hit me — it's meant to be a compliment.'

'Please — I think you ought to stop. People are looking.'

A couple of young businessmen, sharp in expensive suits and carrying mobile phones, were giving them appreciative glances as they walked past. With a last, desperate effort to wrench back some control of herself and the situation, Harriet pulled his hand away and stood up. 'Look, Morgan, I'm sorry, but I have to go.'

'No you don't — I said I'd run you back in the Shogun.'

'Even if you do, I've got to go.' She could see herself reflected in one of the pub's windows, her hair coming out of its plait, glasses skewed, buttons undone, her face flushed with passion. She said urgently, 'It's not because I don't want you — I do, very much. But it's too soon, too sudden, I'm not *ready* for this — please, let me have time to think, I'm not giving you the brush-off or anything, I just want some space to get my act together, OK?'

She was standing between him and the sun, and his face, eyes narrowed against the light, was unreadable. She went on. 'Please don't be hurt or offended — '

'You ought to know by now, I don't get offended.'

'I do know.' With something between a laugh and a sob, Harriet stared down at him. 'I need some time to sort my feelings out, that's all. I'm not saying I don't want to be seen with you or be friends with you.'

'I know you're not.' With the lithe grace she had always admired, he got to his feet and stood in front of her, looking down into her face. 'You're right. We do need time.' He grinned suddenly. 'Time to get to know each other again, OK? It's been ten years, and we've both changed a lot.'

'Yes. As you so tactlessly pointed out just now.'

'I'm sorry, *cariad*. But for the better, huh? We can't go back to the way we were then, but I'm more than happy with the way we are now. And if you need a friend, I'll always be here, darling Hal. *Always*. You know that, don't you?'

'I know,' said Harriet, thinking, But I couldn't trust you before. Have you changed enough that I can trust you now?

'Thanks,' she added. 'I've got to go, or Toby will be wondering where I am. I'll see you soon.'

'Hey!' he called after her as she went hastily through the gate. 'Haven't you forgotten something?'

Maggie, self-abasingly apologetic, was still tied to the drainpipe by the door, where Harriet had left her before going into the pub. Contrite, she rushed back to release her. 'Sorry, old girl, I just wasn't thinking straight.'

'I can't imagine why,' said Morgan, watching her. 'Come on, at least accept that lift.'

'What about your ploughman's?'

'Sod the ploughman's. This is much, much more important.'

'OK, I will,' Harriet told him, smiling suddenly. 'As long as you *promise* not to jump on me when I'm not expecting it.'

'Cub's honour, cross my heart and hope to die.'

'Surely you weren't ever a Cub!'

'Oh yes I was, for all of three weeks — until they kicked me out.'

'What did you do? Smoke in the toilets? Blow up the hut? Handcuff a Brownie to the railings?'

'What d'you take me for, a pervert? No, I

gave two fingers to Akela. And before you ask, I can't remember why, but she was a horrible old battle-axe.'

'She probably had to be, if the rest of the pack was anything like you,' Harriet told him. She tucked her arm in his as they strolled out into the road. 'So where's this fancy car, then?'

'The Shogun? Back by The Pits.'

'Perhaps it might be quicker to walk.'

'Maybe, but then you wouldn't have the pleasure of my company, would you?'

'You're completely impossible, did you know that?'

'Of course I know. Brain and ego the size of a small planet, and *still* you won't let me near you.'

'I might, eventually, if you're very, *very* good.'

'Of course I am. My walls are lined with testimonials from grateful young ladies.'

'Then they can't be ladies.' Harriet felt an irrepressible sense of laughter bubbling up inside her. They had slipped so easily back into the old teasing banter she remembered from the past that the intervening ten years might never have happened. Under the spell of his mood and his sense of fun, all her problems seemed to shrink and wither away.

With his next words, they loomed back

346

again. 'Isn't that Edward, giving us the evil eye?'

They were just passing the entrance to the boatyard, almost opposite the stile into the park. Edward was standing by the canal's edge, staring. Unabashed, Morgan gave him a cheery wave with his free hand. 'That's one in his eye. He won't know what to think now.'

'He'll think I've staged this. Which is true, in a manner of speaking.'

'So what? It doesn't make any difference to the fact that you're not and never have been what he thinks you are, and anyone with any sense can see that. And it won't do any harm to let people assume that we're more than just friends. We can have a bit of fun while we're getting to know each other again.'

And you can get to know Toby, too. The thought was almost spoken, but something made Harriet pause. The prospect of Morgan becoming acquainted with her son implied so many things that he had once rejected: responsibility, commitment, maturity. And she knew that these qualities were essential if their relationship was to have any hope of resurrection. One kiss in a pub forecourt didn't count. What counted was the way he treated Toby. She could imagine, only too clearly, the damage that would be done if he gained the little boy's affections, only to vanish from his life without warning. Her feelings didn't matter. She had coped with betrayal before, and she could do it again. But she could not bear the thought of Toby being deserted by another father figure. It wasn't fair, and she couldn't risk doing it to him, any more than she could risk losing care of him to Edward.

No, nothing less than commitment would ever do. But he had said he had changed. She had already seen convincing evidence of it, up on the hill. So perhaps she would not be putting her son's happiness in danger after all, if she allowed Morgan back into her life and her heart.

24

It took some time to get Maggie into the Shogun, which was much higher off the ground than she was used to. Persuasion, even with the aid of a handful of doggie chocs, proved inadequate, and Harriet found the sight of Morgan trying to heave the dog bodily into the back highly amusing. 'You'll get a hernia if you do it like that — she weighs at least seven stone.'

'What in God's name do you feed her on, cream cakes?'

'She wishes!' Harriet joined him, and eventually they succeeded, with much puffing and panting from all three participants. 'Daphne says there are only three things she definitely *won't* eat — cucumbers, tomatoes, mushrooms and banana skins.'

'That's four. What about what's inside the skins?'

'Oh, she eats bananas. And apples. And carrots. Daphne left her in the car with her shopping once, while she went to the cash point, and when she got back Maggie had scoffed the lot. Three bags full. Including a coffee and walnut gateau, and a piece of

Stilton, still in its wrapper. Needless to say, all came back up later, but it didn't put her off. Dustbins on four legs, that's what Labradors are.'

Knowing she was being discussed, the dog was wearing her embarrassed face, her ears slightly back and a sheepish grin lifting her mouth. Morgan gave her a final pat and shut the tailgate. 'Let's hope the suspension can stand the strain. Which way home? By the road, or across the park?'

'Road,' Harriet said instantly, and knew she had made the safer choice when she saw his face fall. 'Shame. I was looking forward to showing this thing off. Good, isn't it?'

'Beats that awful old van you had.' She climbed into the passenger seat and buckled up her seat belt. 'The tatty blue Transit.'

'That was the rustbucket from hell. Three weeks after I bought it, the gear lever broke off, and I used to drive about with my mate Dave lying in the passenger footwell, changing gear to order with a monkey wrench.'

'How many penalty points on your licence? You did *have* a licence, didn't you?'

'Of course I did. A provisional one. You got me through my test, remember?'

'So I did. And you said . . . '

We must be made for each other, cariad, *if*

we're still together after you taught me to drive.

She glanced sideways as he put the Shogun into reverse and backed it up on to the track which led from the quarry to the driveway of Forfar Towers. If he recalled his words, he gave no indication of it. He said, 'Would you like me to show you round The Pits some time? If you're not too busy, that is.'

'Whatever gives you the idea I'm busy?' She grinned at him as he steered the big car round a prominent lump of slag iron. 'I've only got the illustrations for Daphne's book to finish, and Toby to look after.'

'Well, bring him too, if you like.'

'He's not too keen on the dark.'

'My dear girl, we do have electric light. But I have to admit an ulterior motive. I need your eye for interior design.'

'I don't agree with organ donations from living people.'

'You know what I mean. You turned that dark, poky little flat in Bedminster into something special. Surely you've still got that sense of style?'

'I'm not sure I want to look round your underground house if it's dark and poky.' Harriet tried not to shut her eyes as the car shot precipitately out of the driveway and

351

on to the lane leading between Sanden and Sanden Row.

Morgan gave a shout of laughter. '*Will* you stop deliberately misunderstanding me? Please, *cariad*. I would really appreciate it.'

'All right,' Harriet said at last, not without some misgivings. 'But don't expect me to come up with something wonderful. And why, when the outside of The Pits looks as if it's almost finished, have you not got anything planned for the inside?'

'Of course I know what the floor-plan will be — credit me with a *little* intelligence, *cariad*.'

'I'll try.'

'The gory details, though, aren't so easy. I was waiting for inspiration to strike. The model and drawings I showed Marcus made it look very bare — a few strategically placed plants, the sort of sofa you'd never dare sit down on, acres of cream carpet.'

'I get the picture. And you want me to add a few little homely touches here and there. Like my Chinese parasol?'

'Not a lot. You haven't still got it, have you?'

'No. There wasn't much left of it after you and Dave had the mock sword fight with it and the cardboard tube.'

'Well, don't worry, I've grown out of that

sort of thing, along with throwing used teabags at innocent passers-by and driving dangerous vans in a manner calculated to terrorise other motorists.'

'Really?' said Harriet, as the Shogun scraped perilously close to the park wall in order to avoid a Land Rover coming the other way.

'Don't worry, *cariad*. I know exactly what I'm doing.'

'That's what frightens me. Look out!'

The big car swerved left down Stony Lane, narrowly missing Keith Clark's Mercedes, coming up. 'I'm beginning to wish I'd walked,' Harriet said, glancing behind her. 'Poor Maggie, she's being thrown about all over the place.'

At once, Morgan slowed right down. 'Sorry, I'd forgotten about the dog. Is she OK?'

'Seems to be. She's like all Labradors, if anything awful happens to her she's convinced it's her fault. She'll give you the full grovel when we get out.'

'I can hardly wait to have seven stone of overweight dog on my foot. Here we are, and there's Toby — perfect timing!'

Juliet's car had just pulled up in the driveway of Holly Cottage, and Toby leapt out. Hastily, Morgan stopped the Shogun, and Harriet leaned urgently out of the window. '*Careful*, sweetheart! We could have run you over!'

'Sorry, Mum,' said her son, contritely. 'What are you doing in that car?'

'I met Morgan when I was out walking Maggie, and I didn't want to be late back, so he offered me a lift. Wasn't that kind of him?'

'Morgan?' Toby's voice was doubtful.

'*You* remember — the kite-man.'

'Oh, yes,' said the little boy, his face clearing as Morgan jumped down from the driver's seat and smiled at him. 'I remember. Can we go flying with you again soon?'

'You can attach a long string to me, if you like, and pull me all over Oliver's Castle. Want to help me get Maggie out? It took *ages* to put her in. I shall have to fit a little crane at the back, to lift her in and out.'

'*Really?*' Toby was always entrancingly gullible. 'She'd like that.'

'I hope he's been good,' said Harriet to Juliet, who was hovering with a look of acute curiosity on her face, although she was obviously too polite to express it.

'Of course he has. They just disappeared into Nicholas's room and played with his Action Man all afternoon. It's great having him — I hardly know I've got them. Nicholas on his own is a pain, always whingeing round.

Is Toby the same?'

'Not so much — he's used to his own company, I suppose.' Harriet glanced round, and smiled. 'This is Morgan, an old friend of mine. Morgan, Juliet, the mother of Toby's best friend.'

'Hi,' said her former lover, shaking hands. 'Sorry, but I'd better be getting back. How about tomorrow, Hal? Three o'clock at the site OK?'

'If you're sure you don't mind Toby coming as well, that'd be fine.'

'Great. See you then, *cariad*!'

Juliet gazed after the departing Shogun with interest. 'If I wasn't happily married to Gary, I'd say that was a Grade A hunk. Known him long?'

'We lived together when we were students.'

'Ah.' Juliet's voice spoke volumes. Harriet took the plunge. 'All the rumours going round, you know — about me and Daphne — they aren't actually true.'

'I didn't think they were,' Juliet remarked. 'I *thought* that silly Clark woman had put two and two together and made a wrong number. Not that it makes any difference to me, but I've lived in Sanden for fifteen years and I know how unpleasant some people can be, for very little excuse. I'll spread a few counter-rumours, if you like.'

'It's all right — you don't need to bother.'

'Don't worry, I'll enjoy beating the gossips for a change.' Juliet grinned at her. 'Fancy a coffee some time? How about Friday morning? We could go over to Marlborough, if you like, and you can sample the Polly Tea-Rooms. They have a bottomless coffee pot, and fabulous cakes.'

'That'd be great,' Harriet said, with warmth. If she could make friends with this lively, down-to-earth woman, then at least some good would have come out of the whole unfortunate mess.

She said goodbye, and then went indoors. Daphne met her in the kitchen. 'Phone call. Your solicitor, I think.'

Harriet went into the hall, her heart banging nervously, and picked up the receiver. 'Hallo?'

'Who was that with you at the pub?'

It wasn't Don Potter, but Edward. And he sounded furious. Taken by surprise, Harriet said, 'Morgan. An old friend.'

'He certainly looked pretty friendly. But it won't wash, you can't fool me again. What did you tell him? Or were you leading him on, just like you led me on?'

'Calm down, Edward, please.' Harriet swallowed, trying to be calm herself. She had to win this argument, for Toby's sake. 'I wasn't leading anyone on. Look, can we have a rational discussion without getting worked up, just for a few minutes?'

A snort of disgust at the other end of the line seemed to indicate the impossibility of her request. Determined to state her case before he put the phone down on her, Harriet ploughed on. 'Please, Edward, just *listen* to what I have to say. I'm *not* a lesbian. I *don't* fancy women. I'm *not* having an affair with Daphne. Mrs Clark got hold of the wrong end of the stick, and she's been spreading all this nasty gossip about us because she's got it in for Daphne. Is that clear?'

There was silence at his end, but at least he hadn't hung up. She went on. 'Morgan, the bloke you saw me with today, was my boyfriend when we were students. I met him again a couple of months ago, quite by chance. For your information, I'm not having an affair with him either. He's just a friend. But even if he wasn't, surely all that matters is Toby, and whether I'm the best person to be looking after him. Are you sure *you* are? Do you *really* think you could cope with him full time? Or are you just doing this out of revenge and injured pride?'

Still no response. In desperation, she cried, 'Oh God, Edward, please, *talk* to me! We can sort this whole stupid mess out, I know we can, and it need never get to court! Why can't you just admit you were wrong about me?'

'You don't expect me to believe you, do you?' he demanded scornfully.

'Of course I do, because it's the *truth*! I'll swear it on oath, if you want. And it should be quite easy to convince the judge that you've made rather a silly mistake. If you drop it quietly now, we can just go on as we were before. I don't want Toby to lose touch with you, I don't want hard feelings. But if I have to, Edward, I'll fight you for him, and I might have to say things in court that you won't want people to hear.'

'Such as?'

'The episode with Gina, for a start. That won't go down very well, will it?'

'Are you threatening me?'

'No, I'm just giving you due notice. Please, Edward, just *think* about all this for once. About the consequences, and what it will do to Toby, and to your life, and mine. Think it through. Try and imagine what it would be like if you got that residence order. In the end, your feelings don't matter, and neither do mine. Only *Toby* counts. We have to remember that — we're his parents, we have a responsibility not to mess his life up as well. Please, Edward?'

Again, the long silence. Then his voice

came, gruff and abrupt and utterly devoid of its usual charm. 'You will be hearing from my solicitor in due course. Goodbye.'

And she had no idea, as she put the phone down, whether her arguments had had any impression on him at all.

25

'Are there dragons in this cave?'

Toby was peering dubiously into the widest of the three openings in the side of the concrete bubbles that formed the underground house. Harriet laughed. 'Of course there aren't, sweetheart. It's quite all right. Dragons are only in stories.'

'And in Wales, don't forget,' said Morgan. 'Lots of them there, little 'un, all red and fierce, with fiery breath to fry the English.'

'Are there? Really?'

'He's kidding you,' Harriet told her son, giving him a hug. 'No dragons anywhere, honest.'

'They died out because no one believed in them any more,' said Morgan, walking into the bubble. His voice changed and became hollow and echoey. 'Except in Wales. They live inside the mountains, waiting for Llewellyn the Last to come back. But I promise you, there aren't any in here. See?'

He snapped a switch, and the interior was abruptly bathed in light from a series of naked bulbs, hanging from the ceiling. Harriet, standing on the threshold, beheld a large circular room, about thirty feet in diameter, with three other arched openings, one opposite and one on each side. The domed space above her demanded something to lighten and soften the grim grey concrete. She shivered suddenly. 'It's like being in Wookey Hole.'

'It's very cold,' Toby said, keeping close to her side. She knew he wasn't really frightened, but was enjoying the spooky atmosphere inside the bubbles. 'What's it *for*, Mum?'

'It's a house. To live in.'

'I don't want to live in it,' said Toby, looking round. 'Where's the bed?'

'Fools and children shouldn't see things unfinished,' Morgan said. 'Anyway, this is going to be the living room — the central space. Through there is the kitchen and utility area, and a loo. The main bedroom is on the left, with *en suite* facilities, and the smaller bedroom is on the right, also with *en suite*.'

'You sound just like an estate agent.'

'I intended to. So — got any thoughts?'

'Give me a chance, I haven't been inside it five seconds.' Harriet walked in to the centre, and turned. At once the whole feeling of the room changed. Light poured in through the opening, and beyond it and the level terrace, that magnificent view lay drenched in sunshine.

'How are you going to heat it?' she asked.

'That's a fireplace over there, in case you hadn't noticed. A woodburning stove sends out a lot of warmth. I've designed a set of solar panels to cover the southern side of each bubble, and they should take care of hot water in the summer. Even in winter, you'd be surprised by how much energy you can get from them. And of course the concrete will be fully lined and insulated. Caves can be very snug, which is why Stone Age people used to live in them.'

'And dragons did too,' said Toby. He left her side and went to peer into the furthest opening. 'What's in here?'

'The kitchen,' Morgan replied, going over to join him.

'But where's the cooker?'

'It'll have one, don't worry. Look, can you see the skylight?'

Their voices echoed into the round air. Harriet glanced about her again, trying to visualise what it might look like with a carpet, furniture, pictures . . .

Hanging pictures on an almost spherical wall would be difficult, and yet that expanse of curving blankness urgently needed some kind of decoration. She had never been of the minimalist tendency, she liked rooms that were crowded with the impedimenta of their residents' lives, books and toys and treasured ornaments which could give some indication of the character of the owners. The basement flat she had shared with Morgan had been damp, dark and mildewy, but a couple of tins of paint and the results of trawling jumble sales and junk shops had spectacularly transformed it. She had no idea who would live here — it hardly seemed to be Selina's sort of place — but making it look like a home rather than a clinical experiment was undeniably a considerable challenge. And she knew that she could rise to it.

Suddenly, she thought of Toby's room at the boatyard, where she had let her artistic inspiration run wild. Surely she could do the same here? The walls cried out for a mural, a *trompe-l' oeil* perhaps, though not full of plump cherubs and angels.

The idea came to her in one glorious image, blue skies and puffy white clouds and soaring amongst them, wild and free and joyous, the fierce dragons of Toby's imagination.

Rapidly, Harriet assessed the difficulty of the task. Not quite on the level of the Sistine Chapel ceiling, and she was certainly no Michelangelo. It would mean a lot of scaffolding, and long hours with a cricked neck. But the effect would be worth it. The lower walls could be white, merging into the clouds, and then the dizzying expanse of blue above, and the denizens of the sky in full flight.

So strong was the creative urge that she wanted to start now. She had brought a clipboard along, with several pieces of blank paper and a couple of pencils. She sat down on the stack of timber just inside the opening, and began to sketch feverishly.

By the time Morgan returned with Toby, having obviously given him the grand tour, she had a sheet of paper filled with drawings: dragons, clouds, and a little outline of how it might look when finished. As they approached her, Harriet turned eagerly. 'I've had an idea. What do you think of that?'

Morgan took the paper, while Toby hopped about, demanding to see. Obligingly, he hunkered down beside Harriet, studying the sketches, a small frown between his dark eyebrows. More apprehensive of his reaction than she would ever have admitted to him, she waited for some comment.

'It's dragons!' Toby cried. 'Lots and lots of dragons on the walls!'

'On the ceiling, actually, sweetheart. Up there. To look like the sky.'

'Like my balloons in Daddy's house,' said Toby. 'And they wouldn't be *real* dragons, would they? Only painted ones.'

'That's right. But it all depends on the architect.' She glanced anxiously at Morgan. 'He's got to say yes.'

'It'll take you a long time,' said her former lover slowly. 'But Marcus isn't in any hurry to get it finished — he'd rather have it just right. What sort of paint would you use? Acrylic?'

'That's what I used for the mural I did in Toby's room at the boatyard.'

'Then you've done this sort of thing before.'

'Only that once. I wanted to put lots of painted plants and flowers and pots on Georgia's living room wall, but she wouldn't let me.'

'Now there's a surprise. Your sister has no soul.' Morgan studied the drawings, and then turned to squint up at the top of the dome. 'It *could* work . . . '

Harriet waited for him to finish. When the pause threatened to go on for ever, she said urgently, 'Well? What do you think of it?'

'What do I think of it?' His blue eyes blazed suddenly at her, and his mouth lifted into a delighted smile. 'I'm thinking, darling Hal, that you're a genius. This is brilliant. Wait till Marcus sees it.'

'Marcus?' Lifted into joy by his response, she stared at him in sudden alarm. 'But what if he doesn't like it?'

'I'm sure that he will. He's not afraid of things that are different. He wants this house to be something really special, and your mural will make it wonderful. You don't look very convinced.'

'I'm sorry,' Harriet said. 'I can't help it. He's the generation that likes to say no.'

'Not Marcus — and not Daphne either, for that matter. Come on, Hal, let go, have a little belief in yourself! You can *do* it, you know you can.'

'You don't think it's a bit ambitious?'

'If you don't stretch yourself you'll never get anywhere. I don't suppose Michelangelo was ever troubled by self-doubt.'

'No, but he ended up with a bad back.'

'You're terrible, you are!' said Morgan in exasperation. 'Isn't she, Toby? She comes up with an idea that could lead to fame and fortune, and then refuses to believe that it's any good.'

'I'm not *refusing* to believe,' said Harriet, with a sly glance at him. 'I'm just enjoying hearing you trying to persuade me. It's great for my self-esteem.'

Morgan grinned back. 'I'd be prepared to praise you till the cows come home, you know that. Anyway, by the time I've finished with him, Marcus won't *dare* to say no.'

'You just told me he was bound to say yes,' Harriet pointed out.

'Indeed he is. Shall we go and see him now? I know he's around this afternoon.'

'No. Wait.' Harriet shuffled the paper on the clipboard and then scrambled to her feet. 'I want to see the rest of it, get some idea of what's needed in the other rooms first. Come on, Toby, show me the bedrooms.'

They were very similar, though somewhat smaller, to the main bubble. Harriet gazed round at the bare shell, and frowned. 'I wish I knew who was going to live here. So much depends on that. I presume it won't be Marcus? He hasn't some idea of selling or letting The Towers and moving in here, has he?'

'Not as far as I know. From what he's said to me, this is the place he's going to let. For the sake of argument, imagine that you and Toby were going to live in it. What would *you* like?'

It was an idea so wonderful, and so unattainable, that she could hardly bear the thought of it. And yet Harriet could see herself in this room, with a wide, low bed, and storage and cupboards built against the curving walls, the window draped with yellow muslin, and waking up in a bower of tranquil greenery, arching above her head.

'I could put leaves and flowers all over this one,' she said thoughtfully. 'With some little birds in the branches. And how about a night sky in the other bedroom, with moons and stars and planets? A bit of a cliché, I know, but it wouldn't be very difficult. I could do them in luminous paint, so that they'd glow in the dark.'

'And how about the kitchen? It hasn't got any windows, of course, just a skylight.'

'I don't know. Grape vines? No, too much like an Italian restaurant. Geranium pots? Bowls of fruit?' Harriet stared at him, while the sheer scale of the project threatened to overwhelm her. 'Oh, Morgan, it would take years and years to do it. And I just haven't the time.'

'You would have if Marcus employed you to do it. Your work for Daphne is almost finished, isn't it?'

'There's only a couple more illustrations left, of what we planned. But the publishers haven't seen them yet, and they might not like them. I might have to do some again.'

'Oh Hal of little faith . . . Can't you get it into your head, *cariad*, that you have a gift, and it's wonderful, and people actually *love* your paintings? I certainly do.'

'How do you know? You haven't seen any of them.'

'I have, don't you remember? I've still got the one you gave me ten years ago.' He put his hands on her shoulders and gave her a little shake. 'No one said it'd be easy, you can't wave a magic wand over it all, but I'm giving you the chance, and you'd better bloody well take it, or I won't answer for the consequences.'

'Then I'd better rise to the challenge, hadn't I?' Harriet said. 'Come on, let's go and see Sir Marcus now, before I stop and think about what I'm going to let myself in for.'

Despite her doubts, Harriet's mind kept working busily as they walked up the track to the main house. She could paint undersea scenes in the two bathrooms, with writhing octopuses and fish as bright as jewels in the dark-blue water. Or, alternatively, she could leave them plain, as a rest from all the mural activity elsewhere in the house. It would take a very long time to complete, probably months and months. She'd need to find somewhere else to live, too: she couldn't stay at Daphne's forever, although she certainly wasn't going to move out just because of Edward's accusations. Toby would be starting school in September, giving her much more time to work, and she suspected that if

Marcus did, by some miracle, agree to this, he would pay her extremely generously.

But it all depended on his approval, and despite Morgan's encouraging words, she still could not believe that he would. If she was really honest with herself, she did trust her own power to make her visions real: even she, perfectionist to her fingertips, had been almost entirely satisfied with the balloon mural she had painted for Toby. She knew that she could make the underground house a place of wonder and enchantment for the lucky people who would one day live there. All she needed was the opportunity. But would Marcus grant her what she wanted?

They found him in his office, going through his accounts, and he greeted them with relief. 'Thank God, rescue at last! I loathe and abhor doing my tax return, but it's a vile necessity. Now I can forget about it for an hour or two. Would you like some tea? And how about this young chap?'

'Orange squash, please,' said Toby, after maternal prompting. He was rather overawed by the size and glamour of Forfar Towers: even the little office had an ornate plaster ceiling and a pair of ancestral portraits on the walls. As they followed Sir Marcus towards the kitchens, he clung to Harriet's hand and whispered anxiously, 'Mum, is this a palace?'

'No, it's just a house, Sir Marcus's house. Kings and queens and princes live in palaces.'

'And I'm not a prince, I'm afraid,' said their host, walking into the dining room that Harriet remembered from the night of the ball. It looked rather stark and bare now, with the long table back in the centre, and a dozen chairs arranged primly around it. Their feet clunked on the polished wooden floor, and echoed round the walls. Harriet wondered if Sir Marcus felt lonely, living by himself, save for his housekeeper, in this grandiose building.

'It's Mrs Young's day off, so we've got her domain to ourselves. Trouble is, though, I can never find anything in here.'

The kitchen was almost as large as the dining room next door, but much more cosy. Its two windows faced north, over the garage and outbuildings, but the walls were painted a cheerful shade of yellow, and there were terracotta tiles on the floor, bunches of dried flowers hanging from the ceiling, an Aga, and a big old pine table. The impression of rustic charm was tempered by the wide assortment of modern gadgets, in clinical white, ranked on the worktops, and the dishwasher in the corner. After much opening of cupboards and exasperated muttering, Sir Marcus eventually tracked down a tin of Earl Grey teabags, a pot, some milk and sugar, four mugs and a bottle of fizzy lemonade. Finally, they all retreated to the opulent comfort of the huge drawing room sofas, with beverages to hand, and a big tin of biscuits on the coffee table in front of them. By then, Harriet was in such a state of nerves that she had clenched every muscle in her body to stop herself trembling.

'So, to what do I owe the pleasure of this visit?' said Sir Marcus, smiling at her. She was aware of Toby, on her right, sipping his lemonade cautiously because of the fizz, and on her left, a little closer than was absolutely necessary, the presence of Morgan. And the sense of his support and encouragement gave her the confidence to swallow her nervousness, and begin her pitch.

26

Sir Marcus Grant was not the only person wrestling with his tax return that sunny July afternoon. In the office at the boatyard, now rather less tidy than when Harriet had left it three months previously, Edward Armstrong was staring in angry perplexity round the crowded shelves.

He had everything ready to begin. The neat stacks of invoices, for cleaning materials, fuel, repair work; wage slips and National Insurance records; receipts from the hirers; fees payable to British Waterways for the boats. Harriet had always kept everything in good order, and she had developed a system which Edward, glad to leave everything to her, had only vaguely understood.

Everything, that is, except the actual accounts. He had told her that he knew book-keeping and could see to that side of the business himself, and Harriet, already overwhelmed with the rest of the paperwork, had been happy to let him do the finances. She had handed over all the receipts and invoices, and Edward had always calculated the profits, done the VAT returns, and paid cheques and cash into the bank.

There was a very good reason for this, and one of which Harriet was completely unaware. The Inland Revenue, too, not to mention Her Majesty's Customs and Excise Department, had no idea that the modest profits from Wonderland Boats were, in fact, not modest at all. Ever since taking over the business, Edward had used his knowledge of accountancy to cream off a tidy sum every quarter. Payments in cash were not credited, money coming in was underestimated, expenses were exaggerated. It was cleverly done: individually, the amounts involved were not large. But put together, they had paid for his BMW, his golf club membership, his wine cellar, and all the other luxuries to which Edward assumed he was entitled. While Harriet had struggled to make ends meet and pay household bills, thousands of pounds had lain in his secret deposit account, quietly accruing interest at an extremely preferential rate.

And he had been careful to make no record of what he siphoned off. There were only the monthly statements from the bank, detailing the total, steadily rising even despite the occasional large withdrawals. He had kept them well out of the way of prying eyes, on the high shelf above the fax machine, and in an unobtrusive, tatty old brown A4 envelope. But he could not find them.

For the twentieth time, he examined all the shelves, peered behind them in case the envelope had somehow been pushed to the back, hunted under the desk, looked in the out-tray, the in-tray, the filing cabinets, the photocopier. And eventually, with horror, he was forced to the bitter and obvious conclusion. They were not there. He had not moved them, so they must have been taken. And there was only one person who had had the opportunity and the motive to do it.

He reached for the phone, and punched in Harriet's number with shaking fingers.

It rang for some time before it was answered. To his frustration, the voice at the other end belonged to Daphne. 'Hallo?'

'Is Harriet there?' he demanded furiously.

'No, I'm afraid she's not. She said she wouldn't be back until late this afternoon. Can I take a message?'

'Yes, you can. Tell her it's Edward. She's taken something of mine and I want it back.'

'Has she?' Daphne sounded frankly disbelieving. 'Are you sure?'

'Of course I'm bloody sure. Tell her it's important. I need it today. Get her to ring me the moment she gets in.'

'What is it that she is supposed to have taken?'

'A large brown envelope. It contains some papers I need. I can't find it and she's the only person who could have taken it, and I want it back.' Edward realised that he was almost shouting, and hastily moderated his voice.

'I can't imagine why she should have taken it, Mr Armstrong,' said Daphne, with chilly contempt. 'Perhaps you have mislaid it.'

'No. I've looked everywhere, and it's not bloody there, you stupid woman!'

'There's no need to be so rude,' said Daphne, as if she were reproving a child. 'I shall give her the message when she gets back. In the mean time, I suggest you have a thorough search for it, rather than waste any more time making wild accusations without a shred of evidence to back them up. Good day, Mr Armstrong.'

Edward swore long and hard at the phone, which at least could not answer back. Then he banged the receiver down and put his head in his hands. What a bitch. Bitches, both of them. Of course they were bloody lesbians, man-haters, out to get him. He prayed that if Harriet *had* taken the envelope, perhaps out of spite, she hadn't yet looked inside it: or that, if she had, the stupid little cow didn't understand what the statements implied. They were just rows of figures and dates, that was all. And she'd always said she wasn't too good with finances.

Feeling sick, he tried to concentrate on the legitimate accounts, but his fingers fumbled on the calculator and he needed the statements to ensure that the sums tallied. Finally, after making a complete hash of several totals, he gave up in disgust. If she refused to give the envelope back, he'd make sure he got custody of Toby and she never saw the boy again.

★ ★ ★

'Told you, *cariad*,' said Morgan. 'Told you he'd love it.'

'Doesn't it ever get boring, being right all the time?' Harriet grinned at him, effervescent with delight. 'I can't believe it, I really can't. Pinch me or something, I think I must be dreaming.'

'I'll kiss you instead,' Morgan told her, and planted his lips on hers with gusto. Beside them, Toby gave a small squeak of dismay. 'What are you doing, Mum?'

'Celebrating my new job,' Harriet told him happily. 'I'm going to paint stars and dragons and flowers all over Sir Marcus's underground house. Won't that be fun? And you gave me the idea, about the dragons, so it's all down to you, sweetheart.'

'Me?' said her son, sounding pleased. 'Can I have an ice lolly, then?'

Harriet glanced at her watch. It was after six o'clock: they had spent so long discussing the designs for the murals that Sir Marcus had — after some more searching — provided afternoon tea for them, with cake, sandwiches and scones, washed down with another pot of Earl Grey. Still talking, they had eaten on the terrace in patchy sunshine, while Toby played in the garden. Harriet had found herself closely questioned about the techniques she would use, the type of paint, how long it would take, and the sort of technical details she had assumed would not interest Sir Marcus. It was nerve-racking, but it did make her think hard about how she would cope with the task she had set herself. By the time they had finished, she had pages of notes, and a much clearer idea of what she would paint, and how. Sir Marcus had even scribbled down a brief draft contract which, he said, she could peruse at her leisure. 'Because it's all rather sudden, isn't it? You've sprung this on yourself as well as on me. And I don't want it to go wrong because we've been over-ambitious. I'd like to see some colour sketches, too, and some estimate of the time-scale involved.'

'So would I,' Morgan said. He was leaning back in his chair, looking relaxed and happy, and he smiled at Harriet. The sun gleamed on his dark hair, turning the brief loose curls almost red, and outlining the turn of his neck and the angle of his jaw. Her stomach clenched with the agony of longing, but she knew now, with a lovely feeling of inevitability, that she had only to say the word, and their love, that had never really died, would be returned to her, lying like a glorious jewel within her grasp at last.

'So I'm afraid you'll have to put up with me looking eagerly over your shoulder,' he added.

'I'm sure I can stand the strain,' said Harriet, with a good deal more confidence than she actually felt.

'Ah, but I'm not sure I can,' Morgan had said cryptically, with an eyebrow raised in her direction.

Well, he had always been impatient: that certainly hadn't changed. But she acknowledged now, as the three of them climbed into the Shogun for the journey back to Daphne's, that this Morgan *was* different from the one she'd known before, and not just in his looks either. Seeing him with Sir Marcus, exuding calm control and professional expertise, she had realised that the wild boy had become an impressive and extremely charming man. Her memories of the younger Morgan seemed now to be a pale, wan reflection of this vivid, magnetically attractive person. And amazingly, wonderfully, he still obviously cared very much for her.

So although she didn't usually like people watching her while she worked, she was eagerly looking forward to having him around while she painted Y Wâl Yr Draig. Morgan, unasked, had suggested it as the final name for The Pits, pointing out that it meant 'Dragon's Den' in Welsh, and Sir Marcus, smiling, had agreed. 'What do you think, Harriet? After all, it was your idea.'

'Not mine — Toby's,' she had said, with a glance at her son, who was ten yards away sitting astride a small bronze cannon, chosen by a past Grant to enhance the spuriously martial air of his house. 'But no one will be able to pronounce it — they'll end up calling it Wally's Drag.'

'So four-year-olds do have their uses,' she said to him now, checking that his seat belt was fastened properly. 'Of course you can have an ice lolly. Can we go back via the shop, Morgan? It should still be open.'

'Only if I can have an ice lolly too,' he said,

reversing with a farewell wave to Sir Marcus. 'I promise not to drop it on the seat.'

'Why should I mind? It's your car.'

'So it is. Anyway, it's a good chance to spread some competing gossip.'

Harriet sent him a warning glance. Toby's world did occasionally coincide with the real one, and usually at the most inopportune moments. She said softly, 'You were great with him today, and that time on the hill. How come?'

'Oh, I lived with a woman in Wyoming for a while, she had two kids about his age.' He smiled reminiscently. 'Brittany and Chelsea, they were called. Cute little blonde girls with bows in their hair. They'd be teenagers now. And don't forget, I've got two little sisters myself.'

'I remember.' Harriet grinned. 'Elfair and Angharad. You called them Hellfire and Handgrenade.'

'If I called them that now, they'd thump me. Elfie teaches in Cardiff, and Angharad's just had her first baby. Without any visible partner, much to my mum's disgust. And before you ask, Dad died seven years ago. Heart attack. He had an argument with someone over a parking space, and dropped dead in the street.'

'I'm sorry,' said Harriet, though he did not

sound at all grief stricken.

'No you're not. I'm not, either. And funnily enough, nor is Mum. Since he died she's lost three stone and about twenty years. She's doing an Open University degree, gone on a cruise round the Med, and her social life would make Fergie look reclusive. Sometimes, the people you're supposed to love and respect make it very hard for you to do so. Dad was his own worst enemy, and smoking sixty a day didn't help.' He glanced at her. 'I'm sorry if I seem callous, but he made my childhood a misery, and I can't summon up much grief. What about your family?'

'Oh, my dad took early retirement and spends most of his time in the garden. Mum seems to have volunteered for half the charity shops in Bristol. I go over every couple of weeks, which isn't as often as they'd like, but Mum in particular fusses round me so much. They dote on Toby, of course, because he's their only grandchild.' And likely to remain so, she thought, thinking of Georgia's resolute childlessness, and her own circumstances. At least for a while.

'What about your sister? Still as prickly as ever?'

'More so, I'm afraid. But she's been a really good friend to me, the last few months. I don't know what I would have done without her. Given up hope, I suspect.'

'No you wouldn't,' Morgan said, and touched her knee briefly. 'You're a survivor, *cariad*, and a lot stronger than you give yourself credit for.'

If only that were true, Harriet said to herself wryly, as they stopped outside the village shop to buy Toby's promised ice lolly.

Ten minutes later, the Shogun came to a halt outside Holly Cottage and decanted its passengers, by now slightly sticky round the edges, at the gate. 'It's been a very good day, hasn't it?' said Morgan, leaning out of the car window.

'The best,' said Harriet, smiling up at him, while Toby ran into Daphne's garden. 'Thank you, Morgan. You've been a really good friend too, you know.'

'That's what I'm here for,' he said, his brilliant eyes suddenly serious and unwavering, gazing into hers. '*Always, cariad*. And those paintings will be utterly wonderful. How long do you think it'll take? I know you couldn't give Marcus a definite time-scale, but roughly, off the top of your head?'

'I've no idea,' Harriet said. 'He said he wasn't in any particular hurry, and in any case I can't start properly until September, when Toby's at school.'

'As late as that?'

'Why, is there a problem?'

'You could say.' She saw the sombre cast to his face, and knew suddenly that all her bright hopes for the future were about to be shattered. 'Look, *cariad*, I should have told you this before, I suppose, but somehow the right moment never came along. I've got another commission — another job.'

Despite the warmth of the afternoon, Harriet felt cold all over, as if she had been doused in icy water. She heard her voice, somehow quite calm. 'Oh, have you? Where? In the States?'

'No, not as far as that — in Gloucestershire, up near the Forest of Dean. I've already submitted the design, and it's been passed. They want me to start work on it as soon as I can be spared here.'

'So will you be going soon?' How could, how *could* she keep so composed, when he was breaking her heart all over again?

But surely, she reminded herself, she must have known, deep down, that he was just a bird of passage, a drifter who was congenitally incapable of settling down anywhere, or with anyone. What a fool I was, to imagine that we could possibly have any kind of permanent relationship, Harriet thought sadly. With his past record, I was just deluding myself.

Well, at any rate she knew now what the score was — and before she had revealed too much of her absurd hopes for the future.

'Afraid I will,' Morgan said. 'Much as I'd like to stay around for a bit longer. But I need to live on the job, get the feel of the place, make sure the contractors are up to scratch. It's not like building a house, some of the techniques are very different, and I have to keep an eye on them. Still, Gloucester's not far, is it?' He grinned at her. 'So how about dinner tonight, to celebrate Y Wâl Yr Draig?'

Harriet was tempted — sorely tempted, despite the consequences. But she knew that she had to be strong, and resist. She shook her head. 'Sorry, I can't.'

'Can't, or won't?'

She took a deep breath. Now, of all times, he deserved her honesty. 'It isn't that I don't want to. I do, very much. I'd love to . . . to get closer. But I can't, because you're going. I can't, because of Toby. You do see that, don't you?' She gazed at him urgently, willing him to understand, to accept: and yet, knowing him as she did, the new Morgan almost as well as the old, realizing that it was as unlikely as her dragons, creatures of the spirit and imagination, coming down to dance in the air.

But he said nothing, and she floundered on

despairingly. 'You said earlier that you'd lived for a while with a woman in Wyoming. You were part of her life for a few weeks, a few months. And you were part of her children's lives as well. Even if you and she parted by mutual consent, what about them? What did your going do to them? Did they come to think of you as a father? Did they cry when you left?' She felt her own tears rise hot to the surface, and carried on, desperate to finish before grief overwhelmed her. 'I can't let that happen to Toby, I can't, I *can't*! Edward was bad enough, I can't let him love you, only to have you leave us again. So sorry, Morgan, but no, I can't let you come too close, I can't let myself get involved. I *want* to be, God knows how much I *want* to let you back into my life, but not when we both know it's not going to be permanent.' She managed a smile. 'Sorry, but that's the way it is.'

'I'm sorry too, *cariad*,' he said, and did not smile back. 'Goodbye, darling Hal.'

And as the Shogun roared back up the hill, much too fast, she was aware, with a wry recognition of the irony, that Heather Clark, hedgetrimmer in hand, was watching her weep.

27

Somehow, Harriet had managed to compose herself by the time she encountered Daphne, who was enjoying a mug of tea on the patio, and listening to Toby's high-pitched, breathless account of his day. 'And it's *just* like a dragon's cave, and Morgan said it was going to be called Wally's Drag because that's Dragon's Den in Welsh, and he's Welsh, and Mum's going to paint pictures of them all on the ceiling and moons and stars and things and shells and fish in the bathroom and leaves and *everything*!'

'Did you make head or tail of that?' Harriet enquired, as Toby dashed off to get his colouring pens and paper to draw his own dragons.

'Only vaguely. I gather that, in order of importance, he had an ice lolly with stripes on it that was very cold but melted, and that Marcus lives in a palace, and, oh yes, that you're going to paint things all over the underground house — I presume on the inside, although he didn't actually say as much. There's still plenty of tea left in the pot, if you want it.'

'I'd love some, thanks.' Harriet collected a mug from indoors and sat down opposite the older woman. 'Yes, what Toby was saying was more or less right. I'm still fairly stunned. As soon as the interior is finished, Sir Marcus wants me to decorate it. I've got to produce drawings and sketches of the overall designs in each room, preferably by the end of next week.' She glanced at Daphne. 'That is OK, isn't it? The illustrations for the book are almost finished — unless your editor doesn't like them, in which case I shall have to start again, or do alterations.'

'Nonsense,' said Daphne robustly. 'They're splendid, as you ought to know very well, and Jennifer will love them. No, my dear, that's quite all right, and I'm very pleased for you. Quite an ambitious project, isn't it?'

'Yes, but I've got plenty of time to do it. The plastering and the rest of the inside won't be finished until the end of August, and Toby starts school in September. I can spend six weeks perfecting the designs, and then start straight in on them. They should be done before Christmas.'

'And your friend Morgan? What does he think?'

'Oh, he loves them.' Harriet was making strenuous efforts to appear cheerful. 'But he can't hang around until they're finished. He's got to build another underground house, somewhere in Gloucestershire.'

'Well, that's quite near,' Daphne observed, with a shrewd glance at her. 'He might even be able to commute in that huge four-by-four of his.'

'I doubt it,' said Harriet. 'He said he needed to be as close to the job as possible, in case of any problems.' She managed to smile quite successfully. 'So he'll be off in a couple of weeks.'

'You'll miss him a lot.' It was a statement of fact, not a question. 'I was wrong about him — he seems a thoroughly likeable young man.'

'He is.' Harriet marvelled at how she could discuss Morgan's planned departure with such equanimity, when it felt as if her heart was breaking. 'But not very reliable, I'm afraid. Not a hope of pinning him down to anything. And that's not what I want, not with Toby to think about.'

'Ah.' Daphne surveyed her over the top of her spectacles, but did not elaborate. In any case, the little boy came running out, his colouring pens in one hand and a thick wodge of paper, part of the book's discarded first draft, in the other. 'I'm going to draw lots and *lots* of dragons, Mum!'

Harriet cleared a space for him, and he

settled himself down with his customary neatness, lining all the pens up beside the paper, and putting his name, in rather wobbly red letters, at the top. 'What colour are dragons, Mum?'

'They can be any colour you like. Some have wings and some haven't. Some breathe fire and smoke. Use your imagination.'

'I'm going to do a pink one,' Toby announced, picking up the appropriate pen. 'Because pink's my *favourite* colour!'

'I hope he never says that in front of Edward,' Harriet murmured to Daphne. 'Or all his prejudices will be amply confirmed.'

'That reminds me.' Daphne rose to her feet, picking up the empty tea pot and mugs, and jerked her head significantly towards the kitchen door. 'I had a very strange phone call earlier.'

'From Edward?' Harriet followed her into the house, where they were safely out of Toby's earshot. Her heart, already low because of Morgan, sank even lower. 'Now what does he want?'

'Apparently you've taken something of his, and he wants it back. Immediately. He was absolutely furious. I told him that he must have mislaid it, and of course you wouldn't have taken anything, but he wasn't at all convinced. He wanted you to ring back as soon as you got in.'

'What on earth was it?'

'A large brown envelope, as far as I could make out. I don't know what was supposed to be inside it, but he was getting extremely worked up about it. And extremely rude, too.'

'An *envelope*? I haven't got any envelope of his. He probably hasn't looked hard enough, but that's Edward all over. Very quick to assume the worst, and very slow to accept it isn't.'

'Well, I would advise calling him and telling him, or he'll be round here kicking the door down.'

'And I've spent months constructing this pleasant image of him for Toby, persuading him that Daddy's a nice man who behaves reasonably. I certainly don't want Edward rampaging round the house shattering his illusions.' Harriet sighed. 'You're right, of course. I'd better do it now, and get it over with.'

The phone was answered almost instantly, and Edward's voice, sharp with anger, came down the line. 'Hallo?'

'It's me, Harriet.'

'And about bloody time too! Where have you been all afternoon? I've been sitting here waiting for you to call. Come on, then, where is it?'

'Where's what?'

'You know very well what I'm talking about, you stupid dyke, where's the envelope?'

Even in their worst arguments, Edward had never used that viciously brutal tone of voice before. Like a whip, it roused Harriet's own anger, but she knew she must not give way to it. 'I don't know what envelope you mean.'

'Of course you do! You've taken it and I want it back. Now. Or I'll come over and search your perverted little love nest for it.'

'Listen, Edward. For God's sake, calm down and *listen*.' Harriet tried, with only limited success, to inject some restraint into the conversation. 'I don't know what envelope you're talking about. And I haven't taken *anything* of yours.'

'Don't lie to me! Where is it?'

'I haven't taken it,' Harriet repeated. 'But it would help if I knew what it looked like and what was in it.'

'A large brown envelope, of course. It's got some — some papers in it, that I need urgently. It was in the office, and now it's gone. And if you don't hand it over, I'm coming round right now to get it!'

'No. No, I really wouldn't do that if I were you, Edward,' said Harriet, thinking fast. 'Toby's here.'

'So?'

'Well, for a start, he'd be very upset. And it's not going to look very good if you ransack the place when he's around, is it?'

Not even this could deflect her former partner from his purpose. 'Well, that's your look-out, you'll just have to keep him out of the way, won't you? Now are you going to hand it over, or do I have to come and get it?'

'For the last time, Edward,' Harriet cried, her patience exhausted, 'I haven't *got* your stupid envelope! I don't know what you're talking about, and I swear to you that if you come over and threaten me, I'll call the police. Is that clear? I *mean* it, Edward, so get that into your thick head. I haven't taken anything of yours, I don't *want* anything of yours. And if you keep harassing me, I'll get a court injunction to stop you. Understand? I don't want to do it, but I will if necessary, OK? Is that clear, Edward? Savvy? Comprende? Got it?'

'You're bluffing,' said Edward, but something of the bullying certainty had left his voice. 'If you haven't got it, then who has?'

'How about *looking* for it a bit harder, before you accuse me of stealing? Goodbye, Edward.'

Harriet replaced the receiver with exaggerated care, and took a deep breath. This was, she realised with some surprise, the first argument with him in which she could be said to have won. But the puzzle remained. What *was* this envelope? And why did he want it so badly?

'Any joy?' Daphne enquired, coming into the hall.

'Well, I hope I persuaded him not to come over and ransack the place, but only because I said I'd call the police if he did. I haven't got his wretched envelope, and I told him so. Several times. I hope something eventually penetrated, but I'm not sure.'

'He's not very intelligent, is he?' Daphne observed drily. 'Or perceptive. Not only is he unable to judge when you're telling the truth, but he's making such a fuss about something apparently so trivial that you're bound to wonder why it's so important to him.' She paused. 'I suppose you haven't actually got it by mistake, have you? It didn't somehow get mixed up with your things when Georgia collected them?'

'I don't *think* so,' Harriet said slowly. 'But I suppose it could have done.' She grinned suddenly and mischievously. 'What on earth shall I do if I *have* got it?'

'Look inside it, first of all,' said Daphne.

'You never know — it could be the full and unexpurgated record of his dealings with the Mafia.'

'*Edward*? They'd eat him for breakfast. Fiddling his VAT return is more his style.'

'I was joking, of course. Anyway, why not go and have a look? And I'll keep watch in case he does decide to come and get it.'

'He said it was in the office. So if I do have it, it's most likely to be in my watercolour box,' Harriet said. 'Hang on a minute, I *do* remember something.' She ran upstairs and into her bedroom. Of course, she had removed her paints and brushes and the rest of her equipment, but her old sketches and drawings still remained in the box, now stowed away on top of the wardrobe. She dragged a chair over, climbed up, and brought it down.

Her folders were stacked neatly inside. She lifted them out one by one, and then drew her breath in sharply. Underneath, and exactly the same size, lay a large, tattered brown envelope, addressed to Wonderland Boats, The Wharf, Wharf Lane, Sanden, Wilts.

'I *have* got it,' she said to Daphne, who, driven by extreme curiosity, was standing in the doorway. 'Look. He must have put it on top of the box, and Georgia thought it was mine and brought it along. So I've had it all

395

the time. God, he'll never believe I didn't take it deliberately.'

'With any luck, he'll be so glad to see it again that it won't matter.' Daphne looked at her with raised eyebrows. 'Well, aren't you going to have a look and see what he's so desperate to get back?'

'A load of papers, he said.' Harriet drew them out and looked at them in perplexity. 'They're all bank statements, in his name. But I didn't know he had an account with *them*, I thought he only banked with Barclays.'

Daphne came forward to peer over her shoulder. 'Well, these are definitely current. That one's for last March. And he's got a very healthy balance, too.'

Harriet was flicking through them in growing bewilderment. 'I don't understand. He always said that money was tight, but look at this. He withdrew forty thousand pounds at the end of February, and still had nearly twenty-five thousand left! That must have been to pay for the BMW, he bought it at the beginning of March. But when I had to ask him for a cheque to pay the credit card bill, he accused me of being too extravagant. What's going on?'

'At a guess, he's been creaming off the profits.'

'To the tune of well over a thousand a *month*? No wonder he was so keen to get them back.' Harriet glanced at the statement on the bottom of the pile. 'This one's dated six years ago. That's before I started working for him.'

'Are they numbered?'

'Yes, in sequence, and this is the first. So it's a complete record of the account.' Harriet stared at Daphne. 'I'm sure the Inland Revenue would be very interested in these. And the Customs and Excise people. He must owe them thousands and thousands.' She giggled rather hysterically. 'When I said he might be fiddling his VAT returns, it was a joke. I never dreamed he'd really be doing it.'

'You do realise the power of what you have in your hand, don't you?' said Daphne. 'You have the proof of wrongdoing that could, at the very least, lead to a criminal investigation. And, quite possibly, put him away for a couple of years. What are you going to do with them?'

At once, Harriet laid them down on the bed and took a step back, as if they were intrinsically dangerous. 'I don't know. Oh God, I don't know. What if he claims I knew about them, tries to implicate me?'

'Well, you said yourself they date back to before you even knew him. And it's not a joint account, is it? It's in his name. It's in Swindon, too. Where's his official account held?'

'In Devizes.' Harriet was still gazing down at the statements, so apparently uninteresting, so anonymous, so banal. And yet they possessed the potential to be as explosive as any bomb. 'I never had anything to do with the financial side of it, you see. He even filled in my tax return for me. He'd done part of an accountancy traineeship in his twenties, he said I didn't need to bother with all that sort of thing. And now I see why.'

'Can you prove it? Or is it just his word against yours?'

'I'm sure anyone we employed would be able to confirm it, because he always signed all the cheques. I hired and fired, I took the bookings, ordered the equipment and generally organised the place, but all the money went through his hands. Diesel was supplied on account, I gave all the hire money to him, and if I wanted any housekeeping expenses I had to ask him for it — and he always handed over less than I wanted, and very grudgingly. That's one reason why I took the job with you — I wanted a separate source of income, so I wouldn't have to depend on him for hand-outs every time Toby needed a new pair of shoes.'

'Do you want to know what I think?' Daphne said, and there was a note of steel in her voice. 'I think you ought to hand those over to your local tax office as soon as possible.'

Harriet looked at her. 'Why?'

'Because the bastard deserves it. Goodness, Harriet, don't look so dubious! He's made your life an absolute misery for five years, he's done dreadful things, he's broken the law, he's tried to rat on his responsibilities — do you really think he doesn't *deserve* his comeuppance?'

'It's not that,' Harriet said slowly. 'If I succumbed to my true feelings about him, I'd want him put away for years. But it's not just me, is it? He's Toby's father. I don't want my son to see him in prison. He's almost old enough to realise what it means. How can I do that to him, however much Edward deserves punishment? I can't, Daphne. I honestly can't.'

There was a pause. Then the older woman smiled at her, shaking her head. 'Well, all I can say, you're more generous than I could ever be. In your circumstances, nothing would have given me more pleasure than to take up the mantle of avenging angel.'

'But he won't have it all his own way,' Harriet said. 'I'm not going to hand them over to the taxman, but I'm not going to give them back to him, either.' She grinned suddenly. 'Or not the originals, anyway.'

Daphne stared at her in considerable admiration. 'Are you planning what I think you're planning? Good grief, my dear, you should be giving lessons to Machiavelli.'

'Hardly. But this way solves everything, doesn't it? And if he steps out of line again, he knows what he can expect. So,' said Harriet, with considerable satisfaction, 'now Toby can draw pink dragons to his heart's content, and I shall be able to sleep at night.'

28

Harriet was shaking with nerves as Georgia's Tigra swept arrogantly into the yard at Wonderland Boats. She still could not quite believe the daring, the sheer insolence, of what she was about to do. It wouldn't work. He would laugh at her. She would run away with her tail between her legs, having made everything infinitely worse.

But in her heart, she knew that she would not. Apart from anything else, her sister wouldn't let her. Georgia, told of her plan, had laughed long and hard, and had expressed her admiration in terms so glowing that Harriet blushed to think of it. Of course, being Georgia, she could not resist a small dig: 'Are you sure this is all your idea, Harry? It's just the sort of thing Morgan would think up.'

It was, of course, but he didn't even know what she was planning. Harriet had made the firm decision not to tell him anything about it. After all, it was none of his business, and in a week or two he would have gone from her life for ever.

But still she regretted telling him so bluntly

401

that she did not want them to get back together. She had seen the look in his eyes, and she knew that she had hurt him — hurt Morgan, who had always seemed so invulnerable, so impervious. She felt agonising guilt for that, because she didn't want to cause him any pain: she cared about him too much. But in the long run, she could see no other way out. Better to make it quite clear where she stood now, and save him, and herself, and above all Toby, so much grief in the future.

She loved Morgan, and only now was she beginning to realise just how deep her feelings ran. But she knew that her action was for the best. The trouble was, she also knew that Georgia would thoroughly approve of what she'd done, which was why she hadn't yet told her.

'Right,' said her sister, switching off the engine. 'Are you OK, Harry?'

'Of course I am.' Harriet took a deep, rather quivering breath, and patted the envelope on her knee. 'Come on, let's get it over with.'

'You're not going to back out, are you?'

'No,' Harriet said, with furious emphasis. 'I'm nervous, of course I am, because I know just how nasty he can be. But now I've turned the tables, haven't I?' She grinned at her sister. 'And with you for moral support, how can I lose?'

'Don't even consider it,' said Georgia, getting out. 'I must say, I can't wait to see the bastard's face when you tell him.'

Harriet had rung earlier that morning, to give advance notice of their arrival, and Edward had obviously been looking out for them, because he came striding across the gravel from the house, his hand outstretched. 'I'll have that. I *knew* you'd taken it.'

'It was all my fault,' said Georgia, with patently false remorse. 'I must have inadvertently brought it away when I fetched Harriet's things. I'm *so* sorry.'

'So you bloody well should be.' Edward, with a look of acute relief on his face, snatched the envelope from Harriet's hand, and pulled the statements out. The two women watched as his expression changed abruptly to one of absolute horror. 'These aren't right! What have you done?'

'They're photocopies, that's all,' said Harriet calmly. 'I had a look at them, and decided that I'd better hang on to the real thing. Shall we go indoors, Edward, and talk about it in private? I've got a few suggestions to make.'

'What? What do you mean? Where are the original statements? What have you *done* with them, you stupid little cow?' He took several threatening steps towards his former partner. 'I want them back, *now*!'

'I'm sorry, Edward, I haven't brought them with me. But don't worry, I've put them somewhere quite safe.' Harriet glanced over at the wharf, where Pete, the mechanic, was watching the scene with interest. 'I think we ought to go inside, don't you? After all, you don't really want anyone else to know what you've been up to, and if you keep on shouting like that I should think the whole of Sanden will hear about it.'

If she hadn't felt so strongly that he deserved this, and more, Harriet might almost have been sorry for Edward. He stamped into the house like a sulky toddler, and flung round to face them. 'So what's all this about? What do you want?'

'It's quite simple, really,' said Harriet, inwardly amazed at her own poise and control. 'I want you to withdraw your application for custody of Toby. At once. I'm not going to deny you access, or anything like that. You can still see him, as often as you like. He's your son, you love him and he loves you, and I don't want him hurt — ever. But I want sole parental responsibility for him, and I want you to continue paying me maintenance for him, on the basis we've already arranged. I'm not being greedy, Edward, or vindictive, though God knows I've been provoked enough. I just want justice. And so far, I've had to fight you for every little scrap of it. That must stop, now and for good.'

His face haggard, his eyes bloodshot, all his easy charm vanquished, Edward stared back at her with a hunted expression. 'And what if I don't?'

'Then I pass those statements on to the Inland Revenue — who'll be very interested in them, I suspect. You've been fiddling the books for years, haven't you? Was that why all your other businesses went bust, because you were milking the profits? It wouldn't surprise me. I don't want to see you in jail, because of what it'd do to Toby, but that doesn't mean I don't think you thoroughly deserve it. And if you *ever* try to cheat or lie to me again, I'll have absolutely no hesitation about shopping you. Understand?'

At last, he nodded reluctantly. 'Yes.'

'I'm glad to hear it. I've no interest in what you get up to at the boatyard any more — as long as I get what's due for Toby, I'll be satisfied. I never did want very much, Edward, but you begrudged me even that. And I wish, I really do wish, that I didn't have to do this, but in the end your vindictiveness forced me to. Because it's Toby who matters most to me, and because I know he'd be much happier with me than with you. Oh, he likes seeing you, he looks forward to it, and you've had a lot of fun together — in fact, I suspect you enjoy his company far more now than when he was under your feet all the time. But you'd find it hard to cope if he was ill, or difficult, or in trouble, wouldn't you? You're a fair-weather father, you know you are if you're honest with yourself. You only wanted custody out of revenge and spite, because you couldn't bear the thought that I'd left you for a woman. And you were wrong, weren't you? I'm not a lesbian, Edward, but even if I was, that doesn't make me a bad mother. Do you see that?'

At last, very unwillingly, he nodded again.

'Good. I'm glad that's sorted out. But just remember, Edward — *any* nastiness, and I'll pass on the statements, OK?'

Suddenly, he found his voice. 'You bitch, that's blackmail!'

'Then go ahead and tell the police. I don't mind.'

'You've got me over a barrel, haven't you!' Edward cried in anguish. 'God, you've stitched me up good and proper between you! I wish I'd never clapped eyes on you, I should have kicked you out when you got yourself up the spout!'

It was extraordinarily difficult to remain still and calm as he raged at her, but with a supreme effort, Harriet managed it. When he had spluttered at last into silence, she said softly, 'I'm sorry, Edward. I really do wish it could all have been different. I didn't want this to descend to a sordid battle over Toby. We were good together once, don't you remember?'

Behind her, Georgia made a muffled sound of contempt, but Harriet ignored her. She looked at her former lover's suffused, desperate face, and found herself feeling genuinely sorry for him. She had won, with a vengeance, but at what cost to him?

'You shouldn't have changed,' Edward said, and she saw, with a pang, real regret in his face. 'You changed too much, don't you see? You're not my sweet little Hattie any more.'

'No,' said Harriet. 'I grew up, and you couldn't cope with that. Goodbye, Edward.'

She glanced back as she got into the Tigra, and saw him standing in the doorway. And somehow, he no longer seemed as tall, or as handsome, or as imposing: instead, she could see suddenly what he would look like as an old, old man.

'You were absolutely brilliant, Harry!' said Georgia, as they drove back to Daphne's house. 'I couldn't have said it better myself.

You certainly gave the bastard something to think about, and all without raising your voice.' She grinned delightedly at her sister. 'I never knew you had it in you.'

'Neither did I.' Harriet stared straight ahead, still in a state of considerable shock. 'I can't believe what I've just done. He was right, wasn't he? It *is* blackmail.'

'I suppose so,' said Georgia, the criminal lawyer. 'But quite justified, in my book. Anyway, you aren't asking for money, are you? Just for what's rightfully yours in any case. Don't waste any tears on him, Harry, he's not worth it.'

'Don't worry, I'm not crying for his sake.' Harriet sniffed valiantly and wiped her nose with a crumpled tissue. 'I'm crying because Toby's safe now, and I've got what I wanted, and I still can't quite believe it's all OK, and yet I know it is.'

'You know your trouble?' said Georgia fondly. 'You're hopelessly confused. Just sit back and relax and enjoy it, that's my advice. Forget about Edward. Forget about Morgan. Forget about men, and get on with your life. It's all coming good for you now, so go with the flow!'

'If only it was that easy,' said Harriet.

Daphne was waiting for them at Holly Cottage. When she saw their jubilant faces, she came out, smiling, to embrace them. 'So it worked! I'm so glad for you, Harriet my dear. Shall we all have a celebratory lunch? I've got a rather nice bottle of wine in the fridge, just waiting to be opened.'

Harriet had arranged for Toby to play with his friend Nicholas after playgroup, so the three women enjoyed a very cheerful, grownup meal on the patio. They worked their way through salads, warm bread and a delicious walnut and Stilton pâté that Daphne had made that morning, and Georgia, with great gusto, described for their host's benefit the details of their meeting with Edward.

'So you've got rid of one useless man,' she said, turning to Harriet, who had been rather quiet during the meal. 'Now what about the other one?'

'The other one? You mean Morgan?'

'Who else could I mean?'

'He seems a very lively and charming young man to me,' Daphne observed mildly, sipping her wine.

'*Morgan?*' Georgia demanded. 'Has Harriet ever told you what he did to her, ten years ago?'

'That was ten years ago, and he was twenty-two and I was twenty,' her sister pointed out. 'Don't tell me you never made any mistakes at that age. How about that total nerd you claimed was so gorgeous, and who turned out to be seeing about six women at the same time?'

'You mean Miles? Oh, that was just infatuation, I was never serious about him.'

'Just as well,' said Harriet drily. 'He liked wearing Hawaiian shirts.'

'Yes, well, we all have a few skeletons rattling in our cupboards,' Georgia said, grinning. 'Anyway, I've given up on men, totally. By the time you get to my age, all the good ones are hooked — married, or living together, or engaged. The rest are either gay, or so creepy no woman would look at them twice. My last relationship ended six months ago, and quite honestly I'm happier without one. The cat's better company, and much, much less trouble. Take my advice, Harriet, and tell Morgan to sling his hook.'

'I already have,' Harriet said.

'Good for you! Now all we have to do is find you a place of your own — you can't go on living with poor Daphne for the rest of your life, now can you? There's a nice little garden flat to let just round the corner from me — '

'Georgia,' said Harriet, 'can you please get it into your head that this is *my* life, and I'll

410

live it how *I* want? I'm very grateful for all your help, both of you, but I'm a big girl now, and I think I've proved that I can cope with most things. I'm not some little wet-behind-the-ears kid any more, you know.'

'I do know,' her sister said, rather huffily.

'Anyway, I've decided what I'm going to do,' Harriet said firmly. 'You are right, Georgia, in at least one thing — I do need my own place. It's been wonderful here, Daphne, and you've been absolutely brilliant, but I think it's time for me and Toby to move on, don't you? We've imposed on your kindness for long enough.'

'I've enjoyed having you both, my dear, but I think you're quite right. And I must say, I could do with a little peace and quiet while I contemplate my next move. In fact, I've even thought of selling up and going somewhere sunnier. Starting a wildlife garden in Provence sounds rather attractive, don't you think?'

'It sounds perfect,' said Harriet. 'Just don't rely on my help, that's all. I can't speak a word of French.'

'If I decide I need your illustrations, well, what are long summer holidays for?' said Daphne, smiling. 'So, what are you going to do, Harriet?'

'I've thought about it a lot recently,' she

said, glancing at Georgia, who was still looking rather indignant. 'I did think about moving away from Sanden, because I didn't like the idea of bumping into Edward all the time. But then I thought of Toby, and how he's so happy at playgroup, and all set to go to school in September, and about him growing up here, with all his friends — there's a lovely sort of stability about it. So I decided that if I could, I'd find somewhere here, in Sanden. Especially as I'm going to be painting the underground house, as well. I thought I would ask Sir Marcus if he has anywhere vacant — I know he owns a few places in the village.'

'Won't it be far too expensive?' Georgia asked dubiously.

'With the maintenance from Edward, and the money for the murals, I should be able to afford somewhere,' said Harriet, with rather more confidence than she actually felt. 'Anyway, I can look after myself. Honestly, George, I *can*. You don't have to do the big-sister act any more. Please, can we clear it all out of the way now, and just be friends, on equal terms?'

'I suppose so,' said Georgia reluctantly. 'But it won't be easy, breaking the habit of a lifetime.'

'Well, have a go,' Harriet told her. 'Because

I don't intend to play little sister any more, either. Deal?'

'Deal,' said Georgia, after a pause, and extended her hand. 'Let's shake on it, shall we?'

So that was that, Harriet thought, as she waved her sister goodbye, much later. Everything apparently cleared up, sorted, finished. Don Potter had called, just after lunch, to say that Edward had withdrawn his application for custody, and so everything would continue as it had before. She and Toby were safe from his interference. She had her life back under control, and her future career as an artist glowed enticingly ahead of her.

But she knew that Morgan's departure would leave an aching void in her life that no one else could fill.

29

Tom, the evening barman at the Wharf Inn, was accustomed to the sight of customers drowning their sorrows. It was not surprising, he thought, that Mr Armstrong was in here knocking back the booze: the poor bloke had been through a lot recently. It would drive anyone to drink, having his partner leave him for another woman. He glanced at the clock. Half past nine. Fortunately, he'd only have to stagger across the road to his house, and in any case he was no trouble, sitting at the bar morosely glaring into his whisky. Tom decided that if Mr Armstrong asked for another one, he'd politely suggest that he think again.

A tall man left his table by the window and came up to the counter to order another drink. Tom knew him by sight: he was Sir Marcus Grant's tame architect, and another good regular customer, though he usually drank no more than a couple of pints of beer. Tonight, however, he had already finished his fifth. He strode straight up to the counter and dropped a five-pound note on it. 'Another pint of Six-X, please.'

Tom, anticipating, was already pulling it, although he did wonder if serving him any more would be a good idea. There was something about the look in his eyes that he didn't like. He put the brimming glass on the counter. 'Anything else, sir?'

'No thanks,' said the man. As he waited for his change, he glanced round the almost empty bar. His eyes briefly rested on Edward Armstrong, a few feet along the counter, with a look that seemed so brimful of loathing that Tom, startled, wondered if he had imagined it, and then he took his beer back to the table by the window.

Edward had seen him, but was too sunk in his own misery to pay much attention. The worm had turned, Harriet had won the battle, and to add insult to injury, Selina Grant had told him, in terms that were neither tactful nor flattering, that she was no longer interested in him. Edward was not used to rejection, and it seemed that he had had a surfeit of it in the past few months. And with the incriminating bank statements in her possession, Harriet had the power to make him do exactly what she wanted.

Where did my sweet little Hattie go? Edward wondered despairingly. He remembered how eager she had been to please him, her gratifying devotion, her sleek, lovely body.

He could no longer recognise her in the calm, composed and formidable young woman who had so comprehensively defeated him that morning. But hardest of all to bear was the bitter realisation that, although this Harriet was cruelly different from the old one, part of him still wanted her. And he couldn't have her, ever again.

All that day, fuelled by increasing quantities of alcohol, he had sought vainly for a way out of his predicament. He couldn't steal the statements back, because they were undoubtedly safely under lock and key at her sister's office. He couldn't call her bluff, because she would certainly carry out her threat to send them to the Inland Revenue. And then the whole can of worms would be opened, and the taxmen would look under every stone. They would investigate not only Wonderland Boats, but all the other, ostensibly unprofitable businesses he had run during the past twenty years: the wine importer, the travel firm, and even, if he was very unfortunate, the dodgy financial advice service that had been rather more lucrative for Edward than for any of his clients. And he, Edward, would face, at best, disgrace and a hefty fine, and at worst, a considerable term of imprisonment.

He had thought of trying to persuade Harriet to come back to him, but he knew that he would never be able to dominate and manipulate her as he had done before. Using Toby as a lever had, in retrospect, been a big mistake. His only hope was that one day, she would relent. But he really didn't fancy the thought that his future rested on her whim. Women were inconsistent, illogical creatures, and Harriet a prime example — why else would she have given up her comfortable existence at the boatyard? Give her the slightest, most trivial excuse and she'd be off to the tax office, intent on ruining his life.

There was only one thing for it — he had to leave. The boatyard should fetch a fair bit as a going concern. And then he could move somewhere more congenial. South Africa sprang to mind: he had contacts there, a legacy of his brief foray into the wine trade, and it was a place where you could still live well, despite the change in government. Or Australia. Somewhere sunny, full of gorgeous women, where he could make a fresh start.

The more he thought about it, the more attractive the idea seemed. The only disadvantage was that he would cut himself off from Toby, and the prospect filled him with real grief. To his secret astonishment, he had found himself genuinely enjoying the brief but intensely happy and fun-filled hours of contact with his only son, and all that uncritical adulation was very flattering.

But I had to miss my golf every Sunday afternoon, Edward reminded himself. And after today's humiliation, the thought of having to be polite to Harriet as she handed Toby over each time made his blood run cold. It was all that Daphne woman's fault, it must be, turning her into a man-hating feminist. He wouldn't be a bit surprised if she *was* a lesbian after all, despite her denials.

Well, he wasn't going to put up with it for much longer. He'd be gone. She wouldn't be able to reach him where he was going. She would have to do without his money. And the child was so young, he wouldn't miss his father for long.

If she doesn't like it, well, that's her look-out, he thought savagely. It's all her fault anyway, so she can't complain. She's driven me to this.

He was sure now. He sipped his whisky, thinking. If he put Wonderland Boats on the market tomorrow, it shouldn't take long to find a buyer. He could be out of her grasp before Christmas.

Then he realised that there was one very major flaw in his plans. If Harriet heard he was selling the yard, she'd be bound to guess what he was up to. And then she'd shop him.

His plans in ruins, Edward groaned, and

gulped down the last of the whisky. He pushed the glass towards Tom, who was polishing tankards. 'Another. Make it a double.'

'Are you sure that's wise, Mr Armstrong?' The barman was looking at him with some concern. 'Don't you think you've had enough already?'

'No, I don't,' said Edward. 'Now give me a double. You don't want me to make a fuss, do you?'

'You'll regret it in the morning, sir,' said Tom, with the wisdom of long experience of other people's hangovers. 'Now why don't you go home and sleep it off?'

'That's my look-out,' Edward said savagely. 'Give me my sodding drink or I'll come round and get it myself.'

'There's no call to be so rude,' Tom said. 'I really do think you've had enough, Mr Armstrong.'

'Trouble?'

It was the architect. He had come over to stand beside the bar. He was a couple of inches taller than Mr Armstrong, nearly ten years younger, and looked considerably fitter. Tom said calmly, 'Nothing I can't handle, sir. I'm quite used to dealing with drunks.'

'I'm *not* a drunk!' Edward shouted, his face dangerously flushed. He swung round to

Morgan. 'And you can piss off out of it, it's nothing to do with you.'

'The way you've treated Harriet is plenty to do with me, you complete and absolute bastard.'

'*What?* That's none of your business, is it?'

'Oh yes it is. I care a lot about Hal, we used to live together when we were students, and you've put her through hell the last few weeks. So I should take this gentleman's advice and go home, before I'm tempted to punch your teeth down your throat.'

'I've put *her* through hell! What about what she's done to me?' Edward cried in fury. 'Leaving me for that bloody dyke — '

'Harriet isn't a lesbian, and if you weren't so boring and selfish in bed you'd have discovered that long ago.'

It was a singularly stupid and inflammatory thing to say, and Morgan realised it as soon as the words had left his mouth. Edward, his eyes bulging with rage, hurled himself off the bar stool, knocking it over, and swung his fist at his tormentor. Morgan, whose reactions were still fast, despite the six pints of beer, promptly stepped back out of his reach.

'For God's sake,' Tom said, backing away towards the end of the bar, where the phone was. 'If you *must* fight then kindly do it outside! Mr Armstrong, *please* be careful — '

Too late. Edward was advancing on Morgan. A table, fortunately unoccupied, lay between them, and he pushed it furiously out of his way. 'Why don't you stand still?' he yelled. 'Come on, stand and take what's coming to you, you bastard!'

Safe, for the moment, behind the bar, Tom was frantically dialling 999. Morgan glanced around. He had no doubts about his ability to pulverise Edward if it came to blows, and ten years ago he'd have done it quite happily. But it was different now. He had something to prove, and knocking his assailant into the middle of next week was not the way to do it. Besides, the drunken, desperate figure in front of him was not exactly a formidable opponent. If he could extract himself from this situation without harm to himself or to Edward, then he would.

'Come on, this is stupid,' he said. 'Calm down and think about what you're getting into. You can't win, and you know it.'

'Can't I?' Edward's bloodshot gaze darted round the familiar room. The few other customers shrank into the darker corners, determined not to get involved in the fracas. 'That's where you're wrong, sunshine. I've seen you with that bitch, setting me up, and I know what you're doing. Now STAND STILL!'

Morgan had no intention of obeying, but he took another step backwards and found himself pressed against one of the Wharf's larger and more solid tables. He realised, with a mixture of alarm and wry amusement, that he had nowhere to go, and the gloating sneer on Edward's sodden face revealed that he knew it too. 'Gotcha, you bastard! She won't think you're so pretty when I've finished with you!'

★ ★ ★

Toby was in bed and, hopefully, asleep, supper had been consumed and washed up, and Harriet, her nerves still jumping, was gathering her courage to phone Forfar Towers. After her brave words that afternoon, she must ask Sir Marcus if he could rent her a house. And then she really ought to speak to Morgan and tell him that Edward had withdrawn his application for custody. She wouldn't give him the real reason why for the sudden capitulation, but at any rate he ought to know Toby was safe. She owed him that, at the very least.

She dialled the number, and Sir Marcus answered almost immediately. 'Harriet? How nice to hear from you. Not having second thoughts, I hope, about what you've taken on?'

'No, of course not. I'm really looking forward to it.'

'Good. I'm sorting out the draft contract now, and it should be ready for both of us to sign tomorrow, if you like.'

'That'd be great. Thanks.' Harriet took a deep breath. 'I wanted to ask you something.'

'Ask away.'

'Well, I can't stay at Daphne's house for ever, and I've decided to look for somewhere else to live. I know you rent out a few places in the village, and I was wondering if you had anything coming vacant in the near future?'

There was a brief silence, and then his voice came back, sounding surprised. 'I don't think so — no, no, I haven't. Only the stable flat, and Morgan's living there at present.'

'Oh,' Harriet said.

'I presume he'll be moving out in a week or two, but until then it's occupied. Anyway, there's barely room for one person, never mind two, and it's in a bit of a state — in fact, I've got the builders coming in to do it up once he's gone. Sorry, my dear, but I've nothing else free at the moment.'

'That's all right,' said Harriet, striving to keep the acute disappointment out of her voice. 'It was a long shot, anyway. I'll find somewhere, don't worry. Thanks.'

'Not at all. If anything does come up, you'll be the first person I tell. In fact, there could be something in the pipeline, but not for a while. How desperate are you?'

'Well, Daphne's not exactly throwing me out, but I do think it's time we gave her some space. Anyway, she's thinking of moving abroad.'

'Is she, indeed? Where did she have in mind?'

'Provence, she said. But I don't think it's got any further than vague thoughts.'

'Hmm. Well, I shall have to have a talk with her, find out what's happening. Thanks for tipping me the wink.'

'I hope she won't mind me telling you,' Harriet said.

'Don't worry, I'll be very discreet, I promise.'

'Thanks.' Harriet paused, and then added, her heart thumping, 'Before I go, do you know if Morgan's around?'

'Sorry, my dear, I'm pretty sure he's gone out. To the pub, I think.' Sir Marcus's voice held a note of concern. 'Forgive me if I seem nosy, but have you and he fallen out?'

'Not really,' Harriet said, unwilling to elaborate.

'Well, he's been decidedly grim all day.

Something's obviously wrong. Still, none of my business. I'll let you know as soon as I have any news for you, about a house.'

'Thank you very much,' Harriet said, with considerable gratitude. 'It's really kind of you.'

'Not at all, my dear. The least I could do.'

She said goodbye, and put the receiver back, thinking. It wouldn't be dark for nearly an hour, and although it was still raining, the downpour had dwindled to a soft, fine drizzle. She could take Maggie along the towpath, and meet Morgan at the Wharf Inn. It was only half a mile, she had a torch, and both she and the dog could do with the exercise after being cooped up for most of the day. Decided, she took the lead and her waterproof jacket off the hook and went into the sitting room, where Daphne was listening intently to a play on the radio. 'I think I'll take the dog for a walk, if that's OK. Toby's fast asleep.'

'Go ahead,' said Daphne, with a quick, preoccupied smile.

Outside, the invisible sun was obviously very low in the sky, and the obscuring veil of cloud had a curious brown tinge to the grey. Harriet walked briskly, lost in thought, while Maggie wandered behind her, investigating smells in the hedgerows. It was such a murky evening that even the fishermen, whose rods often lined the canal from Sanden Top Lock to the Wharf and beyond, had all gone home. But at Park Lock, halfway between the two, four boys were sitting on the black and white arm of the top gate. As she approached, Harriet recognised the scrawny figure of her neighbour's son, and smiled at him. 'Hi, Adam.'

He was looking decidedly shifty, and one of the other lads had something very obviously concealed under his jacket. Ignoring it, Harriet said brightly, 'How's your mother?'

'Going spare,' the boy told her, with a quick glance at his mates. 'It's the judging on Saturday.'

'Judging?'

'For the competition. Best Kept Village.'

'I'd completely forgotten about that,' Harriet said, in some surprise. 'So how's her campaign going?'

One of the other boys sniggered, and muttered something to the lad beside him. Adam gave her a rather reluctant grin. 'Not very well. No one's that keen to help any more.'

'I ain't surprised,' said the boy who had laughed. He was tall, with long, floppy dark hair, parted in the middle, and he wore the ubiquitous teenage uniform of baggy jeans, sweatshirt and baseball cap. 'Bossy old cow.'

'Lay off, Ben, that's my mum you're talking about,' said Adam, but he didn't sound very disapproving. Harriet paused, wondering whether to mention drawing lessons, and decided that he might not appreciate her talking about it in front of his peers. Instead, she called Maggie, who was still wandering along behind her, and gave the boys a cheery wave. 'See you!'

'See yer,' said Adam, slouching back against the lock gate, and giving a very good impression of not caring whether he did or not. As she walked on along the towpath, she glanced hack. The four lads were in a huddle again, obviously examining whatever it was they didn't want her to see.

God, I hope Toby isn't like that in ten years' time, Harriet thought, with some apprehension. She could easily deal with his whingeing and his temper tantrums, which were anyway becoming increasingly rare, but the thought of trying to cope single-handed with a surly teenage boy whose overriding concern was to look cool in front of his mates was a grim one.

At the Wharf Lock, she had to wait again for the dog to catch up, so she sat down on the black and white arm of the bottom gate. It was so quiet, so peaceful. She could hear a pheasant calling as it prepared to roost, and the distant lowing of cattle up at Quarry Farm. If she turned her head, she could see the red scar on the hillside above her which marked the position of the underground house, and beyond it, further up and to the left, a light on the ground floor of Forfar Towers.

What am I going to do about Morgan? Harriet thought unhappily. I can't just avoid him for the next few weeks, if I'm working on the dragons. At the least, I shall need to go over to Y Wâl Yr Draig to take measurements and make notes. I just hope he can accept what I've decided.

From Sir Marcus's description of his present mood, she rather doubted it. Like Edward — it was probably the only characteristic they had in common — Morgan was used to getting what he wanted. And he had never coped well with failure, or rebuff.

Well, he's going to have to learn to live with it, she thought sadly, as Maggie came panting up to her. And so am I.

By now, it was rapidly growing dark. Harriet put the dog back on the lead, and climbed the steps to the road bridge. As she reached the top, she had to leap back as a police car, blue lights flashing, roared past and screeched to a halt outside the pub, just along the road. With a sudden, awful presentiment of catastrophe, Harriet sprinted along the bridge, the dog lumbering beside her, and into the Wharf Inn's forecourt. She tied Maggie up to one of the empty wet benches, and ran inside.

There had been a fight. Her frantic gaze swept over upturned tables, smashed glass, horrified customers. Someone was sitting on the floor, with several people bending over him, and a big policeman and his female colleague were grappling with a man in the centre of the room. As the struggling, heaving group in front of her turned, Harriet saw, with horror, that the man they were attempting to restrain was her former partner.

30

She shouted his name in horror, and Edward turned, his face distorted with blind rage. Taking advantage of his momentary distraction, the policeman grabbed his flailing arms. 'That's quite enough of that, sir. Cuff him, quick!'

Harriet watched, appalled, as the two officers employed a series of efficient moves which left her former lover lying on the floor, his hands safely secured. Then she stumbled to the nearest chair, her legs shaking, and sat down.

'Do you know him?' The WPC was standing in front of her, looking concerned. 'Are you all right?'

Harriet nodded. 'He's my ex-partner. His name's Edward Armstrong.'

'Have you any idea why he would suddenly have gone berserk like this?'

'I — I — it's a long story,' Harriet stammered, the utter impossibility of explaining it all overwhelming her. 'I mean, we split up a few months ago — it hasn't been very pleasant — but I never dreamed — I mean, this isn't like him at *all* — '

The policewoman's radio gabbled something, and she bent her head to speak into it. 'Yes, back-up, ASAP. Ambulance too, one casualty. Suspect now secure, could be looking at GBH, plus resisting arrest, drunk and disorderly, criminal damage.' She glanced up at Harriet. 'I'll need to take statements here. Yes. Over.'

'Let me *go*!' Edward snarled breathlessly from the floor. The copper beside him had his knee on his back, holding him still. 'Now, sir, calm down. I should just lie quiet if I were you.'

'There's another car coming, and an ambulance.' The WPC went over to the man sitting on the floor amongst the tables. Harriet noticed, for the first time, that he was wearing jeans that looked familiar, and rather muddy dark trainers which, surely, she had seen before . . .

Feeling curiously remote, as if she had somehow strayed on to a film set, she got up and walked across the bar. She avoided looking down until she was standing beside the WPC, afraid of what she might see.

She was right. It was Morgan sitting down there amongst the overturned stools and the shards of broken glass. He was bleeding profusely from a cut above his bruised left eye, and his face was ashy pale.

She gasped his name, and he looked up, with something approaching a smile on his face. 'Hi, Hal. What are you doing here?'

'Marcus said you'd gone to the pub, and I wanted to talk to you.' Her voice cracked, and to hide her acute distress she knelt down beside him. 'For God's sake, Morgan, what's happened?'

'I told him a couple of home truths, and he attacked me,' Morgan said, with the ghost of a grin. 'Do tell me, *cariad*, is my beauty still intact?'

'You picked a fight with him?' Now that she could see that the damage wasn't too serious, Harriet's fear for him was rapidly changing to anger. 'What in God's name did you want to do that for?'

'I didn't have a lot of choice. Apart from anything else, he's as pissed as a newt.'

'And you aren't, I suppose.' Harriet stared down at him, furious. 'God, Morgan, I thought you'd grown out of this sort of caper! That's what brainless yobbos do, fighting in pubs. What am I going to tell Toby about what you and his father have been up to? Honestly, the pair of you are behaving like a couple of cavemen, only probably not half as intelligent!'

'It wasn't exactly like that,' Morgan began, but Harriet swept on. 'To be quite honest, if

432

this is the sort of thing you're going to do, then I'm *glad* you're getting out of our lives, because it's not exactly the kind of example I want Toby to follow, is it? It's about time you got a grip on yourself, Morgan Price, and just grew up a bit and started behaving like a civilised human being!'

'Hal, listen — '

'I've no intention of standing here listening to your pathetic excuses,' Harriet said, her voice wobbling. 'I'm going home.'

As she stumbled outside, the WPC caught up with her. 'Listen, I'm sorry, I know this isn't a good time, but I might need a statement from you. Either now, or at a later date, when you're less upset.'

'OK.' Feeling drained and utterly exhausted, Harriet leaned against the bench that she had tied Maggie to, only a few minutes earlier. 'I didn't see anything, I only arrived after it was all over.'

'I know, but you may be able to fill us in on a little of the background to all this. If it was the culmination of a long-standing dispute, for instance . . . '

Harriet shook her head, still dazed with shock and disbelief. 'Not really. Morgan and Edward hardly know each other.'

A siren wailed suddenly, and an ambulance, followed by a second police car, shot

433

over the bridge and halted outside the pub. Hastily, the WPC pulled out her notebook and wrote down Harriet's name and address. 'I'll be in touch, probably tomorrow. In the mean time, here's my card, OK? Thanks, Miss Smith.'

She followed the paramedics and the other police officers back inside, leaving Harriet alone in the dark. Like a sleepwalker, almost unaware of her surroundings, she turned and walked across the bridge. Somehow, she negotiated the steps down to the towpath, and set off back in the direction of Holly Cottage.

She had gone perhaps fifty yards before she realised that, for the second time in three days, she had left poor Maggie tied up to the bench outside the pub.

She would have to go back. And suddenly, pushing painfully into her consciousness, came a sharp and agonising spear of guilt. What had she done? Morgan was in there, hurt, in need of her. And instead of comforting him, and helping him, she had covered her fear with anger, told him to grow up, and then abandoned him.

Sick with remorse and self-loathing, Harriet turned and ran back up the steps. She was just in time to see Edward being pushed into the back of the second police car, which then drove off at speed. Immediately afterwards, the ambulance shut its doors and followed it.

She was too late. Miserably, she walked back to the bench, and sat down. Maggie, aware of her distress, pushed a sympathetic cold, wet nose into her hand, and was rewarded with an absent fondling of her ears. 'Oh, Mags, what shall I do?' Harriet whispered. 'I've been utterly horrible to him, and perhaps he didn't deserve it, and how I wish I hadn't!'

The dog put a comforting paw on to her thigh. Normally, it wasn't a reaction she encouraged, but this was emphatically not a normal occasion. Overcome with confusion and anguish, Harriet buried her face in the soft, wet fur, and tried not to weep.

'Miss Smith? It *is* Miss Smith, isn't it?'

She looked up, startled, and hastily took her glasses off to wipe her eyes. This meant that the dim blur in front of her became even less recognisable. She swallowed hard, trying to get herself back in control, and said, 'Yes, it is. Sorry, I don't know who you are. I can't see you very well in this light.'

'Keith Clark. Heather's husband.'

Harriet pushed her glasses back on her nose and gazed at him warily. 'Yes?'

'I . . . ' The man paused, and cleared his throat with some embarrassment. 'Miss Smith, I want to apologise. I feel that my family may have done you and Miss James a considerable injustice.'

Astonished, Harriet stared at him. She could only see the orange street light reflected off the lenses of his own glasses, and they gave her no clues. She said at last, 'Why — why have you decided this?'

'I was in there, earlier.' He nodded at the pub behind him. 'I saw and heard everything that happened. I must say, Mr Armstrong's behaviour this evening has opened my eyes, and I am sure that if my wife had also seen it, she would say the same.' He had a rather clipped, formal way of speaking that put Harriet in mind of Don Potter, and she seemed to remember Adam saying that he was an accountant.

Still mightily confused, she shook her head in bewilderment. 'So what was the fight about?'

Keith Clark coughed drily. 'I gained the impression that it was about *you*, Miss Smith.'

'About *me*? Why on earth would they quarrel about *me*?' Harriet demanded, and then paused. 'Don't tell me. Morgan can be very protective at times. I expect he was raring to slug Edward because of the way he'd treated me.'

'Well, no, actually, Miss Smith, he wasn't. Certainly, drink had been taken on both sides, and to considerable excess on Mr Armstrong's part. And heated words were exchanged. But once Mr Armstrong became aggressive, your other friend, Mr Morgan — '

'Mr Price. Morgan's his Christian name.'

'Mr Price. He seemed very keen to avoid a fight. In fact, he was backing off and trying to calm things down when Mr Armstrong hit him.'

'Oh,' Harriet said. The feelings of guilt intensified. She added miserably, 'And I tore him off a strip for picking a fight, and it wasn't his fault at all.'

'He did say some pretty unpleasant things to Mr Armstrong,' Clark pointed out. 'But in view of the circumstances, I think I'd have done the same in his place. Fortunately, no lasting harm seems to have been done, and it certainly enlivened a rather dull evening. Now, may I offer you a lift home? It's getting late, and I wouldn't want to think of you walking along that towpath on your own.'

'Not quite on my own — I've got the dog. Not that she'd be any use in a crisis.' Harriet gave Maggie an affectionate pat. 'But anyway, yes, thanks, I'd love a lift. As long as you don't mind having her as well, she's a bit damp and doggy.'

'Of course not. I feel we owe you something, and in any case it's a company car, so I'm not too worried about its condition. It's over there.'

The car was a brand-new Mercedes, even larger and more luxurious than the BMW which was Edward's pride and joy. Harriet persuaded Maggie to sit in the footwell between her knees, hoping that she wouldn't make too much mess of the upholstery. When Keith turned the lights on, the dashboard lit up like the Regent Street Christmas display, and the engine hummed throatily. They glided out of the Wharf's car park and crossed the canal bridge.

'I've been hoping for the chance to ask you or your wife about Adam,' Harriet said, as the car squeezed into the side of the road to avoid an oncoming van.

'Adam? What's he been doing?'

'Nothing. I like him, he's a nice boy.'

'Goodness me,' said Keith, with genuine surprise. 'He usually hides it extremely well.'

'I gave him a lift, a few weeks ago, and we got talking. I don't know if you were aware of it, but I'm an artist.' Harriet could not suppress the thrill of pride with which she said the words. 'And he's very keen on drawing, he said.'

'Yes, he spends hours up in his room producing wads of the stuff. They don't look bad to me, but then I know nothing about it — figures are my thing.' Keith, his rather prim face eerily lit by the glowing dashboard, glanced at her. 'He says he'd like to go to art school, and Heather and I have been trying to dissuade him.'

'But what if he has real talent?'

There was a slightly uncomfortable pause. Keith said at last, 'I'm not the best judge of that. But I do know that with the job market so competitive, he needs proper qualifications and training. There's a place earmarked for him, at my firm, when he's done his A-levels.'

'Even if he'll hate it?'

Again, the slight pause. Then Keith smiled suddenly. 'So what are you suggesting, Miss Smith?'

'Please call me Harriet. I'm suggesting that I have a look at what he does, and see if it's any good. And if he has got talent . . . well, I promised him that if you and your wife agreed, I'd give him drawing lessons.'

'But he's doing art GCSE at school. We tried to put him off, but he can be very stubborn. Why should he need extra? It's hard enough to get him to do his homework as it is.'

'He says his teacher doesn't know anything about what he wants to do.' Harriet looked at Keith's face, wondering whether its impassive expression concealed unexpected sympathy. 'Nor do I, much, but I've been to art school and I can give him some pointers. He's very keen.'

'All right.' Keith smiled again, more broadly this time. 'You've persuaded me — now I have the unenviable task of talking my wife round. And I warn you, that might be difficult.'

'Mr Clark.' Harriet paused, choosing her words carefully, and then continued. 'Neither Daphne nor I ever wanted this dispute to get out of hand in the way it has, and I don't think your wife does, either. If we can find a way to declare a truce, then I'm happy to do it. It would be nice if everyone could accept that people are different, and have different priorities, and just live and let live.'

'I agree entirely,' said Keith. The Mercedes purred over the canal bridge, and its headlights threw the two verges, shaggy and flower-strewn outside Holly Cottage, shorn and viridian outside its neighbour, into appropriately sharp relief. 'But Heather has always been, how shall I put it, very

440

wholehearted in her likes and dislikes. However, Miss Smith — Harriet — I shall endeavour to do my best to persuade her that you and Miss James are not fiends or ogres.'

'And not lesbians, either,' Harriet reminded him.

'Personally, I couldn't care less whether you and Miss James dress up as witches and celebrate the Sabbat by dancing round a bonfire,' said Keith, and his smile reminded her suddenly of Adam. 'I don't think I could ever persuade Heather to adopt a similarly broad-minded viewpoint, but you are right — more toleration all round wouldn't come amiss.'

'It certainly wouldn't,' Harriet said. The car had halted outside Holly Cottage, and she opened the door. Maggie, smelling powerfully of wet dog, crawled out with some difficulty, and shook herself vigorously.

'Goodbye,' said Keith, with another smile.

'Goodbye — and thank you, very much, for the lift. I hope Maggie hasn't made too much mess.'

'It doesn't matter if she has. My pleasure, Harriet. And I hope that this is the start of a more cordial and neighbourly relationship between us.'

'So do I,' Harriet said. But she didn't put much faith in it. Both Heather and Daphne were surely too set in their ways, too convinced that they were right, for any compromise.

But for Adam's sake, she hoped that Heather could be persuaded.

31

By coincidence, the phones in both Holly Cottage and Cypress Lodge rang at about eleven that evening.

Keith Clark had had a frustrating time since his return. He had done his best to persuade his wife that neither Miss James nor Miss Smith was irredeemably wicked, and had failed to make any impression whatsoever on the ramparts of her closed mind.

'That Woman,' Heather announced furiously, 'has had it in for me from the start. She deliberately set out to wreck my life. She deserves everything she gets, in my opinion.'

'And what about Miss Smith? Harriet?'

'You're very friendly with her all of a sudden, aren't you? No better than she should be, that's plain for all to see, the shameless little tart. She couldn't even be bothered to marry poor Mr Armstrong for the sake of her precious son.'

'Poor Mr Armstrong,' Keith pointed out, 'has just drunkenly and violently attacked one of Miss Smith's friends, as well as two police officers. And in any case, it's hardly logical to accuse her of being a lesbian one day, and a tart the next.'

But Heather, sitting bolt upright in bed, was riding her hobby horse with gusto. Keith, looking at her distended eyes and rigid mouth, wondered, not for the first time, whether his wife was entirely rational. In one of their more unpleasant arguments, Jessica had accused her mother of having a screw loose. At the time he'd thought his daughter was just exaggerating. Now, he was not so sure.

'No better than she should be, that's obvious,' said Heather, warming to her theme. 'I can't believe that someone like that could be living in a place like this. I thought we had moved to a *nice* area, with the right sort of people. I thought we were coming up in the world. And now it seems it's no better than anywhere else!'

Just then, the bedside phone rang. At such a late hour, he always expected the worst: that his mother had been taken ill again, or that Jessica needed bailing out of another drugs charge. He was relieved when the voice at the other end said, 'Hallo, Keith, it's Christine. Can I speak to Heather, please?'

Her eyes bright with the residue of righteous anger, his wife leaned over to take the phone. Keith could not hear what Christine was saying, but an extraordinary change came over Heather. She drew herself up, and her face became mottled with outraged fury. Several times she seemed about to speak, but Christine rattled on. Keith, puzzled, thought that it was not often that Heather was unable to get a word in edgeways. At last she said, through stiff lips, 'Thank you, Christine, thank you very much for letting me know. Yes. Yes, at once. Yes, I know it's only two days away. Well, we must do what we can, mustn't we? They must not be allowed to get away with this, Christine. And if I catch the people responsible, I shall have no hesitation in handing them over to the police at once. Yes, of course. Yes, I'll meet you there. Goodbye, Christine.'

'What was that all about?' Keith enquired as she banged the phone down.

'Vandals,' said Heather, concisely and uninformatively. 'Don't wait up.'

Before he could ask any more questions, she had got out of bed, and he heard her marching purposefully down the stairs and into the hall. Bewildered, and not a little uneasy, Keith followed her. She was putting on her raincoat, over her floral cotton nightgown, and turned as he approached. 'I said, don't wait up!'

'I'd just like to know what's going on, that's all,' said her husband mildly.

445

'Can't stop,' said Heather, tying a transparent plastic rainhood over her curlers. 'Now go to bed and don't ask stupid questions.'

She went out into the wet darkness, slamming the door behind her. Keith heard the sound of the garage being opened, and the familiar cough of his wife's Peugeot coming to life. He considered going out to try and stop her, but he knew that in this sort of mood, Heather was quite capable of running him down — not from malicious intent, but simply because she was utterly fixated on one thing, to the exclusion of everything else.

Not for the first time, he wondered how long it would be before continuing his marriage became more difficult than the trauma of separation.

★ ★ ★

At more or less the same time, Harriet was making herself a cup of hot chocolate in the kitchen. She had spent some time telling Daphne what had happened at the Wharf, and afterwards, and as she related the story, she could feel her nerves winding up, taut and full of apprehension. She should have stayed with him. She should have gone with him in the ambulance. She shouldn't have said those things. Guilt and anxiety and regret filled her, but she found it impossible to admit as much to Daphne. She made light of the incident, and focused instead on her conversation with Keith Clark. 'He was really very pleasant and kind. I got the impression he knows exactly what Heather's like — '

'And so he should, he's been married to her for at least twenty years, and he probably realised what he'd let himself in for on the first night.'

'Anyway, he seems really sympathetic. I told him we wanted to live and let live.'

'If his wife will let us.' Daphne finished her nightcap, a glass of ten-year-old malt whisky, and rose to her feet. 'I have only ever wanted to be left in peace, Harriet. This dispute was all of her making, and quite honestly I don't feel like holding out an olive branch now. I'm sure she would throw it back in my face.'

'Well, perhaps I can be a sort of go-between,' Harriet suggested.

'You can try, my dear, but I've given up. I'm afraid I have never found it very easy to forgive and forget. And when I think of the lies and the spite she's poured out about us, I am almost tempted to go round and rotovate her lawn.'

Harriet smiled, although she felt as though she had been gently rebuked. 'Anyway, would you mind if I gave Adam drawing lessons?'

'Good heavens, no, you do what you want. Though I would be astonished if that surly lout excels at anything besides hanging around and getting up to no good. Anyway, I'm going up to bed. And don't worry about Morgan. His sort always land on their feet.'

Harriet knew it was true, but she could not rid her mind of the appalling memory of him sitting on the floor, white and bloodstained. Nor of Edward, his once handsome face scarlet and twisted with rage, struggling with the police who were trying to arrest him. She had no idea what Morgan had said to him, but it must have struck a very raw nerve. Edward had always been contemptuous of violence and aggression: his dominance of her had been based on more sophisticated methods. She could not find any sympathy for him, though. However sorely Morgan had provoked him, fighting with the police could not be excused.

She had already decided not to reveal his fraudulent activities. The list of offences he was likely to be charged with was long enough already. At the very least, he faced a sobering night in the cells, a hefty fine, and a detailed and humiliating report in the local paper. Now that she was certain that Toby would stay with her, she could not summon up her old anger. Edward would be punished enough for what he had done tonight. And if he ever threatened her again, she still had the bank statements, securely locked away in a filing cabinet at Georgia's office.

The phone rang just as she was pouring boiling milk into a mug. Swearing under her breath, Harriet put the saucepan on the draining board and ran to answer it. She already knew who it was likely to be.

She was right. 'Hi,' said Morgan's voice down the line. He sounded disgustingly cheerful. 'Are you coming to get me, then?'

Daphne, in striped pyjamas and red flannel dressing gown, was standing at the top of the stairs. Harriet indicated in vigorous sign language that the call was intended for herself. When her friend had gone back to bed, she sat down on the chair by the phone table, and said rather hesitantly, 'I'm really sorry.'

'Doesn't matter, I'll get a taxi.'

'No, not about that, I *will* come, no, I'm sorry about what I said to you earlier.'

'That doesn't matter either, *cariad*. You were right. I should never have accused him of being boring and selfish in bed.'

'You did *what*?'

'I accused him of being boring and selfish in bed. He must have been, if you were so unresponsive he thought you were a lesbian.

449

Whereas I,' said Morgan, and she could almost see his grin down the phone, 'am quite, quite certain that you can't possibly be.'

'You smug bastard!'

'Aren't I just? Anyway, are you coming to get me, or not?'

'You know what I think you deserve? I think you deserve to *walk* all the way back from Bath.'

'I'm not at Bath, I'm at Trowbridge Hospital. Two stitches and an all-clear from the X-ray. It'll only take you twenty minutes. Please, *cariad*?'

Harriet had never been able to argue with him in this mood. 'OK,' she said, grinning reluctantly. 'But the slightest misbehaviour and I *will* make you walk.'

'I'll be as good as gold. Butter won't melt in my mouth. Cross my heart and hope to die. After all,' Morgan added impudently, 'I *was* injured in defence of your honour.'

Harriet said a very rude word, and put the phone down. If she had any sense, she'd go to bed and let him trudge the rainy miles back to Sanden.

If she had had any sense, she'd never have gone to the cinema with him, ten years ago. She would never have let him kiss her, in the double seats in the back row. She would never have taken him back to her flat for coffee, and spent all night talking and laughing. And she would never have made love to him as the sun rose, unleashing a passion that she had never suspected within herself, that even betrayal and separation could not destroy. Like it or not, he was part of her past, and her present. And as for the future, it seemed harder to get rid of him than she'd thought.

She ran upstairs to tell Daphne where she was going. Toby had slept through the sound of the telephone, and she listened to his deep, regular breathing with a smile on her face. Then she hurried down to her car.

It took her some time to find Trowbridge Hospital, which was in a part of the town she didn't know very well. Fortunately, at this time of night there were plenty of parking spaces. She locked up the Polo and went into the bright fluorescent light of the A&E department.

It was empty, apart from Morgan. He was lying full-length across four chairs, and he appeared to be asleep. The nurse on the desk looked up as Harriet entered. 'Have you come to take Mr Price home?'

'For my sins, yes. Is he OK?'

'Nothing that a good night's sleep won't cure,' said the nurse, astringently. She was small and spare and grey-haired, and looked as if she stood no nonsense. 'If he complains of a headache, it's probably the beer rather than the injury. Mr Price?'

Morgan opened his eyes and then sat up, wincing theatrically. 'Christ, that hurts.'

'And so it should,' said Harriet, without sympathy. She stood looking down at him, her hands on her hips and a frown on her face. 'Honestly, you're impossible. Impossible, unreliable, incorrigible.'

'That's all right,' said Morgan, with a sly glance from under his unfairly long and thick eyelashes. 'Just as long as I'm adorable, too.'

'I should keep quiet if I were you, Mr Price,' advised the nurse. 'Or your long-suffering friend might be tempted to leave you here, and I'm not sure if my nerves can stand you much longer.'

'Don't worry,' said Harriet. 'I'd never hear the end of it if I did. If he's any trouble, I'll turf him out on the Hilperton bypass and let him walk home.'

'Do whatever you like,' the nurse told her, with a wink. 'Just make sure he doesn't come back here while I'm still on duty.'

'Whatever did you do to the poor woman?' Harriet demanded, as she led Morgan out to her car. At least he seemed to be walking straight, but she was not deceived. 'And how much did you have to drink?'

'A few beers, that's all. Your Edward must have sunk the best part of half a bottle of whisky. And I didn't do anything to that nurse. I may have buttered her up a bit, but where's the harm in that?'

'Where you're concerned, plenty.'

'Jealous?' Morgan enquired, an unholy gleam in his eyes. 'At last!'

'Oh, don't be ridiculous,' Harriet said, trying not to laugh, and failing dismally. 'Just get in the car and shut up.'

To her astonishment, Morgan seemed to take her at her word. He folded his long length into the rather cramped confines of the Polo's front passenger seat, leaned his head back, and closed his eyes. As she wrestled with the gear lever, which was always difficult to persuade into reverse, she sneaked a glance at him. The orange street lights gave his face a deceptively healthy glow, but the bruised left eye had become magnificently spectacular, like a pirate's patch, and he was still deathly pale. A worm of worry sneaked into the back of her mind, and she could not quite suppress it. She said, 'Are you going to be OK if I drop you off at the Towers?'

'I'm not dying,' Morgan said, his eyes still closed. 'I'm a big boy, I can handle a hangover.'

'Well, it's not as though you're not used to

them,' Harriet pointed out. 'I just wanted to make sure before I abandoned you. I'm rather too good at guilt.'

'Go on, say it. And I'm not.'

'I wasn't going to say anything!' Harriet protested indignantly.

'Oh, come on, *cariad*, you don't have to — you just look at me reproachfully with those big dark eyes. Do you really think I'm that low in the food chain?'

'Somewhere down between the virus and the bacteria,' said Harriet. She risked a grin. 'And that's giving you the benefit of the doubt.'

'One day,' Morgan said, 'you'll see me for what I really am.'

'That's what I'm afraid of. Aren't you worried?'

'I can't please you, can I?' His voice took on a pathetically plaintive note. 'No matter what I do . . . '

No matter what you do, I will always love you. I love your voice, and your eyes, and your body, and your smile, and above all, the silly things you say.

But she would never admit it, because she couldn't afford to be vulnerable again. Better to adopt this light, teasing manner, that gave absolutely nothing away. One day, she'd meet someone else, someone who could give her and Toby the stability they needed, and she would forget all about Morgan Price.

She drove out of Trowbridge and along the road that led to Sanden. It was late, and there was little traffic about. The rain had started again, and the swish of tyres on the wet road and the steady beat of the windscreen wipers were the only sounds in the little car. Harriet concentrated on driving, acutely aware of the man sitting beside her. Sometimes, she wanted him so much that she was sick with it. What would happen if she pulled into one of the dark little byways along the route, and began to touch him?

They would make love, without a doubt. And it would be absolutely wonderful. She would be even deeper in love with him than she was now, and then he would go off to Gloucestershire with that insouciant smile, and turn his charm on some other poor gullible female. And if that wasn't enough to put her off, after months of celibacy she didn't have any condoms, and she was quite certain that Morgan wouldn't either. Take the risk, and the possible consequences just didn't bear thinking about.

'What's happened to that bus stop?'

Lost in her thoughts, driving on automatic pilot, it took a while for Harriet to register what Morgan had said. 'What bus stop?'

'That one, back there. I thought your nosy neighbour took a paint-brush to it a few weeks ago.'

'She did.'

'Well, she isn't going to be very happy. It's completely covered in very rude graffiti.'

Harriet couldn't help laughing. 'You're right. She'll be *furious*. I wonder who did that?' As she drove up the hill, past the turning for Sanden Row, a sudden and vivid memory came into her mind, of Adam and his mates, and the boy hiding something beneath his coat.

'Isn't the judging for the competition supposed to be this weekend?' Morgan asked.

'Yes, it is.' At the top of the hill, she had to turn left at the crossroads, opposite the King's Arms. A car came the other way, its headlights unbearably brilliant, and Harriet cursed it under her breath. For a moment, swinging into School Lane, she was almost blind. Then Morgan said suddenly, 'Stop!'

Fortunately, there was no one behind her. Harriet stamped on the brakes so hard that the little car almost stood on its nose. Her heart thumping, thinking of loose dogs or children, even at this time of night, she peered into the gloom ahead. 'What? What is it? What's the matter?'

'Look,' said Morgan, and pointed at the school.

In common with many other villages in Wiltshire, the local recycling bins were lined up in the school car park, to the left of the main building. And a shadowy figure seemed to be busy around the dark bulk of the paper bank, at the far end.

'Vandals in action?' said Harriet in astonishment.

'Looks like it, doesn't it!' Morgan was undoing his seat belt. 'Come on, kiddo, let's catch them red-handed. Kill the lights. Have you got a torch? Bring it. I don't think they've noticed us.'

'Do you really think this is a good idea?' Harriet demanded. But Morgan was already creeping stealthily across the road.

I've got a bad feeling about this, Harriet thought. But someone had to make sure that Morgan didn't get in any more trouble tonight. And at least one of Adam's friends had looked capable of thumping anyone who crossed his path.

With a sigh of resignation, she took the torch out of the glove compartment, and got out of the car.

32

Morgan had made himself very thin and straight against the concrete post holding up the gate to the car park. To Harriet's amused but exasperated eyes, he looked like a parody of a film spy, or, alternatively, Tom the cat: any moment, she thought, he would slink across the tarmac as though transmuted into a river of oil. But as she came up to him, he glanced at her, put his finger to his lips, and walked normally but softly towards the dim shape of the vandal. Without much confidence in her ability to defuse any violence in the imminent confrontation, Harriet followed him.

She was amazed that their quarry still didn't seem to have noticed their presence, but just before Morgan reached it, the figure turned. There was an exclamation, a brief tussle, and then he said triumphantly, 'Gotcha! shine the torch, Hal.'

She switched it on and directed the beam straight at his captive's face.

There was a moment of total astonishment. Then Morgan dropped his arms as if a string holding them had been cut, and said, 'Good

God, it's the nosy neighbour!'

Squinting in the glare, Heather Clark drew herself up in a manner which Harriet had come to know all too well, and said coldly, '*Will* you turn that thing off? And go away.'

Harriet lowered the torch. The downward track of its beam illuminated Heather's expensive beige raincoat, its shoulders dark with moisture, and below it, incongruously, the hem of a pretty floral nightgown, and pink plastic fur-lined bootees. She began to wonder if she had strayed into some surreal alternative world, of the kind invented by *Monty Python*, in which the bizarre became commonplace and too insignificant to invite comment.

'Not until you've told us what you're doing here,' Morgan said, with rather more front, Harriet thought, than was good for him. 'After all, you have to admit, your behaviour is highly suspicious.'

'Doing? I'm doing my duty as the chairperson of the Sanden Neatness Action Group,' said Heather, with dignity. 'After all, I cannot let vandalism flourish unchecked.' She waved an arm at the huge dark bulk of the paper bank, behind her. 'Just look at that!'

Bewildered but obedient, Harriet shone the torch. Scrawled all across the dark-blue metal, below the slots for newspapers, sprayed silver writing two feet high advised anyone reading it that wanking was good for you.

'*And* on the other side!' said Heather, her voice quivering with affront. Harriet walked round and discovered the immortal slogan, *Sex'n'drugs'n'rock'n'roll*, with, amazingly, every apostrophe correctly positioned.

'Well, at least they're educated vandals,' she said, trying not to catch Morgan's eye: if she did, she knew that she wouldn't be able to keep the laughter bottled up any longer.

'Hang on a minute,' said her ex-lover, with wilful mischief. 'Did *you* do this, Mrs Clark?'

'*I?* Don't be ridiculous, young man. Of course I didn't.'

'Then what are you doing here?' Morgan persisted, with what Harriet considered to be a highly dangerous lack of perception, especially as it was obviously spurious.

'I would have thought that was perfectly clear,' said Heather, with scathing contempt. 'I am painting the graffiti over, of course. What do you think that is?'

Harriet shone the torch on the object on the ground beside her. It proved to be a large can of pale-peach vinyl silk emulsion.

'I'm not sure I approve of the colour scheme,' said Morgan. 'Won't that look worse than the graffiti?'

'Nothing,' Heather said heavily, 'could possibly be worse than that kind of vulgar and obscene scrawl. Now if you will kindly let me finish — '

Several large drops of rain chose that moment to splash down on them, and a mutter of thunder disturbed the air. Harriet said, 'You can't possibly paint in a downpour at this time of night, Mrs Clark. If I were you, I'd go home and do it tomorrow.'

'It really is none of your business, is it, Miss Smith?' said Heather.

The stare from her rather protuberant blue eyes made Harriet feel suddenly and distinctly uncomfortable. She said in bewilderment, 'But the judging isn't until Saturday. You've got loads of time to do it tomorrow, in daylight — '

'I am doing it *now*,' Heather snapped. She picked up the loaded paintbrush from the top of the open can, and advanced on them threateningly. 'It wouldn't surprise me if *you* weren't behind all this. You've been looking for a way to have your own back on me, haven't you, after I told Mr Armstrong about what you'd been getting up to. Nothing would suit you better than having Sanden shown up for the sort of place you'd like it to be.'

'Oh, for God's sake,' said Morgan,

suddenly losing patience. 'You must have a screw loose, you bigoted, petty-minded old bat. Of course Harriet had nothing to do with it — though after all the trouble and grief you've caused her, I wouldn't blame her if she had. Come on, Hal, let's go home and leave her to get drenched.'

He took Harriet's arm and steered her away. For once, she wasn't tempted to shake him off. By the time they reached the car, it was raining heavily, and the dim western sky was suddenly illuminated by a prolonged flicker of lightning. Harriet flung herself inside and shut the door as if something malevolent was after her. Despite her wet hair and damp clothes, she wasn't cold, but she found herself unable to stop shivering.

'She's lost the plot,' Morgan said beside her. 'Did you see her eyes? She's got so obsessive about that bloody competition that it's taken over her life. God, I feel sorry for her husband and kids.'

'So do I.' Harriet turned the key in the ignition and the car spluttered apologetically. 'Oh God, come *on*, I want to get home!'

'Pull the choke out,' Morgan advised helpfully.

'It's got an automatic one. It's the rain, it never likes the rain. Oh, *please* start, nice, kind car, I'll get you serviced if only you'll *start*!'

But when she turned the key again, the engine coughed sadly into silence, and refused to oblige.

'I don't think you're going to get anywhere,' Morgan said. 'Come on, I'll walk you home, it isn't far.'

'But it's pissing down, and you'll have to walk back to the Towers afterwards.'

'A little bit of rain won't hurt. Remember that Glastonbury Festival we went to? After that, nothing will ever seem as cold or wet or muddy again.'

'How could I ever forget? Mind you, the loos were the worst. I still can't look a walnut whip in the eye,' Harriet giggled suddenly. 'And we certainly can't stay here all night. The car should be OK till the morning.'

'Unless that woman decides to let the tyres down. I wouldn't put it past her.'

'Well, if we get back to it and find peach paint all over it, we'll know who to blame.' Harriet peered through the rainy dark. 'I can't see her. Is she still there?'

'Yes, I've been keeping an eye on her. She went round the other side of the paper bank a couple of minutes ago. If she gets any paint to stick in this, it'll be a miracle. Come on, Hal, let's go.'

They scrambled out, locking the doors behind them, and set off down the road at a run. As they passed the school car park, Harriet glanced at the paper bank, but there was still no sign of Heather, and she was glad. Somehow, she didn't want her neighbour to see them forced to walk home in the rain, and although Heather's own car, a two-year-old blue Peugeot, was standing just down the road, she would have waded waist-high through torrential floods rather than ask for a lift.

It was now past midnight, and although there was still some traffic on the main road behind them, the lane was dark and lonely, with no street lights beyond the school. Where the road bent round to the right, heading for Sanden Row, a footpath struck off across the fields, cutting off two sides of a triangle, and Harriet paused at the gate, 'How about a short cut?'

'In this?' Morgan demanded, stopping and turning to face her. She couldn't see much of his face because it was too dark, but she could discern a sudden, wild grin that boded no good. 'You must be mad, but I'm willing to give it a go. I wouldn't put it past that woman to try and run us down in the dark, and think she'd done the public a service.'

'Don't be ridiculous,' said Harriet, with a

cheerful scorn which disguised the fact that she, too, had entertained similar thoughts. Tomorrow, it would all seem totally absurd and over the top, but there, alone in the rain and the dark, with thunder menacing and the memory of those blank, relentless eyes, anything that Heather might do seemed entirely possible.

Harriet had come this way once with Maggie, but the dog had been too big to squeeze under the stile, so they hadn't tried again. Morgan went first, vaulting over it with surprising agility, considering everything that had happened that evening. Then he turned and held out his arms. 'Come on, Hal, I'll catch you.'

'That's what I'm afraid of,' Harriet said, climbing over cautiously. The wood was wet and slippery, and as she spoke, one of her shoes slid abruptly from underneath her, and she pitched forward with some force, knocking him to the ground as he tried to break her fall.

'You always did like to be on top,' Morgan said, sounding rather breathless.

Harriet, lying across his chest, gasping with surprise, began to giggle. 'Can't you *ever* forget?'

'No, of course I can't, *cariad*. And you can't, either.' He rolled over in the wet grass, taking her with him, his arms holding her close. 'But all the same, perhaps you could do with another reminder.'

His lips were cold, but there was an infinity of warmth within. She had searched for ten years, and found nothing and no one else to match him, and the power he had to make her feel like this. And then reality intruded, she realised what was happening to her, and remembered what she had decided.

It was the most difficult thing she had ever done, to wrench her mouth away from his, and pull herself out of his embrace. Breathing hard, her mind ferociously at war with her senses, she stood up.

'Hal? *Cariad*, what's the matter?'

The rain was falling heavily now, and her hair was soaked. Water ran down her face and neck, trickling under her shirt. Harriet wiped her streaming glasses and put them back on her nose, although in the wet darkness she couldn't have seen very much anyway, even with twenty-twenty vision. She said jerkily, 'It's no good, Morgan. It never has been any good.'

He got up and came to stand in front of her, looking down. A distant flash of lightning briefly illuminated his face. Like her, he was breathing wildly, his short wet hair sculpted to his head, but his eyes were shadowed. He said, 'Why? What's wrong? Don't you want to?'

'If I didn't want to, I wouldn't feel like this.' Harriet paused, trying to restore some calm, trying to find the words to explain herself without giving him irrevocable pain. 'Look, don't get me wrong, I *do* want to, even out here in a soaking downpour, which shows how mad I must be — I want to more than anything else I've ever done. I'd forgotten what it was like and now I can remember so clearly, it's agony — but it won't *work*, Morgan, don't you understand?'

'Tell me, Hal — talk to me.'

'I'm not after a quick roll in the hay,' Harriet said, with quiet desperation. 'Nor even two, or three, or four. I want something you can't give me, if you're honest with yourself. I want commitment. I want you to share my life with me. I want love, but I also want reliability, stability, responsibility. I don't want someone who makes me feel more wonderful than I ever dreamed possible, and then swans off out of my life a few days later as if we were just ships passing in the night. Do I make myself clear?'

'Clear as day,' Morgan said.

'In a week or so you'll be gone, and OK, I'm tempted, I'm really, really tempted, to throw myself into loving you and sod the consequences, but I can see that in the long run I'd be doing none of us any favours — not me, not Toby, not even you. You couldn't tie yourself to us, and I don't want you to end up hating me because I tried to change you into something you're not. Do you see? I don't want to hurt you, I love you too much for that, I know how good it could be, but I want long-term, Morgan, not a brief, wild, wonderful fling. I always did love that U2 song,' Harriet said, her voice wavering suddenly, 'but I never really understood what it meant until now. You see, I'm not at all sure I can live without you, but you can't live with me. So it just isn't possible.'

'How can you be so sure?'

'Because I *know* you, Morgan Price, I *know you* through and through, and you're just not cut out for the cosy domestic bit, you know you're not if you're honest with yourself. It's not that I don't love you — I do, I'm so much in love with you all over again that it hurts, I want you so badly I'm shaking with it, but it won't work, and so I don't want to take the risk of wrecking all our lives. You did it to me once, and you'll do it again, you've already told me you will, and I can't cope with the consequences. I'm really, really sorry, but I can't. So please,' Harriet said, trying to smile, 'don't try to persuade me again. Not if you honestly love me. Just accept that we're too different, and that it just isn't meant to be, OK?'

'I can't,' Morgan said, his voice low, furious, impassioned. 'I can't believe you'd throw it all back in my face. God, *cariad*, what's the problem? We love each other, we want each other, no one else will be hurt, so why not?'

'It's not as simple as that, is it? You know it isn't, I've told you often enough. And still you won't take no for an answer, you never did.'

'I'm not taking it now,' Morgan said. His hand came up to caress her cheek. 'Hal, darling Hal, we can sort this out, surely — '

'I don't want you to touch me,' she said, taking a quick step back.

'What in God's name do you think I'm going to do to you!' Morgan cried furiously. 'Do you think I'm going to rape you or something? I want to hold you, that's all — '

'And then what would happen? I'd end up regretting it, and so would you, so what's the point? *Please*,' Harriet sobbed desperately, 'just let me go home?'

There was a long, despairing pause, accompanied by the unceasing hiss and beat of the rain, and the insistent clamour of the thunder, rolling remorselessly nearer. She couldn't see his face, she couldn't read his expression, and she felt a disturbing twinge of fear. Not of him, but of the power he had over her, the power to make her cast aside all reason, all rationality, to do as he desired. If he did touch her again, she doubted her ability to resist him.

'All right!' he shouted suddenly, into the wind. 'Have it your own way, then — go back to your snug, safe little life and forget I ever existed, forget all about what we had, and I just hope you don't regret it, Hal, because I sure as hell will, because you're wrong, so wrong I could wring your bloody neck, but I won't, even though God knows you deserve it!'

'I'm sorry!' she cried, the tears mixed with rain on her face. 'I didn't want to hurt you!'

'Oh, forget it!' Morgan snarled, and he turned and walked back to the gate. 'Just go home, you bloody idiot, and if you wake up in a few months' time wondering what you've done, well don't come crawling back to me.'

'I wouldn't dream of it!' Harriet yelled back, but her words were drowned by a raging roar of thunder, almost overhead. Another barbed streak of lightning showed him climbing over the gate: and then he was gone, and she had never felt more alone in all her life.

She wanted to howl her misery to the storm, but some lingering sense of the absurd came to her rescue. Deliberately, she turned and marched off down the field. There was a gate in the hedge at the end, another stretch of pasture beyond it, and then the stile leading into Stony Lane. She fell over several times, stung herself, stepped in countless cow-pats, but the thought of the warm, dry bed waiting for her kept her going. By the time she reached Holly Cottage, the storm had moved on to trouble Devizes, and the rain was no longer falling with such fervour, but she felt so cold and wet it seemed as if her very soul was frozen.

She had almost, insanely, hoped that he would be waiting for her under the shelter of the holly trees, but no dark figure lingered, urgent to put her through more torment. She felt relieved, and also desperately sad. It's really over now, she thought, letting herself in as quietly as she could. Done, finished, ended. After what we've said to each other, how could we even be friends again, let alone lovers? But oh, how I wish, how I wish it could have been different.

Fortunately, Daphne had not been waiting up for her, and Toby was still fast asleep, apparently undisturbed by the thunderstorm. Harriet slunk into the bathroom, and was horrified to see her image in the mirror. There was mud on her face, her wet hair was hopelessly tangled and full of grass, and her soaked white shirt clung to her body far more revealingly than a scanty bikini top.

Just as well it was so dark Morgan couldn't see me properly, or he really wouldn't have taken no for an answer, she thought. Carefully, she peeled off her clothes, towelled herself dry, cleaned her face and managed, after several painful minutes, to persuade her hair that it was better off wound neatly and tidily back into its usual plait. Now, the face that stared back at her from the mirror was almost, but not quite, the usual Harriet, confident and in control.

It was, of course, completely bogus. If she was in true possession of her wits, she wouldn't be regretting all the things she had said to Morgan. She would be dusting her hands and preparing to make a fresh start with her life, determined to forget all about him.

She tiptoed to bed. It was wonderful to be horizontal, and even better to be warm and dry, listening to Toby's soft breathing, and the regular tick of the clock. But although she was totally exhausted, somehow sleep evaded her. Over and over her feverish mind reviewed the extraordinary events of the evening, from Edward fighting in the pub to the feel of Morgan's hands, and his kiss, and the ragged pain in his voice when he finally understood that she was rejecting him.

She had hurt him. She had spoken to him so bluntly that he had finally realised there was no hope. And it had been the hardest and cruellest thing that she had ever done in her life.

Because he loved her deeply. She had seen it in his eyes and heard it in his voice. And she had thrown it back in his face, for reasons which he, and anyone else who didn't have children, would probably regard as ridiculously honourable — or cowardly.

It was dawn before she slept.

33

When Heather Clark had finally finished her self-appointed task of cleaning up all the graffiti, single-handed — Christine, with reprehensible faint-heartedness, had refused to join her — it was past three in the morning, and she was soaked to the skin. She had painted the paper bank, four bus stops, and the post box in the wall outside the church, which had had a particularly rude word sprayed on it. She was not aware, because only the perpetrators knew about it as yet, that every arm of the set of three Sanden lock gates had also been defaced with a variety of signs, symbols and four-letter words.

There, Heather thought, returning to her car after dumping the now empty paint tin and soggy brush in the school rubbish bin. A good job well done. She shone her torch on the refurbished paper bank. Admittedly, the peach paint looked odd daubed over the dark blue, but at least she had covered over the obscenities. And tomorrow evening, she would mount a guard on all the sites, to make sure that the vandals didn't return.

Full of satisfaction, she drove home. The lounge light was still on, and she shook her head in irritation as she locked the car in the garage. Really, she must have told Keith and Adam a thousand times to switch everything off when they went to bed! No wonder the electricity bill was always so high.

The television was still on, too: she could hear it as she came in through the front door. As she hung up her sodden raincoat, and placed her ankle boots neatly on the newspaper laid down in the hall, her husband, clad in his pyjamas and dressing gown, appeared silently from the kitchen, carrying a steaming mug. He put it down on the hall table, and Heather, with an exclamation of annoyance, immediately snatched it up and thrust it back at him. 'Not *there*, it'll make a mark!'

'To be quite honest, I couldn't care less,' said Keith. He sounded tired, and angry, but Heather was more concerned about the table. 'Really, Keith, you should know better by now. Anyway, what are you doing down here? You should have been asleep hours ago.'

'I was waiting for you,' said her husband. 'Heather, we really do have to talk. It's ridiculous — '

'Not now, Keith, can't you see what time it is? You may want to sit up all night watching rubbish on the television, but I'm going to bed. I've had an *exhausting* evening.' Heather glanced at him to see if her words had evoked any sympathy, but he was staring at her with a deep frown on his face. 'Quite *exhausting*,' she repeated, with emphasis. 'Good night, dear, and don't forget to turn all the lights out.'

Her husband stood in the hall, watching her ample figure marching up the stairs. Then, with a shake of the head that might have indicated anger, or despair, or resignation, he turned, carrying the mug, and went back into the lounge. And, like Harriet in the house next door, he too had a wakeful night, but for very different reasons.

★　★　★

After less than four hours' sleep, Heather was up bright and early the next morning, but Keith had already gone to work, leaving the unmistakable and unhealthy smell of fried eggs and bacon in the kitchen, and the debris from his breakfast dumped in the sink. Despite his illness earlier in the week, Adam seemed surprisingly keen to go to school: he needed no persuasion to get ready, and set off for the bus stop at least five minutes before he needed to. Heather, her mind already planning the rota of SNAG members for guard duty that evening, hardly noticed: as both her children had long ago discovered, the only certain way to attract her undivided attention was to misbehave.

With a certain sense of apprehension, and also considerable glee, Adam jogged up Stony Lane, his rucksack bouncing on his back, and past the school. A quick glance at the recycling skips brought him to an abrupt and astonished halt. For a moment, dumb-founded, he stared at the paper bank, now daubed amateurishly with peach paint that had run in streaks and smears down the metal and puddled on the tarmac beneath. It looked awful. It looked almost as bad as the graffiti. And he knew who had done it. The lounge at home was exactly that colour.

'Adam!' His mate Ben hailed him from across the road. 'What yer looking at?'

The head teacher's car had just turned into School Lane. Adam hissed urgently, 'Don't look as if yer looking, you prat!'

Ben came over to join him, and stared in disbelief at the car park. 'Effing hell, who's done that, then?'

The car drove past them, and turned into the school. Trying to appear nonchalantly innocent, Adam carried on walking towards the main road. 'Me sodding mum, of course.

Must've done it last night.'

Ben began to snigger. 'She ain't half made a mess of it, eh?'

'Serves her right, bossy old cow,' said Adam. He often found himself speaking of his mother in such brutal terms when he was with Ben, who made a great parade of how much he loathed his own parents, but always, in retrospect, the memory of such disrespect made him deeply uneasy. 'I'm sick of her trying to run my life for me, and I reckon Dad is as well. I heard them arguing last night.'

'If I were him, I'd give her summink to remember,' said Ben, whose own father had received several police cautions for doing just that to his wife. 'That'd sort her out.'

'Yeah, well, I don't suppose my dad's got the bottle,' said Adam, continuing his spuriously swaggering, macho pose. 'Like I said, I'm sick of them both — can't wait to leave home.'

'Me brother's got a flat in Bristol,' said Ben. He glanced slyly at Adam. 'You're nearly sixteen, ain't yer? Old enough to tell 'em to stuff it and bugger off. I'm thinking of doing it meself.'

'What about school and that?'

'School never did me no good,' said Ben, who, though precociously streetwise, was in

478

the lowest stream for almost everything, and had a reading age well behind a bright ten-year-old's. 'They wouldn't miss me anyway. Tell yer what, Ad, why don't we bunk off and go to Bristol?'

It was undeniably tempting, but Adam, despite his bravado, had so far failed to cut free of his upbringing. 'Haven't got any money, have I?'

'We can hitch, no problem.'

'Too late, anyway,' Adam said, with concealed relief. 'Bus is coming, and that Heidi Lane has seen us.'

'Snotty cow,' said Ben. 'She's a looker, though. Wouldn't mind some of that.'

'Not going to school today, boys?' Heidi was in the year above them, a tall and elegant young woman with sleek hair, infinite legs and a poised confidence that many women twice her age would envy. She paused on the steps of the bus and gave Ben and Adam a scornful glance from under thick dark lashes. 'Come on, then, what are you waiting for?'

'Prick-teaser,' said Ben under his breath, but he climbed aboard the bus. Adam followed him, flashing his pass briefly at the driver. As they sat down behind Heidi, Adam hissed to his friend, 'Looks like me mum did the bus stop an' all.'

'So what? We can do it again tonight,' said

Ben. He grinned unpleasantly. 'I've still got a couple of cans left. And if the judging's tomorrow, she won't have time to paint everything out.'

'It'll finish her, good an' all,' said Adam, with considerable relish. 'And then perhaps she'll stop poking her nose into everyone else's lives.' And think a bit more about me and Dad for a change, he added to himself, with an unhappiness he would never dare to express in front of Ben.

'Not talking about me, I hope,' said Heidi, without bothering to turn round.

'Nah, darling, but we will if you like,' Ben said, grinning, and the two boys settled down to fifteen minutes of concentrated innuendo and sexual harassment, before the bus dumped them outside the school.

★ ★ ★

In common with Harriet, Morgan had had very little sleep the previous night. He woke much later than he had intended, with a pounding headache and a mouth that felt as if he had been eating sand, and lay for a moment, staring at the stained ceiling of the stable flat's single bedroom, wondering why he felt so awful.

Memory returned in a sickening surge of

anguish. He had held her in his arms. He had felt her response, known she was within his grasp. And then, with a torrent of hard words more potent and deadly than any blow, she had escaped him.

And she was right. The truth hurt, and hurt bitterly. She wanted a father for Toby, as well as a lover. And he, Morgan, who since leaving college had never stayed in one place or stuck with one woman for longer than a few months, was not good enough for her.

He lay on his back, looking long and hard into the future. He was not worried about his career: word was already getting around, and the forthcoming commission in Gloucestershire would be, he knew, the first of many after finishing Y Wâl Yr Draig. But he had a clear and terrible vision of the life he would lead, drifting from job to job, from woman to woman, until he became a sad, ageing Casanova, deluding himself that he was happy until the sheer loneliness and pointlessness of his existence overwhelmed him.

It was not a comfortable prospect. But the alternative was almost as frightening. He didn't think he could do it. He *knew* he couldn't. He was rootless, restless, just as Harriet had said. He would make no one a good father, least of all another man's child, however delightful. She had accused him of fearing commitment, and she was right.

But if he could ever commit himself to anyone, it would be Harriet. He closed his eyes and thought of her: the lovely, short-sighted hazel eyes behind those endearingly unflattering glasses; her round, voluptuously inviting figure; her generosity and unselfishness and warm, loving heart; the tears she had wept for him, even as she rejected him. His own heart ached for her pain and loss, for what he had done to her ten years ago, and for what she was doing to him now. He knew she didn't see it in those terms, but another, more vindictive woman would have considered this to be sweet revenge.

He had treated her very badly, and so had Edward. Small wonder that she couldn't trust any man, let alone the two who had betrayed her. At least Edward had received his just deserts, and was probably even now waking up in the bleak, unpleasant surroundings of a police cell. With a sudden, disturbing flash of insight, Morgan could see that the man he had goaded last night, drunken, despairing, pathetically deluded, was just the man he himself might become, if he allowed it to happen.

It was such an unnerving idea that he got up and went to look in the bathroom mirror.

A sorry face stared back, bereft of its usual devil-may-care charm. Edward's fist had given him a truly magnificent shiner, and the bags under his eyes, the lines of strain round his mouth, and the inexorable growth of stubble completed the disreputable reflection.

Morgan had never been particularly vain, but he was well aware of his attractions. He imagined the same features in ten years' time, the jowls beginning to sag, the thick dark hair greying and receding, the lean, muscular body softened with fat, just like Edward.

But ten years was a long time. He'd packed a great deal of highly pleasurable living into the last decade, and he didn't, just yet, want to give up his carefree, hedonistic lifestyle. He would miss Harriet, but he had missed her before, and survived. I can handle it, he thought, with a welcome return of his usual arrogant certainty. No problem. Still lots more fun out there, just waiting for me.

With sudden, vigorous determination, he turned on the shower, and went to find himself a towel. And if any doubts recurred to shake his bravado, he gave no indication of it.

34

At roughly the same time that Morgan was indulging in self-deception, Edward lay on his hard, narrow bed in the police cell in Trowbridge, and contemplated with a shamed and entirely unwelcome honesty the shambles he had made of his life. Like most successful con-men, he was rather too good at conning himself, and it had taken a dreadful night, full of nausea and bad dreams, to bring him, however briefly, to his senses.

It wasn't my fault, he thought defensively. Harriet drove me to it. But in his deepest, darkest heart, he knew that wasn't true. He had made a mess of it. He had lost her, and Toby, forever. He had been charged with being drunk and disorderly and two counts of assault, one on a policeman. His solicitor, curtly unsympathetic, had told him that a hefty fine was the least he could expect. Gerald's manner had been the first indication to Edward that he had drastically overstepped the bounds of acceptable behaviour. From now on, he would be considered *persona non grata* in the civilised, masculine world from which he had derived so much comforting status.

With shame and horror, he imagined the comments as he was inevitably expelled from the golf club, and the expression of distaste on the face of the Rotarian chairman as he informed Edward, with chilly formality, that he was no longer welcome . . .

He couldn't face the humiliation. He had to escape. And through the long, cold hours of night, as rational thought began to clear away the alcoholic fog that had clouded his brain, he knew what he had to do. The sacrifice would be worth it, however much he disliked making it. And then he would be free to start his life afresh.

At last, exhausted by his unaccustomed bout of introspection, he drifted into a surprisingly pleasant doze, in which he dreamt that he was lounging on a sun-drenched yacht, surrounded by the blue sea and sky of the tropics, with a blonde even more gorgeous than Selina Grant, and more compliant than Harriet as he had first known her, attending to his every need.

⋆ ⋆ ⋆

Harriet took Toby to playgroup. The term had only three more weeks left to run, and then, after the long summer holidays, he was due to start school. He would be five in November, and he was growing up fast. Harriet, looking down at his blond head, listening to his eager chatter as they walked up the lane, wondered what he would be like in a year, two years' time. Would he still display that entrancing mix of wild imagination and sober reality? Would he still be a normal, happy little boy? Or would he begin to suffer all the disadvantages that being the child of a single mother entailed, according to certain newspapers and social commentators?

She doubted it. Toby was himself, and as long as she gave him the love and care he needed, she knew instinctively that he would flower as brightly as children who were apparently more fortunate. The thought of how she might have lost him still made her shiver. But that danger was past now, and she did not have to fear Edward any longer.

Her car was still parked outside the school. Harriet felt sick to think of how nearly she had succumbed to Morgan's temptation, although her emotions were still inextricably tangled with a mixture of relief and regret. But it's done now, she thought sadly. No going back. I can only look forward, and take comfort in what I've got.

'What are you going to do with that,

486

Mum?' Toby enquired, as she raised the car's bonnet. 'What is it?'

'Some stuff called WD-40. It makes dead cars come back to life again — I hope.' Harriet sprayed the chemical liberally all over the plugs and distributor, and then slammed the bonnet shut. 'There. That should sort it. Poor little car, the rain was too much for it last night, and it got all wet inside and wouldn't start.'

'Poor car,' Toby echoed, stroking it sympathetically. 'Will it start now? I've run out of energy.'

'You've only walked up the lane — you'll lose the use of your legs if you're not careful.' Harriet got into the driver's seat and turned the key. The first attempt raised the same apologetic noise she had heard last night; the second, to her delighted surprise, was successful. With a cheering Toby securely strapped into the back seat, she turned the car round and drove the short distance to the village hall, and playgroup.

As she parked, she noticed a car, right in the far corner, that looked like Edward's BMW. A quick glance at the numberplate confirmed that it *was* Edward's BMW, and that he was sitting in it. With a feeling of acute nervousness, Harriet got out and shepherded Toby briskly inside. If there was going to be an unpleasant scene, she wanted her son well out of the way beforehand.

She spent five minutes or so settling him in. Juliet Moss came up to her, smiling. 'Still all right for this morning?'

The momentous events of the previous evening had driven all memory of their planned outing from Harriet's mind. She stared at the other woman blankly for a few seconds, then remembered. 'Oh, yes, of course — we were going to Marlborough, weren't we?'

'If it's not convenient — ' Juliet began, though she looked disappointed.

'No, no, it's fine, I've just got to pop out and see someone for a few minutes, that's all.'

'OK,' Juliet said. 'Come round to my house as soon as you're ready, and we can go in my car.'

'Great. See you in a bit,' said Harriet, and went outside, wondering apprehensively what Edward wanted.

He was waiting for her, beside the Polo. She walked towards him, trying not to let her uneasiness show. After her terrible argument with Morgan, she did not think she could cope with another tirade.

But to her astonishment, his face was heavy with contrition. 'Harriet, I want to apologise for what happened last night. What I did was quite unforgivable.'

I wonder if he's only saying it because he thinks I might hand those statements over to the Inland Revenue, Harriet thought instantly, and was ashamed of her cynicism, although none of her recent dealings with Edward had made her inclined to trust him, ever again.

'You should be saying sorry to Morgan and the police, not to me,' she said, determined not to appear too lenient. 'And I hope you've learned your lesson. I'd have thought you should have known better, at your age.'

'I'm sorry. I was drunk, I didn't realise what I was doing.' Edward held out his hand, which shook slightly. 'Forgive me?'

'You just said yourself that what you did was unforgivable,' Harriet pointed out. 'I will gladly accept your apologies, Edward, but that's all.' She ignored the hand and moved towards the car, but he forestalled her.

'I want to talk to you, Harriet. I've got a proposition for you. Just five minutes of your time. Please?'

She knew that wheedling voice of old, but it no longer had any power over her. She said briskly, 'Is it urgent? I'm going out for coffee, with a friend.' The prospect of an hour or two of Juliet's carefree, lively conversation with no emotional baggage attached was wonderfully exhilarating.

'Yes. You don't have to do anything, just listen, and then you can tell me to bugger off if you like — but I don't think you will,' Edward said, his voice almost pleading. 'Come on, Hattie, just five minutes? Please?'

'OK,' she said. 'We can sit on the bench over there, by the cricket pavilion.'

'Thank you.' Edward looked so pathetically grateful that she was instantly suspicious. But she had plenty of confidence now in her ability to resist his blandishments if she wanted to, however persuasive he might be, and in any case he was a pathetic sight, obviously unwell and hungover.

Edward sat down at one end of the bench, and Harriet, determined not to give any impression of friendliness, sat as far away from him as she could at the other. 'Well?' she demanded. 'What do you want to talk about?'

'I didn't get a lot of sleep last night,' Edward began, rather hesitantly.

You and me both, thought Harriet, but probably for very different reasons. 'The bed in your cell a bit hard, was it?' she said tartly. 'So?'

Edward flushed with embarrassment. He's really ashamed of what he's done, she realised, with some astonishment. And so he bloody well should be.

'So I did a lot of thinking. About what's happened, and about my future. I want to make a fresh start. I'm sick of Sanden, and the boatyard. I'm sick of this country. I want to sell up and follow the sun. I've got friends in South Africa, in the wine trade, and I'd like to go there, start a new life.'

'What about Toby?'

'I'll miss him, of course — I'll write to him, I promise, send him things, I'll come and see him when I get the chance.' Edward stared at her urgently. 'Please, Harriet. Please let me go. The boatyard should fetch quite a lot, and I'll give you a lump sum for Toby instead of maintenance. You can invest it, or use it to buy a house. On one condition.'

He paused, and she knew exactly what he was going to propose. 'Don't tell me. You want the statements back.'

'Yes. Will you agree, Harriet? You said yourself you didn't want to be vindictive. You can't lose. Please say yes.'

'So you want to buy me off.'

'I want to buy you *out*. I haven't been very fair to you, have I? You worked hard to make a success of that place. I've only realised how much was down to you since you left. Look on it as your due, for all you put into the business. And as maintenance for Toby, too.

In return, I'll be out of your life forever, if you want it.'

'Doesn't Toby matter to you *at all*?'

'Of course he does,' said Edward defensively. 'But he's so young, he won't miss me for long.'

'I hope he won't,' Harriet said. 'Because if that's what you really want, Edward, I'm not going to stop you. I never wanted revenge or anything like that. I only ever wanted what was fair, and right. And if you're prepared to give me a lump sum in acknowledgement, then fine. I won't refuse it.'

'Then you do agree!' Edward smiled at her suddenly, and for a brief moment she saw the man she had once loved. 'I knew you would. As soon as the yard's sold, I'll give you a cheque. It should be at least thirty thousand — '

'*What?*'

'I can make it more if you want.'

'It's all right,' Harriet said faintly. 'Go on.'

'At least thirty thousand. You can give me the statements once the cheque has cleared. Is that OK?'

It was much, much more than OK, but she wasn't going to tell him that. Her one regret was that Toby would inevitably lose contact with his father, but she suspected that would have happened eventually in any case,

492

whether Edward lived in South Africa or next door.

'Yes,' she said at last. 'I'm sorry that you feel you have to sell the boatyard, but if you really want to leave, then I won't stop you. But please, please do your best to keep in touch with Toby, won't you? He does love you, you know. And I don't want him to be hurt.'

'I'll write, I promise,' Edward said. 'And I can phone him at Christmas and birthdays. I won't abandon him altogether, I swear I won't. I really need this chance, Harriet, I want to make a good life for myself, and the opportunities are there, I can invest in a couple of vineyards, start exporting in a big way . . . '

He hasn't really changed at all, thought Harriet wryly, listening to her former lover's grandiose plans. He'll throw vast amounts of money at his new project but he won't put any actual effort into it — he's only interested in get-rich-quick, not in hard work.

But at least she wouldn't have to watch, or help, or tie herself to a sinking ship. She would be free of him, finally and for ever. And the money, whether thirty thousand or five, would help her to make a new, better life for herself and Toby. There was a little terraced house for sale in Sanden Row, she had noticed the sign outside. It had two bedrooms, and a lovely cottage garden. She could grow vegetables, and Toby could have a kitten, and they could make themselves into a real family.

So, despite everything he had done to her in the past, in the end she would have real cause to be grateful to Edward. It had all, almost, come right. She smiled at him, and he held out his hand. 'It's a deal, then, Harriet? Shake on it?'

And with real appreciation, she did.

35

At eight o'clock that Friday evening, Heather Clark marshalled her troops in front of the school, and surveyed them with a dissatisfied eye. She and Christine had, between them, phoned nearly twenty people about this meeting, but only three had bothered to turn up.

There was a disco on at the village hall, but that didn't explain it. Heather, completely unaware of the effect her increasingly unbalanced obsession was having on lesser and more tolerant mortals, decided that the inhabitants of Sanden must actually want their beautiful village defaced with obscene graffiti, and consequently turned into a laughing stock when the Best Kept competition was judged the following morning.

'Is this all there is?' she demanded of Christine. 'Well, we'd better do our best with what we've got, I suppose. I'll keep watch here, by the school. You can patrol the high street, Mrs Bentley, and Mr Gardner can take Sanden Row.'

'I'm not sure I can manage that,' said the gentleman in question, who was well over sixty and walked with a stick.

'You've got a car, haven't you? Well, cruise up and down, then. Christine, you look after the area by the village hall.'

'Heather, please, I'd rather not. There are usually some very rough lads hanging about outside on disco nights.'

Heather fixed her crony with a gimlet eye. 'I'm afraid you have no choice. It's either that, or the canal towpath, and I think Mr Bentley ought to do that, it's an isolated area.'

'Very well,' said Christine. 'I just hope that Ben Jarvis isn't there, his language is appalling. Isn't he one of your Adam's friends?'

'Of course not,' said Heather, though she had often seen her son in Ben's company. 'I do not allow Adam to consort with louts like that. It would not surprise me in the least if the Jarvis boy wasn't at the back of all this. Now, have you all got your mobile phones? Good. Don't forget, at the first sign of anything suspicious, dial nine-nine-nine. We want to root this dreadful vandalism out before it swamps us all. Now, to your posts, everyone, and good hunting!'

Unaware of what awaited some of its residents, Sanden lay sleepily relaxed in the evening sunshine. After the storms and rain of the previous night, the forecast promised a glorious few days, and everyone was looking forward to a weekend in the garden or out and about. In Holly Cottage, Harriet was putting Toby to bed, still hardly able to believe that Edward would carry out his promise, and determined not to mention anything, either to her son or to Daphne, until the money was safe in her building society account. Up the hill, in Forfar Towers, Sir Marcus Grant had invited his architect to dinner, and had noticed, with some misgivings, that Morgan had already got through half a bottle of wine before the arrival of the first course.

And outside the village hall, its windows already rattling to the thump of the music within, Ben Jarvis had called his gang, Lee, Jack and Adam, to their own council of war.

They spotted Christine's car straight away, crawling down the narrow lane towards them, but her arrival made no difference to their plans. Adam, who had loitered outside the school for a while on his way past to the village hall, had already told them what his mother had arranged for the evening — it had not crossed Heather's mind that her son was one of the vandals — and they were ready. They allowed themselves the luxury of insolent, intimidating stares as Christine got out of the car, glancing nervously round, her mobile phone clamped tightly in her hand.

'Wanna dance, love?' Ben called, as she made her way across the car park to the cricket pavilion, which seemed to be the safest vantage point. 'Come on, live a little!'

'She's no problem,' Jack Baldwin said cheerfully. 'She wouldn't say boo to a fly, that one.'

'Give her half an hour,' said Lee, who lived next door to Ben. 'She'll get fed up and go home.'

'Not with my mum breathing down her neck,' Adam pointed out. 'Anyway, I've got a better idea. Wait until it gets nearly dark, and then this is what we do . . . '

Christine, hovering on the steps of the pavilion, heard their raucous laughter and shivered. She really, really did not want to do this, but Heather had brooked no opposition. Not for the first time, she wondered whether the Best Kept Village award was worth all the time, effort and sheer unpleasantness involved in the process of winning it. Several people whom she had thought of as friends had been very offended by Heather's manner, and many of the rest just couldn't see what the fuss was about. It's all very well campaigning against litter and vandalism, Christine thought unhappily. But not by treading on everyone's toes and causing a lot of ill-feeling. That business with Heather's neighbours was really most disagreeable.

''S a nice evening, innit, Mrs Howell?'

Startled, Christine jumped back, her hand on her chest. 'Goodness me, Adam, you gave me such a fright, creeping up on me like that!'

'Sorry,' said Heather's son, though he did not look it. 'She put you on guard duty, then?'

'I'm just enjoying the sunshine,' said Christine, although this side of the pavilion faced east, and lay in deep shadow.

'You don't have to do anything you don't want to,' Adam said. 'She ain't Hitler, you know. Why don't you go home? Me and my mates will keep a good look-out for them vandals. And if they do try anything, we can sort it better than you, eh, lads?'

Three grinning faces nodded assent.

''Cause I wouldn't wanna see you getting hurt or anything like that,' Adam went on, earnestly. 'Some of the lads round here can be a bit rough. Me mum can soon sort them, but you're not like her, are you? You don't want any trouble.'

And she does. The thought popped into Christine's head, and would not be dislodged. Suddenly, she realised that he had a valid point. Why on earth was she giving up

499

her evening, when she could be doing some gardening, or watching that new series on BBC1, or just having an early night? Heather could do it. Heather was the one who was obsessed. If anyone did try anything, Adam was right, the boys were better able to stop them. Admittedly, Ben Jarvis was one of their number, and Lee, who had been in all sorts of trouble at school, but she knew that Jack came from a good, responsible family. And if the worst happens, Christine thought, with a twinge of shame, at least Heather won't be able to blame me.

'Thanks, boys,' she said, with a smile of relief. 'You've taken such a load off my mind.'

'That's all right, Mrs Howell,' said Ben, so pleasantly that she began to feel she had misjudged him. 'You go along home and we'll mind the fort.'

'It's very good of you.' Christine hesitated, still beset by misgivings. 'You will be careful, now, won't you? Don't go getting into trouble, or fights, or anything like that.'

'Of course we won't,' said Adam, with a look of injured innocence. 'That'd be stupid.'

'I'm glad to hear it. Well, goodbye, and good luck!'

Carefully concealing their glee, the four boys watched as she climbed back into her car and drove home to her comfortable house in Sanden Row.

'Swallowed it,' said Ben, as soon as Christine was out of sight. 'Hook, line and sinker. That was a great idea of yours, Ad.'

'Yeah, well, she was the easy one. She's a few sarnies short of a picnic, always does whatever Mum tells her.'

'Just like you, eh, Ad?' Lee sneered.

'Oh, shut up. Come on, we ain't finished yet. One down, three to go. The Bentleys, and old Gardner. Who's gonna do him? He ought to be a push-over too.'

'You can, Ad,' said Ben. 'Since you're so good at it. I'll do Ma Bentley.'

'What about her husband? He's no fool, he'll know we're up to something.'

'Yeah, but he's down by the canal, ain't he? I reckon just leave him there. 'S not as if the judges are gonna go down that way, anyway. And with all the others out of the picture, we can do what we like everywhere else. All we gotta remember is to keep well clear of your mum.'

'D'you think there's a Worst Kept Village competition?' asked Lee, sniggering. ''Cause by the time we've finished, I bet Sanden will win it.'

★ ★ ★

501

Blissfully unaware of the cunning plot that her son was hatching behind her back, Heather had already taken up her station in the school car park, setting up a folding garden chair unobtrusively behind the dustbins. The paper bank gleamed with fresh paint; she had bought some from the hardware shop in Devizes that morning, and covered the peach emulsion with a colour that nearly matched the original blue. Just let them try it again, Heather thought, bristling with renewed rage. I'll be waiting for them!

She waited a long time. The sun set, the air grew cooler. Darkness settled softly over Sanden with summer slowness, the sky overhead deepening gently from azure to purest indigo, scattered with emergent stars, while in the west the crimson glow lingered as if reluctant to slide away from the world. After three hours, even Heather's vigilance was trickling away with the last of the light, and her lack of sleep the previous night began to take its toll. Her head grew heavy, and her eyelids drooped, then closed.

The distant chime of the church clock brought her abruptly to wakefulness. It was fully dark, and a sombre silence lay over the village. How long had she been asleep? In sudden anxiety, she got up and shone her torch all around the paper bank. Her paintwork was still immaculate. Nothing, thank God, had happened. Heather did not like to think of the humilation she would have suffered if the vandals had struck whilst she had been sleeping at her post.

So, her stratagem had worked. Word had obviously got around, and the enemy had prudently decided to retreat. Heather turned the torch beam on to her watch, and found with some astonishment that it was two in the morning. Well, they obviously wouldn't do anything now. And since there had been no calls on her mobile, they hadn't tried it anywhere else, either. The village was safe. The award was as good as in the bag, and it was entirely due to her efforts.

With a feeling of enormous satisfaction, Heather folded up her chair and got into her car. The route home was short, and avoided the rest of the village: and so she arrived back at her house completely unaware that the contents of several dozen dustbins had been liberally spread around the sports field, along the high street, and over the verges of all the houses in Sanden Row.

★　★　★

By the following morning, Harriet had begun to wonder whether her discussion with

Edward had actually been one of the unlikely, restless dreams which occasionally disrupted her sleep. Surely he hadn't, unprompted and of his own free will, offered her a sum of money so large that it would make all the difference to her precious dreams? Why this astonishing change of heart?

But of course, she reminded herself cynically, a night in the primitive discomfort of a police cell had probably concentrated his mind wonderfully. And Edward was a proud man who would take his humiliation very much to heart. No wonder he didn't want to stay in Sanden. A fresh start in sunnier and more congenial climes would be, for him, the perfect way out: Edward had always preferred to run rather than face the reckoning. And if he wanted to sell up and move to South Africa, then he needed her co-operation.

He must have decided that paying me for the statements — which is what it boils down to — is the only way to get what he wants, Harriet realised, not without considerable misgivings. And if I were a judge, I think I'd call it blackmail — even though I never asked for the money. But I'm still going to take it off him, so I must be guilty.

But she didn't feel guilty. She had worked like a slave for Edward and the boatyard, and without her they would both have gone under. Morally, she was entitled to every penny of that thirty thousand — if that was what Edward was really going to give her. And, more importantly, so was Toby.

But she knew Edward. It was one thing to promise the money, quite another to deliver it. For a start, he had to sell the boatyard, which might prove more difficult than he had thought, especially if the doctored books showed that the profits were apparently modest. And she wouldn't put it past him to change his mind and call her bluff.

If he did, she wouldn't sit tamely by and watch him swan off to South Africa, breaking his promise, ratting on his obligations, and evading his responsibilities. He had spent much of their relationship taking her for granted. But if he hasn't realised by now that it's unwise to underestimate me, then he'll just have to suffer the consequences, she thought. I meant exactly what I said.

'Are you all right, Harriet?' Daphne enquired, breaking in on her reverie. 'I've asked you three times if you want another slice of toast.'

'Sorry, I was miles away.' Harriet smiled at her friend. 'No thanks.'

'Isn't it the judging for the tidiness award today?' Daphne enquired reflectively, buttering her own slice. 'I expect Heather is all in a fluster. To be quite honest, I couldn't care less.'

'I must admit, I'm not that bothered either. I've got plenty of better things to think about. Like the designs for Y Wâl Yr Draig, for a start. Now your book is almost done, I can start thinking about them seriously.'

'It sounds a splendid idea,' Daphne remarked. 'But won't it take you a very long time to complete? I thought Marcus was dying to see the place finished.'

'He said he didn't mind how long it takes,' said Harriet. 'He just wants to see it done properly. And so do I. It's a lovely building, and I want to do it justice.' For Morgan's sake, she thought, the memory of that final, furious quarrel still agonisingly vivid in her mind. If I can't do anything else for him, and us, I can still make Y Wâl Yr Draig as beautiful as I can. Like the Taj Mahal, in memory of our love. And she mustered a wry smile at the comparison, so absurdly inappropriate and extravagant in the circumstances.

Toby, who had been playing with his cars on the patio, came running in through the back door. 'Mum, look who's here, Mum!'

She knew who it would be before she saw him. It was inevitable. He was like one of those toys — knock him down in one place, and he'd pop up again somewhere else. And despite all her brave, false, hollow words, just the look of him, unshaven, disreputable and all too obviously hungover, was enough to make her knees knock and her palms sweat.

'Hallo, *cariad*,' said Morgan Price.

36

'What are you doing here?' Harriet demanded.

'Can't you be a bit more original?' His normally vivid blue eyes were hooded and bloodshot, and there was a crease between his quirky eyebrows, betraying the probable presence of a headache. 'Why not try, for example, 'Sorry, I'm not buying any blue budgies today?' Or even, 'No, thank you, I'm a practising white witch.' ' He peered at her suddenly. 'You're not, are you? That would explain a lot. I wouldn't be surprised if you had a little Morgan doll hidden under your pillow, with more pins in it than a porcupine.'

As Harriet was startled into laughter, Toby, hovering within earshot, said earnestly, 'Mummy's grown up now, she hasn't got any dolls.'

'Of course I haven't. Morgan was just being silly, that's all, sweetheart.'

'Not entirely,' said the man she could not help loving, his voice very low and intent. 'God knows I couldn't feel any worse than if you did. Hal, can we talk?'

'I thought we did all our talking the other night.'

'That was shouting. It doesn't count.'

'Why were you shouting, Mum?' Toby interrupted.

'Because we couldn't hear each other if we didn't, it was in the middle of a thunderstorm,' Harriet surveyed her inconveniently curious child. 'Toby, I'd like to have a chat with Morgan. For grown-ups only, very boring. You stay here and play with your cars, OK?'

'Yes, *sir*,' said Toby, who was very fond of Action Man. He gave what he fondly imagined to be an immaculate salute, and went back to his game.

'You can show me what's at the end of the garden,' Morgan suggested. 'Fairies, perhaps?'

'Chickens, actually. Sorry, I shouldn't call them that in front of a certain person.' She moved away, out of range of her son's acute hearing. 'Hens are those nice birds who kindly lay big brown eggs for his breakfast. Chicken is what appears on his plate.'

'It's a beautiful garden,' Morgan said, glancing round as they made their way across the shaggy lawn. 'There must be a hundred butterflies around those purple flowers.'

'That's a buddleia — it's often called the

butterfly bush. I painted it a few days ago, for Daphne's book. It's all finished now.' She paused to draw down one of the flower spikes. 'I love the smell. So sweet.'

'I didn't come to make small talk,' Morgan pointed out. 'I want to discuss our future.'

'*Our* future? Didn't you *hear* what I was saying the other night? Or were you still too pissed?'

'I wasn't.'

'But you were last night too, weren't you? I've seen you with a hangover before, I know the signs. You're just like Edward, you never learn.'

'That's not fair,' Morgan said indignantly. 'Look, I admit it, I had a few too many. It wasn't the first time and it won't be the last. So what? Your trouble is that you spend too much time judging people and finding them wanting. OK, I'm not good enough for you. But can't you at least get your head round the fact that I might change?'

'Oh no you won't,' said Harriet, stung by his accusations. 'You're just the same as you were ten years ago. Here today and gone tomorrow.'

'That isn't true either, and you know it. Come on, Hal, what do I have to do to convince you? You love me, I love you, where's the problem?'

510

'You're the problem, can't you see that? You're not permanent. You *can't* be permanent. And I need someone who'll still be around in a year or two, not a week or two. Please, Morgan,' Harriet cried in anguish, 'it's not going to work, so don't even try to persuade me. You're just tormenting both of us. Why can't you accept there's no hope?'

'Because I don't like to walk out on the best thing I've ever had in my life,' said Morgan. He stood quite still, staring down at her, his eyes narrowed. 'I made that mistake once, but never again. I want you, Hal, I love you and need you and want you. And one day I'll win you round, whatever it takes. I'll show you you're wrong about me.'

'No, I'm not,' said Harriet resolutely. 'Please go, Morgan. There isn't any point in prolonging the agony.'

'OK,' he said at last, and bent forward suddenly, before she could move away, and kissed her gently on the mouth. 'But remember, *cariad*, I don't give up so easily.' The smile he flashed at her was a poignant reminder of all the reasons, good and bad, that she loved him. 'I'll be back!'

She watched him striding through the long grass. He ducked under the apple tree with a wave of his hand, as if they had parted friends, as if she hadn't just given him the brush-off for the umpteenth time.

At this rate, I shall be glad when he leaves, Harriet thought unhappily. I'm not sure I can bear it if he keeps arriving on my doorstep, begging me to take him back.

Some women would think she was mad, turning him down. He had even won Daphne over. He was attractive, funny, different, creative, maddening, and utterly impossible to ignore. He could bring her to a frenzy of exasperation, and then defuse her annoyance with a smile, or a humorous remark, or some outrageous gesture. Some women would be happy to go to bed with him for a night or two, and hang the consequences. But she, Harriet, was not like that. She needed a long-term relationship, and so did Toby, especially when his real father was about to vanish from his life, probably for many years. And nothing that Morgan had said or done had yet persuaded her that he wasn't the last man on earth to give her what she wanted.

The back door of the cottage was hidden by the pear trees, so she didn't realise until she reached the gravelled drive that Morgan hadn't left. He was crouched down on the patio, talking to Toby and doing something to one of the little boy's cars. As Harriet checked in surprise, Daphne appeared at the door with a mug of coffee, which she handed to him. 'You look as though you could do with it,' she observed drily.

'Thanks. I didn't even have time for breakfast this morning,' said Morgan, batting his eyelashes at her in shameless appeal. He saw Harriet, and grinned at her mischievously. 'Sorry, *cariad*, I did mean to leave you in peace, honestly. But Toby wanted me to put a wheel back on one of his cars, and then Daphne offered me coffee, and you know me — I can never resist temptation.'

'Surely you're old enough to feed yourself without having to scrounge breakfast off Daphne,' said Harriet, surveying him with considerable exasperation. 'Or did last night's booze-up scramble your brains instead of your eggs?'

'Scrambled eggs, now there's a thought,' said Morgan happily. 'I suppose you wouldn't — ow, that hurt!'

'It was meant to,' Harriet said, grinning despite herself.

'Mum, it's very naughty to throw things at Morgan!'

'I know, but sometimes a woman gets provoked beyond endurance. Anyway, it was only a little pear, and I didn't mean to hit him on the head.'

'Now why do I have trouble believing you?' said Morgan. He sat down on one of the wooden chairs, and took a long, grateful sip of coffee. 'This is a lovely place, Daphne. Apart from the dubious neighbourhood, of course. Which reminds me, aren't we all being assessed by the tidiness police today?'

'I'm trying to forget about it,' said Daphne drily. 'I'm sorry, but I refuse to bow to that woman's pressure. In any case, they're hardly likely to come down here.'

'It might be just as well if they did. Stony Lane looks absolutely spotless compared to the rest of the village.' Morgan looked at both women over the top of his mug, and gave them a sly grin. 'Come on, aren't you going to ask me what I'm talking about?'

'Is he always like this?' demanded Daphne. 'No wonder you've been trying to fend him off, Harriet. I expect his mother never smacked him when he was cheeky.'

'You're right, she didn't, but my dad more than made up for it. Go on,' Morgan said. 'Ask me what's happened.'

'OK,' said Harriet, giving up the struggle to contain her curiosity. 'What's happened?'

'Sanden looks as though it's been hit by the fall-out from a litter bomb. There's rubbish absolutely everywhere,' said Morgan, not without a certain regrettable note of glee in his voice, 'and they'd need an army to clear it up. You can hardly see the grass on the sports field for old cans and plastic bags. Someone had a lot of fun last night.'

'It isn't very amusing,' said Daphne. 'Litter is dangerous as well as unsightly. Who on earth could have done a stupid thing like that?'

'Making a wild and unsubstantiated guess, someone who's got it in for Heather,' said Harriet. 'And I can't summon up much sympathy for her, really. She's only got herself to blame.' She thought of the disturbingly single-minded woman she and Morgan had encountered two nights ago. 'God knows what she'll do when she finds out about this.'

'That's immaterial,' Daphne said. 'Whether that silly prank is her fault or not, the fact remains that it should be cleared up. I suggest that we go and make a start.'

Harriet stared at her in some surprise. 'But I thought that you didn't care about the competition.'

'I don't. But I do care about the children and animals who may be hurt by broken glass, or sharp-edged tins, and although nature may be untidy, there's nothing natural about a free-range plastic bag.' She gave them a challenging stare. 'Well? Are you two going to help?'

'Nothing I like better,' said Morgan, rising effortlessly to the demand, 'than spending a beautiful Saturday morning with a hangover, picking up rubbish. Reminds me of Maggie Thatcher in her heyday.'

'And I warn you,' said Daphne, getting up, 'any further attempt to compare me with that woman will *not* be gratefully received. We'll need gloves, for a start. If you go down to the hen-run, Morgan, and look in the little shed beside it, you'll find lots of large stout empty paper bags marked *Poultry Feed*. They're stronger than bin liners, and hold nearly as much. We'll need all of them. And if either of you knows of anyone who might be prepared to turn out and help us, I should give them a ring.'

In fact, they did not need to. By the time Morgan's 4 × 4, with Harriet, Daphne and a very excited Toby as passengers, arrived at the village hall, a large working party had already assembled, apparently spontaneously, and the football field was thick with people bundling litter into bags, and children pursuing errant pieces of paper. Juliet was there, with her husband and two boys, and a lot of other people whom Harriet knew by sight. She recognised the Bentleys, and several play-group mothers, and, to her considerable surprise, Sir Marcus Grant, in baggy green cords, a Viyella shirt, and a bright-red neckerchief with white spots, industriously collecting filthy cans. He straightened and smiled at them as they made their way towards him. 'I thought I'd see you here, Daphne. Hallo, Morgan. You're up remarkably early, considering. Feeling all right?'

'I've got a very slight headache,' said his architect, with a grin. 'That was an excellent bottle of claret.'

'*Two* bottles of claret,' Marcus corrected him. 'And the next time you feel the need to sink them in short order, warn me before you start, and I won't give you the vintage stuff.'

'Wasted on a pleb like me, anyway,' Morgan said, with a droll glance for Harriet's benefit. 'Well, shall we get started?'

It was not possible, of course, to clear all the litter before the judging, even with the assistance of a large proportion of the village. But at least, thought Harriet, taking a brief respite for the sake of her aching back, they had made the effort. And there was a pleasant spirit of camaraderie amongst the workers. People she hardly knew had addressed her as if they were old friends, and the air was filled with laughter and good-humoured jokes. Quicker than she would have believed possible, the football field had been cleared, and the rubbish tipped back into the big plastic bins outside the village hall.

'Like the war all over again, dear,' said an

elderly lady to Harriet, with a smile. 'Nothing like a crisis to bring people together, is there? It's a shame about the competition, of course, but there's always next year.'

I don't suppose Heather is feeling so philosophical about it, Harriet thought. She glanced round the field, realising for the first time that the Clarks were conspicuous by their absence. But there was no time to wonder about the reasons. Led by Juliet, who, unlike Heather, had the ability to enthuse and organise people without treading on toes, the villagers were moving purposefully towards the high street, which had been strewn with refuse from end to end. Fortunately, the churchyard had escaped the vandals, probably because it stood well back from the road, but the clock had struck twelve before Sanden's main thoroughfare, lined with beautiful old Georgian buildings, had been restored to its usual state of tidiness.

'What about the Row?' Harriet asked the man whose dustbin she had just refilled. 'Was that hit as well?'

'So I hear, but the residents there are sorting it out. I reckon we've done.' He looked wearily around his front garden, now devoid of litter. 'God, if I ever get my hands on those kids . . . '

'Kids?'

'Must've been kids. You know who I think was at the bottom of it? That Clark boy. He and his mates have been acting suspiciously all week. I bet they were the graffiti merchants, as well. No wonder his mother hasn't shown her face this morning. I hope she gives that lad a good hiding. And if she doesn't, I will.'

Harriet felt rather sorry for Adam: whether he was the culprit or not, he had evidently been found guilty. And if he had done it, then she could understand, only too well, the pressures which had driven him to take such drastic action against his mother.

'I'd give my right arm to be a fly on the wall in that household right now,' her informant added. 'I bet he's getting an earful.'

A fly on the wall in Heather's sitting room would have stood no chance of concealment against the peach emulsion, but it would have seen, and heard, that although his part in the litter-spreading had already been detected, it was not Adam who was being rebuked. He was sitting on the window-seat, crimson with shocked embarrassment, listening to something he had never heard before in all his fifteen years of life: the sound of his father in a blistering rage.

Heather, too, could obviously scarcely believe her ears. She sat bolt-upright on the sofa, her face white with shock under the thick layers of foundation, as Keith — mild-mannered, wouldn't-say-boo-to-a-goose Keith — shouted at her so loudly that the noise banged round the lounge, desperately seeking escape.

'I've had it up to here with your stupid trivial obsessions!' Adam's father yelled. 'For years I've put up with it and now I just can't stand it any longer! You've driven Jess away, Adam can't wait to go either, and if you're not bloody careful you'll drive me away too!'

'Don't swear, Keith,' said Heather, her voice pleading rather than expressing her usual robust disapproval. 'Not in front of Adam.'

'I'm willing to bet he's forgotten more four-letter words than you or I will ever know. Do you *realise* what he gets up to? Do you *care*? Oh no, you don't, you care more about your precious sodding committee and your status in the village and what people think of you than you do about your own family! Well, I've had enough, Heather. I've put in for a transfer to the Chester branch. It's a step up the ladder, and a nice area. You can stay in Sanden if you like, I won't prevent you. But if you decide to come with me, you can stop all your committees and action groups and all your bullying too. No more, understand? I don't *want* people pitying me for being henpecked. I don't *want* to feel like an intruder in my own home. I don't *want* a house so clean I could eat my dinner off the floor. You make me feel as if I'm being a nuisance just for sitting on the sofa and disturbing the cushions. For God's sake, loosen up a little, woman, let go, stop trying to lord it over everyone, or you'll end up with no husband, no children, and no friends either. Although I don't actually suppose you've got any, all you've got is cronies who are too scared of you to say no.'

'Keith, please stop,' said Heather, and suddenly, disturbingly, her voice cracked with distress. 'Stop saying all those awful, terrible things, they're not true — '

'Of course they're true, you stupid woman! Haven't you understood yet? I am going to Chester. You can come or not as you choose, but if you do come, you've got to change your ways, or I'll leave again, and next time there won't be any option — you won't be joining me. Understand? I'm fed up with it, Heather, and I'm fed up with you. No wonder Adam's getting up to no good, with you out at all hours of the night thinking you can set the world to rights. And quite honestly, if I'd known what he and his mates were going to do last night, I think I'd have given them a helping hand!'

'Keith!' Heather cried in horror. 'You can't mean that!'

'Oh yes I do.' He turned to his son, still crouched nervously on the window-seat. 'Look, I'm sorry about all this. I didn't mean to explode like that, but I've just had it up to here.'

'I know, Dad,' said Adam thinly. 'It's OK. So have I. Can *I* come with you to Chester, even if Mum doesn't?'

'Adam!' his mother cried. 'Adam, you can't! I'm your *mother*!'

'Yeah, but that doesn't give you the right to sling all my cartoons in the bin. You did, didn't you? Well, I'm *glad* I wrecked your stupid competition, that's all you ever think about, and it serves you fucking well right!' He leapt to his feet. 'You two can do what you like, I'm going out.'

'No, Adam, please, listen to me, I'm sorry!' Heather cried. She struggled to her feet, a hand outstretched to stop him, but Adam pushed past her and ran out into the hall. He heard his father saying, 'For God's sake, leave the boy alone, Heather,' and his mother's anguished cry of protest. He flung the door back so hard that the handle crashed against the wall, denting the plaster, and ran down the driveway to the road.

The big black and silver Shogun that belonged to Harriet's friend was waiting outside Holly Cottage, and she was standing beside the driver's door, talking to him. As Adam stumbled into the road, she stepped back with a gesture of resignation, and the Shogun roared off over the bridge. The boy stopped, but she had already seen him, and smiled. 'Hi, Adam. Are you OK? What's up?'

Adam prayed that he wouldn't burst into tears. He tried to affect an air of nonchalant unconcern. 'Nothing. Mum and Dad are having a row, that's all. I thought I'd get out of the way for a bit.'

'Oh dear,' said Harriet. She paused, glancing at him thoughtfully, and then added, 'Anything to do with what happened last night?'

'Yeah, a bit.' Adam stared miserably down at the ground. It felt as if there was a huge weight inside his chest, and he had to get rid of it, talk to someone about it, or be crushed. And he liked Harriet, she was friendly and sympathetic, and she knew how awful his mother could be. She would listen. Heartened slightly, he continued. 'And about what Mum's been doing, too. Dad doesn't like her spending so much time on the action group. She didn't get in till after two last night, and he was cross about that. And then . . . ' He swallowed, and went on. 'Then her friend Christine rang this morning, to tell her about all the litter and that. She was *furious*.' For the first time, a slightly lighter tone invaded his voice. 'Eight o'clock this morning, it was, and she was ranting and raving and foaming at the mouth — you should've seen her!'

'I don't think I should,' Harriet remarked. 'Adam — *did* you and your friends spread all that rubbish around?'

He looked up at her, and she saw the answer in his face, a curious combination of pride and dismay. 'Yeah. It was my idea. Ben wanted to re-do the graffiti, but I said this'd be easier, it wasn't what they were expecting. We told all the people on watch that we'd do their job for them, and they were glad to get off home. Then we waited till dark and emptied all the dustbins.' A small, reluctant grin appeared. 'I s'pose we shouldn't have done it really, but it wasn't half fun at the time.'

'I bet it isn't now, though.'

Adam shook his head vehemently. 'No, it isn't. I couldn't help laughing when Mum went ballistic, and Dad guessed it was me and blew his top too, but he said it was Mum's fault for getting so obsessed with it. And now he's saying he's going to leave, and she can come with him if she wants, but she's got to be different from now on, and she can't understand what he's getting at, and I just wanted to get out of there.' He sniffed. 'If Dad goes I want to go with him, but Mum won't hear of it. But I don't want to stay with her, she'd drive me mad, just like she's driven Dad mad. She threw all my cartoons away, all the best stuff I'd kept to show you. She doesn't care about *me*, not really, she only cares about being good and clean and tidy all the time.'

'Oh, Adam, I'm sure she does love you, she just doesn't always show it,' said Harriet. Beside his open confusion and misery, her own problems seemed petty and self-inflicted. 'Look, why don't you come back to Holly Cottage and have some lunch and a cup of tea or something? You can do some more cartoons for me, if you like, afterwards. And then with any luck your parents will have sorted themselves out and you can go home. How about it?'

'Yeah, great, thanks,' said Adam, with a perceptible lifting of his drooping shoulders. 'And I'm sorry about the litter.'

'It's all right. It's all cleared up now — we've been helping, pretty well everyone in the village must have been there — and I don't think there's any lasting harm done.'

'They won't have won the award, though, will they?'

'Not unless the judges were visually and intellectually challenged, no,' said Harriet drily. 'But it's only a plaque, Adam, it doesn't mean anything, not really. It's like an exam. It just shows that the winning village looked nice and neat on the day, that's all. And quite honestly, I'd rather live in a place which is a bit untidy and smelly and *real*, instead of some artificial showpiece with all the wild flowers and mud cleaned up and not a butterfly to be seen. Wouldn't you?'

'Yeah, s'pose so, but try telling that to me mum.'

'Daphne already has, several times, with no discernible effect. Anyway,' said Harriet, 'come and have some lunch. And cheer up. I'm sure once your parents have thought about it, they'll find a solution that suits everyone. Nothing's ever as bad as you think it is. It'll all come right in the end, you'll see.'

But as she walked into Holly Cottage, she knew that she was trying to convince herself even more than him. Standing at the roadside, she had said to Morgan, 'Can't we just be friends, without making demands on each other? Isn't that an option?'

'It may be for you,' he had said, his eyes bleak. 'But it isn't for me. So you won't be seeing me from now on, *cariad*. I'm going over to Gloucestershire on Monday, to start work on the new house.'

'Why?' she had asked. 'Surely you don't have to leave so soon?'

'I've got to, or I'll go mad here. Haven't you ever wanted someone so badly that you're ill with it, you see them every day and yet you can't touch them and you can't bear it? That's what it's like,' Morgan had said, his voice soft and desperate. 'And I *can't* bear it, so I'm getting out. Goodbye, *cariad*. See you some day, perhaps.' And then he had added, so quietly that she hardly heard him, '*Rydw i'n dy garu di.*'

She knew what it meant: 'I love you.' And the sense of loss she felt now, knowing that finally her rejection had driven him away, was almost more than her own heart could bear.

37

After the episode which became known in Sanden as The Great Litter Day, the village settled back into summer somnolence. Although it had not, of course, won the award, the villagers' efforts to clear up the rubbish had earned them a special commendation from the judges, for their obvious community spirit, and also gave the vicar subject matter for at least two sermons. The gossips, too, were kept busy for much of August, speculating on the consequences of that momentous day. Most residents, however, were too intent on their own immediate concerns to bother much about what was happening in the lives of people they barely knew.

In the second week in July, a For Sale sign appeared outside Cypress Lodge. Christine, who was still Heather's confidante, told everyone that Keith had been given a splendid promotion, and that the family was moving to Chester. She did not know, because Heather would have died rather than reveal to her crony the true reason for their departure, that a great deal of anguish, home truths and hard talking had preceded this momentous decision, although she did notice that her formidable friend had become unwontedly quiet and subdued since the litter episode.

More than one person on the action group, which was now discreetly dissolving, heaved a sigh of relief at the news, and hoped that the new inhabitants would be less domineering. Fortunately for the Clarks, demand for luxurious country property was buoyant, and their home sold for the asking price within a few days of coming on the market. By the last week in August, Daphne had met her new neighbours, a family relocated from Yeovil, with three small boys and a very much more relaxed attitude to gardening than their predecessors. The emerald velvet lawn was given over to riotous games of football, dens were made in the shrubbery, and the cheerful racket of children at play enlivened the quiet of Stony Lane.

Elsewhere in the village, but more discreetly, Wonderland Boats had also been put up for sale. To Edward's relief, it was quickly snapped up by a hire-boat company based at Rugby, doing very well and looking to expand to a convenient new yard on the Kennet and Avon. The price wasn't as good as he had hoped, but he couldn't very well show them the bank statements which proved that the business was doing much better than the official accounts indicated. With boyish enthusiasm, he booked his flight to South Africa, fired off dozens of letters to anyone he knew in that country, and then, reluctantly remembering his promise, wrote Harriet a cheque.

It was for twenty thousand, not thirty, but to his intense relief she didn't seem to mind when he explained the reason. In fact, he wondered afterwards whether he could have got away with giving her less. But he was free now, and she had kept her part of the bargain. He closed the secret bank account, burnt the incriminating statements, and boarded the plane to his new life with hardly a backward glance.

Unfortunately, the demand for houses meant that Edward's money arrived too late for Harriet to buy the little cottage in Sanden Row. She was only mildly disappointed. There were plenty of others, and she was looking forward to the hunt. In any case, she was busy. Daphne's editor had loved the book and her illustrations, and was keen to give her another commission. She had stalled before accepting it, very conscious that she should do the work on Y Wâl Yr Draig first, and unwilling to take on too much until she was sure that Toby was settled at school. But Sir Marcus, invited for dinner at Holly Cottage for the third time in as many weeks, had reassured her. 'No, you should never turn anything down, not at this stage of your career. The house can wait for a bit, or you can do the two together. Either way, they'll both get finished — it's just that my job will take a little longer. Anyway, all the plastering's done, so the place is ready for you whenever you feel like starting.'

'You can't let your entire life revolve around Toby, you know,' Daphne had added, unexpectedly. 'Like it or not, he'll begin to grow away from you now he's at school. You don't want to wake up when he leaves home in fifteen years' time and find your life is full of empty regrets. And believe me, *if only* and *I wish* are very poor companions in your old age.'

'I hope you're not speaking from experience, my dear,' said Sir Marcus.

'I'm not now,' Daphne said, and they exchanged glances so warmly that Harriet was filled with sudden understanding. She was glad for them, and delighted by the new, softer expression in her friend's face. Had she, too, once rejected a lover and then regretted it? And had Sir Marcus come back into her life, to give her a second chance?

As if he knew where her thoughts had travelled, Sir Marcus had turned to Harriet with a smile. 'Have you heard from that architect of mine recently?'

Harriet, who had been desperate, yet afraid, to ask him that very question, shook her head. 'No, not since he left.'

'Hmm. I haven't either. I wasn't expecting it, mind you, not for the pleasure of polite conversation at any rate, but I would have thought he'd have been in touch with you before now.'

'I can't think why,' Harriet said wryly.

'It's a shame,' said Sir Marcus, still gazing at her ruminatively. 'You really did seem made for each other, and I know from what he said the night before we cleared up all the litter that he was pretty cut up about the situation.'

'It just wasn't on, I'm afraid,' Harriet said. But how I wish it was, she thought. What is he doing now? Where is he? How is he coping? Probably getting pissed in the nearest pub, if I know Morgan.

In this, as it happened, she was doing him an injustice. Certainly, the temptation to drown the furious ache of his parting from Harriet every night was very strong, but Morgan, with greater self-control than he had demonstrated in his life so far, had managed to resist it. Instead, he had thrown himself with desperate energy into the new commission, fulfilling every deadline and driving himself into an exhausted sleep every night.

It didn't work, just as alcohol hadn't worked. As the summer dwindled into a wet, cold autumn, he faced the truth. He would never get over Harriet. Nothing on earth could obliterate this overwhelming sense of loss, and it wasn't fading away with time. He couldn't go on like this. He had to do something about it. He had to prove to her that he was the rock she had always wanted, the man whom she could trust. But at first he had no idea how he could convince her, when all his most desperate arguments had already failed.

And then he had a phone call from Sir Marcus Grant, late in October, and suddenly the answer lay cupped like a jewel in his hand.

★ ★ ★

Toby wore his new uniform with shining pride, and loved every minute of school. With delighted relief, Harriet began the paintings that Daphne's editor had wanted, illustrations for a book of rural reminiscences, but she knew that she should also make a start on the murals in Y Wâl Yr Draig. She owed it to Sir Marcus, and to Morgan, to carry out the work she had promised to do.

But she didn't want to. She was reluctant to go back to the place which had come to mean so much to her, even though she had only seen it twice, and unfinished. Every turn of the walls, every glimpse of the view, would remind her of what could never be. And, like the man who loved her, she didn't want to subject herself to such pain.

It began to loom so large in her life, though, that she had to remind herself that this was absurd. She was a grown-up, not a scared child. It was only a house. This apprehension was her own fault, and no one else's. The pain of his absence was an ache, no more, and she could live with it. So she would stop this nonsense forthwith, and sally forth to lay her ghosts.

She obtained the key from Sir Marcus, and he looked at her quizzically. 'I thought you were too busy, with your other project. And aren't you supposed to be house-hunting, too?'

'Yes, but I haven't seen anything I like yet, or that I can afford. Most places in Sanden are way out of my reach. Lots of people want to live here.'

'I've heard there's a cottage in The Croft

coming on the market soon. But it's quite unmodernised — an old lady lived in it for fifty years, never did anything to it. You'd need to spend a fortune on it to make it habitable.'

'And I haven't got a fortune, or the time.' Harriet grinned at him. 'Thanks, anyway. I'll find somewhere eventually, I know I will. I've just got to keep looking.'

She went down alone to Y Wâl Yr Draig, walking along the narrow driveway that led to the site. She hadn't seen it at close quarters since that day with Morgan and Toby, two months ago, and she almost didn't notice it, because the three round roofs had been turfed over, and were growing daisies and thistles and even a few small shrubs. The track swept round to the side, where a garage had been hollowed unobtrusively out of the hill, and she walked on down to the level terrace at the front of the building.

Now, the rough earth and weeds had been replaced by a broad paved strip, and there were creamy muslin curtains draped across the three tall windows. She turned the key in the central door, and slid it open. With a feeling of wondering curiosity, she tiptoed inside.

Last time, the place had been a bare husk, but even so she had thought herself able to imagine how it would look with plaster over the curving walls, and the specified wood-block flooring covering the expanse of grey concrete. But the reality exceeded even her dreams. The hollow white space floated above her like the delicate inward curve of a shell, crying out for embellishment. The gauzy curtains drifted in the gentle September breeze, diffusing the light and lending their fluid grace to soften the bare starkness of the rooms within.

It was marvellous, and Morgan's vision had created it. He had drawn it and modelled it, but no miniature representation could possibly have done justice to the actual building. He possessed the power to bring his dreams to life, and make them real. And it was an achievement that no restless, rootless, irresponsible lightweight drifter could possibly have achieved.

For the first time, the full impact of what she had done to him struck Harriet with terrible force. Overwhelmed with grief, and regret, and vivid memories, she stood in the centre of the room, and the tears poured down her face.

She managed to calm herself eventually, of course. Crying wouldn't change things, or bring him magically back into her embrace. She wiped her face, and unpacked her equipment: pencils, rubbers, the stencils she had made for the decorative borders, acrylic paints, brushes and sponges, and the tins of cloud-white and sky-blue emulsion. She set up the stepladders that Sir Marcus had told her were stacked in the utility room, and laid scaffolding boards across them. Finally, she unrolled the designs on the floor, weighted down with pots of paint, and studied them for a long, long time. They were good, but she was almost frightened to begin putting them into effect. What if she spoilt this wonderful, magical place?

'You want to give yourself a damn good kicking,' said Harriet, aloud, in Georgia's best bossy manner. 'Now get a grip on yourself and get cracking!'

And of course, once she had made that first, brief, tentative mark on the wall, she found it impossible to stop. Heedless of the passage of time, she slapped on sky, then sponged drifting white clouds across the blue. When she first thought to look at her watch, it was a quarter to three, Toby would be coming out of school in fifteen minutes, and she hadn't even thought about lunch.

For the next few weeks, Harriet worked on the mural during every hour she could scrounge. It was almost impossible to tear herself away from it, even to spend time with

Toby. Despite their fierce protests, she forced the dragons to the back of her mind when she was with him, but once he was in bed she would take a torch, and sometimes Maggie for company, and walk across the park to put in another couple of hours. Her back ached, she had given herself tennis elbow, and often her eyes felt so sore and strained with the effort of concentration that she thought she wouldn't be able to carry on. And dragons, as wild, free and joyful as the man who had inspired them, filled her dreams.

She didn't know if Sir Marcus, who was the only other person who had a key, had kept an eye on how the paintings were progressing, although she had told him that she didn't mind him coming down to see, as long as he didn't turn up when she was actually working. She had always hated people looking over her shoulder.

So she was a little perturbed when, one wet, gloomy evening early in November, she came up through the park and saw that there was a light glowing behind the central window. Harriet paused for a moment, wishing that she hadn't left Maggie behind, although it had seemed a perfectly sensible decision earlier, because of the rain. Then she walked cautiously up to the door, found it unlocked, and slid it gently open. It was perfectly balanced, and obeyed her touch smoothly and silently. The heavy torch ready in her hand, she peered suspiciously through the curtains.

The room was empty, but someone had been in it. The ladders and scaffolding had gone, along with the dust sheets, which had protected the polished floor from spilt paint. At opposite sides of the room, two tall branched cast-iron candelabra provided the subtle, flickering light that she had noticed from the park. The wide, bare space between them was filled by two huge white cushions, a yellow and white checked Indian rug, and a low white table. On it stood a yellow vase, filled with freesias, a flower Harriet had always loved. Their rich, sweet scent pervaded the room, and above her head, the dragons, almost finished, whirled in their fierce, exuberant dance amongst the clouds.

There was an ice bucket beside the vase, with a gold-capped bottle in it. Someone had gone to a great deal of trouble, and an incredible suspicion was beginning to wake in Harriet's mind. She closed the door softly behind her, took off her coat and laid it neatly on the floor. For a moment she stood quite still, listening, letting senses and instinct roam free in search.

And music began to steal into the room.

She recognised it instantly. Brought up on rock and pop, she had only a sketchy knowledge of the classics, but if she had to take just one recording to a desert island, this would be it. The cello spoke, deep and dark, and the violins, interrupting, took up the tune and embellished it with glory.

Long ago, listening to a string quartet playing this outside the Pump Room in Bath, she had wept for the beauty of it, within Morgan's encircling arms. And when, now, she had brushed the tears from her eyes, and looked up, he was standing in front of her.

38

For a moment, so strong was her sense that she had strayed into a fantasy that she could hardly believe that he was solid, and real. Surely he was taller than she remembered, and his hair had grown longer since the summer. He was wearing a loose shirt and dark trousers, and the smile on his face was uncharacteristically tentative, as if he was unsure of her reaction. And all around them, the violins sang and wove and repeated the intricate cadences of Pachelbel's Canon, rising in a crescendo of delight.

'Dance, *cariad*?' he said, with the look she had loved for so long, full of reckless mischief, as if he had asked her to waltz along the edge of an abyss. And with a joyous leap of her heart, she took the hand he held out to her.

She wanted to talk, but words would spoil this wondrous atmosphere of romance. She had never thought she needed the conventional sentimental trappings of love: flowers, champagne, sweet music. Yet he had provided them all for these few, brief, perfect moments of reunion, and because neither of them had ever considered these things to be necessary, that made it all the more special.

Too soon, as always, the music drew to its triumphant close, and the soaring melody seemed to sing the phrase within her head: *I'll love you all my life, I'll love you all my life*. Her senses were overflowing, the sounds of the strings filled her head, her arms held his body so close they seemed to have become one, she breathed in the scent of him, clean and unique and so long familiar, her eyes looked into his, and could no longer evade the truth they conveyed. And finally, she tasted the warmth of his kiss, at once gentle and urgent, and knew she had come home at last.

'Have you missed me, *cariad*?' he whispered, his mouth so close that the touch of his lips spoke the words against hers. 'Because I have missed you, past all bearing.'

'Yes, I missed you,' she said, drawing back a little so that she could see his face. 'And I was wrong about you, and I am so very, very sorry.'

'If I'd known that music and flowers could work this magic, I'd have tried them long ago,' he said softly. 'Come on, *cariad*, come and sit down. I've got something to give you.'

Her hand still in his, she was drawn to the cushions and guided into them with as much courtesy and grace as if she were a great Victorian lady in a crinoline, instead of ordinary Harriet Smith in jeans and paint-stained shirt. Morgan knelt down in front of her, and brought out an envelope from the back pocket of his trousers. He smoothed out the creases, and handed it to her. 'Darling Hal, this is for you. And whether you say no, or yes, at least you'll know how much you mean to me.'

Bewildered, she opened it, and stared down at the paper inside. She had taken her glasses off, and the sentences wavered blurrily before her, refusing to make sense. She caught the words *Official Registrar* and *special licence*, and their names: Morgan Llewellyn Price and Harriet Susan Smith. Utterly confused, she looked up at him. 'What is this?'

'It's the result of a hell of a lot of thinking and soul-searching, over the past few months. It's a special licence. *Cariad*, I'm asking you to marry me.'

In all her most insane dreams, this moment had never occurred. It was beyond all imagination, all she knew, or thought she knew, of him. She remembered him saying once, in a Bristol pub long ago, that marriage was for people so conventional that they were afraid of the alternatives. She found her voice at last, and said hoarsely,

'Why? You didn't need to do this.'

'Aw shucks — all that dosh down the drain! Why? Because I love you, Hal. Truly, madly, deeply, I love you. Because we've carried a torch for each other for more than ten years, and I at least am tired of longing. And because I couldn't think of any other way to convince you that I was serious. I'm not going to leave you again, *cariad* — I'm not going to walk out. I'm here, permanent, for good, a fixture in your life. If you want me, you can have me.'

'But what about the house you're doing in Gloucestershire?' Harriet said in bewilderment.

'An hour away along the M4, that's all. I never said I would stay with you every hour of your life — but I will always come back to you, *cariad*. *Always*. Because I have got roots, and they're embedded in you.' His eyes were bluer than the painted sky above them. 'Is that good enough for you?'

'But you've always been good enough — more than enough,' Harriet said. 'And it was stupid and arrogant of me to think otherwise. I misjudged you, and I'm sorry, so very sorry, and I don't deserve this, I really don't.' She was crying, or was it laughing? Tears ran down her cheeks, and Morgan offered her a pristine snow-white handkerchief. 'You don't have to marry me,' she went on, wiping her face. 'I'll gladly have you without. I've changed my mind, you see. It had nothing to do with all this, I changed it weeks ago, but I thought you were sick of all my excuses, because that's what they were, excuses, because I was frightened of the way you make me feel — I gave you all of my heart before, and you broke it, and I didn't want it to happen again.'

'But I *want* to marry you,' Morgan said. He leant forward and took her hands in his, his voice impassioned. 'OK, I know what I used to say about it. I know we don't *need* it. But I want to marry you because I love you and there will never be another woman in all my life that I'll love as much — never has, and never will be. And I want all the world to know about it. I want us to settle down and have kids and a garden and a dog as daft as Maggie. I want Toby to call me Dad, and mean it. I want us to trust each other, and know that whatever happens, we'll still be able to rely on each other. I want us to laugh and be tolerant and take each other for granted, and still be able to make whoopee in bed when we're drawing our pensions.'

'That's a tall order,' said Harriet, suppressing a giggle. 'I'm not sure I could *ever* take you for granted. You're too unexpected.' She glanced round at the lovely room, the candles and flowers, and added, 'You must have been planning this for ages.'

'Oh, yes — at least a couple of days.' He was still gazing at her, and she realised suddenly that he was waiting for her response: and that what she said was of desperate importance to him.

And so she had no doubts, because he had so obviously done this for her, from his heart and his soul. She said softly, teasingly, 'I suppose I ought to give you an answer.'

'I suppose so.' He was smiling, trying to pretend it didn't matter. 'But if you want some time to think — '

'I don't. Of course I'll marry you, Morgan Llewellyn Price, because I love you to bits, and any other reason just doesn't matter.'

'Oh, *cariad*.' His smile grew suddenly and dazzlingly wide. 'Oh God, I wasn't sure — I didn't think you'd agree to it — '

'And why wouldn't I? You're all I've ever wanted, for the last ten years and more.' She pulled him close to her. 'But enough of all this idle chit-chat. How did that song go? 'Don't talk, just kiss'.'

'Good advice. Let's take it.' His lips met hers, tasting her, gently, teasingly, yet with increasing hunger. Her own desire was melting her bones, feeding their mutual passion. He unbuttoned her shirt with playful slowness, and then his mouth and hands began to caress her breasts, while she struggled with his clothes, desperate to feel the touch of his skin against hers. Her jeans were cast aside, with considerable laughter, and rather more difficulty than the shirt, and then there was no barrier between them.

'Wait,' she said breathlessly, as his mouth travelled further down her body, and desire threatened to overwhelm her. 'Did you mean what you said about kids? Because I haven't got anything with me, I wasn't expecting this — '

'I have.' He glanced up at her, his face filled with joyful amusement. 'Always be prepared, that's my motto.'

She gasped as his fingers explored her. 'I didn't know you'd been a Scout.'

'They don't teach you this in the Scouts.'

'If they did, there'd be a waiting list a mile long . . . ah, that's wonderful, don't stop — '

This time, there was no thunderstorm, no anguish, no guilt to hinder them. Now, they were free to enjoy each other without restraint, and take delight in the pleasure they could give and receive, for the first time in ten years. She had thought she had forgotten how their bodies fitted together, the exquisite tingling sensation as he caressed her breasts, the feel of him inside her, their long, slow movements in perfect harmony, gathering urgency as their passion soared, uniting them in an emotion so wild and shattering that its culmination engulfed them both in sensations wonderfully more intense than ever before.

And as she came slowly back to full consciousness, his head on her shoulder and his warm body lying heavily on hers, she looked up and saw her dragons, dancing for joy above them.

'Did you really mean that, about kids?' she asked softly.

'Of course I meant it. You can have any number of small goats.'

'*Be* serious, you lunatic!'

'Sorry. Yes, I've always wanted kids — the human sort, that is. I like them, believe it or not.'

'I know you do — I can see it when you're with Toby.'

'Would he like a little brother or sister?'

'I expect so. He used to ask me if he could have one for his birthday. He said he didn't want to be a lonely child. He meant *only* child, but lonely seems more appropriate, somehow.'

'When's his next birthday?'

'This Thursday. He's having a party and he

wanted to invite his entire class, so I've hired the village hall and a bouncy castle.'

'Thursday's a bit soon. I reckon we could manage the conception before then, but delivery takes a while longer. If that's all right with you, of course.'

'It's very all right.' She kissed him lovingly. 'I can't believe this is really happening — if I'd asked a genie to give me three wishes, he couldn't have done as well.'

'Sorry, I'm not blue and I don't talk like Robin Williams.'

'Just as well — I don't fancy him at all, and I fancy you something rotten.' She smiled at him. 'So tell me — how long have you really been planning this?'

'Since last week. I got a call from Sir Marcus, and it put all my thoughts into place.'

'How come?'

'He offered me this house.'

The room became suddenly very quiet. Harriet said at last, hardly daring to trust in the truth, 'He did *what*?'

'He offered me this house. On a long lease, low rent. Selina doesn't want it, she's quite happy partying in Bath. He knows how I feel about you and what happened between us. That night I had dinner with him, I got rather drunk — '

'On vintage claret, wasn't it? Wasted on a pleb like you.'

Morgan laughed, his arms tightening around her. 'Anyway, I talked rather too much about you, and me, and I think he decided to play matchmaker. He knew you were looking for somewhere to live, and this seemed the perfect solution. I built it, and you're making it a cave of wonders.' He glanced upwards. 'I love the dragons. They're superb — even better than I thought they'd be.'

'They're not finished yet.'

'Then imagine what they'll be like when they are. Unwary visitors will think they're going to swoop down and carry people off. You've made them so real.'

'But dragons aren't. They're in my imagination, that's all.'

'Best place for them. They're altogether too fierce for comfort — but then that's how dragons should be. They're not easy, or cuddly, or predictable — they're wild creatures, untamed and free.'

'Like you.'

Morgan laughed again. 'No, I'm not. You've tamed me, just a little.'

'I never wanted to do that.'

'Well, I wanted you to. So — how about it? Shall we live here? I know it's not going to be suitable for ever, it's not big enough for more than a couple of kids, and there's no garden, just the park, but I reckon we could manage for a year or two, very happily.'

'Breakfast on the terrace,' said Harriet wonderingly. 'I came here once to see you, back in the summer, and I found myself imagining so strongly what it would be like to live here that I couldn't believe I wasn't. I think I must have been remembering the future — does that sound silly?'

'Not a bit of it, *cariad*.'

'But then, I thought it was just a stupid, impossible dream.' She smiled. 'Like having you to share it. And I was wrong, on both counts.'

'So shall we?'

'Oh yes, of course, you idiot — how could you ever have thought I'd say no?'

'I didn't — you're putty in my hands, you are.'

'You've got a lot to learn about me, Morgan Price.' Harriet glared at him. 'I'm not a pushover.'

'Aren't you?'

'Absolutely not.' She grabbed his hands and wriggled round until she was sitting astride him. 'Flowers and music and champagne won't get you everywhere, you know.'

'It might — we haven't even opened the bottle yet. In the mean time, how about flattery? The view's wonderful from down here.' His hands came up to cup her breasts. 'Round and soft, as delicious as a peach, although not quite so furry, of course — ow!'

'Serves you right, you cheeky rat,' said Harriet happily. 'Now, about our earlier topic of conversation.'

'Which was?'

'Conception. I'm warning you, I intend to take you at your word.'

'Good. I was hoping you would. Shall we start now?'

'Why not? I can't think of anything I'd rather do. Mmm, that's nice.'

'It's meant to be. I hope those dragons aren't easily shocked, because they've got a grandstand view.'

'I doubt it. They've seen it all before, at least ten minutes ago.'

'And they're probably dying for a replay. Let's do it so often they get sick of it. Imagine them saying, 'Oh no, they're not at it *again*! Let's close our eyes and think of St George.' '

'You're silly, and wonderful, and I love you so much.' Harriet leaned down and kissed him, long and hard, exulting in the pleasure she was giving him.

And Morgan, before he drowned in her, was sure that one of the dragons had winked at him.

PLAIN DEALER

William Ardin

Antique dealing has its own equivalent to 'insider trading', as Charles Ramsay finds out to his cost. Offered the purchase of a lifetime, he sees all his ambitions realised in an antique jade cup, known as the 'Loot'. But as soon as the deal is irrevocably struck he finds himself stuck with it like an albatross around his neck — unable to export it without a licence, unable to sell it at home, and in a paralysing no man's land where nobody has sufficient capital to take it off his hands . . .

NO TIME LIKE THE PRESENT

June Barraclough

Daphne Berridge, who has never married, has retired to the small Yorkshire village of Heckcliff where she grew up, intending to write the biography of an eighteenth-century woman poet. Two younger women are interested in her project: Cressida, Daphne's niece, who lives in London, and is uncertain about the direction of her life; and Judith, who keeps a shop in Heckcliff, and is a divorcee. When an old friend of Daphne falls in love with Judith, the question — as for Cressida — is marriage or independence. Then Daphne also receives a surprise proposal.

SEARCH FOR A SHADOW

Kay Christopher

On the last day of her holiday Rosemary
Roberts met an intriguing American in the
foyer of her London hotel. By some extraordinary coincidence, Larry Madison-Jones
was due to visit the tiny Welsh village
where Rosemary lived. But how much of a
coincidence was Larry's erratic presence
there? The moment Rosemary returned
home, her life took on a subtle, though
sinister edge — Larry had a secret he was
not willing to share. As Rosemary was
drawn deeper into a web of mysterious
and suspicious occurrences, she found
herself wondering if Larry really loved her
— or was trying to drive her mad . . .

THREE WISHES

Barbara Delinsky

Slipping and sliding in the snow as she walks home from the restaurant where she's worked for fourteen years, Bree Miller barely has time to notice the out-of-control lorry, headed straight for her. All Bree remembers of that fateful night is a bright light, and a voice granting her three wishes. Are they real or imagined? And who is the man standing over her bedside when finally she wakes up? Soon Bree finds herself the recipient of precisely those things she'd most wanted in life — even that which had seemed beyond all reasonable hope.

WEB OF WAR

Hilary Grenville

Claire Grant, a radar operator in the WAAF, still mourning the death of her parents and brother in an air raid, finds coming on leave to her grandmother's home difficult to face. Martin, a friend from her school days, now a pilot in the RAF, helps her to come to terms with her grief and encourages the flimsy rapport between Claire and her grandmother. War rules their lives and it is some time before they meet again. Claire is in love, but there are many quirks of fate yet to be faced.